...country for granted and loving the ...llenge of pursuing her writerly dreams.

Abby Green spent her teens reading Mills & Boon romances. She then spent many years working in the Film and TV industry as an Assistant Director. One day while standing outside an actor's trailer in the rain, she thought: *there has to be more than this.* So she sent off a partial to Mills & Boon. After many rewrites, they accepted her first book and an author was born. She lives in Dublin, Ireland and you can find out more here: abby-green.com

Louise Fuller was a tomboy who hated pink and always wanted to be the prince. Not the princess! Now she enjoys creating heroines who aren't pretty pushovers but strong, believable women. Before writing for Mills & Boon, she studied literature and philosophy at university and then worked as a reporter on her local newspaper. She lives in Tunbridge Wells with her impossibly handsome husband, Patrick and their six children.

Sins and Seduction

Sins and Seduction:
Terms of Surrender

ANGELA BISSELL

ABBY GREEN

LOUISE FULLER

MILLS & BOON

First Published in Great Britain 2022
by Mills & Boon, an imprint of HarperCollins*Publishers* Ltd,
1 London Bridge Street, London, SE1 9GF

www.harpercollins.co.uk

HarperCollins*Publishers*
Macken House, 39/40 Mayor Street Upper,
Dublin 1, D01 C9W8

SINS AND SEDUCTION: TERMS OF SURRENDER
© 2022 Harlequin Enterprises ULC.

Defying Her Billionaire Protector © 2017 Angela Bissell
The Virgin's Debt to Pay © 2018 Abby Green
Claiming His Wedding Night © 2016 Louise Fuller

ISBN: 978-0-263-31820-3

MIX
Paper | Supporting
responsible forestry
FSC™ C007454

This book is produced from independently certified FSC™ paper
to ensure responsible forest management.

For more information visit: www.harpercollins.co.uk/green

Printed and Bound in Spain using 100% Renewable electricity at
CPI Black Print, Barcelona

DEFYING HER BILLIONAIRE PROTECTOR

ANGELA BISSELL

For my friend Lisa, a brave, beautiful and inspiring woman. Thank you for your valuable insights—and for letting me have a spin in your wheels. Here's to many more Princess Days in the sun!

CHAPTER ONE

'*MAMMA MIA!* HERE they come.'

Marietta's hands stilled over the keys of her computer, her assistant's warning—low-voiced yet laced with an unmistakable thread of anticipation—shattering her train of thought like crystal under a hammer. She looked up in time to see the courier pushing open the glass doors of the gallery she managed in the heart of Rome's affluent Parioli district. In his arms he cradled a huge, hand-tied bouquet of roses.

'*Bellissimo.*' Lina moved from the storeroom doorway and stood by Marietta's desk at the rear of the gallery. 'They are the best yet!'

Marietta would have liked to disagree with that assessment, but Lina was right. The long-stemmed roses *were* beautiful, each head—at least two dozen of them—exquisite, the velvety petals a vivid red that in the whiteness of the gallery made Marietta think, perversely, of blood.

Her thoughts snapped to the elegant spray of white orchids that had been delivered earlier in the week—surprisingly, because until then the flowers had always arrived on a Friday. Pretty and delicate, the orchids, like the roses, had been lovely to look at, but their sweet, cloying scent had lingered in her nostrils and left her feeling faintly ill long after she had disposed of them.

Even the note that had come with them had been heavily perfumed, and she'd wanted to destroy that too. Had wanted to rip the card and its intimate typewritten message into tiny, indecipherable pieces and flush them down the toilet.

But she'd been told to keep the notes in case they held any clues, so she'd shoved the card into a drawer, along with all the others, and vowed that when this was over—when her secret-admirer-turned-stalker was caught or simply grew tired of his antics—she would set a match to those cards and enjoy watching them burn.

The courier strode over the polished concrete towards them, and Marietta felt her stomach doing a little surge and roll. She didn't want to touch the roses. She definitely didn't want them near enough for her to smell.

'Ciao.'

The young courier's broad smile did nothing to quell her dread. His gaze shifted sideways—drawn, unsurprisingly, to Lina's tall, willowy form—and Marietta saw the predictable flare of male appreciation on his face give way to surprise—or maybe *shock* was a better word—the moment the man sitting behind her stood.

He strode around her desk, straight into the courier's path, and she imagined she heard the young man's jaw crack, his mouth dropped open so fast. His face lost its colour, paling several shades as he took in the large, imposing man before him. She felt a twinge of sympathy for the guy; Nicolas César, ex-legionnaire, head of the widely revered global conglomerate César Security and her brother's good friend, could scare the wits out of most people—and that was on the days he *didn't* look hell-bent on throttling someone.

He stared down at the courier from his massive height and extended a large, capable-looking hand. A hand that appeared elegant and bone-crushingly strong all at the same time. 'Give them to me.'

Nico's deep voice rumbled with the kind of natural authority only a fool with no thought for self-preservation would dare to challenge. Wisely, the younger man didn't hesitate. He handed over the roses with a haste that might have amused Marietta had anything about this situation been remotely funny. His eyes darted back to Lina, but her attention was firmly fixed on the other man, and, as if understanding he couldn't possibly compete with all that eye-popping masculinity, the courier shot Marietta a bemused look and hurried out of the gallery.

She gripped the titanium hand rims on the wheels of her custom-made chair and reversed a few feet from her desk. Although Nico stood on the other side, with a great slab of horizontal glass between them, she needed the comfort of the extra distance before she looked at him.

Not, she told herself, because she wasn't used to looking up at people. Thirteen years in a wheelchair had accustomed her to seeing the world from a diminished height, and she'd long ago reconciled herself to that aspect of her disability. And although able-bodied people often thought of her as being *confined* to a wheelchair—as though the chair and not her paralysed legs were the prison—for Marietta the use of her modern, ultralight chair for mobility was a choice. One that gave her the freedom to work and travel. To live her life with a level of independence any single, career-focused woman of thirty would wish to enjoy.

But Nicolas César wasn't anything like the people Marietta encountered on an ordinary day, and it wasn't only his unique physicality that set him apart—wasn't only the impressive breadth of his shoulders, the fact that he stood taller than most. On par with her six-foot-four brother—or the fact that his dark trousers and close-fitting black shirt moulded the kind of lean, hard-muscled physique that spoke of discipline and sweat and the good fortune of strong, resilient genes. Rather, it was the raw power he exuded from every inch of that undeniably masculine frame—the overriding impression that here was a man few others dared trifle with—that made Marietta's hormones sit up and take notice.

Which irritated her enormously.

Sexual attraction was a complication she didn't need in her life right now—or *ever*, for that matter. Especially to a man so far out of her physical league her pride smarted just to look at him.

'Are you not going to interrogate him?' she asked, and her annoyance with herself—with that hot, inescapable lick of feminine awareness—lent her words a much pithier edge than she'd intended.

Dark blue eyes thinned and settled on her, making her aware that her sarcasm wasn't lost on Nico, and guilt instantly pricked her. He was here to help because her brother had asked him to. That Leo had done so without consulting her first was no fault of Nico's. Unleashing her frustration on him was childish. Unfair.

He held her gaze, his silent, prolonged eye contact causing her skin to flush and her insides to squirm with something far more unsettling than guilt. She didn't look away and wasn't sure she could even if she wanted to. His eyes were such a dark, mesmerising blue. Staring into them made her feel as if she'd been dragged beneath the surface of a vast, bottomless sea and could no longer breathe.

She opened her mouth to offer an apology—and drag some much-needed air into her lungs—but Nico spoke first.

'Bruno has cleared the staff at the florist's shop and vetted the couriers they use. There is no need for me to...' he paused for a fraction of a beat '...*interrogate* him.'

That slight yet deliberate emphasis on the word *interrogate* elevated Marietta's discomfort. Looking at him, it wasn't at all difficult for her to visualise Nicolas César in the role of interrogator—nor did she have any trouble imagining that anyone on the wrong side of that arrangement would quickly find themselves either pleading for mercy or spilling their deepest, darkest secrets to him. Or both.

At the same time, she imagined any man who possessed that degree of dark, potent magnetism would rarely, if ever, want for female companionship. Women flocked to him wherever he went, no doubt, drawn like hummingbirds to nectar by his hard-edged looks and his big, powerful body.

And that would be *before* he opened his mouth.

Before that deep-timbre voice, with its French accent and slight North American inflection, poured over them like heated syrup and turned their insides all gooey.

Marietta suppressed a little shiver.

Did Nico make his lovers plead?
Did he make them scream?

The shiver turned into a hot flush that cascaded through Marietta's body and scalded her from the inside out. *Madre di Dio.* What was wrong with her? She had no business allowing her thoughts to veer in that direction. No business entertaining hot, lurid fantasies about her brother's friend. Life had taught her some harsh lessons—lessons that had moulded her into a realist—and realists like her did not waste their time fantasising about things they would never have.

And yet she wasn't without aspirations. Cementing her place in the art world, achieving success and recognition as an artist in her own right, supporting herself independently of her brother's wealth and generosity—*those* were her goals, the dreams that got her out of bed in the mornings.

Plus she had a wish list tucked away—a 'bucket list', some people called it. Everyone had one, didn't they? Everyone wanted to see things and do things that breathed some excitement, some *magic* into their ordinary lives.

Marietta was no different. As an incomplete paraplegic she could no longer walk, but living with a spinal cord injury didn't mean she couldn't push her own boundaries, do things that were a little adventurous or wild.

Paraplegics around the world skydived and flew planes and competed in rigorous sports.

Every item on Marietta's wish list was doable. Some more challenging than others, given her physical limitations, but all of them realistic. She certainly didn't have her head in the clouds. She knew what was possible and what wasn't. And there was no reason whatsoever that she couldn't tandem skydive. Or float in a hot air balloon. Or travel to Egypt to see the pyramids.

But what were the chances of a man who could crook his finger and have any woman in the world—any *able-bodied* woman in the world—he wanted desiring her?

Now *that* was pure fantasy—a pointless, fanciful daydream she needn't waste her time indulging.

What she did need to do was stay focused, remember what was important: her job, her independence, her art.

Especially her art.

But now all of that was under threat. In danger of being disrupted by some anonymous admirer who *must* be mentally unstable, or, if she were being less kind, completely deranged.

Six weeks. That was how long she'd been receiving the bunches of flowers and the notes she'd thought quaint and amusing—even flattering—at first. But over the weeks the messages had gone from sweet to intense, their content growing more personal, more intimate. More possessive.

It was the note that had come with a bouquet of thirteen crimson tulips on a Friday two weeks ago, however, that had for the first time left her truly spooked.

Such a beautiful dress you wore yesterday, amore mio. *Red is perfect on you—and my favourite colour. You see? We were made for each other! S.*

Those words had clamped a cold fist around her throat and squeezed hard as their import had slowly sunk in. And she had realised something she hadn't considered before then—that he, whoever *he* was, was following her, watching her, *stalking* her.

Gooseflesh rose on Marietta's forearms and she resisted the urge to rub them, to scrub away the sensation of something unpleasant crawling over her skin.

She'd been so shaken she'd confided in her sister-in-law, Helena—which in hindsight had been a mistake. Helena, in spite of Marietta's pleas for her not to, had told her husband—Marietta's brother—who had, of course, flipped. Within minutes Leo had been on the phone, severely chastising her for not going directly to him and urging her to involve the police.

Advice she'd promptly ignored. She hadn't wanted to create a fuss and her big brother was, as always, being over-protective. The fact he'd waited an entire forty-eight hours before calling on his friend Nico for assistance was, she reflected now, nothing short of astonishing.

That Nico, whom she'd last seen at Leo and Helena's wedding two years before, had, in the first instance, sent his man Bruno rather than handle the matter himself, was something Marietta had *not*, she'd assured herself, been a little disappointed about.

Nicolas César was, after all, a busy man—CEO of a renowned global network that provided security and protection services to some of the world's most powerful corporations and influential figureheads. Dealing with an overzealous admirer was never going to figure high on his priority list, no matter how solid his friendship with her brother.

And yet…here he stood. Or perhaps *towered* was the better word, she thought, conscious of a crick in her neck. Of the warm pulse of blood beneath her skin. Her heartbeat had not quite settled back into its normal rhythm since he'd walked, unannounced, into the gallery some forty minutes earlier.

After a brief, polite greeting he'd asked to see the cards Bruno had told her to keep, and then, despite the fact they were written in Italian, had proceeded to read every intimate word until Marietta's face had burned with mortified heat. Then—since it was mid-afternoon on a Friday, and that meant another bouquet was likely on its way—he'd commandeered one of the soft chairs reserved for the gallery's clientele and artists and waited for the flowers she had silently prayed wouldn't come.

'Where's Bruno?' she asked now. Not because she missed the rigid presence of the dark-suited man, but rather because she could see the small white envelope attached to the roses and wanted to delay, if only for a minute longer, having to open it.

'Following up a lead.'

A lead. That sounded vague. 'What sort of lead?'

He didn't answer her. Instead he turned to Lina, as if he'd not heard the question or had simply chosen to ignore it.

Marietta tamped down her annoyance—only to feel it flare again when she glanced at her assistant. *Santo cielo!* Had the girl no pride? No sense of dignity? Marietta wanted to snap her fingers at her. Tell her to wipe that silly doe-eyed look off her face. To straighten up and pull her hip back in, instead of jutting it sideways in a come-hither pose she probably wasn't even aware she'd adopted.

Nico detached the envelope from the roses, his strong fingers snapping the straw ribbon like a strand of cotton, and handed the bouquet to Lina. 'Get rid of them.'

Lina—foolish girl—beamed at him as if he'd paid

her a compliment rather than barked an order at her. Marietta bristled on her assistant's behalf. Lina, however, was oblivious. Without so much as glancing at Marietta for confirmation, she took the roses and disappeared out to the back—heading, presumably, for the outdoor dumpster behind the building.

Marietta couldn't help herself. 'That was rude.'

Nico's eyes narrowed on her again...so blue. So disconcerting. 'Pardon?'

'Lina,' she clarified. 'You could have asked nicely. Barking commands at people is rude.'

One heavy eyebrow arced, ever so slightly, towards his dark brown hairline. 'She did not look upset.'

Of course she hadn't looked upset. She'd looked smitten and flushed and...*ravenous*. As if she'd wanted to drag Nico into the storeroom, bolt the door shut and tear his clothes off—with her teeth.

Marietta was sure Nico knew it, too.

And yet, to his credit, he hadn't encouraged her attentions. Hadn't seemed to give out any inappropriate cues. In fact he'd seemed barely to notice her—unlike some of the male visitors to the gallery, who appeared more entranced by Lina's legs than by the sculptures and paintings on display.

And the girl had good legs—long and shapely—and a good body that she dressed, or on occasion *under*dressed, to showcase. Why shouldn't she? She was tall and graceful. Feminine, yet lithe.

Unbroken.

Everything Marietta might have been and wasn't, thanks to one fateful split-second decision. One irreversible moment of teenage stupidity. A moment that had altered the course of her life and shattered what little had remained of her childhood innocence.

Still—as a few well-intentioned if slightly insensitive people had pointed out during the long, excruciating months of her rehabilitation—she'd been lucky.

She had survived.

The three teens in the car with her—including the alcohol-impaired driver—had not. Two had died on impact with the concrete median barrier, the third on a gurney surrounded by the trauma team trying desperately to save her.

For Marietta, the sole survivor of that tragic car crash, a long string of dark, torturous days had followed. Days when she'd lain unable or sometimes unwilling to move, staring at the ceiling of the hated rehab unit. Reliving those final moments with her friends and wishing, in her darkest moments, that she had died alongside them.

But she had not died.

She had fought her way back.

For the brother whom she knew had taken the burden of responsibility—and blame—upon himself. For the second chance at life she'd been given that her friends had not. For her mother—God rest her soul—who would have wanted Marietta to fight with the same courage and determination with which she'd battled the cancer that had, in the end, cruelly won. And—even though she'd stayed angry with him for a long time after he'd died—for her father, who'd fought his own grief-fuelled demons after his wife's death and tragically lost.

Her chin went up a notch.

She had faced down every brutal obstacle the universe had thrown at her and she was still here. She would *not* let some stranger, some clearly unhinged individual, disrupt the life she'd worked so long and hard to rebuild. And she certainly wasn't afraid of some pathetic words on a little white card.

She held out her hand for the envelope. Nico hesitated, then handed it over. Willing her hands not to shake, she tore open the flap and pulled out the card. She sucked in a deep breath and started to read—and felt the cold pasta salad she'd had for lunch threaten to vacate her stomach.

Marietta's hands had started to shake.

She glanced up, her espresso-coloured eyes so dark Nico couldn't differentiate between iris and pupil. They were glassy, enormous—larger than usual—and, he noted, unblinking. Combined with her sudden pallor, the tremor in her slim hands, they conveyed an emotion Nico had more than once in his life been intimately acquainted with.

Fear.

He cursed under his breath, reached over the glass-topped desk and whipped the card out of her hands.

His Italian wasn't impeccable, like his native French or his English, but he had no trouble reading the typewritten words. His fingers tightened on the card but he took care to keep his face expressionless. Marietta was a strong woman—something he'd intuited the first time they'd met in passing at her brother's office, and again at Leo's wedding—but right now she was shaken and he needed her to be calm. Reassured. *Safe.*

Anything less would be a disservice to her brother, and Leo was a good friend—had been ever since their paths had crossed via a mutual client eight years ago.

Nico had recognised in the Italian the qualities of a man he could like and respect. Leo's company specialised in cyber security, and his people occasionally lent their technical expertise to Nico's own. Outside of business the two men had become firm friends—and Nico did not intend to let his friend down.

He slipped the card into a plastic folder along with the others. Aside from an insight into their composer's mind, the notes offered nothing of real value and no means by which they could track the original sender. The flowers were always ordered online, the cards printed by the florist, the words simply copied from the order's electronic message field.

Bruno had been confident at first. Online orders meant a traceable digital trail to IP addresses and credit cards. But whoever Marietta's stalker was he was careful—and clever. Their tech guys had chased their tails through a series of redirected addresses and discovered the account with the florist had been opened using bogus details. The invoices were sent to a rented mailbox and payments were received in cash via mail.

It all indicated a level of premeditation and intent neither Nico nor Bruno had anticipated. And Nico didn't like it. Didn't like it that he'd underestimated the threat—assuming, at first, that they'd be dealing with nothing more troublesome than a jilted boyfriend. It galled him now to accept that he'd been wrong because he knew better than to assume.

But he was here now, in Rome, with the meetings he'd had scheduled for today in New York cancelled after Bruno's call twenty-four hours earlier.

And they *would* find this guy. They'd break some

rules, sidestep some local bureaucracy, and they would find him.

He strode around the desk and dropped to his haunches in front of Marietta's chair, bringing his eyes level with hers. She jerked back a little, as if she wasn't used to such an action, and he wondered briefly if it were not the accepted thing to do. But he'd have done the same with any woman he sought to reassure, conscious that his height, his sheer size, might intimidate.

'We *will* stop him, Marietta.'

Her eyes remained huge in her face, her olive complexion stripped of colour. 'He's been in my home...'

Nico ground his jaw. 'Perhaps.'

'But the note—'

'Could be nothing more than a scare tactic,' he cut in. Yet the tension in his gut, the premonitory prickle at his nape, told him the truth was something far less palatable. More sinister.

I have left you a gift, tesoro. *On your bed. Think of me when you unwrap it. Sleep well,* amore mio. *S.*

On impulse he took her hand—small compared to his, and yet strong rather than dainty or delicate. Her fingers were slender and long, her nails short and neat, manicured at home, he guessed, rather than by a professional.

Incredibly, Nico could still remember clasping her hand on their very first introduction—four, maybe five years ago at her brother's office. Their handshake had been brief but he'd noted that her skin felt cool, pleasant to the touch, her palm soft and smooth in places, callused in others. He remembered, too, seeing her at

Leo's wedding a couple of years later. Remembered watching her, intrigued and impressed with the way she handled her wheelchair—as if it were a natural extension of her body.

In the church she'd glided down the aisle before the bride, composed and confident, unselfconscious—or at least that was the impression she'd given. Her sister-in-law, a beautiful English woman, had looked stunning in a simple white gown, but it was Marietta to whom Nico's attention had been repeatedly drawn throughout the ceremony.

In his thirty-six years he'd attended two other weddings—his own, which he preferred not to dwell upon, and an equally lavish affair in the Bahamas to which he had, regrettably, allowed a former lover to drag him—but he could not recall a bridesmaid at either who might have outshone Marietta in looks or elegance.

With her thick mahogany hair piled high on her head, the golden skin of her shoulders and décolletage bare above the turquoise silk of her long bridesmaid's sheath, the fact she was in a wheelchair had not diminished the impact of her beauty.

And then there were the shoes.

Nico could not forget the shoes.

Stilettos.

Sexy, feminine, four-inch stilettos in a bright turquoise to match the gown.

That Marietta could not walk in those shoes had made him admire her all the more for wearing them. It was a statement—a bold one—as though she were flipping the bird to her disability…or rather to anyone who thought a woman who couldn't walk was wasting her time wearing sexy shoes, and it had made him want to smile.

Hell, it had made him want to grin.

And that was an urge he rarely experienced.

'Nico?'

Marietta's hand twitched in his, jerking his thoughts back to the present. He refocused, realised his thumb was stroking small circles over her skin. Abruptly he broke contact and stood. 'Stay here. Keep Lina with you.'

She wheeled back and looked up at him. 'Where are you going?'

'Your apartment.'

She frowned, a smudge of colour returning to her face. 'Not without me, you're not.'

'It is better that you stay here,' he said evenly.

'Why?'

When he hesitated a fraction too long, her fine-boned features twisted into a look of horror.

'*Mio Dio*. You think he might be there, don't you?' She stared at him accusingly. 'But you said the note was just a scare tactic.'

'*Could* be,' he corrected. 'I won't know for certain until I've checked it out.'

'Then I'll come with you.'

'I'd prefer you didn't.'

Her shoulders snapped back, her eyes, wide with shock and fear only seconds before, now narrowing. 'It's my apartment. I'm coming whether you *prefer* it or not.' Her delicate chin lifted. 'Besides, you need me. You won't get in without my security code and key.'

'Both of which you are about to give to me,' he told her, keeping his voice reasonable even as he felt his pa-

tience slipping. He was unaccustomed to people argu-
ing with him—especially women.

Marietta folded her hands in her lap. The gesture
combined with her conservative attire—a sleeveless
high-necked lilac silk blouse, long black pants and,
perhaps less conservative, a pair of purple high-heeled
suede boots—made her look almost demure. Yet there
was nothing demure in the set of her shoulders or the
bright glint of defiance in her eyes.

'Do people always jump when you bark?'

He crossed his arms over his chest. Outwardly he
was calm. Inside, impatience heated his blood dangerously close to tipping point. *'Oui,'* he said, injecting a
low note of warning into his voice he hoped she had the
wisdom to heed. 'If they know what is good for them.'

Her eyebrows rose at that, but the shrug that rolled
off her shoulders was careless. 'Well, I'm sorry to disappoint you—' she looked pointedly at her legs and
then back at him '—but you might have noticed I can't
jump very high these days.'

Nico flattened his mouth, returned her stare. Channelled his trademark control—or tried to. 'You are wasting time, Marietta.'

'Me?' Somehow she managed to look utterly innocent. 'You're the one holding us up, Nico. We could
have been halfway there by now.'

He sucked in a breath and exhaled sharply. Leo had
warned him that Marietta could be stubborn. Resolute. Headstrong. No doubt those qualities had served
her well through some difficult times, helped her overcome the kind of obstacles most people, if they were
fortunate, would never have to face in their lifetime.
He respected those qualities, admired them, but right

now he'd settle for a lot less lip and a great deal more acquiescence.

The determined glitter in those liquid brown eyes told him he had zero chance of getting it. Nico couldn't decide if that surprised him, impressed him, or angered him.

People did not defy Nicolas César.

They *obeyed* him.

Fortunately for Marietta he had neither the time nor the patience to stand there and argue. He uncrossed his arms. Muttered an oath. 'Wait here,' he growled. 'I'll bring my car to the front of the gallery and collect you.'

A smile broke on her face that almost made the pain of his capitulation worth it. He blinked. *Mon Dieu.* Did she give that smile freely to everyone she met? If so, he wouldn't be surprised to find a thousand infatuated admirers lurking in the wings.

'No need,' she said, and rolled her chair forward to a small cabinet beside her desk. She pulled out an enormous leather handbag. 'I have my car in the lane out back. I'll drive myself and meet you there.'

Lina reappeared at that moment, minus the roses. She tossed her blonde hair over one too bony shoulder and gave him a smile that lacked even a fraction of the impact of Marietta's.

'Can you please close up tonight, Lina?' Marietta said to the girl. 'I doubt I'll be back. Call me if you need anything. I'll see you in the morning.' She lifted her gaze to Nico's. 'I suppose you already know my address?'

'Oui,' he said, and noted with a small punch of satisfaction how her pretty mouth tightened at that.

'Okay. Well, I'll see you there, then.' She wheeled past him, towards the rear of the gallery.

'Marietta.'

She stopped, glanced over her shoulder at him. '*Si?*'

'If you get there first, wait for me. Do not go in.'

Her mouth pursed. 'Is that an order?'

'You may consider it one.'

Only the flare of her fine nostrils betrayed her annoyance. 'Very well,' she said, then continued on her way.

For a moment Nico watched her go, her long dark hair swinging behind her, her olive-skinned arms, defined by muscle yet still slender and feminine, propelling the wheels of her chair forward with strong, confident movements.

She disappeared through a rear door and Nico spun away, making his own exit through the front of the gallery and down a short flight of stone steps. He strode along the wide tree-lined street to where he'd parked the silver sports car Bruno had had waiting at the airport for him this morning when his jet had landed.

He wrenched open the driver's door and scowled.

He would very much enjoy giving Marietta a lesson in obedience, but he had no doubt her brother would kill him—slowly and painfully—if he knew the methods Nico had in mind.

CHAPTER TWO

MARIETTA DROVE HER bright yellow sedan into the basement of her apartment building and swung into her
reserved space near the elevator. She cut the engine,
pushed the door open and used her arms to shift herself
around until her legs dangled out of the car.

She loved her modified car. In addition to its cus-
tomised hand controls, the rear passenger door on the
driver's side had been altered to open in the reverse
direction, so she could reach around from the driver's
seat, open the door and pull her wheelchair out of the
back. She did so now, and with a little shuffling, some
careful hand placements and a couple of well-executed
manoeuvres she transferred herself out of the car and
into her chair.

It was a routine refined and perfected through years
of practice, and one she could probably perform in her
sleep.

She put her handbag in her lap and took the elevator to the lobby, confident Nico couldn't have beaten
her there despite the extra minutes she'd needed to get
in and out of her car. He probably had a faster, flashier
set of wheels, but she knew the roads between here and

the gallery like the back of her hand—not to mention
half a dozen shortcuts only a local would know to use.

And yet when she rolled out of the elevator onto the
lobby's shiny sand-coloured marble, there he stood. She
frowned, confused as much as miffed. The building,
she knew, was secure, the double doors from the street
controlled by keypad access day and night. 'How did
you get inside?'

'One of your neighbours was on his way out and let
me in.' His voice was dark. His expression, too. *'Imbécile.'*

His deep scowl deterred her from jumping to the
defence of whichever neighbour had earned his disapproval. The man had no doubt thought nothing of it,
but even Marietta had to admit that giving entry to a
stranger off the street showed a dreadful disregard for
security.

'I'm on the ground floor,' she said, deciding to leave
that subject well enough alone, and wheeled her chair
around.

Silent, his big body radiating tension like ripples
of heat from a furnace, Nico followed her through the
lobby, across the quiet interior courtyard with its great
pots of manicured topiaries and into a small vestibule
housing the front doors of her apartment and one other.
As soon as they stopped his hand appeared, palm up,
in front of her face.

'Key.'

For a second—just a second—Marietta contemplated
ignoring his curt command, but this, she acknowledged,
was not the time for bravado. Her stalker might have
been in her home.

Her stalker might *still* be in her home.

Her stomach gave a sharp, sickening twist and she promptly handed over the key and watched, heart thumping, as Nico unlocked the door.

'Stay here,' he ordered, and she nodded, her mouth suddenly far too dry to protest. He went in, leaving the door an inch ajar behind him.

Marietta clutched her handbag in her lap and waited. Endless minutes ticked by, followed by more endless minutes. When Nico still hadn't reappeared and she could no longer stand the suspense, she nudged the door open, inched forward and hovered on the threshold.

'Nico?' she called out, her voice echoing off the parquet wood flooring in the entry hall.

Nothing.

'Nico!' she tried again, louder this time.

Still nothing.

This was ridiculous. She wheeled down the hallway, a hot mix of impatience and adrenaline spurring her on.

'I told you to stay put.'

Nico's deep voice slammed into her from behind. She turned her chair around and blinked, her brain instantly grappling to interpret what her eyes were seeing. The sight of Nico standing in her bedroom doorway—which, in her haste, she'd sailed straight by—was easy enough to compute. The rest—the blue latex gloves sheathing his large hands, something red and lacy dangling from his fingers—was enough to send her senses into a floor-tilting spin.

She stared at the bizarre image before her a moment longer, until her breathing resumed some kind of normal rhythm, then gripped the hand rims of her chair and started forward—only to have Nico plant his feet firmly in the doorway and block her path.

She hiked up her chin, wishing there was a way to plough through that imposing wall of muscle. 'Let me in,' she demanded, and reached for the scrap of red lace.

He jerked it out of reach. 'Marietta—'

'No. This is *my* home, Nico. Whatever he's done, whatever he's left for me, I want to see.'

It took every shred of determination she possessed not to back down under the full force of Nico's reprimanding stare. Finally, just as she began to think he wouldn't budge, his rigid stance loosened.

He pointed a latex-clad finger at her. 'Do not touch anything. There could be DNA and prints to lift.' Then he stepped aside, allowing her to enter.

Marietta's gaze went straight to the bed. To the crimson box lying open on her cream cotton coverlet and the items of luxury lingerie spilling haphazardly from between layers of soft white tissue. Scattered around the box and all across her bed were dozens upon dozens of red and white rose petals.

She moved closer, made out a red satin and black lace chemise, a sheer negligee and a pair of skimpy scarlet knickers. She closed her eyes, turned away, fighting a sudden stab of nausea. When she opened them again, her gaze landed on the item in Nico's hand. A bra, she registered now. A lacy, see-through concoction designed to be sexy and revealing as opposed to any kind of practical.

Her gaze jerked up, collided with Nico's, and for a fleeting moment it seemed as though something arced in the air between them. Something hot and bright and electric.

Which just went to prove how easily stress could affect the mind—because surely she had imagined that strange ripple of energy in the room that had felt almost like… What? Sexual awareness?

Heat flooded her face. *Si*, she was definitely stressed—not to mention embarrassed and *horrified*.

She yanked her gaze away from Nico's and took one last look at her bed. Did her stalker think he would one day share it with her? Thick bile coated her throat and the heat drained from her face, leaving her cold and clammy.

'Was there a card?' she managed to ask.

Nico turned away from her to lay the bra on the bed. 'No,' he said, snapping the gloves off his hands. He turned back to look at her, his blue eyes dark and unreadable. 'You're pale, Marietta. Do you have anything to drink?'

She nodded. *Si*, a drink…something to wash the bile out of her throat, shave the edge off her nerves. She wheeled out of the room. She wouldn't be able to sleep here tonight. Perhaps she could stay at Leo's penthouse for the weekend? He'd be travelling to Tuscany this evening, back to Helena and their adorable baby boy Riccardo. Leo's apartment building—a stunning renovated historic structure in the heart of the old city—wasn't as wheelchair-friendly as this one, but there was an elevator at least. Or perhaps she could telephone a girlfriend?

Her mind spun in jerky circles until she reached her lounge and paused. She looked around the cosy, light-filled room. Had her stalker been in here, too? Had he snooped through every inch of her beloved home? Had he *touched* her things?

Angry and sickened, she dumped her handbag on her plum-coloured sofa and headed for the solid oak sideboard. The cabinet housed a small selection of spirits—brandy, *limoncello*, and a bottle of whisky for her brother when he visited.

She grabbed two cut-glass tumblers and, hearing footsteps on the hardwood floor behind her, twisted her chin round to look at Nico. 'What will you have?'

He shrugged, the movement accentuating the breadth of his shoulders under his black open-necked shirt. 'Whatever you're having.'

She chose the brandy, unscrewed the cap and started to pour. But her hands shook and the liquid sloshed out too fast, hit the rim of the glass and splashed onto the sideboard. She cursed, the mishap pushing her to the verge of ridiculous tears, and then Nico's hand was closing over hers. Without a word, he removed the bottle from her grip and poured a generous measure into each tumbler.

Feeling foolish, she took the glass he handed her and tried to ignore the lingering effect of his touch. It was the same hot, static-like sensation she'd experienced at the gallery, when he'd crouched in front of her and taken her hand in his. Except his touch then had lasted longer, she recalled, and his thumb had rubbed gentle, delicious circles on the back of her hand, setting off a chain reaction of tiny sparks under her skin.

She took a gulp of brandy and welcomed its distracting burn. 'I don't understand,' she blurted when the heat had abated. 'Why me?' It was a question with no logical answer, she knew. She threw up a hand in helpless frustration. 'Your company provides protection services to public figures,' she said. 'You must know something about this sort of thing. Why would he go to such lengths to get my attention and yet keep his identity a secret?'

Nico stood with one hand wrapped around his glass, the other shoved in his trouser pocket. He paused, as if carefully weighing his response. 'In his mind, he's courting you, and he wants total control over this stage of his fantasy,' he said finally. 'The longer he remains anonymous, the more time he has to build the perfect relationship with you in his head and avoid the risk of real-life rejection.'

Marietta grimaced. 'That is totally twisted.'

Nico knocked back his brandy in a single swallow that made the muscles in his strong throat visibly work. 'I agree,' he said, then put the glass down and pulled his mobile phone from his pocket.

'Who are you calling?'

'Bruno, the police—' he tapped the screen and pressed the phone to his ear '—and your brother.'

Marietta sighed. *Eccellente.* An army of men was about to invade her beloved home. She chafed at the intrusion—at the very knowledge that she could no longer handle this situation by herself—but, loath as she was to admit it, she had no choice. She'd have to accept help.

Her brother arrived first, and he must have driven like a madman to complete the journey from his office in less than twenty minutes. He looked like a madman, too, with his tie skewed, his hair on end, his handsome face creased with worry—an expression that grew considerably darker the moment he looked in her bedroom.

'I'm fine,' she told him as he tipped up her chin and searched her face with dark, probing eyes. His jaw clenched, as if he didn't trust himself to speak, then he simply dropped a kiss on her head and stalked across the room to Nico.

Shortly afterwards, Bruno turned up, with a thin

middle-aged man he introduced as a private forensic specialist, and, surreal though it all seemed, her lovely peaceful home began to resemble an official crime scene.

Marietta reached again for the brandy bottle and refilled her glass. She'd suffered through countless indignities during the painstaking months of rehabilitation and therapy after her accident, but this was a violation beyond her experience—beyond anything she'd equipped herself to deal with.

And it was so unfair—even though she knew life *was* unfair. Life didn't owe her anything. Which was why she had worked so hard for everything she had: her job at the gallery, which provided a steady income, the loft she'd bought and turned into a nice little earner by converting it into an art studio and hiring out the space to working artists, and her own art career—which, with a few exhibitions of her paintings and some lucrative commissions under her belt, was finally taking off.

Admittedly she'd accepted some help from Leo in the early days, but she'd repaid him every euro she'd borrowed—despite his vociferous protests. While her dear brother had never understood his little sister's need to assert her independence, he had finally accepted it.

She looked around at her apartment, filled with strangers. For years she'd prided herself on her strength and resilience, but she didn't feel at all strong and resilient today. She felt helpless and afraid and she hated it. Her gaze travelled across the room to where her brother and Nico stood by the window, deep in conversation, their dark heads bowed. Leo had already swooped in like a man possessed, bent on taking control. How long before he tried to smother her in a suffocating blanket of protectiveness?

And then there was Nico. A man so commanding, so authoritative, she imagined the world would stop on its axis if he so ordered it.

As though sensing her scrutiny, the men stopped talking and looked up, two sets of eyes—one midnight-dark, the other a startling blue—settling on her. At once unease bubbled up inside her. She didn't like the looks on their faces. Didn't like the determined set of Nico's jaw or the hint of something too much like apology in Leo's eyes.

Marietta lifted the brandy she'd poured without spilling a drop this time and took a large, fortifying gulp.

Those expressions told her the men had decided something—and she wasn't going to like it.

Nico had lied. First to Marietta and then, by omission, to her brother. Her stalker *had* left a note, and it was now in the hands of the forensic technician who was under strict orders to keep it out of sight. Leo already looked white-lipped and murderous. If he saw the sexually explicit language in the card he would undoubtedly lose the tight rein he held on his temper.

And Marietta—well, she'd already seen more than Nico had intended her to, thanks to a stubborn streak as wide as the Atlantic. Why she couldn't have simply obeyed him and stayed put, he couldn't fathom. Most of the time women were eager to please him, not defy him, and yet Marietta seemed to have a unique talent for the latter.

He handed his friend a double shot of whisky and Leo tossed the liquid down his throat, then glared at the empty glass as if he'd like nothing more than to smash it against a wall.

'How the hell did he get in?'

Guilt sliced through Nico's gut like a jagged knife. He'd failed to anticipate this turn of events. Failed to predict accurately the threat to Marietta's safety. Not least of all, he'd failed his friend.

And Nico didn't *do* failure—not on any scale. He had tasted that bitter elixir ten years ago and his failure then had cost him his wife's life.

He jammed his fists in his pockets. Focused his thoughts with the same ruthless discipline that had seen him survive that brutal plunge into darkness and come out the other side—eventually.

'The windows don't appear to have been tampered with.' He gestured with his chin to the secured latch on the window by which they stood. 'My guess is he took an old-fashioned approach and picked the lock on the front door.'

'And the building?' Leo's scowl darkened. 'It should be secure twenty-four-seven.'

'He could have talked his way in.' Tension bit deep into Nico's shoulders. *He* had gained access the same way; it had been appallingly easy. 'Or waited and slipped in behind someone.'

'*Dio.*' Anger billowed from Leo in palpable waves. 'This is insane. What did the *polizia* say?'

Nico balled his hands more tightly in his pockets. The attitude of the two plain-clothes officers who had turned up at the apartment had reeked of apathy. 'They'll file a report, but don't expect too much action from that quarter,' he warned. 'They're viewing it as a romantic prank, at worst.'

Nico hadn't missed their exchange of lascivious grins over the lingerie and he'd wanted to knock the officers' heads together, plant his boot firmly in the seats of their pants. Just as he'd wanted to kick *himself* earlier, when he and Marietta had been in her bedroom and his thoughts had gone to a dark, carnal place they'd had no right to go. Not with Marietta. She was a victim, he'd had to remind himself, a woman who needed his help— and wondering how her ample breasts would look encased in that barely there bra had been wrong on too many levels to count.

Leo swore now—a vicious expletive that drew not so much as a blink from Nico. Five years in the French Foreign Legion as a young man, followed by several stints as a private military contractor, working alongside war-hardened ex-soldiers, had broadened his vocabulary to include every filthy word and crude expression known to man in half a dozen languages.

'Find him, Nico,' Leo grated, his expression fierce. 'Do whatever you have to to keep her safe.'

Do whatever you have to.

Those five words seemed to strike Nico in the gut one by one, like the consecutive blows of a steel mallet, and they left him savagely winded. He'd heard those same words before, ten years ago, from his former father-in-law's mouth.

Do whatever you have to.

And Nico had.

He'd utilised every resource within his power. Called in every favour owed him. Employed every conceivable tactic within the law—and beyond—to get Senator Jack Lewisham's daughter back.

But it wasn't enough. It all went belly up. And Nico

committed one critical, unforgivable sin: he underestimated the men who had taken her.

He failed. Failed to bring the senator's daughter home. Failed to save his wife's life.

Her father, who'd only grudgingly accepted Nico as a son-in-law in the first place, was inconsolable—a man irreparably broken by the loss of his only daughter.

He had not spoken to Nico since.

Do whatever you have to.

He glanced over at Marietta, nursing her brandy in her hand, quietly studying them. She was pale, but beautiful, those dark, intelligent eyes sizing him up. No doubt she was a little annoyed that she was not privy to his and Leo's conversation. She was a woman of undeniable strength, yet the pallor of her skin, the obvious tension around her eyes and mouth, belied her show of composure. He could see it in the rigid set of her shoulders, her too-tight grip on the glass, the unblinking wideness of her eyes.

Marietta wasn't afraid.

She was petrified.

Nico turned back to Leo, an idea seeding, taking shape in his mind. An extreme idea, perhaps, for it would mean sacrificing the sanctity of his personal space for a time, but extreme circumstances called for extreme measures. He clamped a hand over his friend's shoulder. 'Do you trust me, *mon ami*?'

Leo looked him in the eye. 'Of course,' he said at once, his voice gruff. 'You do not need to ask me that, Nicolas.'

Nico nodded. It was the answer he'd hoped for. *'Très bien,'* he said. 'I have a suggestion.'

CHAPTER THREE

'ABSOLUTELY NOT!'

Marietta looked from her brother to Nico and back to Leo. *They had to be joking.* Yet neither man wore an expression she could describe as anything other than deadly serious. They both looked stern, formidable, standing side by side with their feet planted apart, their arms folded over their broad chests. Looking at them was akin to seeing double, and she wanted to slap them both.

'Pazzo!' she cried, gesturing with one hand in the air to emphasise just how crazy she found their proposal.

They had the gall to stare at her then, as if *she* were crazy. As if the idea of disappearing to some island off the coast of France until her stalker had been caught was the perfect solution and they couldn't understand why she didn't agree.

And not just *any* island.

Oh, no.

Nico's island.

Nico's *home.*

With Nico.

Heat that had nothing to do with anger and everything to do with the idea of being holed up on a remote island with Nicolas César scalded her insides.

Torture. That was what it would be. Exquisite torture of a kind she didn't dare contemplate.

She swigged down her brandy, set the glass on the sideboard and wheeled towards her kitchen. Enough alcohol. *Coffee.* That was what she needed. An injection of caffeine to hone her senses—and her tongue—for the showdown she was about to have with her brother.

He followed, his dark mood like a gathering thundercloud at her back.

'Marietta, just stop for a minute and think about this.'

'I don't need to stop in order to think.' She yanked the lid off a tin of coffee beans, unleashing a rich, nutty aroma that failed to please her the way it normally did. 'I'm a woman, so I can multitask, and I *am* thinking about it. I'm thinking what a stupid, *stupid* idea it is.'

She ignored his heavy sigh.

'You can't do this,' she ploughed on, pouring a handful of dark beans into her cherished *caffè* machine—her first port of call in the mornings, when strong coffee was a prerequisite for coherent speech. 'You can't just sweep in here and go all Big Brother on me. I'm not a rebellious, out-of-control teenager any more. I'm thirty years old. You're not responsible for me.'

An abrupt silence fell.

Marietta spun her chair around, regret, hot and instant, welling in her throat. 'Leo, I…I'm sorry.'

His jaw tightened. 'I will always feel responsible for you.'

'I know.'

Instantly she hated herself for hitting that sensitive nerve—the one that had been flayed raw by her accident thirteen years ago and had never completely healed. Leo blamed himself. Believed he should have tried harder to keep her at home that night.

The truth was no one could have saved Marietta except herself. *She* was the one who had sneaked out of the tiny flat she and Leo had shared. *She* was the one who'd gone to the party he'd expressly forbidden her to attend. *She* was the one who'd climbed into the back seat of a car with an inebriated driver.

Her decisions that night had borne consequences she had no choice but to live with, but the hell she had put her brother through was a heavy cross she would always bear.

The last of her temper dissolved. Leo loved her... wanted to keep her safe. How could she stay angry with him over that?

'I can't just drop everything and disappear.' She tried for a softer, more reasonable tone. 'I have a job. Responsibilities. And Ricci's party is a week from tomorrow. Helena's had it planned for months. What if this guy hasn't been caught by then?' She shook her head. 'I can't stay away indefinitely—and I won't miss my nephew's first birthday.'

Leo crossed his arms, perched his lean frame on the edge of her low granite bench. 'Your life could be in danger, Marietta. Have you considered that?'

Now she wanted to roll her eyes, accuse him of being melodramatic—but *was* he? What had happened today felt serious, even if the *polizia* were inclined to view it as a prank. And after today's performance who could predict what kind of sick encore her stalker had planned?

A dull throb started up behind her eyes and she pressed her thumb and forefinger against her lids.

'When you cannot eliminate the source of danger your best defence is to remove yourself from its path.'

Nico's deep voice rumbled into the room and she jerked her hand down from her face. He loomed in her kitchen doorway, his sheer presence so commanding, his physique so powerful, that for a moment she couldn't help but feel a sense of reassurance—of safety—steal over her.

Still. That didn't change anything.

She couldn't put her life on hold indefinitely.

'A week, Marietta,' Leo urged. 'Give Nico a week.'

She looked at Nico. 'And how exactly are you going to catch my stalker if you're on an island with me?'

'I have faith in my people. He's upped the ante and so will we.'

'And if I insist on staying in Rome?'

'Then I'll appoint a bodyguard who'll shadow you day and night, wherever you go.'

'And I will stay,' Leo said. 'For as long as necessary.'

No. She gave an adamant shake of her head. 'You can't, Leo. It wouldn't be fair to Helena—or Ricci. You should be in Tuscany with them this weekend, not babysitting me.'

He shrugged. 'They'll come to Rome.'

Marietta pressed her fingertips to her temples. She knew her sister-in-law well. Helena was a kind, capable woman who wouldn't hesitate to uproot her domestic idyll for Marietta's sake. But Marietta's conscience wouldn't allow it. This was *her* problem to handle. How could she justify disrupting their lives when she had an alternative?

A week. Could she forego her independence, abandon her life, for a week? She looked at her brother and saw the deep lines of worry etched into his face. Her safety would give him peace of mind and didn't she owe him that much? He'd made so many sacrifices when they were younger, worked himself ragged to give them both a chance at a better life. Doing what he asked of her now seemed a small thing in return.

She pushed her hands through her hair. Released her breath on a long sigh. '*Si.* Okay,' she said. 'One week.'

Marietta sat in the front passenger seat of her brother's car the next morning and chewed the inside of her cheek, fighting the powerful urge to blurt out that she'd changed her mind and all this was too sudden, too unexpected, and she couldn't possibly travel at short notice like this. Travel—for her—required careful planning, special considerations, and they hadn't given her a chance to plan a damned thing.

'Quit fretting, *carina.*' Leo glanced over, then returned his attention to negotiating the chaotic morning traffic. Even on a Saturday Rome's roads were flat-out crazy. 'Nico has everything under control.'

She cast him a sideways look. 'Will you stop doing that?'

'What?'

'Reading my mind.'

He grinned. 'If I knew the secret to reading women's minds, I would be a very rich man indeed.'

Had Marietta been in the mood for banter she would have reminded her brother that he *was* a rich man. Instead she turned her gaze out through the side window and watched the blur of busy streets and *piazze* and sidewalk cafés go by. She believed Leo when he said his friend had everything under control—and that was the problem. Nico had all the control and she had none. It made her feel adrift, somehow. Alienated from her life. She didn't even know where exactly in the Mediterranean they were going. Until yesterday she'd never heard of Île de Lavande.

She rested her head against the soft leather seat.

Island of Lavender.

At least the name was pretty.

Perhaps she'd find some inspiration there for her next series of paintings? The European summer was in its twilight, but Nico had said the island was still warm, so she'd gone light on clothes and made room for packing her brushes and a set of fast-drying acrylic paints, a sketchpad and a small canvas. She'd even squeezed in a collapsible easel.

She supposed a few quiet, uninterrupted days of sketching and painting wouldn't be so bad—but only a few. She'd agreed to a week, no longer, and she still planned to be back in time for little Ricci's party. Nico's men would just have to pull out all the stops to find her stalker, because she wasn't compromising on that.

As for the gallery—she'd made two phone calls from Leo's apartment last night: one to her boss, the owner of the gallery, who'd expressed her support and understanding once apprised of the circumstances, and the other to Lina, who'd assured Marietta that everything would run smoothly in her absence.

Too soon, the powerful car decelerated and the runway of the Aeroporto dell'Urbe came into sight. They drove through a security checkpoint and then they were on the Tarmac, headed for a sleek silver and black jet with the circular logo of César Security emblazoned on its tail.

Nico appeared in the open hatchway and Marietta leaned forward in her seat for a better view of the aircraft—and him.

And, *mamma mia*, he looked good. Faded jeans clung to long, muscular legs, he wore an untucked, open-necked white shirt, and a pair of dark shades obscured those deep blue eyes. His dark brown hair was stylishly mussed and his angular jaw sported a layer of stubble that only exaggerated his masculine appeal. He looked less formidable than yesterday. More relaxed, despite the ever-serious expression he wore.

Edible, an inner voice whispered, and she felt her face flame. *Santo cielo!* Her mind was *not* going there.

He jogged down the steps with an easy masculine grace, and he was pulling open the car door before her cheeks had even had time to cool. He hunkered down beside her.

'*Bonjour*, Marietta.' He removed his sunglasses and the impact of that blue gaze arrowed all the way to her stomach. 'Are you ready for our journey?'

The morning breeze ruffled his hair and carried into the car the scent of soap and lemons, along with something more earthy and rich. Marietta tried not to breathe in, but the need for air prevailed. She frowned, growing more irritable by the second. No man should smell that enticing. That delectable.

'Do you have half-decent coffee on board?'

A muscle quirked at the side of his mouth—a mere flicker of movement that might have turned into a smile if he'd allowed it.

Had she ever seen Nico smile? It occurred to her that she hadn't—not properly.

'The coffee is *exceptionnel*,' he said, and she wished he wouldn't speak French.

It did squishy things to her insides and there was nothing good about squishy. *Nothing*.

He slid his shades back on. 'There's a lift on standby if you want it.'

She shook her head. '*Grazie*, but Leo will carry me on,' she said, preferring that simple, no-fuss solution over the mechanical platform that could raise her, wheelchair and all, to the door of the plane. Besides the ground crew there were few people around, but all the same she hated anything that created a spectacle or shone a spotlight on her disability. People often stared without meaning to, and though she'd grown inured to the curiosity of others, occasionally the attention still bothered her.

Minutes later her luggage was stowed and she was settled in a large, soft leather seat, her wheelchair reassembled and within reach should she wish to move about the plane's roomy interior once they were airborne. Out on the Tarmac, Nico and Leo exchanged final words. A moment before, when Leo had kissed her goodbye, silly tears had pricked the backs of her eyes, and she blinked now to clear her vision, annoyed because she rarely allowed herself to cry. She'd taught herself to be strong, to handle whatever challenges life threw at her, and all *this*—this was just another obstacle to overcome.

'I hear you're after some good, strong coffee, honey.'

Evelyn, the flight attendant who'd earlier introduced herself and then disappeared to give Marietta and Leo privacy, stood now by Marietta's seat, her cherry-red lips stretched into a friendly smile.

Marietta pulled herself together and looked up at the slender uniformed blonde. '*Si. Grazie.* Black and very strong, please.'

Not how she'd have ordered coffee in a bar in Rome—requesting a *caffè* in Italy automatically got you what the rest of the world labelled espresso—but Evelyn wasn't Italian, and Marietta wasn't in the mood for weak, watery coffee.

Evelyn tilted her head. *'Un caffè ristretto?'*

Marietta felt her brows climb and the other woman laughed. It was a pleasant laugh. Bubbly and bright.

'I know.' Evelyn winked. 'Who'd have thought a gal from Mississippi would know how to make proper Italian coffee.'

Marietta couldn't hold back a smile. 'You just improved my morning.'

Another long-lashed wink. 'My pleasure, honey. One coffee coming up,' she said, and Marietta decided right then that she liked Evelyn. Very, very much.

A short while later they were airborne. An hour after that they were cruising at forty-one thousand feet above sea level, halfway between Rome and their destination of Toulon, on the southern coast of France. Marietta knew this because Evelyn was a veritable fount of information. Unlike Nico who, aside from enquiring about her comfort prior to take-off, had uttered scarcely a word in the time since.

He sat in one of the cushioned club-style seats on the other side of the cabin, facing in her direction, so that if he looked up from his laptop they could easily converse. He hadn't. Not once in the last sixty minutes.

Which made the challenge of snagging his attention almost impossible to resist.

'Here you go, honey.'

Evelyn placed a glass and the bottle of mineral water Marietta had asked for on the shiny walnut table in front of her. Marietta smiled her thanks. The *honey* might have sounded patronising from anyone else. From the tall, statuesque American it was just part of her charm.

Marietta watched her return to the other end of the cabin. It had to be an exciting life, jetting around the globe. Evelyn wore no rings, so presumably she was single, free of ties. Marietta didn't doubt she worked hard, but the perks had to be rewarding.

She waited until Evelyn was out of earshot before speaking. 'I like her.'

Nico's head came up and in her mind Marietta did a little self-congratulatory air-punch. Finally she had his attention.

'Pardon?'

'Evelyn,' she said, and watched to see his reaction. Because he had to know how beautiful his flight attendant was. No man could fail to notice a pair of legs as long and toned as Evelyn's, never mind that everything else about her was flawless and elegant.

Though Marietta felt sordid even thinking it, she couldn't help but wonder what level of 'personal service' Evelyn gave her boss. They were two beautiful people in the prime of their lives; they *had* to be aware of each other. Evelyn embodied the kind of physical perfection a man like Nico would no doubt look for in a sexual partner.

And yet he was frowning at her as if he hadn't a clue what—or whom—she was talking about.

'Your flight attendant,' she said, and stared at him, astonished. 'You don't *know* the names of your flight crew?'

He shrugged. 'I have many hundreds of employees,' he said, his tone implying that he considered that a perfectly adequate excuse—and then he returned his attention to his computer.

End of conversation.

Marietta sniffed. 'Well, I like her,' she said to the top of his head. 'She's very good at her job. And she has spectacular legs.'

That got his attention back.

He looked at her and she shrugged. 'I'm an artist,' she said. 'I appreciate beauty in all its forms. And you have to admit Evelyn has great legs.'

'I hadn't noticed.'

'Really?' Her voice rang with disbelief.

'Oui,' he said, holding her gaze for a drawn-out beat. 'Really.'

And then something happened that she wasn't prepared for. His gaze dropped. First to her mouth, where it lingered for several seconds—long enough to make her self-consciously moisten her lips—and then down to her chest, where it rested only briefly. And yet the effect of that very deliberate scrutiny was so shocking, so profound, he might as well have touched her.

Heat prickled over her skin, from her neck to her breasts, and her heart pounded so hard, her pulse beat like the wings of a moth trapped in her throat.

Then his gaze came back to her face and she knew he must see the heightened colour there. One side of his mouth did that flickering thing again. That quirk that wasn't quite a smile.

'I'm a breast man myself,' he said, as casually as if he'd said he preferred beans over peas, or his steak medium rare, and then he went back to his work as if the air all around them *wasn't* sizzling and popping in the wake of that brief, electrifying exchange.

Marietta pressed her lips together. *Touché*, she conceded silently. Because shocking her into silence had no doubt been his intent. She uncapped her mineral water, filled her glass and took a long swig. But the cool liquid didn't douse the heat in her cheeks. Or the embarrassment washing through her. She had pushed him—deliberately provoked a reaction. Because... *Why?* Because she was bored? Because she felt ignored? Because Nico was the most beautiful, aloof man she'd ever met and some needy, feminine part of her craved his attention?

Oh, now, *that* did not sit well.

Marietta did not need a man's attention. She did not need a man, full stop. Her body might be broken beyond repair, but she had rebuilt her life regardless and it was everything she wanted. Everything she needed. Her job, her success as an artist…it was enough. It had to be enough.

Because she was done with wanting things she would never have. Things that couldn't be. Things that were simply not written in her destiny.

You are a realist.

And Nico… Nico was just a fantasy.

CHAPTER FOUR

THE WEATHER IN Toulon was clear when they circled in
for landing, the bright blue of the sky stretching as far
as the eye could see along the Côte d'Azur, enhancing
the beauty of a coastline that was coveted by holiday-
makers and frequented year-round by the world's famous and rich.

Nico had no interest in the glamorous beaches and
glittering nightlife that gave the French Riviera its reputation as a decadent playground. Toulon featured on his
itinerary several times a year only because it was the
nearest mainland airport to Île de Lavande, the quiet,
secluded home he retreated to when he wasn't residing
in Paris or New York or travelling across continents
for business.

On occasion, however, when his mind grew restless
and his body demanded a certain kind of release, he'd
linger on the mainland for a night and venture into a
glitzy casino or high-end bar. He'd order a shot or two
of something—whatever he fancied on the night—and
wait for them to come. And they always did. Those
women with no hidden agendas who, like him, were
simply looking for a good time. He would choose one—
only ever one…gluttony wasn't his thing—and take her

to a luxury hotel suite, order champagne and anything else she desired from the menu and let her flirt and tease for a while if that was her wont.

But not for too long.

He could be a gentleman when he chose, but he was no saint. Not when his thoughts were dark and his body primed and the only way to obliterate his memories was by losing himself in the pleasure of soft flesh and tight, wet heat.

Sometimes, if the sex was outstanding, he'd take a number, hook up with the same woman again, even indulge in the occasional dinner or outing. But only if she understood that pleasure was the only offer on the table. He had nothing more to give. Nothing beyond the physical certainly.

Julia had been his one love.

His one chance at a normal, happy life.

He didn't deserve another. Didn't want another only to have it brutally torn from him.

The jet touched down and he channelled his thoughts back to the present as they taxied to a stop on a private strip of Tarmac, close to where his helicopter awaited. He released his seat belt and stood, glancing over to where Marietta sat, as silent now as she'd been for the last hour of the flight.

He still didn't really know what their conversation in the air had been about. He'd wasted no time shutting it down, sensing it was going nowhere good, nowhere *safe*, but in so doing he'd spiked his awareness of her, and that awareness was still humming in his body like an electric current he couldn't switch off.

Was she upset with him? Hard to tell. Her gaze was focused out of the large oval window so that all he could see was her proud, elegant profile. *Dieu*, but she was lovely. High cheekbones. Straight nose. Flawless skin. Hair like burnished mahogany. And her lips were soft and full—ripe for tasting.

He clenched his jaw. *Not helpful.*

'Marietta?'

He half hoped she *was* annoyed. A little reserve, a touch of coolness between them, might be a good thing. He had one objective and that was to keep her safe. This spark of attraction he felt—there was no room for it.

She turned her head then and his hopes met a swift end. She didn't look angry. Didn't even look mildly irritated. Hell, she was *smiling* at him.

'Are we flying to the island in that?'

For a moment he didn't register the question, blindsided as he was by that smile. The pretty flush on her cheekbones. The breathless quality to her voice that seemed to stroke right into him.

She looked out through the window again and he leaned down, followed the line of her gaze to where his chopper sat on the Tarmac, its long rotor blades and black paintwork gleaming in the sunshine. A man in blue overalls and a fluorescent orange vest moved around the craft, completing a thorough safety check that Nico himself would repeat prior to take-off.

'*Oui,*' he said. 'The island is accessible by boat, but the chopper is faster.'

'I've never been in a helicopter.' Her gaze swung to his. 'Will you pilot it?'

'Of course.'

She fired another look out of the window and then undid her seatbelt and smoothed the creases from her grey linen pants. 'Okay. I'll wait here while the luggage and my wheelchair are transferred,' she said, her voice turning brisk. 'Take me last.'

'There's a lift—'

'No,' she cut across him. 'No fuss. Please.' Her gaze didn't quite meet his. 'It will be quicker and easier if you carry me.'

Easier, Nico reflected ten minutes later as he settled Marietta into the cockpit of the chopper, was a relative term. Because the effort of willing his groin not to harden in response to holding a soft, warm woman in his arms—a woman who smelled enticingly of strawberries and vanilla and something faintly exotic—had not come anywhere close to being easy.

He strapped her into the harness, made a couple of adjustments that brought his fingers dangerously, agonisingly close to her breasts, then hastily withdrew his hands.

'Comfortable?' She nodded and he handed her a black helmet. 'This has a built-in headset so we can communicate. I need to do a final weather check and then we're set.'

Her gaze turned skyward. 'The weather looks perfect.'

'*Oui*. But we're flying twenty miles south over open sea. The marine winds can be unpredictable.'

Rather like his body, he thought grimly.

Marietta's heart raced and she gripped the edges of her seat. She looked down at the deep, surging swells of the Mediterranean Sea, then up again to the lone mass of land looming in the distance. Silhouetted against a bright blue sky, the island's long, uneven shape teased her imagination and made her think of a great serpent slumbering on the horizon.

She'd always wanted to fly in a helicopter and now she was hurtling over the ocean in one and struggling to hold back a grin. Which was crazy. What reason did she have to smile or feel breathless and giddy?

Yesterday her life had been turned upside down, her home invaded by a man who at worst was a predator and at best was a disturbed individual in dire need of a shrink. Yet somehow, right at this moment, all of that seemed very distant and she really was fighting an insane urge to grin.

She let her gaze roam the cockpit's interior, fascinated by the dials and buttons and levers. Beside her, Nico looked at home in the pilot's seat, his large hands working the controls of the powerful machine with dexterity and ease.

Strong hands, she thought, recalling how he'd carried her from the jet to the helicopter as if she weighed next to nothing. As if carrying a woman was something he did every day and the experience left him unaffected. While *she* had been hyper-aware of *everything*. From the hardness of his body and the citrusy scent of his cologne to the tanned triangle of chest in the opening of his shirt and the glimpse of dark hair at the base of that V.

She'd wondered whether the texture of that hair was soft or coarse. If it thickened and spread across his chest or was merely a dusting. If it arrowed into a fine line that bisected his stomach and travelled into the waistband of his pants and lower.

Inappropriate thoughts she should not have had then and should not be having now. Not about the man she was going to spend the next few days cooped up with on an island.

She dragged her attention off his hands and back to the mass of land ahead of them that was appearing more substantial by the second. Running her gaze along the nearest stretch of coastline, she made out three separate white sand beaches and, nestled into the lee of a lush hill range, a large village and a port, where rows of colourful boats were moored to long wooden wharves jutting into clear turquoise waters.

'You own a whole *village*?'

A short burst of static came over the headset before the rich timbre of Nico's voice filled her helmet. It was an odd sensation—as if he was inside her head and all around her at the same time.

'No. I own sixty percent of the island, including the southern and western coasts. The rest—including the northern beaches, the olive groves to the east and a small commercial vineyard—is now owned by various locals whose families have lived on Île de Lavande for hundreds of years.'

'*Now* owned?' she said. 'Did they not always own it?'

'*Non*. For several centuries the island was owned by a single aristocratic French family. They employed caretakers and servants who settled on the land with their families. It wasn't until a wealthy American industrialist bought the island in the early nineteen-hundreds and decided to sell off some parcels of land that the locals finally had the opportunity to become landowners instead of leaseholders.'

Fascinated, she took a moment to absorb it all. 'How do the islanders make their living? Fishing?'

'*Oui*. And from olives and wine. Most of which they sell to the mainland. Plus a controlled level of tourism.'

'Controlled?'

'Limited numbers of tourists, and only at certain times of the year. During those months a passenger and car ferry visits twice a week—no more. The villagers rely on the revenue, but they also want to protect the environment—and their privacy.'

'Are most of them descended from the original settlers?'

'Many of them, *oui*.'

'That must be amazing—to know the history of generations of your family.' Silence crackled in her headset. 'Do you have any familial links to the island?' she asked.

'*Non,*' he said.

'So…you have family living in France?'

'*Non.*'

The message in that second abrupt no was clear. *Subject off-limits*. Marietta bit down on her tongue—and her curiosity—and focused on the scenery.

Ahead, an old sturdy fishing vessel rode the ocean swells as it chugged slowly into the calmer waters of the harbour. Nico flew the chopper directly over the boat, low enough to see the broad smiles on the fishermen's upturned faces. They raised their arms and waved and Nico waved back—and Marietta's surprise lasted only a second. Mr Security Conscious *would* know his neighbours, she realised. Even a whole village of them.

They neared land and he banked the helicopter to the right, angling them over the port and the outskirts of the village. She glimpsed red-tiled roofs and open shutters on whitewashed houses, an old stone church and the crumbling remains of a sprawling derelict structure on the crest of a hill.

'Where's your home?'

'Further around the coast,' he said. 'Twenty-five minutes by road from the port.'

The village fell behind them and she looked down, saw rows upon rows of pine trees extending into the island's interior. It was lush and dense—much more fertile and beautiful than she'd expected.

'Will you show me some of the island while we're here?'

'Perhaps. If time allows. We have work to do first.'

She turned her head to look at him. 'What kind of work?'

'Questions and answers.'

Her brows knitted. 'I don't understand…'

'We are going to dissect your life, Marietta. Day by day. Hour by hour. Minute by minute. You are going to break down every routine for me—everything you do, everywhere you go, everyone you meet—until we have ruled out the possibility that your stalker is someone you know or have met.'

A groan rose in her throat. 'But I've answered all of Bruno's questions. *And* yours.'

'And you will answer them again,' he said. 'As many times as I need you to. Until I am satisfied.'

His tone was uncompromising and a shiver rippled through her. *How ironic.* Yesterday she'd spared a thought for anyone unfortunate enough to find themselves interrogated by Nicolas César—soon she would experience for herself that very ordeal.

Her mood well and truly dampened, she stayed silent for the rest of the flight, even stifling her exclamation of *wow* when she spotted the house perched on a high plateau above a steep limestone cliff.

Sleek, white, and über-modern, the expansive single-level dwelling might have dominated its surroundings. Instead, its simple understated design complemented the landscape, with acres of glass reflecting the sky and the rich, fertile land all around it. On the ocean side a flat terrace featured a large swimming pool, which sparkled like a sheet of cobalt glass in the sunshine. On the inland flank, a circular courtyard sat at the head of a long winding driveway which descended into a thick forest of towering pines.

Marietta surveyed the property as Nico set them down on a dedicated helipad a short distance from the courtyard.

It was, she decided after a moment, just like its owner.

Stark. Remote. And beautiful.

CHAPTER FIVE

'ENOUGH!'

The shrill note in Marietta's voice brought Nico's head up. He laid his pen on the legal pad he used for old-fashioned note-taking and leaned back in his chair. 'Take a breath, Marietta.'

'Don't patronise me,' she snapped, a flash of Italian temper darkening her eyes to the colour of hot, bitter espresso. She squeezed them shut and pinched the delicate bridge of her nose.

Nico stretched out his denim-clad legs, crossed his bare feet at the ankles and waited for her to calm down.

'I'm sorry.' She dropped her hand, opened her eyes. 'I didn't mean to snap. I just don't see how where I choose to buy my fruit and vegetables on a Saturday morning can possibly be relevant.'

A warm, gentle Mediterranean breeze rippled the surface of the pool and swayed the enormous umbrella which shaded the outdoor table where they sat. Sighing, Marietta scraped her long hair back from her face and secured the lustrous swathe into a high ponytail which she fastened with an elastic band from her wrist.

Toying with his pen, Nico studied her. He couldn't

detect a scrap of make-up on her this morning and still she was beautiful. 'More coffee?'

She nodded. 'Please.'

He refilled her cup from the heavy silver coffee pot his part-time housekeeper Josephine had set out for them, along with a selection of fruits, thick yoghurt, freshly baked croissants and homemade jams.

It had been good of Josephine to drive up from the village on a Sunday morning. She and her son Luc had already been at the house in the hours prior to Nico and Marietta's arrival, cleaning, stocking the kitchen and installing special handrails in the guest en-suite bathroom at Nico's request. He appreciated their commitment; he'd given them only a day's notice and yet they hadn't complained at a time when their family-run bistro had to be busy with the final late-summer run of tourists.

Josephine had said she'd returned this morning to check that everything was satisfactory, but Nico figured it was curiosity as much as solicitude that had brought her back. In the four years since he'd built his home on Île de Lavande, he'd never invited a guest there—had never allowed anyone inside his sanctuary aside from the select few he employed for its upkeep. In that respect Marietta was something of a novelty, and she had—not surprisingly—charmed his housekeeper.

It was a charm she had not extended to *him* for the last hour and a half, he noted dryly. He sat forward, picked up his pen. 'Tell me more about Davide,' he said, and watched her expression instantly shutter.

'There isn't much to tell. We had a relationship and then we broke up. End of story.'

'You were together for two years.' The same length

of time he and Julia had been married. 'It must have been serious,' he said, ignoring the sudden sharp clench in his chest.

Her shoulders, bare aside from the straps of her pale blue tank top, hitched up. 'For a while, *si*.'

'Who broke it off?'

'I did.'

'Why?'

'That's personal.' She picked up her sunglasses from the table and pushed them onto her face. 'And if you think Davide could be my stalker, you're wrong. He's moved on. Married. Started a family. What is it the English say? You are barking into the wrong bush.'

His mouth twitched despite himself. 'Up the wrong tree.'

She flicked a hand in the air. 'Whatever. Anyway, it can't be Davide. The cards are always signed off with an *S*.'

He put down his pen again. Worked to keep the impatience out of his voice. 'First, the *S* could stand for anything,' he said. 'Second, I know this is difficult, but any previous romantic partners must be considered as potential suspects until they've been definitively ruled out.'

Her graceful chin took on that stubborn tilt he was learning to recognise. 'How do you know my stalker isn't a complete stranger?'

'I don't. And I haven't discounted the possibility. But the majority of stalking victims are stalked by someone they know—two-thirds of female victims by a former or current partner.' He paused before driving home his point. 'It is extremely likely that you have met or know your stalker in some capacity. He could be your neighbour. Someone you've met through work. Maybe the guy who sells you fruit at the market on a Saturday morning.'

She shuddered visibly. '*Santo cielo*. It could be anyone.'

'*Exactement*. And the sooner we narrow the field of potential suspects, the closer we get to identifying the real perpetrator.'

She sat a little straighter in her wheelchair, pulled in a deep breath and slowly expelled it. 'Okay.' She folded her hands in her lap. 'What do you want to know about Davide?'

'How did he react when you ended the relationship?'

She hesitated. 'He was upset.'

'Angry?'

'A little,' she said, quietly. 'Mostly hurt, I think.'

'He didn't want it to end?'

She reached for her coffee, took a careful sip, then replaced the cup before answering. 'He'd asked me to marry him.'

Nico blinked.

'I know,' she said, before he'd fully processed that potentially critical piece of information. 'A perfectly normal, eligible, good-looking guy asks a crippled girl to marry him and she says no.' She laughed, but the sound wasn't at all pretty. 'You're thinking a girl like me can hardly afford to be choosy, right?'

A flash of anger—and perhaps indignation—snapped his brows down. 'That is not what I was thinking.'

'But you were thinking *something*,' she challenged.

He felt a pulse leap in his jaw. 'I was thinking you should have told me this sooner.'

'Is that all?'

'*Non,*' he said tersely. 'I was also thinking the poor bastard must have been crushed when you turned him down.'

Marietta's chin jerked back—with surprise or scepticism? He couldn't tell.

'Why did you reject his proposal?'

She picked up her coffee again, took another sip, as if buying time to compose herself. When she put the cup down her hand wasn't quite steady. 'Davide wanted to *fix* me.'

'What do you mean?'

'He was obsessed with the idea of curing me.'

'Your paralysis?'

'*Si.*'

He frowned. 'And that was a bad thing?'

'For me it was. It made our relationship untenable.'

'Why?'

Her slim shoulders lifted, dropped. 'Because I didn't share his obsession.'

Nico rubbed his jaw, assimilating that. 'So you don't believe in the possibility of a cure?'

A small groove appeared on her forehead. 'I believe there's hope for a cure. Technology and medicine will always advance, and people who are passionate about finding a way to reverse spinal cord damage will always be looking for the next major breakthrough. But at some point you have to stop chasing the miracle and get on with the business of living. And that means learning to accept the hand you've been dealt. Davide couldn't do that. He couldn't accept that I wouldn't one day get out of this chair and walk. Instead he spent every spare minute researching medical journals and the latest treatments he thought I should try.'

Marietta paused. She was glad suddenly that she'd put her sunglasses on, because if eyes truly were the windows to the soul she didn't want Nico seeing into hers. Didn't want him seeing the hidden part of her that still hurt whenever she thought about Davide and his obsession with 'fixing' her.

She might have shared his enthusiasm if she hadn't already travelled that same road with her brother in the early years after the accident, when Leo convinced himself—and her—that there was a real chance she would walk again. His tenacity and determination were contagious and she let herself get swept up in the possibilities—agreed, once Leo convinced her he could afford it, to travel to Germany and undergo the experimental treatments he'd researched.

But in the end it all turned into nothing more than a wild rollercoaster of shattered hopes and dreams. An enormous, heartbreaking reality check that devastated her for a time—until she picked herself up and fiercely told herself that from then on she was going to be a *realist*, not a dreamer.

And then, scarcely a year later, she met Davide and became that naive, hopeful fool all over again. The one who was stupid enough to think she could have something as ordinary as a husband and a family. The doctors had told her years before that she was physically capable of bearing children but she'd firmly quashed that dream—because what man would want to have a family with *her*?

But then Davide had come along, and at some point during their relationship she'd forgotten that *ordinary* didn't exist for her. That *ordinary* was a fantasy. That *ordinary* was something she had forfeited the night she'd climbed into the back seat of that car with her young, ill-fated friends.

'He said he loved me, but the woman he loved was the version of me in his head,' she said now, unable to stop a hint of bitterness creeping into her voice. 'The one he wanted to turn me into. The one who could walk.'

Nico shifted in his chair. 'Were you not tempted to consider any of the treatments?'

And now he was delving deeper than he needed to go. Deeper than he knew he should go. Finding Marietta's stalker and keeping her safe until then were his only concerns. He needn't care about anything else. Caring, he reminded himself, made people vulnerable, weak—and in his line of work, there was no room for weakness.

'I've been down that road,' she said. 'I had several surgeries and experimental stem cell procedures at a specialised clinic in Berlin. The results were negligible. A tiny bit of muscle movement, some increased sensation—that's all.'

'And Davide knew this?'

'*Si*. He said I gave up too easily.'

Nico's mouth settled into a grim line. She'd made the right decision to ditch the *imbécile*. Any man fool enough to label this woman a quitter didn't deserve her.

He closed the pad, pushed his chair back from the table. He would call Bruno, relay the information he deemed useful and tell him to take a closer look at the ex. Bruno had already compiled a superficial dossier on Davide, but now Nico would give the green light to dig deeper. Pay the guy a visit.

'We're done?' She sounded surprised. Or relieved. Maybe both.

He stood. 'For now,' he said, aware of something like relief coursing through his own veins.

These last two hours had been intense—for both of them—and he suddenly wanted some distance from this woman. Wanted her out of his sight so that he could concentrate on work and stop noticing things about her he had no legitimate need to notice.

Like the way those full lips of hers pursed when she was thinking and one cheek hollowed slightly, as if she were biting the inside of it. Or the way she sometimes used her hands to emphasise a point and at other times clasped them in her lap to give the impression of composure. Or the way she occasionally rubbed her shoulders or the back of her neck, as if the muscles there were cramped and needed loosening. Or—and this was by far the most disturbing of all his observations—how pink and delectable her tongue looked when it darted out to rescue a flake of croissant from her bottom lip.

Nico picked up the pen and pad and stepped back. *Oui.* Distance. A lot of it—and for the rest of the day, preferably. 'You did well, Marietta. Relax now. Enjoy the sunshine.'

She looked up and he saw his reflection in duplicate in her oversized sunglasses. 'What are you going to do?'

'Work.'

'All day?'

'Probably.' He turned towards the house. Pretended not to see the sudden slight pout on those voluptuous lips.

'What about sightseeing?'

He pulled up. 'Pardon?'

'Sightseeing,' she repeated. 'You said you would show me the island.'

He frowned. 'If time permitted.'

Her chin rose in that tenacious way of hers that stirred irritation and something much hotter, more dangerous, inside him.

'I've answered your questions,' she said.

He curled his fingers around the pen. 'My priority is to keep you safe until your stalker is caught, Marietta, not babysit you or play tour guide.' Her head drew back as if he'd spat in her face, but he ruthlessly fought the urge to soften his tone. 'Now, if you'll excuse me, I have work to do.'

He turned and strode into the house. Into his study. Where he tossed the pen and pad onto his desk with such force the pen pinwheeled across the glass surface and onto the floor.

Grunting, he leaned down to pick it up and told himself the burn he could feel deep in his gut was irritation.

Not an attack of conscience.

And *not* desire.

Marietta dropped her sketchpad and pencil onto the solid wooden table where she'd sat earlier with Nico and pulled out her earbuds, trading the orchestral tones of her classical playlist for the natural summer chorus of cicadas and the distant cries of gulls circling over the ocean.

She closed her eyes, breathed in the briny scent of the sea and the distinctive floral notes of the wild lavender that stained the island's clifftops a vibrant purple and gave Île de Lavande its name.

It was beautiful here, peaceful—a world away from the crazy pace and relentless noise of Rome—but the creative inspiration she'd hoped for had proved elusive and her efforts this afternoon had been disappointing, to say the least.

She was in the wrong headspace. Upset with Nico and more so with herself for letting him affect her like this. Allowing him to make her feel guilty and ungrateful simply because she wanted to see more of his beautiful island. She understood that he was busy. Understood that he must have had to rearrange his schedule to bring her here. But this outlandish idea had been *his*, not hers.

And she had tried to co-operate. Had tried to prevent her temper from flaring as she'd answered every personal, invasive question he'd fired at her.

He should not look so gorgeous. Should not have sat there in his worn jeans and his white T-shirt, with his feet bare and that film of dark stubble on his jaw that gave him a deliciously rough, disreputable edge. How could she concentrate with all that flagrant male energy swirling around her like a hot mist, drenching the very air she needed to breathe?

She opened her eyes and let her gaze drift beyond the terrace towards the clifftop and the blue expanse of sea that was so vast Marietta felt very insignificant all of a sudden, and for some reason very lonely.

Her brows tugged together.

Santo cielo.

What was wrong with her?

She didn't wallow like this.

She was strong—a battler like her *mamma* had been—not a dreamer given to fits of melancholy like her father, a man who had become so lost in his grief, so consumed by addiction, that he'd neglected his children and forced his son to assume the role of provider before he'd even reached his teens.

Looking back on those years always reminded her how lucky she had been to have Leo. She'd been only seven when their mother died, so Marietta's memories of her were limited, but she knew in her heart that Estelle Vincenti would have been proud of her son for stepping up.

And would she have been proud of you?

Marietta's frown sharpened as the question popped into her head. She liked to think her mother would have forgiven the fractious, rebellious teenager she'd been— the girl who'd acted out in the absence of a mother's love and influence—and regarded the woman she'd become with pride and affection.

Yet she would never know for certain the answer to that question, would she?

Her eyes prickled and she cursed.

Enough.

It was being stuck here on this remote estate with a man who clearly didn't wish to spend more time with her than was necessary that was plunging her into this funk. A friendly voice and distraction—that was what she needed. She turned her wheelchair and headed for the house. She'd call her sister-in-law, Helena, and see how the plans for Ricci's birthday party were coming along.

Except when Marietta reached the beautiful blue and white guest bedroom she'd been given and fished her mobile out of her bag, she discovered the phone was dead and realised she'd forgotten her charger.

She swore again, and wheeled out of the room. Had she seen a landline phone anywhere in this sprawling modern abode? She rolled along the wide hallway and paused outside the open door to the study where Nico had spent most of the afternoon. He'd emerged half an hour ago and declared that he was going for a short run. She'd pasted on a smile and waved him off as if she couldn't care less what he did.

She looked into the room. It was neat and masculine, with lots of sharp edges and straight lines, glass surfaces and sleek, pale wood. A textured black rug, a tan leather sofa and a matching desk chair were the only soft furnishings.

And on the glass-topped desk sat a phone.

More eager by the second to hear a familiar voice, she glided over to the desk and dialled her sister-in-law's mobile number.

'Helena,' she said a moment later. 'It's me.'

'Marietta!' Helena's posh English voice rushed down the line. 'I've been thinking about you all weekend. This whole business is just dreadful. Is everything all right over there? Is Nicolas treating you well?' A fleeting pause. 'He'd *better* be treating you well.'

Marietta smiled to herself. 'Everything's fine. A little quiet, that's all.'

She stared out of the large window which faced the terrace, her gaze trailing over the pool and the table where she'd sat drawing for much of the afternoon. Her brows pinched. Had Nico watched her from his desk while he'd worked?

'Tell me about Ricci's party,' she said, pushing aside that thought. 'How's the planning going?'

'Great. Except Leo is such a proud *papà* he's invited half of Tuscany—and Rome...'

Marietta was still smiling as she wound up the call, some ten minutes later. 'Give Ricci and Leo my love. I'll see you in six days.'

'Are you sure?'

'Of course. I'll be there,' she said firmly. 'I'm not missing Ricci's first birthday for anything.'

She hung up feeling lighter, less maudlin and more like herself. This ugly business of her stalker would be over soon and she'd have her life back. She reversed away from the desk, turned towards the door—and saw something against the wall on the far side of the doorway she hadn't noticed upon entering. It was a piece of antique furniture totally at odds with the rest of the decor and yet so lovely it commanded her attention for a long moment. She inched closer and recognised it was a vintage rolltop desk, crafted from a rich golden oak which gleamed as if someone had polished it only yesterday.

And, oh, it was *magnifico*. A stunning piece of craftsmanship her artist's eye couldn't fail to admire. Lured by its beauty, she brushed her hand over the intricate gold leaf designs on the drawer-fronts and fingered the little gold lock and key at the bottom of the tambour lid. She'd always adored the idea of these old-fashioned desks, with their hidden nooks and crannies, and before the left side of her brain could issue a caution she had turned the key and pushed up the slatted tambour to reveal the interior.

Immediately Marietta knew she had gone too far— gone somewhere she shouldn't have—because everything inside the desk…every item sitting in its neat, allotted space…was too pretty and feminine to belong to a man.

Unease flared, even as curiosity kept her gaze fixated. One of the central nooks accommodated a pretty peach-coloured writing compendium, with an elegant silver pen lying on top and a bright orange reading glasses case alongside it. In the next cubbyhole sat a large trinket box, fashioned from dark wood with mother-of-pearl inlay, and a smaller silver box with an ornamental lid. A neat stack of hardcover books filled another space, and below them a solid silver photo frame lay face-down on the desk's polished surface.

Don't look.

But the strident command in her head couldn't stay her hand. Her fingers stroked the velvet backing of the frame and then tilted it up. She stared at a photo of a much younger Nico, in profile, gazing adoringly at a striking golden-haired woman in a long white veil and wedding dress.

A door opening and closing, followed by the sound of footsteps and fast, rough breathing, catapulted Marietta's heart into her throat. The footsteps travelled down the hall, then retreated, and seconds later, through the window, she saw Nico emerge onto the terrace.

His back was to her but she could see he was breathing hard, his impressive shoulders lifting with each deep, controlled breath. His T-shirt stuck to his broad back and his running shorts emphasised narrow hips, a taut backside and long, muscular legs. He was hard and honed, every sweaty, musclebound inch of him, and for a few seconds Marietta lost all sense of her surroundings as some visceral response to all that hardcore virility short-circuited her brain and triggered a burst of heat in her belly and breasts.

He turned and strode into the house. 'Marietta?'

She jolted back to herself and looked at the photo, still in her hand. Gently, her fingers shaking a little, she replaced the frame. She'd wasted precious seconds and now it was too late to avoid discovery. She couldn't close up the desk with the necessary care—she'd never risk damaging this beautiful antique—and get out of the study undetected.

She clasped her hands in her lap and swallowed hard. She had trespassed, but not with any malicious intent. This was a minor transgression, she assured herself. She would own it.

'I'm in your office,' she called out.

He was there within seconds, and she saw on his face the exact moment he registered the raised lid of the desk. Saw his nostrils pinch and flare, his mouth flatten into a hard line, and knew with a sharp mix of certainty and regret that he wouldn't simply shrug off the intrusion.

His large body went still—so still it frightened her.

Her heart thundered in her ears. 'Nico, I'm sorry.' The apology spilled out in a breathless rush. 'I came in to use the phone and saw the desk and it was so beautiful...I...I didn't think.'

If possible his features grew tighter, his eyes harder. He said nothing, and the silence, broken only by his harsh breathing, was awful.

'I'm so sorry,' she said again, and her voice cracked. Because this time she wasn't only apologising for opening the desk. This time she was telling him she was sorry about his wife. She knew nothing about his marriage, of course, but the photograph, the desk so lovingly preserved—almost like a shrine—told her two things.

Nico had loved his wife.

And his wife was no longer alive.

Marietta's throat constricted. 'Please say something,' she whispered.

He moved to the desk, carefully lowered the lid and laid his palms on the tambour. He didn't look at her, and somehow that was ten times worse than his hard, silent stare.

'Go,' he said at last, and the command was all the more terrible for its quietness.

'Nico—'

'Get out, Marietta.'

Still he didn't look at her, and the rebuff needled deep, even though she knew she'd earned it. Smothering the impulse to apologise yet again, Marietta turned her chair and wheeled out of the room.

CHAPTER SIX

NICO WALKED OUT to the terrace with two crystal tumblers balanced in one hand and an unopened bottle of vintage cognac from the back of his liquor cabinet cradled in the other.

He paused. Marietta sat in her wheelchair at the table by the pool with her back to him, her slender form silhouetted by the dying light of the sun, which was now no more than a sliver of fiery orange on the horizon. Her long mahogany hair spilled in loose waves down her back, and before he could censor his thoughts he found himself wondering how it would feel to slide his fingers through those thick tresses, wind them around his hands...

He tightened his jaw. Shook off the thought as swiftly as it had surfaced. Marietta was his friend's sister and right now her safety was his responsibility. This incessant awareness of her was an unwelcome distraction and he needed to shut it down. At the very minimum he needed to control his thoughts and reactions around her—especially after today, when he had not reacted well to finding her at Julia's desk...had not known how to handle the unexpected gut-punch of emotion or the glitter of sympathy in Marietta's eyes.

Seeing the woman who'd lit a slow-burning fire in his blood these past forty-eight hours alongside the only mementoes he had of his dead wife had unbalanced him, had fired a shock wave through his brain that had stolen his ability to do more than clip out a few terse words.

And that look he'd seen on Marietta's face... Apology mixed with *pity*, of all things. His gut had hardened, everything within him rejecting that look. Rejecting the idea of Marietta feeling sorry for him. Of *anyone* feeling sorry for him. Nico elicited a range of reactions from people—respect, obedience, trust, fear—but rarely sympathy or pity. If ever. Witnessing both in Marietta's eyes had left him feeling sideswiped. Exposed. Something he had worked hard for the last decade *not* to feel. And yet even now, years later, he didn't always succeed in burying his feelings—did he? Occasionally the darkness would try to claim him. The guilt and the burning sense of failure that had dogged him ever since Julia's death would rise up and torment him.

He strode to the table and set down the bottle and glasses. He'd come out here to make peace, he reminded himself. Not to examine his inner workings.

Marietta looked up, her liquid dark eyes startled at first, then veiled and wary. One graceful eyebrow rose. 'Are we celebrating something?' She looked from the bottle to him. 'Perhaps you've caught my stalker and you're gracing me with your presence to tell me I can return to civilisation tomorrow?'

Nico let the sarcasm slide. He'd avoided her for much of the day and she was upset with him. Women didn't like to be ignored—he remembered that much from his too brief time as a married man. He took in her pale cotton pants, the soft green halterneck top which clung to her generous curves and left her golden shoulders exposed. Had she changed especially for dinner? A needle of guilt pricked him. She'd knocked on his study door an hour ago, offered to fix a meal for them, and he'd grunted a response through the closed door, telling her to eat without him.

He opened the bottle and poured a double shot of cognac into each tumbler, put one in front of Marietta and settled in a cushioned seat beside her. 'You do not consider Île de Lavande to be civilised?' He swirled the cognac in his glass. 'Or perhaps you are referring to the company?'

Colour crept into her cheeks but her chin stayed elevated. 'I'm sure parts of Île de Lavande are very civilised—I'm simply yet to see most of the island. As for the company—so far it's been...' She shrugged minutely. 'Satisfactory.'

Despite the tension in the air Nico felt his facial muscles twitch, and then his lips were stretching into a rare smile. Had a woman ever described him as 'satisfactory' before? No. He didn't think so. On the infrequent occasions when he indulged in female company, he made damn sure the woman was a great deal more than *satisfied* when he was done with her.

He raised his glass. '*Touché*, Marietta.' He swallowed a mouthful of the expensive cognac and noted she hadn't touched hers. 'You are angry,' he observed.

'No...' she began, and then stopped, shook her head and puffed out a quiet sigh. '*Si*. A little,' she confessed. 'I made a mistake and you won't accept my apology. I'm angry with myself *and* with you.'

He lifted his eyebrows. 'That's a candid statement,'

he said, which maybe shouldn't have surprised him. Marietta had never struck him as a smoke-and-mirrors kind of woman. She was headstrong and honest. Unafraid to speak her mind.

She reached out suddenly, and curled her hand around his wrist. 'I didn't mean to intrude, Nico,' she said softly. 'And I truly am sorry—about your wife.'

Heat radiated from her touch—a sharp, unsettling contrast to the inevitable icy chill that swept through him whenever he thought about his wife—and then she was sliding her hand away, sitting back.

'How long were you married?'

His chest grew uncomfortably tight. 'Two years.'

'She was very beautiful.'

So she *had* taken a good look at the photograph. He didn't know how he felt about that. He took another generous sip of cognac, held the liquid in his mouth for a moment before letting it burn down his throat. He *did* know he wasn't going to have this conversation.

'Who did you call?' he asked, and the abrupt change of subject elicited an immediate frown.

'Scusi?'

'You said you went into my study to use the phone,' he reminded her. 'Who did you call?'

'My sister-in-law.'

'Because…?'

Her shoulders stiffened. 'Because I wanted to hear a friendly voice,' she said, her tone turning defensive, faintly accusing.

Nico cursed himself silently. He'd come out here to make peace, to defuse the tension between them before it sprouted claws—not to pick a fight. He had no wish to speak of his late wife, no desire to dredge up the darkness that lurked too close to the surface, but he could have deflected Marietta's curiosity in a less antagonistic manner.

'Forgive me,' he said, his voice gruff, the words alien on his tongue.

Rarely did he apologise or seek forgiveness. The last time had been ten years ago, the day of Julia's funeral, and on that day his father-in-law had been disinclined to forgive.

'You may call whomever you wish, whenever you wish,' he said. 'The house and its facilities are yours to use as you desire. However, I will ask one thing of you.' He held her gaze, kept his voice low. Measured. 'Please do not ever again speak of my wife.'

For a long moment Marietta's gaze didn't falter from his, then her lashes lowered, shielding her expressive eyes from him. She backed her chair away from the table.

'Understood,' she said, glancing up, her gaze reconnecting with his briefly. '*Buona notte*, Nico.'

And then she turned her chair around and wheeled into the house, leaving her drink sitting untouched on the table.

Nico watched her go and something pierced him. Something, he thought darkly, like regret. He reached for her glass, downed the double shot of cognac and scowled into the empty tumbler. That had *not* gone at all how he'd planned.

'It's not the ex-boyfriend, boss.'

Nico leaned back in his chair, his phone pressed to his ear. 'Are you positive?'

'Yes,' Bruno said. 'The guy was in Vienna on business all day Friday. And my gut says it's not him. He's settled, content. Devoted to his wife and kid. The wife's a looker, too.'

Nico ignored that last comment. He ran his hand through his hair, across the back of his neck. A long, restless night had left him edgy. Irritable. 'Forensics?'

'Waiting on a DNA profile from the hair strand found in the bedroom.'

'Chase it up. Today. Then contact those fools from the *polizia* and check their records for a match.' He drummed his fingers on his desk, cast a brooding look out of the window. 'And the neighbours?'

'One left to interview. Female. In her fifties.'

'Okay. *Bien*. Review that list of artists I emailed to you yesterday and get—' Nico broke off, sat forward, then surged up out of his chair. *What the hell?* 'Bruno, I'll call you back.'

He slammed down the phone, strode through the house and out onto the limestone terrace. Raising a hand to shield his eyes against the midmorning sun, he stared beyond the pool to the cliff's edge—and felt his heart punch into his throat.

He paused, drew a deep breath and loosed his voice on a furious bellow. *'Marietta!'*

She didn't hear him—or chose to ignore him. The latter, most likely. Anger spiked and he spat out a curse.

He veered onto a little-used dirt path that meandered through tall grasses and clusters of wild lavender and rosemary. The wheels of her chair had left tracks in the dirt. Tracks that led directly to the edge of the plunging forty-foot cliff.

'Marietta!' he shouted again, and knew she'd heard

him this time because her shoulders flinched. And yet she didn't so much as turn her head.

Another few strides and the pump of adrenaline through his veins gave way to relief. She was sitting farther back from the edge than he'd thought. He reached her side, balled his hands lest he curl them over her slender shoulders and shake her.

'What the *hell* are you doing?'

She looked up, her expression faintly astonished. 'Enjoying the scenery,' she said, her air of calm making his jaw clench.

He jammed his fists in his jeans pockets. 'Is there something wrong with the view from the terrace?'

'Of course not. But I sat on your terrace all day yesterday. I need a change or I'll go mad. Besides...'

She rolled forward and he pulled his hands out of his jeans so fast he heard one of the pockets rip.

'I've been dying to look at the beach down there.'

He stepped in front of her. 'That's far enough.'

She huffed out a breath. 'Seriously, Nico. You're as bad as my brother. What do you think I'm going to do? Push myself over the edge?' She craned her neck to peek around him. 'Are those steps cut into the cliff?'

He ground his molars together. '*Oui*. But they're extremely old. Probably eroded. Unsafe.'

'Probably? You mean...you don't *know*?' Her eyebrows arched. 'As in...you've never been down there before?'

He folded his arms over his chest. 'It's just a beach.'

'But it's *your* beach...and it's a beautiful beach. Why would you not go down there?'

A vein throbbed in his temple. *Mon Dieu.* Had he ever met a woman so infuriating? So unpredictable?

He let his gaze rake over her, from her high glossy ponytail to her sun-kissed shoulders, all the way down to the pink-painted toenails poking out of her strappy white sandals. Her white knee-length shorts left her pale, delicate shins visible and her stretchy pink spaghetti-strap top made her breasts look nothing short of magnificent.

How could a woman look so alluring and be so annoying all at the same time?

He brought his gaze back to her face. Colour flared over those high cheekbones and a pulse flickered at the base of her throat. Their eyes met and hers widened a fraction—and he wondered if she felt it too. That pulse of heat in the air. That pull of attraction.

Belatedly he realised she'd spoken again. 'Pardon?'

'A prisoner,' she repeated, frowning at him. 'I feel like a prisoner, Nico.'

A prisoner.

His gut twisted hard, turning in on itself, and his mind descended instantly to a dark, savage place.

Julia's final, terror-filled days on this earth had been as a prisoner, held captive by the kidnappers who'd extracted a hefty ransom from her father—then left her in a ditch to die.

'Nico?'

Marietta's voice penetrated the sudden thick haze in his head.

'Are you all right?'

He gave himself a mental shake, shoved a lid over that dark, bottomless hole before it sucked him into its destructive vortex. 'I'm trying to keep you safe, Marietta. That's all.'

'I know. But my stalker's in Rome—there's no threat to me here.'

She edged her chair forward until her toes nearly touched his shins. When she tilted her head back the appeal in her huge brown eyes had a profound effect on him.

'Nico...I spent six months of my life in a rehabilitation unit—two of those months flat on my back, staring at the same ceiling and walls, day in, day out. I had no control...no choice...I felt angry and scared and trapped—I guess that's why I get a little stir-crazy when I'm cooped up in one place for too long.'

Guilt coiled inside him. He hadn't considered that the isolation in which he found solace would, for Marietta, feel like captivity.

Silently cursing his thoughtlessness, he dropped to his haunches in front of her. 'Tell me what you'd like to do today.'

Her face broke into a smile and for a second—just a second—Nico felt as if he'd stepped out of the darkness into the light.

CHAPTER SEVEN

'COFFEE TO FINISH?'

Nico's question drew Marietta's attention from the young couple sitting several tables away in the bistro's outdoor courtyard. She looked across the table she and Nico shared, its surface crowded with empty platters and dishes from their delicious seafood lunch. '*Si*. Please.'

A moment later Josephine's son, Luc, came to clear their table and take their coffee order. He was pleasant, relaxed and friendly—like the rest of his family, all of whom Marietta had met upon their arrival at the quaint seaside restaurant.

Nico's presence had drawn the entire Bouchard clan out to greet them—Josephine and her husband Philippe from the kitchen, and her father, Henri, from the cool, shaded interior of the family-run bistro. The old man had smiled broadly and the two men had greeted each other with obvious warmth—surprising Marietta, until she'd reminded herself that people were multi-faceted and Nico was no different.

Until yesterday she would never have guessed he was a widower—a fact that stirred a pang of emotion every time she thought of it.

A burst of laughter from the young couple drew her gaze back to them. Tourists from the mainland, she guessed. The guy was good-looking, his girlfriend pretty—blonde and suntanned, her slender legs long and bare below a short summer skirt. Their faces were flushed, from the sun or maybe from the wine they were drinking, and they looked happy. Carefree. In love.

'I spoke with Bruno this morning.'

She looked at Nico, so big and handsome here in the open-air courtyard, with its colourful potted flowers and its miniature citrus trees in terracotta planters dotted around the tables. Overhead an umbrella shaded them from the sun's brilliance and beyond the broad span of his shoulders the water sparkled in the harbour. She couldn't imagine him looking carefree—not with that constant air of alertness about him—but he did look more at ease than she'd ever seen him before. That rare smile—the one she'd caught her first glimpse of last night—had made a couple of stunning reappearances, and each time it had stopped the breath in her lungs.

'Is there any news?' she asked, wondering why he hadn't mentioned it before now, and yet grateful that he hadn't. For a while over lunch she'd felt like just another tourist, enjoying the island.

'Your ex is in the clear.'

Relief surged, even though she hadn't for a moment suspected Davide. 'So…what now? Are there other leads?'

'A couple.'

She waited for him to elaborate. When he didn't, she suppressed a flutter of annoyance. 'I *am* going back in five days,' she reminded him—because staying on the island beyond Friday and missing Ricci's birthday was still a compromise too far.

Nico remained silent, evoking a frisson of disquiet. But then Luc arrived with their coffee and Josephine came out to ask if they'd enjoyed their meal.

'*Bellissimo!*' Marietta exclaimed.

Josephine beamed. 'You will come and join us for dinner one evening before you leave, *oui*?'

'Of course,' she said, then, fearing she'd spoken out of turn, cast a quick glance at Nico.

But he simply murmured an assent that had Josephine looking pleased before she bustled back to the kitchen.

Marietta sipped her coffee and noticed the young couple get up to leave. The girl giggled and swayed, and her boyfriend caught her but he too was staggering. Grinning, he tossed some euros on the table and then guided the girl out onto the street towards a parked car—and Marietta's belly clenched with alarm.

She dropped her cup into its saucer, reached across the table and grabbed Nico's arm. 'Stop them,' she said urgently, and pointed with her other hand. 'That couple—about to get into the red car. He's drunk.'

Frowning, Nico glanced over his shoulder and then back at her. 'Are you sure?'

'*Si.* I was watching them.' Panic tightened her grip on his arm. 'Nico, please…'

He stood abruptly and strode out onto the street, calling something to the young man, who already had the driver's door open. An exchange in French followed and the younger man's demeanour morphed from jovial to belligerent—and then outright combative when Nico snatched his key away from him.

Nico, looking remarkably cool for a man who had just dodged a wildly thrown punch, pinned the tourist against the car, and then all of a sudden Luc and his father Philippe were there, helping to defuse the situation.

The tension eased from Marietta's shoulders but an icy chill had gripped her and her hands shook. She curled them tight, closed her eyes for a minute.

'Marietta?'

She looked up. Nico was crouched beside her chair, and she searched over his shoulder for the couple.

'They're inside,' he told her. 'Josephine's encouraging them to stay, to drink some water and coffee, have something to eat.'

She nodded, grateful, and yet still the iciness inside her wouldn't abate. She had been that girl once—young and beautiful, with her whole life ahead of her. If only someone had stopped her and her friends from getting into that car…

She shook her head. Dispelled the thought. She knew better than to dwell on *if only*. She picked up her cup, took a fortifying gulp of coffee, felt relieved when Nico stood. He returned to his chair but then studied her, and her skin heated and prickled despite the chill in her veins.

'You did a good thing.'

'*We* did a good thing,' she corrected.

He shrugged. 'You were the one who noticed them— and you were right. The kid's way over the limit.'

Marietta wrapped her hands around her cup. Stared into the dark brew. 'I couldn't watch them get into that car.'

Nico was silent a moment. 'Your accident?'

She looked up. 'You know about that?'

'Only what your brother told me—that your paralysis resulted from a car crash.'

Her stomach gave a hard, vicious twist. It always did when she recalled her fragmented memories of that night. The mangled wreckage and broken glass. The whimpers of the girl dying beside her. Her own pain and then—worse—no pain at all. Nothing but numbness and fear.

Her grip on her cup tightened. 'I was young and stupid…drinking at a party Leo hadn't wanted me to attend. I knew my friend had had too much to drink when he offered me a ride.' She grimaced. It was never easy to admit your own stupidity. 'I still got into that car.'

'And your friend…?' Nico asked quietly.

'He and the two girls in the car with us died.' She pushed her cup aside, her mouth too bitter suddenly for coffee. 'I was the only survivor.'

'I'm sorry, Marietta.'

Nico's voice was deep and sincere, but she told herself the warmth spreading through her belly was from the coffee, not the effect of that rich, soothing baritone. 'I made a mistake and I live with the consequences of that mistake every day,' she said. 'If I can stop someone else from suffering a similar fate, I will.'

Because no one deserved to suffer what she had. To have their life so drastically altered by one foolish, split-second decision. To have to face up to the bitter realisation that their future was going to be vastly different from the one they'd envisaged. She'd always wanted a career in art, and she'd achieved that, but as a girl she had dreamed of other things, too—love, marriage, children—things she'd eventually had to accept were no longer in her future.

Nico's blue eyes were unfathomable, as always, and suddenly she regretted opening up to him. This man knew so much about her already, and she knew next to nothing about him—especially his past. She'd known he'd served in the French Foreign Legion—that alone was fascinating—but knowing he was a widower... It touched something inside her. Made her want to see beneath that tough, formidable exterior. And yet she couldn't imagine she ever would. Nico guarded his privacy like a fortress—and he'd made it clear two-way sharing wasn't on the agenda.

'Anyway,' she said, 'the accident was a long time ago. I try not to dwell on the past.' She brightened her voice. 'Lunch was lovely. Thank you. Can we go and see the old ruins now?'

His thick brows drew together. 'You really want to see a crumbling pile of ancient stones?'

'I thought we were doing what *I* want to do today?'

His eyes narrowed. 'You are a stubborn woman, Marietta Vincenti.'

She raised her chin. 'So I've been told.'

Nico stepped onto the terrace with a bottle and two glasses in his hands and a strong sense of *déjà vu*.

Tonight, however, the bottle was an expensive Burgundy rather than cognac, and the mood in the air—if not entirely tension-free—was an improvement on yesterday.

He couldn't remember the last time he'd spent almost an entire day with one woman. Marietta was beautiful and he couldn't deny she made his blood heat, but she also fascinated him on a level most women didn't. She was strong. A woman who'd fought her way back from a major life-altering trauma—*a survivor.*

She was different from the women whose company he normally sought and that was the attraction, he assured himself. Nothing more.

And he couldn't deny that today had been...pleasurable.

She had charmed the entire Bouchard clan, including old Henri, and though the incident with the young couple had seemed to shake her she'd bounced back—enough to demand he take her to see the old fortress.

Her fascination with the ruins had bemused Nico. The ancient stronghold that had once defended the island against marauding pirates was, to his eye, no more than a dull, crumbling edifice, and yet Marietta had taken the time to snap photos from every vantage point her wheelchair had allowed her to reach.

Then she had asked him to piggyback her up the spiral staircase of the stone tower to see the view.

It had been torture. Sweet, exquisite torture.

Those soft, lush breasts pressed into his back. Her slender arms looped around his neck. Her warm breath misting over his nape.

He had thought that lifting her into and out of his Jeep throughout the day had tested his control. Carrying her on his back, all that feminine warmth and vanilla and strawberry scent enveloping him, had been a hundred times more challenging.

She was wheeling out of the house now, a platter of cheeses, olives and cured meats expertly balanced on her lap. A bread basket filled with the fresh minibaguettes Josephine had given them this afternoon already sat on the table.

A minute later she was piling thick slices of cheese into a baguette. 'I shouldn't be hungry after our enormous lunch,' she said. 'It must be all the sea air.'

Nico watched her bite into the baguette. He liked it that she wasn't overly dainty in the way she ate. She tackled her food with enthusiasm. Appreciation. A sign of her Italian heritage, perhaps?

'The air quality here is pristine,' he said. 'I crave it when I've been in Paris or New York or any major city for too long.'

She swallowed. 'Do you have homes in Paris and New York?'

'Apartments.'

She nodded—as if that didn't surprise her. Her head tilted to one side. 'So, what does a man who runs a multi-billion-dollar global security company do with his time off?'

He fingered the stem of his glass. Tried not to notice how her mouth wrapped around the end of her baguette. 'That depends,' he said finally.

'On what?'

'On what kind of recreation I'm in the mood for.'

He enjoyed the sudden bloom of pink in her cheeks more than he should have.

Her gaze thinned. 'Holidays,' she said. 'Where do you go on holiday?'

'I don't.'

She frowned. 'You don't take holidays?'

'This is where I come to unwind.'

'Alone?'

'*Oui,*' he said. 'Alone.'

Her eyes widened. 'So you don't bring your...friends here?'

He lifted an eyebrow. 'Do you mean to ask me if I bring my lovers here, Marietta?'

The colour in her cheeks brightened. She picked up her wine glass, took a large sip and sat back. 'Do you not get lonely here on your own?'

He shrugged. 'I like the quiet.' Which wasn't strictly true. He craved the isolation more than the quiet itself. The disconnection from the world and the people in it.

Marietta looked towards the ocean and the setting sun. Half a dozen shades of orange and gold—colours she would no doubt give fancy names to—streaked the sky. 'It *is* peaceful here. And beautiful.' Her gaze returned to his. 'Are there no other places you'd like to visit, though? Things you'd like to see?'

He shifted in his chair. 'I've seen more things in this world than you can imagine,' he said. 'And most of them I never wish to see again.'

He heard something dark and bleak in his own voice then. Marietta studied him, and he shrugged off the notion that she could somehow see the darkness inside him…the *emptiness* he'd never been able to fill since losing his wife.

'Well,' she said, 'I haven't seen enough of the world. There's plenty of places I'd like to see…things I'd like to do.'

'Such as…?'

'The pyramids in Egypt.'

His brows dropped. *Was she kidding?* 'Do you have any idea how volatile that region is?'

She lifted her shoulders. 'Isn't the whole world "volatile" these days?'

'*Oui*. Which is why travellers need to be more selective about the destinations they choose. More safety conscious.'

'I agree. But no one can live in a protective bubble, can they? If people did they'd never go anywhere, never do anything. Living involves risk, whether we like it or not.'

'Risk can be minimised through sensible choices.'

Marietta sighed. 'You sound like my brother.'

'That's because Leo is a smart man,' he clipped out.

She flicked her hair over one shoulder. She wore another halterneck top tonight, this one red and floaty and partially see-through. Nico kept his gaze above her collarbone.

'None of that diminishes my desire to see the pyramids,' she said. 'In fact it doesn't change anything on my wish list.'

His brows sank lower. 'You have a *list*?'

'*Si.*'

'Tell me about it.'

Her chin notched up a fraction. 'I'm not sure I want to.'

'Tell me,' he commanded.

Something flashed across her face. Annoyance, he guessed. She took a slow sip of her wine, fuelling his impatience.

'Okay—I want to do a tandem skydive.'

Mon Dieu.

'No.'

The word shot from his mouth of its own volition.

Her eyebrows rose. 'I don't need anyone's *permission*, Nico.'

His jaw tightened. 'It's dangerous.'

'So is getting into a car and driving on the *auto-

strada,' she said, and the significance of that statement didn't escape him. 'Besides...' She flung a hand in his direction. 'I bet *you've* jumped out of a plane plenty of times. Don't elite soldiers do that sort of thing?'

The reference to his soldiering days gave Nico only brief pause. His service in the French Foreign Legion was no secret. The Legion's flame-like emblem and motto—*Honneur et Fidélité*—were inked on his upper left arm and had been for eighteen years. He had knocked on the Legion's door—literally, because that was the only way to gain entry—on the day of his eighteenth birthday, gone on to serve his five contracted years, and then got the hell out.

No doubt he'd mentioned his service to her brother at some point, though Nico never spoke of those years in any detail. Trekking through humid, insect-ridden jungles and dry, shelterless deserts, defending himself and his unit against lethal attacks from rebel forces and random insurgents, policing war zones where their allies had been indistinguishable from their enemies and they hadn't known who to trust—none of it made for idle conversation.

Still, those five years had put into perspective the many childhood injustices he'd suffered as a ward of the French state—had made them seem almost trivial. Insignificant. And, yes, during his time as a legionnaire—and as a military contractor—he'd jumped out of a few planes.

'Irrelevant, Marietta. What else is on your list?'

She sipped her wine, took her time again. 'A hot air balloon ride. Let me guess,' she added. 'That's dangerous, too.'

'You think floating two thousand feet above the ground in an oversized picnic basket is *safe*?'

She rolled her eyes. 'This from the man who flies a helicopter?'

He scowled. No comparison. His chopper was a solid machine, designed and built by aeronautical specialists to exacting safety standards. A hot air balloon was nothing but yards of silk filled with...*hot air*. It would be a frosty day in hell when he climbed into one of those things.

'Is there anything remotely sensible on your list?'

Her lips curved, as if she were actually enjoying this conversation. 'Sensible isn't any fun, is it? But, yes— there are things you'd probably consider low-risk.'

'Like?'

'Swimming in the ocean...' That little smile continued to play about her mouth. 'Naked.'

And just like that, the steady, persistent hum of awareness in his blood intensified—until he felt as if a high-voltage current arced through his veins.

'Somewhere private, of course,' she said, and then her eyes widened as if she'd had an enlightening thought. 'Your beach would be perfect!'

All at once an image of Marietta floating naked in the clear seawater at the foot of his cliff flashed into his head. Heat and lust ignited in his belly, along with the certain knowledge that she *did* feel the same pull of attraction he did. He could see it—in the sudden hectic colour in her cheeks. In the way her eyes glittered and held his in silent challenge.

She was provoking him.

Playing with fire.

He lunged up out of his chair, strode to her side and

seized her chin. The dark look he gave her should have subdued and intimidated. Instead her lips parted, soft and inviting, as though she were anticipating...a *kiss*.

Dieu.

He *wanted* to kiss her. Wanted to crush his mouth onto hers and let her feel the full, unleashed power of the lust she was deliberately inciting. Wanted to punish her for dangling temptation in front of him like an enticing treat he didn't deserve.

He held himself rigid. Controlled. 'Be *very* careful what you wish for, Marietta.'

And then he released her and stalked into the house, back to his study—where he should have stayed in the first place.

Nico stood near the edge of the vertiginous cliff and stared down at the small crescent-shaped beach he had never set foot upon.

On this side of the island the coastline was rocky, precipitous in places, but here and there the cliffs formed inlets with sandy sheltered beaches and calm channels of crystal blue water ideal for swimming.

Yesterday he had told Marietta the steps carved into the ancient rock face might be eroded, but in truth they appeared sturdy—probably as safe now as they had been a century ago. Until this morning he'd never thought about using them. Had never given the beach more than a passing thought.

Had he been in a war zone, he'd have cast his trained soldier's eye over the isolated cove and deemed it a death trap—the perfect location to fall prey to ambush—but he wasn't a soldier any longer and the island wasn't a war zone.

And he wasn't standing here right now thinking about danger hotspots and military manoeuvres.

He was thinking about the woman he had wanted to kiss last night and her damned wish list. About the sand down there on his beach and whether it was coarse or soft. About the temperature of the water—and Marietta's skin... How she would feel pressed against him if they swam together naked.

Ridiculous, *insane* thoughts.

Thoughts he would not normally entertain.

But, by God, she'd got under his skin. Ignited a hunger that hadn't relinquished its grip but rather had burned hotter, fiercer, during the night.

Did she understand what kind of man she was toying with? What sex with him would mean and—more importantly—what it *wouldn't* mean?

He jammed his hands into his jeans pockets.

He was not a tender, romantic man. He was an ex-soldier with a grisly past. A man who had loved and lost and vowed he would never again tumble into that soul-destroying abyss. His liaisons with women served one rudimentary purpose, and for that reason he chose experienced women. Never innocents.

And yet Marietta was no ingénue. She was smart and confident. Strong and resilient. A woman who didn't fear the world, who understood what it meant to accept the consequences of her actions. *A woman who knew what she wanted.*

Did she want *him*?

He closed his eyes, searched the dark, twisted labyrinth of his conscience. Which would make him the better man? Indulging her? Or keeping his distance?

He opened his eyes and studied the ancient steps.

Were they as solid as they appeared?

He pulled his hands from his pockets and moved closer to the cliff's edge. *Only one way to find out.*

CHAPTER EIGHT

MARIETTA CLUNG TO Nico's back as he paused at the top of the cliff, her belly a cauldron of excitement and nerves. She couldn't believe they were doing this.

She peered over his shoulder, all the way down to the crescent-shaped strip of white sand at the foot of the cliff. It was a very, *very* long way down, and the steps hewn into the rock face were much steeper than she'd imagined. Her arms tightened reflexively around his neck.

'I've got you, *chérie.*'

His deep voice seemed to resonate through her chest, and the unexpected endearment made her pulse hitch.

'Ready?' he said.

'Yes.'

As ready as I'll ever be.

And then he started down the steps and the buzz of anticipation turned into a wild flutter. They *were* doing this. And she really couldn't believe it. Not after last night, when he'd stormed off and she'd been certain she had pushed him too far.

She'd sat by the pool, watching the rich golds and ambers and deep purples of the sunset bleed into one another, and tried to attribute her uncharacteristic behaviour to having had too much sun during the day. Too much wine with her supper.

But neither of those excuses was valid.

The truth was she had wanted to provoke him—because a reckless yearning had been building in her all day. A yearning to find out if a man like Nico could be attracted to a woman like her—a woman whom society largely viewed as *disabled*.

She knew the wheelchair frightened most men. Some wrongly assumed she couldn't have sex or wouldn't enjoy it. Others, she guessed, were repelled by her useless legs. Davide had been different in that regard, and their sex-life had been healthy, satisfying—though not the kind of passionate, all-consuming sex she'd fantasised about as a teenager.

She had a feeling deep in her belly, where the butterflies had gathered *en masse* now, that sex with Nico would be the kind of wild, passionate sex she'd long ago resigned herself to never experiencing.

And Nico *was* attracted to her. She had seen the evidence as soon as she'd made that provocative suggestion about swimming naked at his beach. Had seen it stamped on his face—a raw hunger her body had instinctively responded to with its own powerful throb of need.

He had almost kissed her. Standing there grasping her chin and glaring down at her, anger and desire pulsing off him in waves, he had looked like a man fighting for control.

And, oh, she had *wanted* him to kiss her. Even knowing that if he did it wouldn't be gentle. That there would be fire and fury behind his kiss. When he hadn't—when he'd walked away from her instead—her disappointment had been so intense it had felt like a physical blow against her ribs.

He'd negotiated the last few steps now, and Marietta's eyes widened as he carried her across the sand to where a blue-and-white-striped awning stood in a sheltered lee off the cliff. Beneath the awning lay a picnic rug and a bunch of big, comfy-looking cushions, and on a corner of the rug, shaded from the direct heat of the midday sun, sat a large wicker basket.

'Nico!' Her voice came out breathless. 'How many trips did this take you?'

'A few.'

He knelt on the rug and she slid off his back, the friction between their bodies teasing her already over-sensitised nipples into hard, aching nubs. She plucked her tee shirt away from her breasts before he turned, glad that she'd put the loose-fitting white tee on over her yellow bikini top. She slipped her hands under her legs and straightened them out in front of her.

Nico propped two cushions behind her back. 'Comfortable?'

She nodded, looked around her. 'It's beautiful, Nico.'

She ran her hand through the warm sand. The pearly-white granules felt luxuriously soft as they sifted through her fingers. She looked towards the calm water in the inlet. It was a clear, stunning turquoise—the kind seen on postcards of exotic locales that most people only ever dreamed of visiting. Best of all, the cove was utterly, totally private.

'I can't believe you've never been down here before.'

Nico shrugged and kicked off his sneakers. He wore khaki shorts and a black polo shirt and he looked big and vital and masculine. He lifted the lid off the hamper. 'I didn't know what you'd want to eat…' He started pulling out items. 'So I brought a bit of everything.'

He wasn't joking. There were fruits, olives, crackers, breads, pickles and a variety of meats and cheeses in a small cooler, plus water, soda and two bottles of wine—a red Cabernet and a chilled white. Cutlery, plastic plates and glasses emerged as well, along with condiments and a packet of paper serviettes.

Marietta couldn't help but laugh. 'I bet you never go anywhere unprepared.'

Nico opened a water bottle and handed it to her. 'Who's the guy you want to be with when disaster strikes?'

She rolled her eyes. 'You,' she conceded.

A smug look crossed his face. He planted his hands on his thighs and surveyed the enormous spread of food. 'I hope you're hungry.'

'Not *this* hungry.' She reached for a bunch of green grapes and smiled. 'But I'll give it my best shot.'

In the end, however, Marietta found she could eat very little. Thoughts of what they might do together after lunch made her stomach too jittery. She did manage a small glass of white wine, hoping it would lend her some much needed Dutch courage.

Now she lay on her back under the awning, her eyes closed, wondering if she needn't have bothered with the wine. If perhaps she'd been a fool to think anything was going to happen beyond a picnic lunch on the beach. Because Nico hadn't suggested they swim, nor made a move to touch her, nor even so much as uttered a word in the last fifteen minutes.

Yet a definite tension permeated the air. Her sixth sense could intuit it—just as her other senses could detect *him*. The scent of soap and the faint tang of clean, male sweat. The sound of his breathing, deep and even. And his *heat*. She could feel the heat that seemed always to radiate from him, as if his body were a non-stop furnace. Whenever he was close that heat enveloped her, penetrating her skin, sinking into her bones and making her feel as if she were melting.

She opened her eyes and turned her head to look at him. He lay beside her, his eyes closed, but she knew he wasn't sleeping. Nico didn't strike her as the kind of man who indulged in daytime naps. In fact she half suspected that even at night he slept with one eye open. She let her gaze drift down, away from his strong profile, and mentally braced herself for the heart-stopping impact of his bare torso.

He was utter perfection. Hard muscle, smooth skin, dark, crisp hair in all the places a man should have hair—including a liberal sprinkling over his sculpted pecs and a narrow line bisecting his washboard abs. A black ink tattoo adorned his upper left arm and a long rough-edged scar curled over the same shoulder.

I've seen more things in this world than you can imagine—and most of them I never wish to see again.

His words from the previous evening came back to her, sending a shiver through her now as they had then. Nico had sounded so grim in that moment, so haunted, and she'd wanted to ask him what he'd seen that had been so terrible he never wanted to see it again. That had made him into a man who guarded his privacy and kept himself aloof from the world. But she had reined in her curiosity, knowing it wouldn't be welcome. Knowing instinctively that if she probed, their conversation would be over before it started.

Her gaze trailed the jagged line of the scar, and she recognised the tattoo on his arm as the emblem of the French Foreign Legion. Had the awful things he'd seen been the horrors of war? Of course. They must have been. Soldiers who served in conflict zones witnessed first-hand the worst of mankind's atrocities.

'Why did you join the Legion?'

She grimaced as soon as the words were out of her mouth. She hadn't meant to speak them aloud. She opened her mouth to retract the question—but he spoke first.

'Because I was eighteen and full of testosterone and didn't know what else to do with my life.'

Nico kept his eyes closed as he spoke. He'd surprised himself by answering her question. Normally he shut down conversations that ventured too far into personal territory, but right then he figured talking was the lesser of two evils. The greater evil—the dark, sexual desire prowling through him—couldn't be unleashed. Not on Marietta.

He realised that now.

Belatedly.

Hell. What had he been thinking? She wasn't one of the easy, vacuous, forgettable women with whom he occasionally hooked up for the sole purpose of satisfying his physical needs. She was Marietta, his friend's sister—a woman he respected. A woman who was *un*-forgettable.

He had told himself she was no ingénue, and she wasn't. No innocent would have goaded him last night without understanding where such provocation could lead. What she was *inviting*. And yet as they'd sat there on the sand, sharing food and idle small talk—the kind

of simple pleasure his late wife would have loved—
he'd looked at Marietta and thought about the incident
at the bistro, her concern for the young couple. And
he'd realised that after everything this woman had been
through, she was still pure. She still had compassion in
her heart. Still cared about others.

How could he touch her and not taint her with his
darkness? He had nothing to give her. Nothing to offer
beyond the pleasures of the flesh.

'Did your parents not object?'

He slid his right hand under the back of his head and
continued to keep his eyes closed. She'd taken her tee
shirt off after they'd eaten, and seeing her in that yellow bikini top only inflamed his libido.

'I didn't have parents,' he said.

'Oh…I…I'm sorry, Nico.' She fell silent a moment.
'Did you lose them when you were young?'

'My mother died of a stroke when I was six,' he said,
surprising himself yet again. He couldn't remember
the last time he'd spoken of his childhood. Couldn't
remember the last time someone had shown an interest, aside from Julia. 'She was a solo parent—I never
knew my father.'

He heard Marietta shift, felt the weight of her gaze
on him.

'Did you live with relatives after your mother passed
away?'

'My mother didn't have any relatives. I became a
ward of the state and spent the remainder of my childhood in children's homes and foster care.'

'Oh, Nico… That must have been difficult.'

It hadn't been a walk in the park. His mother had
been a good woman, a loving *maman*, and he'd missed

her. But he'd survived. Years of being shuffled around in an indifferent welfare system had thickened his skin.

'Don't go all sympathetic on me, Marietta. Every second person out there has had a difficult childhood.' He opened his eyes, turned his head to look at her. 'I understand you and Leo lost your mother young—and your father a few years later?'

'*Si*. And I missed my mother desperately—which is probably why I acted out as a teenager. But Leo and I had each other. You…' Her voice grew husky. 'You had no one.'

And he hadn't needed anyone. Certainly hadn't wanted to get close to anyone. *Why bother?* he'd thought as a boy. *Why attach yourself to someone just so they could leave you or die.*

It was a pity he hadn't remembered that lesson before he'd married Julia. Instead he'd let life teach it to him all over again—only much more brutally the second time around.

He shrugged, looked up at the awning shielding them from the sun. 'There are worse things in life than being alone.'

'Like going to war?' She touched him then, trailing the tip of one finger over his scar. 'Did you get this when you were in the Legion?'

He sat up, forcing her hand to fall away. '*Oui*.'

'How?'

Mon Dieu. Did her curiosity know no limits?

'It's a shrapnel wound,' he told her, because maybe if he shared something ugly with her she'd see the damaged man he was and realise she didn't want him. Not the way she thought she did.

'From an explosion?'

'A suicide bomber.' He twisted his head around to see her face. 'A twelve-year-old boy.'

'*Mio Dio...*' she breathed, her expression horrified. 'That's awful.'

'That's the modern face of war.' He kept his voice hard, unaffected, *emotionless*. Because that was what he'd learned to do as a soldier. Control his emotions, follow orders, focus on the job and divide those he encountered into one of two camps—ally or enemy. Except that last part hadn't always been easy.

Marietta pressed her palm against his bare back, the contact so unexpected he nearly flinched.

'I'm so sorry for all the terrible things you must have seen, Nico,' she said, in that soft, sympathetic voice that seemed to curl around him, *through* him.

Her hand moved, stroking over his skin, setting fire to a host of nerve-endings which all led like a series of lit fuses to one place. *His groin.*

'Marietta,' he growled, 'what are you doing?'

Marietta wasn't sure she knew the answer to that question. She only knew that she'd felt compelled to reach out in some way, and that once she'd touched him—once she'd made contact with all that smooth, hot skin and sculpted muscle—she hadn't been able to draw her hand away. Hadn't *wanted* to.

He moved with lightning speed. Before she understood his intent he was leaning over her, one hand clamped around her wrist, imprisoning her hand above her head. His expression was dark. Almost angry.

Her heart thumped in her chest.

'You don't want this, Marietta.'

'Want what?' she whispered—but she knew what he meant. Of course she did. She wasn't naive. He hadn't carried her all the way down here just to have lunch on the beach.

But something had changed since they'd got here. Something had caused him to withdraw, have second thoughts.

It felt like a rejection—and it stung.

'Not what—*who*,' he said harshly. 'You don't want *me*, Marietta.'

She pushed up her chin, feeling reckless and bold. Angry even. How *dared* he tell her what she didn't want? 'Why?'

He breathed hard, his nostrils flaring. 'I'm not the kind of man you want to get close to.'

'Why?' she challenged again, her blood thundering in her ears now. 'Because you've seen some terrible things? *Experienced* some terrible things? Things you don't think I could possibly understand?' She struggled to free her wrist. 'Let me go, Nico,' she demanded.

He did, and she levered herself upright, forcing him back from her. 'Do you think you're the only one with scars?' She leaned forward over her legs, exposing her back. 'The one under my left shoulder blade is from the accident,' she told him. 'The rest are from surgeries— *failed* surgeries—and every one of them represents a shattered hope. A shattered dream.'

She dropped back to her elbows, locked her gaze with his.

'I lay in the wreckage of that car for thirty minutes, with two dead friends and another friend dying beside me, before the emergency services arrived.' She hiked up her chin, swallowed down hard on the lump in her throat. 'I haven't been to war, Nico. I haven't seen or done the things you have. But I *do* know something about death and survival.'

Her blood continued to pound, flushing her skin, making the pulse in her throat leap. The after-effects of the wine combined with her anger and the sight of all that potent, half-naked masculinity before her spurred her on to more recklessness.

She reached out and laid her palm against his chest, her fingers nestling in the fine covering of crisp hairs. 'Maybe I *don't* know what kind of man is hidden away in here. But whoever he is—whoever you *think* he is—he doesn't scare me.'

Deliberately she glided the tip of her little finger over his nipple and heard the sudden sharp hiss of his in-drawn breath. But his big body remained taut and rigid, unmoving except for the powerful rise and fall of his chest beneath her hand. She searched his face, looking for signs of desire—for the flash of hunger she'd seen there last night—but the seconds stretched and nothing happened.

The flush receded from her skin and her insides turned cold and then hot again with a horrible, humiliating thought.

She snatched her hand back.

Dio. Had she read this all wrong? Had she imagined something that wasn't really there?

The moment seemed to click into slow motion. Nico's eyes narrowed, his mouth opening as if he was about to speak. But she gave her head a violent shake and fell back onto the cushions, squeezing her eyes closed. She couldn't look at him. He was too perfect. A man like him could have any woman in the world. Why would he take *her*? Unless...

Her face burned. *Stupid, stupid…*

'I think you're right.' She forced the words out between stiff lips. 'I *don't* want this.' Pride made her voice brittle. Defensive. 'I don't need pity sex.'

A sound came from above her—a harsh, ferocious growl of a sound—and she snapped her eyes open.

Nico grasped her wrist, not gently, and pulled her hand to his groin.

'You think *this* is pity?'

A gasp caught in her throat. Nico's eyes blazed into hers, but it wasn't the glittering anger and raw desire she saw that stripped her lungs of air—it was the irrefutable evidence of his arousal, big and thick and rock-hard against her hand. Heat coiled in her belly, and she curled her fingers around his impressive length. *Santo cielo.* He was enormous—and hard. For *her*.

A low, guttural curse shot from his mouth. 'Marietta—' The way he rasped her name was half-warning, half-groan. 'I want you,' he said roughly, tightening his fingers around her wrist, thrusting his groin harder into her hand to encourage her grip. 'Make no mistake about that. But you need to be certain this is what you want—because believe me when I say *this* is the point of no return.'

The fierce heat in his gaze, the solid, rigid length of him in her hand, extinguished her doubts. She squeezed him, giving her answer, and he pulled her hand away from him and loomed above her. Anticipation shivered through her and then his mouth covered hers, and that sudden, shocking clash of lips was ten times more electrifying than she could ever have imagined.

The world spun and she reached blindly for an anchor, until her hands latched on to the hot, hard flesh of his shoulders. He moved and she tightened her grip on him, terrified he was going to end the kiss, but he simply angled his head so he could take it deeper. His tongue stroked over her lips, then thrust between them—and the explosion of heat and earthiness in her mouth was unlike anything she'd ever experienced.

When he raised his head colour slashed his cheekbones, emphasising their prominence, and his eyes had darkened to an inky blue. His gaze raked over her face and lower, down to her breasts in the revealing yellow bikini. He fingered the gold clasp holding the triangles of fabric together and then, with a single flick, unfastened the top. The fabric fell away, exposing her to his scrutiny.

'*Spectaculaire...*' he murmured, and cupped his hand around her right breast.

Her shoulder blades arched off the cushion, her body straining instinctively into his touch. When his thumb stroked over her extended nipple the sensation was exquisite, but nowhere close to being enough. She needed *more...*

She moaned. 'Nico...'

A dark, anticipatory gleam lit his eyes. He lowered his head and sucked her nipple into his mouth, gently at first and then, when she gasped and drove her hands into his hair, harder, using his tongue and his teeth to tease and torment, until she cried out some incoherent words, which he obviously took as encouragement, because he popped her nipple out of his mouth and lavished the same attention on her left one.

Her nails scraped over his scalp. '*Dio...* Nico...'

Something broke loose inside her. Something wild. Demanding. She thrust her chest upwards, urging him on until she was conscious of nothing else besides the heat of his mouth and his tongue and the tight, coiling sensation inside her. Time stopped, ceased to exist, and she didn't know if seconds or minutes had passed when she registered the faint metallic slide of a zipper—realised Nico's hand was at the front of her shorts.

She froze. Only for a moment, but he felt it. His mouth slipped off her nipple, and she wanted to groan.

'I'm not changing my mind,' she said hurriedly, cursing the insecurity that had struck her out of the blue.

She tried pulling his head back down, but he resisted.

He cupped her jaw. 'You froze. Why?'

Inexplicably, her hands trembled. She let go of him and curled them against her stomach, closed her eyes.

'Marietta—'

'My legs,' she whispered. 'They're not...' *Not beautiful.* Her face heated.

'Open your eyes.'

She did, and they prickled dangerously. *Madre di Dio.* What was wrong with her? She *wanted* this. He wanted *her.* Why was she suddenly afraid of revealing her body to him?

'You are beautiful, Marietta,' he said. 'And I want *all* of you.' His hand tightened on her jaw when she would have looked away. 'Do you understand me?'

She stared at him, and then she swallowed and nodded. He dropped a scorching kiss on her mouth. Then he pushed to his feet, removed his shorts and briefs and stood before her fully naked.

The moisture evaporated inside her mouth. Her imagination had not done him justice. He was glorious, every part of him lean and muscled. Her gaze trailed from his broad chest down over the ridges of his abdomen and lower, to where his arousal jutted proudly from the nest of dark hair at the juncture of his thighs. Her belly turned molten. He was so hard. So *big*.

He dropped to his knees, slid the zipper the rest of the way down and removed her shorts and bikini bottoms. Heart pounding, she shrugged off the straps of her bikini top. And then he scooped her into his arms, stood, and carried her across the hot sand into the water.

Kissing, touching, exploring Marietta while immersed in the tepid sea water was the most erotic build-up to sex Nico had ever experienced.

He'd fooled around in water before—taken a woman against the side of a pool more than once—but this...

This was different.

Or maybe it was simply that he was wound so impossibly tight with need for her that he felt as if he might explode at any moment?

God help him.

He hadn't even buried himself inside her yet.

He gave a low, tortured groan, reached between their bodies and pried her fingers from his hard, engorged length before he embarrassed himself and came in the water.

The action earned him a small, petulant frown, but when she reached under the surface, he again seized her wrist.

'*Chérie,*' he growled, 'it will be over before it starts if you keep doing that.'

Her smile was playful, naughty, dialling up the heat in his blood and at the same time reinforcing his sense of relief.

This was the Marietta he knew.

Confident. Spirited. *Pushy*.

The way she'd challenged him on the beach—her boldness, the things she'd said, even her scars—had made him want her even more, until resisting his desire, resisting *hers*, had been impossible. And yet the woman who had frozen beneath him had been vulnerable, insecure—a version of Marietta he hadn't seen before—and his chest had ached with a fierce need to reassure her. To chase the uncertainty from her eyes and bring *this* woman—the one who fired his blood, who challenged him at every turn—back to him.

She wound her arms around his neck now, clinging to him like a silken-skinned mermaid, pressing her lush, caramel-tipped breasts against his chest. He had sucked on those responsive nipples at every opportunity, enjoying her gasps of pleasure as he'd coaxed them into tight, sensitive nubs.

They were ten metres or so from the shore, the water chest-deep, and his feet on the seabed prevented them from drifting.

He kissed her, savouring the warm, salty taste of her mouth and the erotic playfulness of her tongue as it dived between his lips and then retreated, duelling with his.

After a minute he pulled back. Despite his previous claim about the point of no return, he needed to make certain she understood what this was—and *wasn't*. To offer her one last chance to change her mind. Even though it would kill him if she did.

'This is all I can give you,' he said. 'These few days—'

Her fingers landed across his lips. 'I'm not looking for anything more,' she said. 'Here and now—this is all I want…'

And with that the final barrier fell. He dropped an open-mouthed kiss onto the wet, satiny skin between her neck and shoulder and slid his hand under the water, seeking out the silky curls and the velvety V of flesh he'd briefly explored once already—and planned to do so more thoroughly now.

'Tell me where it feels good,' he urged, eager to learn her pleasure points. To understand where she had sensation and where she didn't. He slid his fingers along the seam of delicate flesh, parting, probing, locating the precise spot that made her throw her head back and arch those magnificent breasts against him.

'Oh, *Dio*… There, Nico… *There*…'

He hoisted her higher in the water and clamped his mouth over her nipple, sucking hard while increasing the pressure and movement of his fingers. Her nails sank into his back and the sound she made as she came—something between a purr and a little feminine roar—was the sexiest damn thing he'd ever heard. His body throbbed urgently, almost painfully in response. She dropped her head onto his shoulder, her body going limp in his arms, and cursed in Italian.

Satisfaction rocked through him. 'Was that on your wish list, *chérie*?'

'No…' she mumbled into his neck. 'But I think I'll add it, just so that we can do it again and cross it off.'

'I have some other ideas for your list.'

She lifted her head, her dark eyes slumberous. 'Tell me.'

Nico shook his head, shifted her onto his back and started towards the shore. 'I'm going to show you instead.'

CHAPTER NINE

MARIETTA HAD EXPECTED Nico to lay her down on the cushions beneath the awning and take her right there on the beach—and she'd have been lying if she'd said a part of her hadn't wanted him to. But he had muttered something about sandy blankets and comfort and now they were in his bedroom—a huge room characterised by clean lines and simple masculine decor—lying naked on soft cotton sheets in a bed so enormous it could have slept an entire family.

Her insides were still molten from the orgasm she'd had in the ocean. She had never climaxed like that before—so easily, so *quickly*. With Davide—and on the occasions when she'd experimented by herself—she'd needed a lot more stimulation. But Nico had brought her to her peak with such little effort it had been almost embarrassing.

She stared at him now, unashamedly, her gaze trailing the length of his powerful body as he lay on his side, stretched out beside her. His arousal was just as proud and fierce as it had been in the water, when she'd wanted so desperately to touch him, and it nudged her hip now, so thick and long she wondered a little nervously if she'd be able to accommodate him.

He drew a fingertip over her belly. 'Comfortable?'

Frustration spiralled. She *was* comfortable, lying on her back, one arm thrown above her head, soft pillows plumped under her shoulders for support. But she didn't *want* to feel comfortable. She didn't want Nico to be solicitous—to treat her like a china doll that might break in two if he was too rough with her. She wanted to feel hot and sweaty and breathless. Wanted to feel his weight on top of her, crushing her into the bed as he drove into the hollow place inside her begging to be filled.

His fingertip traced around her belly button and then her nipples, trailing circles of fire over her skin.

'Is there anything I should know?' he said, his voice rough—as though he wasn't quite as in control of himself as he appeared. 'Anything I can do to make it better for you?'

Her thoughts veered towards the tiny niggle of nervous concern at the back of her mind. Heat surged into her face, and his eyes narrowed.

He gripped her chin. 'What?'.

She swallowed. 'I used to sometimes have issues with—' she closed her eyes, her cheeks burning like hotplates '—with lubrication.'

Silence followed. She cracked her eyes open, expecting to see an awkward look—maybe even disappointment—on Nico's face. Instead his blue eyes glittered with something like…*determination*. As if she had tossed down a gauntlet and he was accepting the challenge. Slowly he rose to his hands and knees.

'Are you worried I won't be able to make you wet for me, *chérie*?'

Her eyes widened. 'No! It's not that… It's just—'

Her eyes grew rounder still as he straddled her,

placed his large hands on her skinny thighs and spread them apart.

When he dropped to his stomach, his intent obvious, she babbled again. 'It's not you… It's just that… My body—*oh!*'

Suddenly his mouth was on her—*there*—and the powerful jolt of sensation forced her head back onto the pillow. She caught her breath, clawed her fingers into the sheet beneath her. His mouth was so hot, and his tongue…

Santo cielo!

His tongue was running over and over the spot where her nerve-endings were still very much intact. And then his finger was gently seeking entry, stroking, massaging, sliding deep into…*wetness*. She felt the sweet burn within, the build-up of tension that teased with the promise of a shattering release. Moments later the pressure reached its zenith and she cried out, silence impossible as she split into shards of white light that beamed her skywards and kept her suspended there for a weightless, timeless moment before casting her back to earth.

The bed moved, and she forced open heavy eyelids. Nico was braced above her, his gaze hot. *Satisfied*.

'It's wet down there, *ma petite sirène*.' He kissed her, thrusting his tongue into her mouth, letting her taste herself. '*Very* wet,' he added, and reached over to the nightstand for a condom.

Soon he was sheathed, poised between her legs. He slid his mouth over hers, kissing her long and deep. He lifted his head, his expression as he stared down at her stark. Intense.

'I can't hold back,' he warned, his voice ragged. 'I can't be gentle with you.'

She thrilled to those words. She didn't want gentle—
she wanted wild. *Passionate.* She scraped her fingernails
down his back and dug them into his firm buttocks.

'Don't be,' she said boldly.

And then he pushed inside her and her mouth slackened on a gasp of pleasure. In one long, powerful thrust
he filled her up, and when he started to move, sliding
out and thrusting in, again and again, she had no trouble feeling him.

She knew a moment's regret because she couldn't
wrap her legs around him, couldn't flex her hips to meet
his powerful thrusts. But Nico didn't seem to care; when
she looked at him she saw only lust and fierce pleasure
carved into his stark features.

He went taut above her, and a second later he shuddered and groaned, signalling his release, and then he
was collapsing onto her, pressing his face into her neck.

Marietta wrapped her arms around him and smiled
to herself. The weight of his body crushing her into
the mattress was, she decided, the most delicious feeling in the world.

Nico awoke from an unusually dreamless sleep, and as
he hovered in that place between oblivion and wake-
fulness he was aware of an unfamiliar sense of…con-
tentment.

He turned onto his side and blinked.

Sunlight streamed through the massive bedroom
window and he guessed from the angle that it was late
morning—long past the time he would normally rise.
He wouldn't normally leave the blinds up either, but
last night Marietta had wanted to lie in bed and watch
the sunset and he'd indulged her, spooning against her

as he'd listened to her *ooh* and *aah* over the fiery sky until his body had stirred and he'd given her something much more impressive to *ooh* and *aah* about.

When the sky had finally turned a deep navy blue and the stars had begun to wink he had turned her onto her back and taken her again, watching her moonlit face as she climaxed before giving in to his own mind-shattering release.

He watched her now, asleep beside him, the sheet rumpled around her waist and her breasts bare. Her ebony eyelashes were dark against her skin, her long mahogany hair fanned out in thick waves across his pillow. The night had been warm and humid, but she'd tucked the sheet around her lower half, conscious of her legs even after everything they'd done together—all the ways he'd explored her—over the last twenty hours.

He didn't understand her insecurity. Marietta was a beautiful, sensual woman and he didn't give a damn about her legs.

He curled a thick strand of dark lustrous hair around his fingers. He'd known his attraction to her was strong, but he hadn't predicted just how fiercely and completely his hunger for her would consume him. He had the feeling she had been seared into his memory for life—and yet he knew the danger of collecting memories. Knew how treacherous they could be. How they could lurk in your soul, lying in wait for the moment when you finally thought you were strong and then raising their insidious heads just so they could remind you of what you'd once had—what you'd lost.

Marietta's eyelids fluttered open and she turned her head, blinked sleepy, liquid brown eyes at him.

Nico shook off his maudlin thoughts, curved his mouth into a smile. 'Morning, *ma petite sirène.*'

She stretched her arms above her head. 'What does that mean?'

'My little mermaid.'

She blinked, took a moment to process that, then turned her face towards the window. An adorable scowl formed on her face. 'It can't be morning.'

'It is,' he assured her. 'Late morning, in fact.' He circled a fingertip around her left nipple and the nub of caramel flesh puckered and hardened. 'Time to wake up.'

She stretched again, shamelessly thrusting those perfect breasts towards him. 'Coffee…' she mumbled. 'Mermaids need coffee to wake up.'

He took her hand and guided it to his groin. 'I have something better than coffee to wake you up.'

Her eyes flared, her lips parted—and suddenly his little mermaid didn't look sleepy any more.

Over the next forty-eight hours time slowed and blurred and the outside world ceased to exist—or at least that was how it felt to Marietta. They made love at regular intervals and in between they ate and swam, either at the beach or in the pool. When Nico disappeared to his study every so often to work she would paint, parking herself in front of her canvas and the easel which he'd erected for her in a sunlit corner of the living room.

In no time at all she started feeling as though she were living in one of those protective bubbles, the thought of which she'd scoffed at only nights before. Which was dangerous, she knew. Bubbles were pretty, but they were temporary. Sooner or later they burst—

and hers was about to burst very soon. Because it was Thursday afternoon, and that meant that tomorrow she would return to Rome.

A good thing too, she told herself, slotting tubes of paint into their storage container. This thing with Nico couldn't last. A few days of indulgence—that was all it was meant to be. He'd been up-front about that, and so had she.

She had a life to return to. An excellent, satisfying life where there was no room, no need, for unrealistic expectations.

Plus she had little Ricci's party in two days' time. That would cheer her up. Help her get rid of this silly ache which had settled in her chest this morning and so far had refused to budge.

Nico appeared in the doorway of the living room. He'd been working in his study for no more than an hour and still her breath hitched as if she were seeing him for the first time in days.

She smiled, forced herself to sound brighter than she felt. 'I thought I'd get a head start on packing up my things. I assume we'll leave early in the morning?'

'We're not,' he said.

She paused in the process of wrapping her brushes in a cloth. 'Oh…? What time *will* we leave, then?'

'We're not leaving.'

She blinked at him, and for a fraction of a second her heart soared. Because if they weren't leaving then she wouldn't have to say goodbye to him just yet. She wouldn't sleep with him tonight knowing it was the last time they would ever make love. The last time she would ever feel him inside her, filling her. Making her feel beautiful and desirable and wanton and *whole*.

And then her brain reasserted itself. 'What do you mean, we're not leaving?'

'Exactly that.' He came into the room. 'You're not going back to Rome tomorrow.'

His tone left no room for misinterpretation. He wasn't giving her a choice. He was *telling* her.

For the first time in days, her temper flared. She put her brushes down. 'One week, Nico. I agreed to come here for *one week*.'

He crossed his arms over his chest. The gesture reminded her of the way he and Leo had confronted her six days ago. How they had bulldozed her into coming here. She'd been angry, hating the loss of her independence, the sense of having control of her life stripped away. Which was why she'd laid down her own rules—rules Nico was now completely ignoring.

'Until your stalker is caught, this is the safest place for you to be.'

She folded her arms, mirroring his pose with an equally resolute one of her own. 'And *when* will you catch him?' she demanded to know. 'Next week? Next *month*?'

Something glittered in his eyes. 'Is that an appalling idea, *chérie*? Spending an entire month with me?'

She pressed her lips together before she could blurt out the word *no*. The idea didn't appal her. Not in the slightest. In fact it made her feel light-headed. Euphoric. And that was wrong.

Wrong, wrong, *wrong*.

She wasn't *meant* to want more of him.

'This is hardly a joking matter,' she said. 'I have a job to get back to. A *life*. And it's my nephew's first birthday party on Saturday—I told Leo and Helena I wouldn't miss it.'

'I've spoken with Leo and he agrees you should stay.'

Her anger bloomed, swift and bright and vivid like a bloodstain on cotton. *How dared they?* 'That's not Leo's decision to make—nor, might I add, is it yours!'

She seized the wheels of her chair and propelled herself towards the doorway.

'Where are you going?'

'To call my sister-in-law,' she snapped.

'Why?'

'Because she's got more sense than you and my brother put together!'

And maybe Helena could change her husband's mind. If Marietta had Leo on her side Nico would have to let her go—a thought that only sharpened the ache in her chest.

And that made her angrier still.

Sisterhood, it turned out, was overrated.

Helena had sided with the men. Marietta had wanted to express her anger over the phone but found she couldn't. Her sister-in-law's stance came from a place of caring and concern, and Marietta wasn't angry with Helena. She was angry at the situation—and with Nico for his high-handedness. He hadn't even consulted her first. He'd simply made the decision.

She managed a smile for the young waitress who had arrived at the table with her dessert and then realised the courtesy was a wasted effort. The girl was more interested in casting pretty smiles at Nico, even though she looked as if she was barely out of her teens and he was surely too old for her.

He had that powerful effect on women. She imagined he always would. He'd carry those rugged good looks and that dark sex appeal into his later years and become one of those sexy, distinguished-looking older men to whom women of all ages flocked.

The thought didn't improve Marietta's mood.

And if Nico had hoped a nice meal and the buoyant atmosphere of the Bouchards' seaside restaurant would, he was in for disappointment. She picked up her spoon and cracked the hard caramelised top of her *crème brûlée* with a sharp jab.

'You're still angry.'

She glanced across the table at him. He was clean-shaven for the first time in two days and the skin over his hard jaw looked bronzed and taut in the golden candlelight which flickered from the glass holder on the table.

'Of course,' she said, opting for honesty, because no matter how hard she strove for the kind of composure she'd often admired in her sister-in-law she'd never been very good at hiding her emotions. 'I'm missing an important family event by staying here, Nico.'

His long fingers toyed with his espresso cup. 'You would put a child's birthday party above your own safety?'

'It's not just any child's party,' she retorted. 'It's my *nephew's* very first birthday and a milestone I won't get to share with him now.'

Nico regarded her. 'It means that much to you?'

'*Sì.*'

She laid down the spoon. *Crème brûlée* was her favourite dessert, but she didn't really have the stomach for its rich creaminess right now. The only reason she'd ordered it was to delay the end of their meal and their return to the house. If their post-dinner entertainment followed the trend of the last two evenings they would very quickly end up naked—and she didn't want that to happen. Not yet. She wanted to nurse her anger awhile longer and she knew that as soon as he touched her, the second he was deep inside her, she'd forget she was supposed to be angry with him.

'They're my family,' she added, sitting back in her wheelchair. 'The only family I'll ever have.'

His eyes narrowed. 'What do you mean?'

She shrugged, but inwardly she cringed. That statement had been too honest. Too revealing. 'Exactly that,' she said, tossing his words from that afternoon back at him.

He looked at her for a long moment. 'Can you not have children, Marietta?' he asked quietly, and the intimacy of the question—from a man who routinely avoided conversations of a personal nature—threw her.

She hesitated. 'There's no medical reason I can't have children,' she admitted, pushing her dessert plate away. 'It's possible…physically.'

His gaze narrowed further. 'So there's nothing stopping you from having a family of your own?'

Her chest tightened. He made it sound so natural. So easy. As if having a broken back didn't make her different. 'It's not that simple,' she said, her voice stilted.

'Why?'

She frowned at him. Around them the restaurant was busy, with the clink of tableware, the buzz of conversation and frequent bouts of laughter lending the place a lively air. Josephine had seated them at a private table, however, set in a quiet corner by a large window overlooking the harbour.

Marietta glanced around, assuring herself that their

conversation wasn't being overheard. 'Generally speaking, a woman needs a husband before she has children,' she said.

He lifted an eyebrow. 'And you object to marriage?'

Her frown deepened. Why was he asking her these questions? Why was he interested?

Why should he *care?*

Her breath caught in her throat.

Did he care?

Hastily she crushed the thought. He was making conversation, showing a polite interest in the woman he was temporarily sleeping with.

She cleared her throat. 'Marriage is fine,' she said. 'It's just not for me.'

'Because of Davide?'

'Partly.' She lifted her shoulder. 'When push comes to shove, few men want to tie themselves to a cripple for life.'

Nico's brows slammed down, his face darkening. 'Don't call yourself that,' he said tersely.

'What? A cripple?' She affected an air of indifference. 'Why not? That's how most people see me.'

Which wasn't strictly true. She was fortunate; she had people in her life who saw the woman first and foremost and not the disability. But equally there were those who *never* saw beyond the wheelchair. Never saw *her.*

Blue eyes blazed at her from across the table. 'That's not how *I* see you.'

Her heart lurched. She believed him, but how *did* he see her? As a woman who needed protecting? A perk of the job? She'd already guessed she was one of a long string of short-term lovers he'd taken in the years since his wife's death. She'd told herself it didn't matter to her, ignored the taunting voice that had cried *liar*.

'I know,' she said quietly.

Nico's gaze stayed pinned on her. 'Davide was an idiot,' he said. 'But he's one man. Why write off your dreams because of one bad experience?'

Her shoulders stiffened. 'Because I'm a realist—and some things simply aren't destined to be.' She sniffed. 'Anyway, you have no idea *what* my dreams are. Not every woman longs for the white picket fence, you know.'

He raised his eyebrows. 'So you don't *want* children?'

'No.' But that was a lie. A lie she had repeated in her head so often she'd almost believed it. Her stomach knotted.

'But family is important to you?'

'So are other things,' she said, hating the defensive note in her voice. 'My job—my career as an artist...'

She trailed off. Her words had sounded hollow and they shouldn't have. She was utterly passionate about her art. Determined to make a full-time living from it eventually. In the meantime she had a job she loved, her apartment, her studio for hire... It was enough. Of *course* it was enough.

So why had Nico's questions got her all tied up in knots?

She took the white napkin off her lap, folded it carefully and placed it on the table. 'Thank you for dinner,' she said, avoiding his eye. 'I'm ready to go when you are.'

The Bouchards came out to farewell them, dropping kisses onto Marietta's cheeks, and she wondered what assumptions they'd made about her and Nico's relationship.

Not that it mattered. Sooner or later she'd be gone from Île de Lavande and she'd have no reason to return—a thought she found inordinately depressing as Nico drove them home on the winding mountain road. When they arrived, he parked in the courtyard by the house, went to open the front door, then returned and lifted her out of the Jeep. He carried her towards the house.

'Nico!' she cried. 'My chair!'

He kicked the front door closed, barely breaking stride. 'You won't be needing it for a while.'

Outrage and something else she didn't want to acknowledge sent a lick of heat through her veins.

Her voice rose on a high note of fury. 'I'm *not* sleeping with you tonight!'

He reached his bedroom and dropped her unceremoniously onto his bed, so that she sprawled inelegantly on the grey silk coverlet.

He shot her a dark, blistering look and started unbuttoning his shirt. 'I don't plan on doing much sleeping.'

She pushed onto her elbows, glared up at him. 'I'm still angry with you!' she flung at him.

He shrugged off his shirt and threw it to the floor. The moonlight illuminating the room washed over his powerful torso, making him look like a statue of some demigod cast in pewter.

Marietta's mouth dried.

'Bien,' he said in a low, rough voice, simultaneously toeing off his shoes and unbuckling his belt. 'I like that fiery temper.'

He shoved the rest of his clothes off and when he

straightened the full extent of his arousal was plain to see. He curled his hand around himself and the sight of him doing so was deeply erotic. Utterly mesmerising.

'It turns me on,' he said, quite unnecessarily, and then he was climbing onto the bed.

She shook herself, shot her arm out and slapped her palm against his chest. 'Stop!'

'You don't mean that,' he said, and his lips curved into a smile of such utter carnality that her belly flooded with hot, liquid need. Then he pushed up her top, freed her left breast from its lacy confines and sucked her nipple into his mouth.

Marietta gasped, her traitorous body arching in response to the exquisite sensations he inflicted so effortlessly. She lifted her hands, intending to beat them down upon his bare shoulders, but somehow her fingers ended up buried in his thick hair.

His head lifted, his blue eyes glittering with triumph. 'Do you still want me to stop?'

She gave him a mutinous glare, then dragged his head down and kissed him, sinking her teeth into his lower lip for a second before pushing his head back up.

'This won't make me forget that I'm angry with you,' she warned him.

That wicked smile returned, making her insides quiver.

'Chérie,' he said, lowering himself on top of her, his hard body crushing her into the mattress, 'by the time I'm done with you, you won't remember your *name*.'

CHAPTER TEN

'DID I DRAG you out of bed, my friend?'

Leo Vincenti's voice carried over the video feed with a distinct note of dryness.

Nico thrust his hand through his dishevelled hair and peered at his friend's image on his computer screen. Leo sat in his office in Rome, looking immaculate in a crisp shirt and tie, making Nico even more aware of his unshaved jaw and the rumpled tee shirt he'd hurriedly pulled on after realising he was late for the video call he and Leo had scheduled for this morning.

'Long night working,' he said as he ruthlessly smothered the image of his friend's sister naked and spread-eagled on his bed.

Dieu. He hadn't considered how truly awkward it would be to look his friend in the eye after all the things he had done with Marietta last night.

Never had he known sex to be so… so *combustible*. So all-consuming. And still he wanted more. Still his groin twitched at the mere thought of sliding between her thighs and burying himself inside her wet, welcoming heat.

He moved his chair closer to the desk, concealing his lower body.

'Sorry I couldn't talk longer yesterday,' said Leo. 'I was in the middle of a client crisis meeting. You said you had more news?'

'There's been a development,' Nico confirmed, forcing his mind away from the sleepy, satisfied woman he'd left in his bed. He'd placed her chair within arm's reach, in case she wanted to get up, but he hoped she'd stay put. He wasn't finished with her yet.

He sat forward and gave a brief summary of the information Bruno had imparted yesterday. Late on Wednesday one of the two men they'd shortlisted as suspects had confronted Lina at the gallery and demanded to know Marietta's whereabouts. When Lina had claimed not to know he'd become aggressive and physical. Bruno was convinced they had their man. But now the guy had gone to ground.

Leo's expression was grim. 'Is the girl all right?'

'She's fine. I have a protective detail on her.'

'How will you find him?'

'We have the *polizia* fully on board now.' And his own men continued to work around the clock.

'Does Marietta know?'

'Not yet.' When the perpetrator was in custody—*then* he would tell her. In the meantime she didn't need to know about Lina. She'd only worry. 'I'll give her the details when the time is right.'

Leo dragged a hand over his face, pulled in a deep breath. 'Thank you, Nico,' he said gravely. 'I don't know how I can ever repay you for this.'

Nico shrugged. 'If our roles were reversed you would do the same, *mon ami*,' he said, tamping down on a flare of guilt.

Marietta was a grown woman, he reminded himself. She wasn't answerable to her brother—and neither was he.

He promised Leo to keep him updated and disconnected the call. When he returned to the bedroom Marietta was still in bed, early-morning sunlight streaming over her mahogany hair and golden breasts. He shed his clothes and climbed in beside her.

She stirred, blinked those beautiful dark eyes at him. 'I thought I heard you talking to someone…'

'Just a work call,' he said, cupping a soft, lush breast in his hand and thumbing its nipple. She moaned, and the little nub of caramel flesh peaked into a hard point that begged for the attention of his mouth.

A few more days, he acknowledged, his heart punching hard at the thought. That was all he'd have with her. Right then it didn't seem as if it could possibly be enough, but it would have to be. He had nothing to give her beyond these days on the island, nothing to offer, and she deserved more. She deserved a man capable of love. A man who would tear down the barriers she didn't even know she'd erected around herself and convince her she'd make an amazing wife and mother.

Nico wasn't that man. And for a moment, as he stared into her liquid brown eyes, the knowledge twisted his stomach into a knot of deep, gut-wrenching regret.

Marietta lay on her side on the soft beach rug and watched the steady rise and fall of Nico's magnificent chest as he slept.

He wore only a pair of swimming trunks and she trailed her gaze over his bronzed body, her belly twisting with a physical need she'd thought might have lessened over the last three days but had, in fact, only intensified.

They'd settled into something of a routine. In the mornings they'd linger in bed and make love, before indulging in a leisurely breakfast on the terrace, then Nico would work for two to three hours in his study and Marietta would paint. When her tummy grumbled she'd wash out her brushes and make them some lunch, and afterwards they'd swim and laze by the pool or at the beach. Dinner was usually a light snack, shared at the kitchen table or out on the terrace—and bedtime always came early.

It was indulgent and idyllic and it couldn't last. Marietta knew that, and that was why she planned to enjoy it. Reality would intrude soon enough. For now she was going to accept these extra days with Nico for what she'd decided they were—once her anger over missing Ricci's birthday had worn off. A gift.

She traced her finger over the words tattooed around the emblem on his left arm. *Honneur et Fidélité.* It was the motto of the French Foreign Legion and somehow those words—honour and fidelity—fitted him perfectly. Because he *was* loyal and honourable. Her brother had said so many times, and Leo trusted him implicitly—as did she.

Her heart squeezed every time she thought about what he'd revealed of his childhood. She ached inside for the lonely boy he must have been, and she ached for the man he was now—a man who held himself aloof from the world. A man who seemed very much alone.

He was like a multi-layered gift-wrapped parcel, she decided. The kind that was passed around a circle of children at a party and when the music stopped another layer was unceremoniously ripped off. The excitement—and the frustration—was in not knowing how many layers there would be. Not knowing exactly when you were going to peel off the final layer and reach the heart of the parcel—the true gift beneath.

Nico had many layers—most of them deeply buried. His difficult childhood, the loss of his mother, his time as a soldier and the horrors he must have seen... But she sensed his greatest trauma—and thus the key to understanding him—had been the loss of his wife, and unfortunately that subject had been declared off-limits.

'Ready for a swim, *ma petite sirène?*'

She jumped, her hand jerking away from his arm.

Of course he hadn't been asleep.

She smiled at the endearment. *My little mermaid.* When she swam with him she *felt* like a mermaid, too. Graceful and elegant. Playful and sultry. For a while she'd forget all about her useless legs and simply revel in the freedom of the water. The exquisite pleasure of being skin to skin with him.

'In a bit,' she said, tracing her finger through the dark, crisp hair on his forearm.

Her mind toyed with the question.

Did she dare?

She looked at him, then took a deep breath and plunged in. 'Will you tell me about your wife?'

He tensed, and she held her breath.

He sat up, the lines of his shoulders and back rigid.

'I asked you never to speak about that.'

'I know, but—'

'Leave it, Marietta.'

She swallowed. 'I only—'

'I said *leave it.*'

And he lunged to his feet, stalked across the sand and dived into the water.

When Nico emerged from the sea he had no idea how long he'd been swimming. Fifteen minutes, if he hazarded a guess. Twenty at the most. Long enough for regret to outweigh his anger.

He had been too harsh with Marietta. These last few days they had been totally absorbed in one another, as physically intimate as two people could be. Her curiosity had felt intrusive, uncomfortable—more than uncomfortable—but it wasn't entirely unreasonable.

He padded across the sand. She lay on her back now, the awning shading her from the afternoon sun, her enormous dark sunglasses keeping her eyes hidden. A bright blue sarong draped her legs and she wore the yellow bikini top he'd enjoyed removing on numerous occasions. She must have heard his approach and yet she didn't move a muscle.

He dropped to his knees on the rug and shook his head, spraying droplets of seawater over her.

'Hey!' She whipped her sunglasses off and glared up at him.

He stared back, meeting that fiery little temper of hers head-on. 'You're upset,' he observed.

'You got up and walked away from me, Nico. How do you *think* that makes me feel? Knowing that I can't stand up and follow you?'

Shame pierced him, and he didn't like it. 'You pushed me, Marietta,' he said, taking a defensive tack.

'I asked you a question. That's all.'

Frustration needled under his skin. He grabbed a

towel, dried himself off and sat down beside her. He stared moodily out at the sea. 'I don't talk about my wife with other people.'

A pause. 'Is that what I am to you?' she asked quietly. '"Other people"?'

He turned his head to look at her. 'No,' he conceded gruffly—because she wasn't. She was different—the only person he'd let get this close to him in ten years.

Hell. He pushed his hands through his hair, closed his eyes for a moment. Then he stretched out on his back beside her and took a deep, slow breath.

'Her name was Julia,' he began, 'and we met at a resort in Mexico when I was twenty-four.'

He could feel Marietta's gaze on him but he kept his own pinned on the blue and white stripes of the awning above them.

'She was vacationing with girlfriends and I was blowing off steam with some guys I had just completed a private security contract with.'

It had been a classic case of 'opposites attract'.He'd been a big, rough-around-the-edges foreigner and she'd been a pretty polished blonde from a privileged background. But Julia had been so much more than that. She had been sweetness and light—everything Nico had missed from his life since his mother had died.

Within six months they'd been married, despite her parents' protestations.

'It should never have worked,' he said. 'Our backgrounds were too different. And her father was running for the state senate.' He grimaced at the memory of Jack Lewisham's reaction to the man his daughter had declared she was marrying. 'I wasn't exactly desirable son-in-law material.'

He paused. Marietta was silent, but he sensed her listening intently.

'Things were rocky with her parents at the start, but eventually they accepted me.'

Nico had been determined to prove to Jack Lewisham that he was worthy of the man's daughter. He'd worked multiple day jobs and studied for a business degree at night, with the intention of starting his own company. In the end Jack had been impressed. He'd even loaned Nico a substantial chunk of capital to get the business started.

He closed his eyes and swallowed, his mouth going dry.

'Julia was kidnapped.'

Marietta gasped. *'Mio Dio...'* she breathed. 'By whom?'

'Opportunists. Criminals.' His jaw hardened. 'Her parents were extremely wealthy and high-profile.'

'Oh, Nico...'

He could hear the horror in her voice, blocked it out.

'Her father and I argued over whether or not to involve the authorities. The kidnappers had warned against it and Jack was terrified. He believed that his willingness to hand over the ransom combined with my military experience and resources would be sufficient to get Julia home safely.' He clenched his jaw. 'The man practically got on his knees and begged me to agree.'

'And you did?'

'Reluctantly.'

The absolute worst decision of his life. His biggest, most horrific failure.

She touched his arm. 'What happened?'

'Julia was shot.'

Marietta's hand tightened on his arm, communicating her shock, and somehow her touch grounded him. Kept him from sliding back to that dark place in his head where there was only that filthy ditch and Julia's cold, lifeless body.

'Were the kidnappers caught?' she asked gently.

'Eventually.'

He hadn't rested—not until every member of the gang responsible had been caught, prosecuted and imprisoned.

'They claimed her death had been an accident. Said she'd made a grab for one of their guns and it went off in a struggle.'

'Nico…I'm so sorry…'

Finally he looked at her. Tears streaked her face and he muttered a curse, gathered her into his arms.

'Please tell me you don't blame yourself,' she whispered, pressing her face to his chest.

In the silence that followed she lifted her head and stared at him.

'Nico! You can't possibly—'

'I can,' he said grimly. 'And so did Jack.'

'But that's crazy—how *could* he?'

'He was a man half-demented with grief.' It was something Nico had understood, for he, too, had almost lost his mind. 'He needed to lash out. To blame someone other than himself.'

Marietta put her head back on his chest. 'It wasn't your fault,' she said fiercely.

Nico tightened his arms around her. She was, he thought with an odd feeling of gratitude, the only person ever to try to absolve him of guilt.

* * *

For the first time in days Nico retired to his study after dinner, and when it got late and he still hadn't emerged Marietta went to bed alone.

She lay in his gigantic bed, thinking of everything he'd told her on the beach that day, and her heart ached for him.

How could he blame himself for his wife's death? And how could his father-in-law blame him for a decision the older man had essentially made himself?

It didn't make sense—but when did these kinds of things ever make sense? It was the nature of tragedies. Of how people tried to cope. And she understood something about that. Her friends had died in the accident and she hadn't—how could she not have questioned that outcome? Not felt some degree of survivor's guilt? But in the end she'd had to let it go or it would have destroyed her. She had decided to be strong. To make something of her life—of the second chance her young friends had been so cruelly denied.

And are you? a voice in her head challenged. *Are you making the most of that chance?*

She frowned at the ceiling. She had tried hard for the last three days not to think about her conversation with Nico at the restaurant. He'd pushed some buttons she'd thought were no longer sensitive. Rekindled a longing for things she had convinced herself were out of reach.

But she knew that yearning for things that might never be was dangerous. A guarantee of heartache and disappointment. She had already travelled that road— with the experimental surgeries, with Davide... She couldn't set herself on a path of false hope again.

Which made the little daydreams she'd caught herself indulging in these past few days—silly fantasised scenarios of wheeling down a church aisle in a white gown, or holding a tiny sweet-smelling baby in her arms—all the more ridiculous.

The sound of footsteps coming down the hallway halted her thoughts. Quickly she closed her eyes, feigned sleep. If Nico had wanted to make love to her tonight he'd have joined her sooner; she had too much pride to let him think she'd been lying here waiting for him.

She heard the rustle of clothes being shed, felt the bed compress and then, to her surprise, the press of a hot palm against her breast. She looked up and saw the glitter of blue eyes in the semi-darkness before his mouth claimed hers in a hard, invasive kiss that drove a hot spike of need through her core.

He pushed her thighs apart, slid his hand between her legs and growled low in his throat when he found her wet and ready for him. He rolled away for a moment and then he was back, braced above her this time, his features stark, the glitter in his eyes ferocious as he entered her with a single powerful thrust.

She gasped his name, clinging to his shoulders as he drove deep, again and again. He had never taken her hard and fast like this before—as though he barely had control of himself—and she thrilled to the wild, primitive feeling of being claimed.

Possessed.

She dug her fingers into rippling muscle, feeling the tension and the heat building, spiralling, until a moan rushed up her throat and she crested that blinding peak at the same instant as Nico's big body tensed above her.

He slammed deep into her one last time and pleasure pulsated from her core, obliterating every conscious thought from her head except for one.

One thought that stopped her heart as his weight bore down on her and she wrapped her arms tightly around him.

She loved him.

Marietta put down her brush and studied the canvas. The painting was finally finished and she was pleased with it. Her choice of colours and the way she'd illustrated the fortress's proud, crumbling ruins, with pale shafts of sunlight slanting through the old ramparts, had created the impression of something ethereal, almost otherworldly.

But she couldn't help but wish now that she'd painted something different. Something a little brighter, more uplifting. She had planned on leaving the painting behind—as a gift for Nico—but it seemed too haunting now for a man who was already haunted.

A shiver rippled through her. Their lovemaking last night had been so intense. So *silent*. Nico hadn't uttered a word—not before or during or afterwards—and yet he'd watched her the entire time he had been inside her, with that fierce intensity blazing in his blue eyes.

Her heart twisted painfully in her chest. The emotion she'd been wrestling with ever since her shattering revelation last night refused to be subdued.

She could *not* have fallen in love with him. Not so quickly. So hopelessly. So irrevocably.

Except she had.

And now her heart would break, because she wanted something she couldn't have. *A man.* A man too closed off from his emotions to ever be available to her or anyone else.

And already he was withdrawing.

He hadn't reached for her this morning…hadn't lavished her with kisses and caresses while the sun rose and then joined her for a lazy breakfast on the terrace. Instead he'd got dressed and gone straight to his study, emerging only for a quick lunch before disappearing again.

She put her paints away and folded her brushes into a rag for cleaning. The ache in her chest was her penance, she told herself harshly. She'd been a fool and now she'd have to live with the consequences—a concept she was all too familiar with.

She wheeled down the hall towards the utility room where she usually cleaned her brushes.

Nico stepped out of his study.

'Do you have a minute?'

She stopped and looked at him. He sounded so *polite*. The ache in her chest intensified. For the last three days she'd deliberately avoided asking about her stalker, assuring herself that Nico would tell her anything important.

He had something important to tell her now. Which meant this was the beginning of the end.

Her mouth drying, she nodded, and he stood back so she could wheel herself into the study. She stopped by his desk and he handed her a piece of paper—a printed digital photograph of a man.

'Do you know him?'

She studied the image. The man was clean-shaven, and he wore trendy thin-rimmed eyeglasses and a baseball cap. The photograph was grainy, as if it had been enlarged a few times, but the man's face was clear enough and...*familiar*.

She nodded slowly. 'It's Sergio Berardi. He's an artist.' She studied the photo again, an icy finger sliding across her nape. 'I exhibited some of his work at the gallery about a year ago.'

'Nine months,' said Nico.

The hairs on her arms lifted. 'I've met him a few times socially, through art circles,' she said, and suddenly it all made a horrible kind of sense. She put the photo down on the desk, not wanting to look at it any longer. 'He asked me out a couple of times but I declined.'

He hadn't been unpleasant, or unattractive, but she'd already decided not to waste her time on relationships. She rubbed her forehead. Thinking back, he *had* been intense. A little unsettling.

'*Santo cielo...*' Bile climbed her throat. 'I can't believe I didn't think of him before.'

Nico shrugged, as if it were of no consequence. 'Don't beat yourself up,' he said.

Did he sound distant, or was she imagining it? Being oversensitive?

Her heart lurched. She wanted to rewind. Go back to the beginning and relive her time with him. Relive the fantasy. Because she knew with utter certainty that her life wouldn't be the same when she got back to Rome. Not after Nico.

She swallowed past the lump in her throat. 'What happens now?'

'I'm leaving immediately for Toulon.'

She frowned up at him. 'Don't you mean *we* are leaving?'

'*Non,*' he said. 'I need to get to Rome as quickly as possible, to liaise with the authorities. I can travel faster if I leave at once and go on my own. I'll do a quick round trip and be back late tomorrow. We can stay here tomorrow night and then get you back to Rome on Wednesday.'

One last night with him.

Her heart somersaulted. 'Okay,' she agreed—too readily.

He glanced at his watch. '*Bien.* I'll call Josephine. See if she or Luc are available to come and collect you.' He started gathering together papers on his desk. 'You should go and pack an overnight bag straight away.'

Marietta blinked at him. 'Why would I do that?'

He paused. 'Because you'll be staying at Josephine's tonight.'

She blinked again. 'And why would I do that when I can stay here?'

He frowned. 'Because I don't want you staying here on your own.'

She stared at him. 'Why not? I live alone in Rome. You *know* that, Nico. I'm more than capable of spending a night here on my own.'

'Rome is different. You live in an urban apartment, with neighbours and people nearby. It's too isolated up here. I want to know you're safe while I'm gone.'

'You mean you want someone to babysit me?' Her face heated with indignation. 'I'm paralysed, Nico—not *useless.*'

His expression darkened. 'I did not say you were useless.'

'But you might as well have. Heaven forbid the poor cripple is left to fend for herself!'

Now his face turned thunderous. 'Don't call yourself a cripple!'

'Then don't *treat* me like one!'

'Marietta…' His voice was a low, warning growl.

She pushed her chin up. 'I'm staying here.'

He cursed loudly. 'I don't have time for this.'

'No, you don't,' she agreed. 'So I suggest you get a
move on and go and pack *your* bag.'

A nerve flickered in his temple. He opened his mouth
and closed it again, then scowled and stalked out of
the room.

Nico sat in a leather recliner in his private jet and stared
out at the thickening wall of cloud as the aircraft's powerful engines ate up the miles to Toulon.

It was twenty-six hours since he'd left for Rome and
he was eager to get back to Île de Lavande. Leaving
Marietta alone at the house had not sat well with him,
but she was proud—stubborn as hell—and she'd argued
him into a corner.

He stretched out his legs, rubbed eyes that felt gritty
and strained. Dealing with endless police bureaucracy
in Rome and the vagaries of the Italian legal system
had been an exercise in frustration. But he'd called on
some old contacts, pulled a few strings and in the end
got what he'd wanted: a little one-on-one time in a non-
surveillance holding cell with Sergio Berardi.

Nico hadn't laid a finger on the man and he hadn't
needed to. Berardi had nearly wet himself the second
Nico had locked the door, shrugged off his jacket and
rolled up his sleeves. He intended to do everything
within his power to ensure that the charges against Berardi stuck and he was locked up, but Nico had wanted

to make certain that in the event the man was released he understood *exactly* what kind of retribution to expect if he went anywhere near Marietta.

He swallowed a mouthful of whisky.

He had missed Marietta last night. Missed her sweet, intoxicating smell, her soft warmth, the taste of her lingering on his tongue after making love. Even thinking about her now sent a powerful throb of desire pulsing through him.

Mon Dieu.

He'd crossed a line with her but he couldn't bring himself to regret it. Marietta had been a balm to his tortured soul. A ray of light in the sea of darkness that had closed over his head a long time ago.

He took another gulp of whisky.

Perhaps he was being hasty, confining their affair to these few days on the island? He couldn't imagine his hunger for her dying any time soon—nor could he imagine another woman satisfying him while his need for Marietta still burned in his blood. He could see her occasionally, could he not? A casual arrangement might be the perfect solution. Might suit them both until—

A massive jolt wrenched Nico sideways in his seat. His head hit the wall and the glass flew from his hand, whisky spilling everywhere and soaking the crotch of his trousers. He swore, looked up, and saw his flight attendant, Evelyn, clutching a seat-back. He barked at her to sit down and strap herself in, then picked up the built-in handset that gave him direct access to the cockpit.

'Severe unexpected turbulence, sir,' his pilot informed him. 'It's the edge of a category three storm— coming through a couple of hours earlier than expected.'

Expected? Nico swore again. He always checked the

weather forecasts when he was headed to the island. *Always*. But this time… This time he'd forgotten. He'd been preoccupied. Distracted.

'We have clearance from Toulon, provided we land in the next fifteen minutes,' the pilot advised. 'After that everything's grounded or diverted.'

Which meant he had zero chance of flying the chopper to the island. He stared grimly out of the window. The cloud was menacing and black, darkening the interior of the plane.

'What direction is the storm coming from?'

The pilot rattled off the latest update—and Nico felt the blood drain from his face.

The storm was headed straight for Île de Lavande.

CHAPTER ELEVEN

THE PHONE LINE was dead.

With clammy hands Marietta put the receiver back in its cradle on Nico's desk.

This is just some bad weather, she told herself for the umpteenth time—then jumped as the entire house shifted and groaned under the onslaught of the powerful wind. She looked out of the window at the angry sky. *Dark.* It was so dark. Yet it was only late afternoon. She tried the light switch in the study, then a couple out in the hall—nothing. The house had no power.

Dio. Please let Nico be safe, she prayed. He wouldn't do anything crazy, would he? Like try to fly in this weather?

She wheeled herself to a window in the living room, looked out at the sea, which had been whipped into a seething grey-green frenzy, then back at the clouds—which looked wilder, even blacker now if that were possible.

No. Of course Nico wouldn't try to fly in this. He was too safety-conscious. Too sensible.

If only *she* had been sensible. If only she hadn't argued with him. If only she hadn't been so stubborn and proud and oversensitive about her independence.

She could have been warm and comfortable with the Bouchards right now. Instead she was here. Alone and, yes—she'd swallow her pride and admit it—*just a tiny bit terrified.*

Rain came down—thick, horizontal sheets of it lashing the glass—and the wind roared like some kind of vicious animal howling for blood. It raised the hairs on Marietta's nape. Made her want to curl up in Nico's bed, pull the covers over her head and breathe in his scent. Pretend that he was there and she was wrapped in his strong arms, protected and safe.

She pulled in a deep breath.

Nico wouldn't travel in this storm. She was alone—at least for tonight. Which meant she'd need to be calm, practical. Prepared. She'd start by looking for a torch, she decided. Then she'd recheck the windows and doors to make sure the house was secure, and hunt out some candles and matches.

She found a lantern torch in the utility room and started her check of the house in the study. She wheeled to the window and glanced out—just as the large terrace table at which she and Nico had shared so many meals by the pool started to slide across the limestone pavers. Her eyes rounded with disbelief. The table was heavy— a solid piece of outdoor furniture—yet it might as well have been plastic for all its resistance to the wind.

Her heart surged into her throat as another wild gust shook the walls—and then the table simply lifted into the air like a piece of driftwood and flew towards the house.

Marietta backed her chair away as fast as she could and spun around. But the torch slipped off her lap and caught under her wheel. Her chair lurched and tipped and she threw her arms out to break her fall, crashing to the floor at the same moment as the table slammed into the study window. She locked her arms over her head, protecting her face from the splintered glass that showered all around her.

Fear clawed at her chest and a sob punched out of her throat. Clapping her hands over her ears, she tried to block out the violent cacophony of wind and rain. And started to pray.

Nico paced the floor of his hotel room in Toulon.

The room was tiny, compared to the hotel suites he normally stayed in, but the city was full of stranded travellers and last-minute accommodation was scarce. Not that he cared one iota about the room. He barely noticed the tired decor and frayed furnishings. Barely registered the cramped confines that forced him to spin on his heel every ten steps and pace in the other direction.

The floor beneath him shook and the glass in the windows shuddered. The wind was gaining strength, becoming brutal in its capacity for damage even with the full force of the storm yet to hit the mainland. Toulon and the other coastal cities and towns were in a state of lockdown; in this part of Europe storms of this category were rare and people were cautious and nervous.

A cold sweat drenched his skin.

He was nervous.

He stopped. No. *Nervous* didn't do justice to what he was feeling right now.

He picked up his phone from the floor, where he'd thrown it earlier in a fit of fury and frustration. But he still couldn't get a connection; the network was either down or overloaded.

He tossed the phone aside.

His house was strong, he reminded himself. Architecturally designed and built to withstand the elements. And yet bricks and mortar were no match for Mother Nature at her worst. If she was so inclined she would demolish everything in her path.

Hell.

He resumed his pacing. *Josephine.* Josephine and her family knew Marietta was alone at the house. He'd called his housekeeper yesterday, before he'd left, to let her know—just as a precaution. The Bouchards would check on Marietta, wouldn't they? If they'd been forewarned of the storm…

But the weather predictions had been wildly off—the storm was hitting land two hours sooner than expected…

Nico's head threatened to explode. He felt useless. Helpless. And he knew this feeling. He *knew* it. Remembered it. Had sworn he would never feel it again.

Suddenly Julia's face swam in his mind—laughing, eyes dancing…and then glassy, lifeless, her pale skin streaked with dirt. And cold. *So, so cold.*

His legs buckled beneath him and his knees slammed into the cheap carpet, the impact jarring his entire body.

Loving Julia had made him weak, left him open and defenceless, so that when the worst had happened—when she'd been taken from him—he'd had nothing inside him to fight the pain. And the pain, the agony of losing someone he'd loved, had nearly destroyed him.

Mon Dieu.

He couldn't do this again.

His mother.

Julia.

Marietta.

A wild, rage-filled roar tore from his throat and he picked up an ugly vase from the coffee table and hurled it across the room.

Marietta navigated her chair around the tree branches and clumps of debris strewn across the Bouchards' front yard and cast yet another anxious look towards the hills.

She couldn't see Nico's house from the village, but every so often throughout the morning she'd taken a break from helping in the kitchen to come outside and scour the skyline for signs of his chopper. Thankfully power had been restored to most of the village, but the phone lines were still down and mobile coverage was intermittent.

A gentle hand squeezed her shoulder. She looked up, and Josephine smiled down at her.

'He'll be fine.'

Marietta nodded. 'I know.'

Josephine gave her an understanding look. 'It is too easy to worry about the ones we love, *oui?*'

Marietta felt her smile stiffen. Was it really so obvious that she loved him?

'How are you feeling?' asked Josephine.

'Fine, thanks.'

And she *was* fine. She had a cut on her forehead, scratches on her arms and some bruises from falling out of her chair. But otherwise she was healthy and safe—thanks to Luc and Philippe, who had driven into the hills as the storm had descended on the island and rescued her.

She cast another look at the sky—a clear vivid blue in the wake of the storm—and then returned with Josephine to the kitchen. They'd been baking all morning, preparing a mountain of food to sustain the men who were tackling the massive job of cleaning up the village.

It was good to feel useful, to do something constructive, but her thoughts kept drifting back to Nico.

She wanted more time with him. Wanted to explore the possibility of seeing him once she was back in Rome. It was crazy, and extending their affair would only delay the inevitable heartbreak, but she wanted it all the same. Because as much as her feelings for him frightened her, the thought of tonight being their very last together frightened her even more.

A commotion outside the house pulled Marietta from her thoughts. She paused with a tray of pastries in her hand and heard car doors slamming, then male voices speaking in rapid French. She thought she recognised Philippe's voice, deep and firm, and then another, even deeper but louder—and agitated.

Marietta almost dropped the tray.

Nico's voice.

Josephine had hurried outside and now Nico appeared in the doorway. And he looked—*terrible*. Bleary-eyed and unshaven, his hair and clothes rumpled. A hint of wildness in the blue eyes that instantly zeroed in on her. He reached her in three strides.

She put the tray down. 'I'm fine,' she said, hurriedly, because she could see that he wasn't and it was scaring her.

He didn't speak. He just tipped up her chin and examined the cut on her forehead, then lifted her arms, one by one, scrutinising the many nicks and scratches she'd sustained when the window had shattered over her. His mouth thinned.

'Nico, I'm *fine*,' she repeated, wanting to erase the awful bleakness from his face.

Still he didn't speak and his silence unnerved her.

'I'm afraid there's been some damage at the house,' she said. 'Your study—'

'I don't give a damn about the study.' Finally he spoke but his voice was harsh. Angry, even. 'I've already seen the house. I thought—' He broke off. '*Mon Dieu*, Marietta,' he resumed after a moment. 'I thought...' He dragged his hand through his hair, stepped back, his expression shuttering. 'Do you have any belongings to collect before we leave?'

'Just my clothes,' she said, referring to those she'd arrived in last night.

There'd been no time to grab anything else. When the men had found her in the study, Luc had scooped her off the floor while Philippe had grabbed her chair, and then they'd driven at once to the village. The clothes she wore now had been borrowed from Josephine who, minutes later, hovered as Nico bundled Marietta into the Jeep, followed by her chair and a bunch of supplies from Philippe for the house.

Marietta thanked the other woman—for everything—then sat in silence as Nico drove them back up the mountain.

Several hours later Nico's gut still churned with a mix of emotions, some clear-cut—like relief and anger—others not so easy to distinguish.

It had taken him two hours to clear the debris from the pool and terrace, another two to get the study back into some semblance of order. The repairs he'd made to the house were only temporary; he'd need a glazier to install a new window, some furnishings replaced and the flooring fixed, thanks to a fair amount of water damage.

The antique desk that had belonged to his wife had survived mostly unscathed, but in truth he had barely spared it a thought when he'd arrived at the house this morning and discovered the carnage. And—worse— Marietta gone. The violent punch of fear and panic had almost doubled him over. Until rational thought had resurfaced and he'd realised the only logical explanation was that she was in the village with the Bouchards.

He'd felt raw, volatile with emotion. So much so that he'd struggled for words when he'd first clapped eyes on her in the Bouchards' kitchen. On the drive back to the house, when she'd asked him what had happened in Rome, he'd managed to clip out a brief, sanitised version of events, but then he had kept his jaw tightly locked, afraid of what would spill from his mouth if he opened it again.

Since then he'd largely avoided her, rejecting her offer to help with the clean-up and suggesting she pack her things in preparation for leaving tomorrow. The hurt in her eyes had cut him to the bone, but it was safer this way. If he got too close to her he'd drag her into his arms and never want to let her go. And that terrified him.

Now, showered, wearing jeans and a fresh shirt, he stood in the living room and studied Marietta's painting of the old stone fortress. It was a stunning piece of work. Beautiful and evocative, he surmised. Not unlike the artist herself.

'Nico?'

He stiffened… *God help him*. Even the sound of her

voice challenged his resolve. Made him think twice about what he must do.

'Nico, please…'

Her tone was plaintive and it tore at something inside him.

'Talk to me.'

He turned, hands jammed into his jeans pockets. 'What would you like me to say, Marietta?'

Long shafts of late-afternoon sunshine streamed in through the tall windows, gilding her olive skin, picking out the amber highlights in her mahogany hair. She'd changed out of the borrowed clothes into long black pants and a sleeveless white blouse and she looked beautiful. She *always* looked beautiful. She rolled closer and he clenched his jaw, fisted his hands to stop himself from reaching for her.

'You could start by telling me why you're angry.'

He shot her an incredulous look. Did she really have no idea what she'd put him through?

'I went through *hell* last night,' he bit out, his resolve to remain calm, impassive, flying out of the window. 'Knowing the storm was approaching and you were here alone while I was stuck on the mainland—' He broke off, jerked a hand out of his pocket and thrust it into his hair. '*Mon Dieu*, Marietta!'

She pulled her lower lip between her teeth. 'I can imagine how worried you must have been,' she said, and for some reason her placatory tone of voice only riled him further. 'I was worried about *you*, too,' she added. 'But we're both fine—aren't we?'

He begged to differ. He did *not* feel fine. He felt as if someone had mashed up his insides with a chainsaw.

'You could have been seriously injured—you *were* injured,' he ground out.

'A few scratches,' she dismissed. 'Nothing more.'

'Thanks to Luc and Philippe rescuing you—which they wouldn't have needed to do if you hadn't been so damned stubborn and insisted on staying here by yourself.'

She bit her lip again, her eyes clouding. 'I'm sorry, Nico…'

She reached out, closed her fingers around his wrist, and he thought that simple touch might be his undoing.

He forced his hand to hang by his side. 'Forget it. It's over now,' he said. And he didn't mean only the storm. He watched Marietta's face, saw the flicker of understanding in her eyes.

She withdrew her hand.

'Does it have to be?' she asked after a moment.

He stared down at her. 'I told you—'

'I know what you told me,' she interrupted. Her chin lifted. 'And I'm not suggesting any kind of commitment. I'm just suggesting that maybe…once I'm back in Rome…we could see each other occasionally.'

An uncomfortable pressure built in his chest. Had he not contemplated that very arrangement just yesterday? He suppressed a humourless laugh as an even greater irony occurred to him—having Marietta on a casual basis wouldn't be anywhere close to enough.

He hardened his voice. 'I don't do relationships—casual or otherwise.'

'Why?'

Her soft challenge poked at something inside him. Something that already felt bruised. Raw. 'Don't push, Marietta,' he warned. 'I made it clear from the outset that I couldn't offer you anything more. I thought you understood.'

She rolled forward and he stepped back.

'I understand that you're afraid, Nico,' she said softly, and stopped in front of him, meeting his gaze with another firm lift of her chin. 'I understand that you've loved and lost and now you're afraid of getting close to people, afraid of caring for anyone—because if you do you might lose them.'

Nico's blood ran cold. He felt as if she'd crawled inside him. Into the darkness he tried so hard to keep hidden.

It was shocking. Exposing.

Anger rose, swift and defensive. He paced away, turned back. 'Are you calling me a coward, Marietta?' He stalked towards her. 'That's rich, coming from you.'

Marietta's head snapped back. Nico's comeback was harsh, unexpected, landing a sharp dent in her bravado. Not that her courage had been bulletproof to start with. Mustering the nerve to seek him out and talk so frankly with him after he had avoided her all afternoon hadn't been easy.

'What do you mean?' she said.

He shook his head. 'You don't see it, do you? You're so goddamned proud, so independent—you wear it like a suit of armour so that no one can get inside it.'

She stiffened. 'I've said I'm sorry about last night—'

'I'm not just talking about last night!' He cut across her, a vein pulsing in his right temple as he stared down at her. 'You accuse *me* of being afraid—'

'It wasn't an accusation!'

'But what are *you* afraid of?' he finished.

She gripped the arms of her chair, her heart hammering wildly in her chest. 'Nothing.'

'I think that you're afraid to admit you can't do everything on your own,' he carried on, as if she hadn't spoken. 'To admit that you might actually need someone.'

Her stomach twisted. His words sliced too close to the bone. Except she wasn't afraid of needing. She was afraid of *wanting*. Or was there really no difference?

She wheeled backwards, but he followed. 'You use your independence to isolate yourself,' he said. Relentless. Ruthless. On the offensive now because she'd pushed and he had warned her not to. 'To cut yourself off from what you really want.'

She balled her hands into fists. 'You don't *know* what I want—and you're a fine one to talk about isolation. This from the man who chooses to sit up here in his house all alone and wallow in his misplaced guilt.'

Fury darkened his features. 'You know nothing about my guilt.'

'Don't I?'

A fierce ache ballooned in her chest. This exchange of harsh, angry words wasn't what she'd imagined for their last night together. She dropped her shoulders, defeat and weariness washing over her. How had they ended up here? What were they *doing*? The sudden urge to retreat tugged at her, but she loved this man—too much not to serve him a final painful truth.

'I survived a car crash that killed three of my friends,' she said. 'So I *do* know something about guilt, Nico.' She paused, took a moment to choose her next words carefully. 'What happened to Julia was tragic and horrific but it wasn't your fault—and it wasn't your father-in-law's.'

His frown deepened ominously but she forced herself to finish.

'I think it's sad that you haven't spoken to each other in ten years, and while I never knew Julia I can't believe it's what she would have wanted—nor can I believe she would have wanted you to spend the rest of your life blaming yourself for not saving her.'

Nico was tight-lipped, but the emotion she knew he tried so hard to suppress swirled in his eyes.

'You need to let go of your guilt,' she said gently. 'And if you can't do it for yourself—then do it for her.'

And for me.

She turned her chair and wheeled away from him—before the tears threatening to overwhelm her could spill.

CHAPTER TWELVE

THE NEXT MORNING they travelled in the helicopter from the island to the airstrip in Toulon, the entire journey conducted in tense, agonising silence.

Marietta's chest ached from the emotion she was bottling up inside. Tears threatened at regular intervals but she forced them back, determined to remain stoic. Even throughout the long night, as she'd lain alone in the guest bed, she'd refused to succumb, afraid that if the tears started to fall they might never stop.

When Nico carried her from the helicopter to the jet and lowered her into one of the soft leather seats she clung to him for a few seconds too long, desperate to imprint every detail of him onto her memory: his clean citrus scent, his hard male body, the bone-melting heat he exuded.

He straightened. 'Leo will collect you from the plane in Rome.'

She nodded; he had told her this morning that he wouldn't be travelling to Rome with her. Impulsively she reached for his wrist.

'Thank you,' she said. 'For…for keeping me safe.'

Flimsy, inadequate words—yet what more could she say? She couldn't tell him she loved him. Not when she knew she wouldn't hear those same words in return. And everything else—hurtful or otherwise—had been said the day before.

His gaze held hers for a long moment. Then he leaned down, cupped a hand around the side of her face and dropped a brief kiss on her mouth that brought those foolish tears springing into her eyes again.

'*Au revoir*, Marietta.'

And then he was gone.

A solitary tear escaped and she dashed it away, her insides twisting with the bitter irony of it all. Yesterday Nico had flung her fears in her face, and now he was validating them by walking away. Denying her the thing she wanted most. *Him*.

Twenty minutes later the powerful jet was soaring, and Marietta blinked as a glass half filled with amber liquid appeared on the table in front of her. She looked up. Evelyn stood by her chair, her mouth curved in a gentle smile.

'I know you like your coffee, but right now I figure you could do with something stronger.' She touched Marietta's shoulder. 'I'll give you some space, honey. Buzz if you need anything.'

Marietta murmured her thanks, then sniffed the drink and blinked at the eye-watering fumes. It was whisky rather than her favoured brandy, but she sipped it anyway, hoping the potent liquid would warm the cold, empty space inside her.

It didn't.

Nico swung the sledgehammer high above his head and smashed it down onto the centre of the beam. The wood split under the force of the blow and he finished the job off with the heel of his boot. The violent sound of splintering wood was gratifying, as was the burn in his muscles—the kind of burn only hard physical labour could induce.

It was almost a month since he'd been back here on Île de Lavande. After sending Marietta to Rome he had set himself a gruelling work schedule of back-to-back meetings and international travel, which had, for a time, kept him focused on work and nothing else. But in the end, no matter how deeply he buried himself in work, no matter how many meetings and travel destinations he piled into his schedule, he couldn't escape the simple truth.

He missed her.

'Nico!'

He looked up. Luc stood a few metres away, surrounded by the detritus of his family's boat shed. The storm had rendered the small building unsalvageable and the Bouchards had decided to knock down what remained and rebuild from scratch.

Nico had offered to help with the demolition. He needed the distraction. Needed to escape the house he had once valued for its privacy and isolation but which now felt curiously empty and too silent.

'Break time,' said Luc, gesturing with a thumb over his shoulder towards the bistro. Josephine stood at the entrance to the courtyard, waving to catch the men's attention. Luc grinned and threw Nico a towel. 'Let's get cleaned up and grab a beer.'

Half an hour later the two men sat in the courtyard, along with Josephine's father Henri. Chilled bottles of lager sat on the wrought-iron table between them and appetising smells wafted from the kitchen. A middle-aged couple dined in the far corner of the courtyard and a small group of locals drank inside, but otherwise it was a quiet afternoon at the bistro.

Luc cradled his beer and tipped his chair back on two legs. 'How's Marietta?'

Nico's hand froze with the bottle halfway to his mouth. For appearance's sake he lifted it all the way and took a swig he hoped wouldn't choke him. 'Fine,' he said.

The younger man gave a couple of slow nods, exchanged a look with his *grandpère*, and then—to Nico's profound relief—switched the subject to football.

Ten minutes later Josephine dragged Luc away to help his father unload some supplies, leaving Nico alone with Henri.

The old man regarded him. 'You are troubled, *mon ami*.'

Nico tried to blank his expression. Henri might be long in the tooth but he was wise. Astute.

'I am fine,' he said.

Henri nodded slowly. 'So…you are fine… Marietta is fine…but things between you are *not* so fine, *oui*?'

Nico picked up his beer, realised the bottle was empty and put it down. He folded his arms over his chest.

'Things between us are…'

Over. Forgotten.

A peal of bitter laughter echoed in his head. Marietta *forgotten*? No. Far from it. She was in his mind every hour of every day, testing his resolve to forget. Only last week he'd been on the brink of flying to Rome. He'd travelled from New York to London for meetings and decided to spend the weekend at his penthouse in

Paris. At the last minute he'd almost told his pilot to change the flight plan. Had entertained for a crazy moment the flawed notion that if he could have Marietta one more time, for one more night, he'd get her out of his system. His *head*.

Realising Henri was waiting for him to finish, he cast about for a suitable word and settled on, 'Complicated.'

Henri slapped his thigh and chuckled. 'Women *are* complicated, son.' He sat back, studied Nico's unsmiling face and grew serious again. 'You do not strike me as the kind of man to fear a challenge,' he said.

Nico's chest tightened. Henri's assessment of him was too generous. He feared a good many things—things Marietta had driven home to him, when she'd ruthlessly dished up a few unpalatable truths on that last night. Angry and offended, he'd accused her of labelling him a coward, but she was right. He *was* a coward. Because that night in Toulon during the storm, when he'd been out of his mind with worry, the truth of his feelings had struck with heart-stopping clarity.

He loved her—and the realisation had gripped him with unrelenting fear.

And instead of finding the strength to fight that fear he'd allowed it to control him. Had clung to his belief that loving someone again would make him weak because the fear of losing them would rule him, consume him.

But was it love that made him weak?

Or was it allowing the fear to win?

Mon Dieu. He had done exactly that. He had pushed Marietta away out of fear, to protect himself, and it wasn't only cowardly, it was selfish.

He swallowed. 'I have made a mistake, Henri.'

'Perhaps you should tell her that.'

Nico stood. *'Oui,'* he said, his thoughts clear, his mind focusing for the first time in weeks. 'But first there is someone I must see.'

The Georgian mansion nestled in the heart of the sprawling Hudson Valley estate was unchanged from the way Nico remembered it, its distinguished brick façade with its shuttered windows, columned portico and black front door as pristine and imposing as ever. The lawns were still manicured, the gardens meticulously kept, and as he walked up the white-painted steps to the door Nico's hands felt as clammy as they had the first time Julia had brought him here.

Before he could knock, the door opened and Barbara Lewisham stood before him.

A fist clamped tight around Nico's heart. Julia and her mother had always looked alike, both of them blonde and petite in size. Barbara's genteel face was older now, and lined with the remnants of grief, but still she reminded him of his late wife.

He braced himself, unsure of how his former mother-in-law would receive him in person. He had called ahead and, despite her obvious shock, she had been civil, polite to him over the phone. But then Barbara had always been a woman of manners and natural reserve. Even at her daughter's funeral she'd held her emotions in check.

She looked up at him and for a moment he thought her grey eyes glittered with anger. Then she stepped forward, took his hands in hers, and he realised it was tears making her eyes shimmer.

'Nico…' she said, her smile tremulous. 'It is so good to see you.'

The genuine warmth she conveyed threw him. He'd expected coolness from her at best. Hostility at worst. They hadn't spoken much in the days leading up to Julia's funeral, or afterwards. He'd assumed that she shared her husband's view of things. Had he been wrong?

'And you, Barbara,' he said.

She led him into the grand foyer and closed the door. 'Jack's in the study.'

'You told him I was coming?'

'He's expecting you.' She gestured towards the wood-panelled hallway that Nico remembered led to Jack Lewisham's study. 'Go ahead.'

The door was closed when he got there—which was not, he thought, a particularly welcoming sign. He took a deep, even breath, knocked once and entered.

'Hello, Jack.'

Jack Lewisham turned from the window where he stood across the room, and Nico kept his expression impassive as he registered the physical changes time had wrought in the man. He was still tall—six foot—and broad-shouldered, but the deep lines scoring his face and the grey streaking his hair made him look as if he'd aged twenty years rather than ten.

He didn't stride forward to shake Nico's hand. Instead he nodded a silent greeting, walked across the Persian rug to an antique sideboard and poured whisky from a crystal decanter into two cut-glass tumblers.

He took the glasses to a small table set between two deep leather chairs, and finally spoke. 'Will you join me?'

The invitation was stiff, the words wooden, and yet more polite than Nico had expected. Wary, his palms still clammy, he crossed the room and sat down.

Jack sipped his whisky. 'I see your company is doing well.'

Nico picked up his glass, inclined his head. 'It is.' He paused, then added, 'I'm not here to talk about my company, Jack.'

The older man eyed him for a long moment. He took a larger slug of whisky. 'I tried to talk her out of marrying you, you know.'

'I'm aware,' Nico said flatly.

'As a kid, she always had a thing for strays.'

Nico slammed his glass onto the table and stood. *Dieu.* What insanity had brought him here? He turned and started towards the door.

'Nico.'

Jack's voice halted him. He turned back. The man was on his feet, his mouth set in a grim line.

'I apologise,' Jack said hoarsely. 'It wasn't what I meant to say. Please…' He ran his hand through his hair. 'Stay.'

Nico hesitated, tension vibrating in every muscle, his gut churning with anger and indecision. After a moment he walked back, sat again.

'Thank you,' Jack said, lowering himself to the edge of his chair. He rested his elbows on his knees, scrubbed a hand over his face before speaking again. 'Julia had a good heart, is what I was trying to say. And she was smart—an excellent judge of character.' He paused, looked Nico in the eye. 'Despite my reservations in the beginning it didn't take me long to realise she'd chosen a good man.'

Emotion punched through Nico's chest, so swift and powerful his lungs were left airless for a moment.

'Losing her was the worst thing that had ever happened to me,' Jack went on. 'I didn't know how to handle it. The anger, the grief...' He bowed his head. 'I blamed you, but it was my fault... *my* fault,' he repeated, his voice bleak, filled with self-loathing. 'I was arrogant, stupid—'

He broke off, his body heaving with a sob that seemed torn from him, and Nico instinctively reached over, gripped the man's shoulder.

'You tried to save her,' he said. 'We both did—and we failed. But we are not to blame for her death. That responsibility lies with the men who took her.'

And for the first time in ten years, he truly believed that.

Jack looked up, his eyes deeply shadowed, his face ravaged by years of grief and self-recrimination. 'I don't know how to move beyond it.'

Nico firmed his grip on Jack's shoulder. 'You have to let go of the guilt,' he said, his throat thickening as Marietta's voice echoed in his head.

Jack nodded and they sat in silence for a moment. And then they talked—until the whisky decanter was nearly empty and the shadows outside had lengthened across the manicured lawns.

Barbara ventured in to ask Nico if he would stay for supper. He accepted, and then excused himself to place a call.

Though it was already evening, his assistant at his New York office answered on the first ring.

'I need to travel on the jet out of LaGuardia first thing tomorrow,' he said.

'Yes, sir. Destination?'
'Rome.'

Marietta stared at the printout of the ultrasound image and felt all the same emotions she'd experienced the *first* time Helena and Leo had announced they were expecting: joy, excitement, happiness, and envy.

That last one she tried not to feel too keenly.

'Oh, Helena!' She leaned forward in her chair and threw her arms around her sister-in-law. 'I'm so happy for you. A little sister or brother for Riccardo.'

Helena hugged her back. 'I know—I'm so excited.'

Marietta was thrilled for her brother and his wife. They deserved every happiness. Their road to love had been rocky, and eight years ago their first child—an unplanned baby—had been stillborn. The tragedy had affected both of them deeply, even though Leo hadn't learnt about his son until some years after the event.

Ridiculously, her eyes began to prickle.

Helena looked at her. 'Marietta—what's wrong?'

'Nothing. I'm happy for you, that's all.'

She blinked the tears back and forced a smile. She'd left Île de Lavande over a month ago and still she was an emotional wreck. She needed to pull herself together, get back to being her old self, and yet she'd started to suspect with an awful sinking sensation in her stomach that her 'old self' was long gone and wasn't ever coming back.

Because her 'old self' would have celebrated the lucrative commission she'd recently landed with a night out with friends, instead of sitting at home alone with a glass of brandy and the DVD of a silly romantic movie—and, worse, *crying* over that movie.

Her 'old self' would have gone about her day with her usual vigour and would *not* have felt her heart surge every time she saw a tall dark-haired man, only to feel it shrink again when she realised it wasn't him.

Her 'old self' would have noticed the black vehicles with their tinted windows and the occasional watchful man in the shadows and felt outraged, instead of feeling her heart swell with the knowledge that he was still protecting her, from a distance.

And her 'old self' definitely *wouldn't* be sitting here feeling envious of her sister-in-law, wishing she had a handsome husband and children of her own to shower with love and affection.

Helena was still looking at her and she slipped her sunglasses on. They were sitting in the landscaped garden at Leo and Helena's Tuscan villa, enjoying the late morning sun and some 'girl time' while Leo entertained Ricci indoors. Autumn had arrived but the days were still warm, and the air carried the fragrance of flowers and fruits from the neighbouring orchards. Marietta had travelled up for the weekend, hoping a change of scenery would lift her mood.

'How far along are you?' she asked.

'Ten weeks.' Helena frowned. 'You know, you haven't seemed like yourself since you came back from the island.'

Marietta tried to keep her smile intact but the very worst thing happened—her lips quivered.

'Oh, Marietta.' Helena reached for her hand. 'What is it? Tell me.'

'I slept with Nico,' she blurted out, because she simply couldn't keep it secret any longer. She needed to talk about it with someone or she'd lose her mind. She stared at her sister-in-law, waiting for the look of shock. Of censure.

'Well,' said Helena, 'I can't say I'm surprised.'

Marietta's jaw slackened. 'You're not?'

'No. I'm not.' She let go of Marietta's hand and re-filled their glasses from a pitcher of homemade lemonade on the table. 'I saw the way he looked at you on my wedding day, Marietta.' She picked up her glass, sat back and smiled. 'He couldn't take his eyes off you.'

Marietta frowned. She remembered Nico from the wedding day. He'd been impossible to miss. Aside from her brother he'd been the tallest man there, and by far the most eye-catching in his tux. But she'd taken one dry-mouthed look at his powerful body and his chiselled features, reminded herself that men like him were out of her league, and then steadfastly kept her gaze off him.

'I take it things didn't end well?' Helena said gently.

Marietta shook her head. 'I ended up wanting more than he could give.'

Helena exhaled on a sigh. 'Don't tell me he's one of those men who's allergic to commitment.'

'He's a widower,' she said, and this time her sister-in-law's face *did* register shock.

'I had no idea.'

'Leo doesn't know?'

'If he does he's never said anything. I'm guessing Nico has some issues, then?'

'A few.'

She wanted to share more with Helena, but Nico was an intensely private man and talking about his past—particularly the gruesome story of his wife's death—felt wrong. And then Leo appeared, carrying Ricci in his arms, and the little boy gurgled and squealed when he saw his mother.

Helena stood to take him, and he squealed again when she blew a raspberry kiss on his plump rosy cheek.

Leo put his hand to his wife's back, said something in her ear. Helena looked at Marietta and frowned. Her mouth opened, but Leo cut her off with a few quietly spoken words and then urged her indoors. Helena resisted, gave her husband a stern look and walked back to Marietta.

'I'll be right inside if you need me,' she said, squeezing Marietta's shoulder, and then she took Ricci into the house.

Confused, Marietta looked to her brother.

'Nico's here,' he said without preamble. 'He wants to see you.'

Her brain stalled. Nico was *here?* She blinked, trying to process the fact. 'How did he know where I was?'

'He called me and I told him.'

'Why didn't you say anything?'

'Because he asked me not to. And, frankly, he sounded…desperate.' Leo scowled. 'Do you want to tell me what the hell is going on, Marietta?'

She pulled in a deep breath, her heart pounding. 'Not particularly.'

A muscle flexed in her brother's jaw.

'Do you wish to see him?'

She hesitated. Briefly. *'Si,'* she said, and instantly her stomach quivered.

Leo strode into the house and a minute later Nico emerged. He walked towards her, smart and handsome in black trousers and a grey button-down shirt, his strong jaw clean-shaven, his dark hair cropped short.

Her heart somersaulted. How could he look so good, so *unchanged*, when she felt so fundamentally altered? It wasn't fair.

'*Bonjour*, Marietta.'

His deep voice washed over her and just like that, with a few velvety syllables, all the heartache of the last month was swept away by a surge of heat and longing she was helpless to prevent.

'*Buongiorno*, Nico,' she managed, her voice cool. Composed. Silently she congratulated herself. No need for him to see how he affected her.

He gestured to the seat Helena had vacated. 'May I?'

She nodded, and he moved the chair closer to her before he sat. His proximity made her skin tingle. Her pulse race.

'I've missed you.'

Her insides clenched on another surge of longing. *I've missed you too*, she wanted to say.

'Did you come all the way to Tuscany to tell me you missed me, Nico?'

The corners of his mouth tilted, as though he were amused, and she wished he wouldn't smile. It weakened her.

'I did,' he said simply.

And that made her eyes sting, because she wanted so very badly to believe him.

Suddenly he moved, reaching towards her, and before she could stop him he'd pulled her sunglasses off her face.

His gaze narrowed. 'You don't believe me, *ma petite sirène?*'

'Please don't call me that.'

'Why not?'

Did he really need to ask?

'Nico, please…just tell me why you're here.'

He hesitated. 'I'd like to take you somewhere.'

'Where?'

'It's a surprise.'

Her stomach fluttered. 'I don't like surprises.'

'Please,' he said, and she heard the distinct note of uncertainty, of vulnerability, in his voice.

It weakened her.

Still, she made him wait a few seconds more. 'Okay,' she said at last, and his features relaxed a fraction.

He stood. 'Do you trust me, *chérie*?'

She nodded, because she did. She had always trusted him and she always would. All the same, she wasn't expecting him to do what he did next—which was to lean down and scoop her out of her chair.

'Nico!' she exclaimed.

He carried her through the garden and round the side of the villa to the courtyard out front. A large black vehicle was waiting, a man dressed in black standing beside it. He opened the rear passenger door and Nico slid her into the back seat, closed the door, and a few seconds later climbed in beside her from the opposite side. He rapped on the dark glass partition that separated them from the driver and the vehicle started to move.

Nico reached across her—to strap the seatbelt over her, she assumed. But he hauled her into his lap.

'Nico—'

He kissed her, and shamefully, wantonly, she made no effort to resist. Instead she surrendered, snaking her arms around his neck and kissing him back.

It was a hot, hungry meeting of lips, and when they finally broke apart he was breathing hard. His large hands cradled her face, his blue eyes heated and glittering. '*Mon Dieu*, I missed you.'

Marietta trembled. 'Nico,' she pleaded. 'Tell me what's going on.'

He pressed his forehead to hers, the gesture so sweet that her chest flooded with tenderness and something else. Something she was too afraid to acknowledge.

'I don't know where to start,' he said.

'Start at the beginning,' she said softly.

He nodded, and took a deep breath. 'The morning after the storm, when I got back to the house and found the shattered window and you nowhere in sight, it was like Julia all over again—arriving home, finding her gone…I couldn't breathe…couldn't think…'

Marietta's throat ached. She laid her hand along the side of his face. 'I'm so sorry for putting you through that,' she whispered.

He placed his hand over hers, turned his head and kissed her palm, then tucked her hand against his chest and held it there.

'Losing her inflicted wounds I thought would never heal, and I was determined to never feel that pain again. To never feel that sense of loss and devastation.'

He fell silent. Marietta waited.

'You were right, *chérie*. I was afraid. Afraid to care for someone. Afraid to love again. But then…' He gave her a crooked smile. 'You came along.'

A jolt of warmth, of hope, went through her.

'And you were right about something else,' he said. 'I needed to deal with my guilt—confront the past.' He paused. 'I went to see Jack.'

Her eyes widened. 'And…?'

He grimaced. 'It wasn't easy, but we talked. Laid some demons to rest.'

'Oh, Nico…I'm so proud of you.'

'Don't be.' His mouth flattened. 'I pushed you away, and that's nothing to be proud of. I told myself it was the logical thing to do but it was logic driven by fear—a weak man's excuse.'

She frowned. 'You're *not* weak,' she declared. 'And you're not the only one who's been driven by fear.'

Nico shook his head. 'I shouldn't have said—'

She pressed her fingers to his lips. 'But you were right. I isolated myself, just like you did—but in a different way and for different reasons. I was afraid, too. Afraid of wanting what I couldn't have.'

Nico took hold of her slender fingers and kissed their tips one by one. He loved this woman. When he'd walked down that garden path and caught his first glimpse of her—beautiful in a simple white top and long skirt, her glorious hair flowing loose over her shoulders—he'd thought his chest might implode.

'And what *do* you want, *ma belle?*'

'You,' she said, a fierce light shining in her eyes.

He cupped her face in his hands. 'Marietta Vincenti, will you do me the honour of letting me love you?'

Tears welled in her eyes. She placed her hands over his. 'If you'll do me the honour of letting *me* love *you.*'

The car stopped and he kissed her, briefly, but with enough intensity to let her know there'd be more to come.

'I love you,' he said.

Then he lowered the window and pointed towards the middle of the large meadow by which they'd stopped.

She blinked, and her eyes widened as she saw a fully inflated, brightly coloured hot air balloon.

'Will you come fly with me, *chérie*?'

Her mouth stretched into a grin. 'I thought you said hot air balloons are dangerous.'

He'd also said it would be a frosty day in hell when he flew in one. Well…today hell was having a cold snap.

A short while later the 'oversized picnic basket'— as Nico was fond of calling it—lifted off the ground. Marietta felt like a child. Breathless, giddy, excited. Or maybe like a woman in love. She sat on a special stool, high enough to enjoy the stunning view of the Tuscan countryside, with Nico's arms circling her from behind, his chest solid and warm against her back.

She jumped at the sudden loud whoosh as the pilot fired the burner, and Nico's hold tightened.

'I've got you, *chérie*.'

She smiled up at him. 'I know. I've got you, too.'

For ever.

EPILOGUE

'PAPÀ! PAPÀ!'

A flash of pink and lime-green hurtled through the doorway of the study.

Nico swivelled his chair around. 'Amélie, don't run in the—*oomph!*'

His six-year-old daughter catapulted herself into his lap, and the moment she grinned up at him he forgot to finish scolding her. He closed his arms around her wriggling body and grinned back.

Amélie was a brown-eyed, dark-haired mini-version of her mother, and too damned adorable to stay cross with for very long—even when she pushed his patience to its limits. Which she did—frequently—because she'd inherited not only Marietta's beauty but a good deal of her stubbornness as well.

'Can we go to the beach now, Papa?'

And, like her mother, she loved to swim in the sea.

'In a bit, *ma petite sirène.*'

Her little lips formed a pout that was no doubt designed to weaken her *papà*. 'But I want to go *now*. Enzo's already there, with Remy. Why can't I go down the steps by myself like they can?'

'Because they are older and bigger.'

The tiny scowl on her face looked a lot like the one her mother occasionally wore when Nico earned her disapproval. Fortunately for him, those occasions were rare—and he always enjoyed it when they made up afterwards.

He scooted his daughter off his lap. 'Go and help *Maman* prepare the picnic hamper.'

He watched his daughter fly out of the room. Her energy was boundless, and these days it seemed she was incapable of *walking* anywhere. Enzo, his ten-year-old son, had gone through a similar stage, which had included climbing anything in sight that looked remotely scaleable.

Nico had been convinced he was destined for heart failure—especially in those first few years of parenting. On the day his son had been born he'd known fierce pride and elation, but also a sort of quiet terror. A fear that he would somehow fail to protect this tiny life in a world increasingly fraught with danger and risk.

Marietta had known. Whether she'd seen something in his face or simply sensed his inner turmoil, she had understood. And she had talked him down. Helped him to wrestle his fear into something less daunting, more controllable. And as their son had grown, she had insisted they did not wrap him in cotton wool. Had insisted that their son be allowed to experience the world. To grow up as safely as possible, yet with an understanding of risk and consequence.

It was Marietta, too, who had convinced him they should have a second child. Nico had been hesitant after her first pregnancy. Blood pressure problems and other issues related to her paralysis had dogged her from the second trimester onwards. He had watched her struggle with long months of enforced bed rest and vowed he wouldn't see her suffer like that again.

But she was resilient, and strong, and she'd set her heart on a little sister or brother for Enzo. And his wife had, of course, proved very persuasive in bed...

Nico closed his laptop. He had cleared enough emails and reports for today. Marietta growled if he spent too much time working during their family vacations on Île de Lavande.

He stood and his gaze caught, as it sometimes did, on the antique rolltop desk in the corner of the study.

Julia's ghost had been laid to rest many years before. Very occasionally the darkness and the guilt would stir in some deep corner of his soul, but the emotions never lasted for long—not in the face of the light and the laughter that his children and his wife brought to his world. He'd considered at one point getting rid of the desk, but Marietta had convinced him not to and he was glad she had.

He found his girls in the kitchen. Amélie launched herself into his arms again and he lifted her up.

'Now, Papa? Can we go *now?*'

He looked to Marietta and felt the familiar jolt in his blood. Her hair, still long and lustrous, was pulled into a ponytail and she wore a sarong and a crimson bikini top, ready for the beach. Into her forties now, she was as beautiful as ever—and she still made his body hum with desire.

'Are you finished with your little helper?'

She wheeled back from one of the low marble benches they'd had specially installed for her and smiled. '*Si.* And the hamper's ready. Take Amélie and the basket down—and don't forget to come back for your wife.'

He slid a hand around the back of her head and dropped a quick kiss on her teasing mouth. 'Funny, Mrs César.'

She grinned and his heart expanded—and he wondered, not for the first time over the years, how his chest could feel so full and yet so incredibly, amazingly light.

Marietta lay on a towel on the sand with her eyes closed, enjoying the sun on her face and the sound of her husband and children playing in the ocean. Nico had already taken her in for a swim and she was content now to relax and let the kids frolic under his watchful eye.

This was her reality now. The one that in the early years of her marriage she had secretly feared wasn't reality at all, but a fantastical dream of some sort. A great big bubble of joy that would sooner or later burst and send her crashing back to her *real* life.

But the bubble hadn't burst. It had only grown bigger and stronger—like her love for her husband—and eventually she'd stopped waiting on tenterhooks for the fairy tale to end and allowed herself to truly enjoy the life she'd never thought she'd have.

She smiled at the sound of Amélie's high-pitched squeal and guessed her *papà* was throwing her into the air. She could hear the boys too. Her son and Remy Bouchard—Luc's son—were firm friends, and Remy usually stayed with them for a few nights when they vacationed here.

She could not believe she and Nico had been married for almost thirteen years. They had finally settled in Paris, and they lived there in a beautiful home they'd renovated and fully modified for her wheelchair. They'd sold her apartment in Rome, but retained Nico's apartments in London, New York and Singapore, all of which he used when travelling for work.

Marietta happily divided her time between motherhood and her art career, which had flourished in the early years of their marriage and continued to keep her busy now, with several lucrative commissions each year.

She heard Nico's deep voice telling Enzo to watch his sister and then her son's obedient response. She smiled again. Enzo was becoming more like his father every day—serious and intense—but he also had a strong streak of curiosity about the world which showed he had something of his mother in him.

'What are you smiling about, *chérie*?'

She looked up through her sunglasses at her husband and her stomach clenched, because he was still the most magnificent man she knew. Dripping wet, he stretched out on a towel beside her and she marvelled at how hard and toned his body had remained over the years. Physically, he really hadn't changed. A few distinguished-looking grey hairs at his temples and some deeper lines on his face due to his secretly worrying about his wife and children, but otherwise he looked the same.

And he still loved her—as fiercely and passionately as he had in the beginning.

'I was just thinking,' she said, tracing her index finger along the strong line of his jaw, 'that Enzo is very much like his *papà*.'

Nico grinned—and she melted. She always did when her husband smiled at her.

His chest puffed out. 'But of course. He is good-looking, intelligent, irresistible—'

She slapped her hand over his mouth. 'And lacking in modesty!'

Her took her hand and pressed a kiss into her palm. 'And our daughter is very much like her *maman*.'

'*Si*. Beautiful, talented—'

'Stubborn, wilful—and her wish list is already longer than her mother's was!'

She laughed. 'A girl needs to dream.'

And yet her own wish list was practically non-existent now, because she had everything she could possibly want—and more.

All the things that had originally been on her list had been ticked off early in their marriage, before they'd started trying for children. Nico had taken her to Egypt to see the pyramids and the Valley of the Kings, and the trip had been magical—despite a team of his security men shadowing them everywhere they went. They'd gone up in a hot air balloon again—on their honeymoon—and eventually, after much persistence on her part, he'd agreed to her doing a tandem skydive. But not before he'd vetted the skydiving company and warned the operator that if anything happened to his wife he would personally throw the man out of a plane *without* his parachute.

The only things she wished for now were health and happiness for her family.

She looked at Nico, propped on his elbow, staring down at her. 'And why are *you* smiling, *tesoro mio*?'

He trailed a fingertip over her bare belly, inciting a flurry of goosebumps on her skin. 'Because I've arranged for Luc to collect the children in an hour's time and take them to his place for the night.'

A hot spark of anticipation ignited in her belly. She arched an eyebrow. 'And what will you do then?'

'Then, *ma belle*,' he said, his blue eyes smouldering, 'I will spend the night showing my wife how much I love her.'

* * * * *

THE VIRGIN'S DEBT
TO PAY

ABBY GREEN

I'd like to dedicate this story to my go-to Equestrian Experts, Peter Commane and Nemone Routh. Any inaccuracies are all my own fault! And I'd like to thank Heidi Rice, who gave me the moment of inspiration I needed while walking down Pall Mall in London. x

CHAPTER ONE

NESSA O'SULLIVAN HAD never considered herself capable of petty crime, and yet here she was, just outside a private property, under the cover of moonlight, about to break and enter to steal something that didn't belong to her.

She grimaced. Well, to be accurate, she wasn't really going to be breaking and entering, because she had her brother's keys to his office in the Barbier stud farm offices. *Luc Barbier.* Just thinking of the owner of this stud and racing stables made a shiver of apprehension run through Nessa's slim frame. She was crouched under an overhanging branch, on the edge of a pristine lawn in front of the main reception buildings. She'd left her battered Mini Cooper a short distance away from the gates and climbed over a low wall.

Nessa's own family home was not far away, and so she knew the land surrounding this stud farm very well. She'd played here as a child when it was under different ownership.

But any sense of familiarity fled when an owl hooted nearby, and she jumped, her heart slamming against her breastbone. She forced herself to suck in deep breaths to calm her nerves, and cursed her hot-headed older brother again for fleeing like he had. But then, could she really blame Paddy Junior for not standing up to Luc Barbier—the intimidating French *enfant terrible* of the thoroughbred racing world, about whom more was unknown than known?

His darkly forbidding good looks had rumours abounding...that he had been orphaned by gypsies, and that he'd lived on the streets, before becoming something of a legend in the racing world for his ability to train the most difficult of horses.

He'd progressed in a very short space of time to owning his own racing stables outside Paris, and now he owned this extensive stud farm in Ireland attached to another racing stables, where his impressive number of successful racehorses were trained by the best in the world, all under his eagle-eyed supervision.

People said his ability was some kind of sorcery, handed down by his mysterious ancestors.

Other rumours had it that he was simply a common criminal who had grown up on the wrong side of the tracks, and had managed to climb out of the gutter to where he was now by using a fluke talent and ruthless ingenuity to get ahead.

The mystery of his origins only added to the feverish speculation surrounding him, because along with his racing concerns, he had invested in myriad other industries, tripling his fortune in a short space of time and securing his position as one of the world's wealthiest entrepreneurs. But racing and training remained his main concerns.

Paddy Jnr had talked about the man in hushed and awed tones for the last couple of years, since Barbier had employed Nessa's brother as Junior Stud Manager.

Nessa had seen him herself, once or twice, from a distance at the exclusive Irish horse sales—where there was a regular attendance of the most important names in racing from all over the world. Sheikhs and royalty and the seriously wealthy.

He'd stood out, head and shoulders above everyone around him. Inky black hair, thick and wild, touching his collar. A dark-skinned, hard-boned face and a stern expression, his eyes hidden by dark glasses. Thickly muscled arms were folded over his broad chest, and his head had followed the horses as they'd been paraded for the prospective buyers. He'd more resembled the taciturn security guards surrounding some of the sheikhs, or a mysterious movie star, than an owner.

He'd had no obvious security around him, but even now Nessa could recall the faint air of menace keeping people away. He would be well capable of protecting himself.

The only reason she was even here tonight, indulging in this hare-brained exercise for her brother, was because he'd assured her that Luc Barbier was currently in France. She had no desire to come face to face with the man himself, because on those occasions when she had glimpsed him from a distance she'd felt a very disconcerting sensation in her belly—a kind of awareness that was totally alien to her, and very inappropriate to feel towards a complete stranger.

She took another deep breath and moved forward from under the tree, across the lawn to the buildings. A dog barked and Nessa halted, holding her breath. It stopped, and she continued moving forward. She reached the main building and went under the archway that led into a courtyard, around which the administrative offices were laid out.

She followed Paddy's directions and found the main office, and used the bigger key to unlock the door. Her heart was thumping but the door opened without a sound. There was no alarm. Nessa was too relieved to wonder why that might be.

It was dark inside, but she could just about make out the stairs. She climbed them to the upper floor, using the torch app on her phone and breathed a sigh of relief when she found his office. She opened the door with the other key, stepping inside as quietly as she could, before shutting it again. She leant against it for a second, her heart thumping. Sweat trickled down her back.

When she felt slightly calmer she moved further into the office, using her phone to guide her to the desk Paddy had said was his. He'd told her that his laptop should be in the top drawer, but she pulled it open to find it empty. She opened the others but they were empty too. Feeling slightly panicky, she tried the other desks but there was no sign of the laptop. Paddy's frantic words reverberated in her head: *'That laptop is the only chance I have to prove my innocence, if I can just trace the emails back to the hacker...'*

Nessa stood in the centre of the office biting her lip, feeling frantic now herself.

There was no hint of warning or sound to indicate she wasn't alone, so when an internal door in the office opened and light suddenly flooded the room, Nessa only had time to whirl around and blink in shock at the massive figure filling the doorway.

It registered faintly in her head that the man filling the doorway was Luc Barbier. And that she was right to have been wary of coming face to face with him. He was simply the most astonishingly gorgeous and intimidating man she'd ever seen up close, and that was saying something when her brother-in-law was Sheikh

Nadim Al-Saqr of Merkazad, as alpha male and masculine as they came.

Luc Barbier was dressed all in black, jeans and a long-sleeved top, which only seemed to enhance his brooding energy. His eyes were deep-set and so dark they looked like fathomless pools. Totally unreadable.

He held up a slim silver laptop and Nessa looked at it stupidly.

'I take it this is what you came here for?'

His voice was low and gravelly and sexily accented, and that finally sent reality slamming back into Nessa like a shot of adrenalin to her heart. She did the only thing she could do—she pivoted on her feet and ran back to the door she'd just come through and pulled it open, only to find a huge burly security guard standing on the other side with a sour expression on his face.

The voice came from behind her again, this time with an unmistakable thread of steel. 'Close the door. You're not going anywhere.'

When she didn't move, the security guard reached past her to pull the door closed, effectively shutting her in with Luc Barbier. Who patently wasn't in France.

With the utmost reluctance she turned around to face him, very aware of the fact that she was wearing black tracksuit bottoms and a close-fitting black fleece with her hair tucked up under a dark baseball cap. She must look as guilty as sin.

Luc Barbier had closed the other door. The laptop was on a desk near him and he was just standing there, arms folded across his chest, legs spread wide as if to be ready for when she bolted again.

He asked, 'So, who are you?'

Nessa's heart thwacked hard. She kept her mouth

firmly closed and her gaze somewhere around his impeccably shod feet, hoping the cap would hide her face.

He sighed audibly. 'We can do this the hard way, or the harder way. I can have the police here within ten minutes and you can tell them who you are and why you're trespassing on my property…but we both know it's to get this, don't we?' He tapped the laptop with long fingers where it sat on the desk. 'You're obviously working for Paddy O'Sullivan.'

Nessa barely heard the last phrase. Totally ridiculously, all she could seem to focus on were his beautiful hands. Big and masculine but graceful. Capable hands. *Sexy hands.* The quiver in her belly became something far more disturbing.

Silence lengthened between them again and suddenly Barbier issued a low, violent-sounding curse in French and picked up the laptop, moving towards the door. He was almost there before Nessa realised that involving the Irish Gardaí would be even more of a disaster. The fact that Barbier hadn't called them yet left a sliver of hope that something of this situation could be salvaged.

'Wait!' Her voice sounded very high in the silence.

He stopped at the door, his back to her. It was almost as intimidating as his front. He slowly turned around. 'What did you say?'

Nessa tried to calm her thundering heart. She was afraid to look up too much, using the lip of her cap to keep herself hidden as much as possible.

'I said wait. Please.' She winced. As if a nicety like *please* would go over well in this situation.

There was more silence and then an incredulous-sounding, 'You're a *girl*?'

That struck Nessa somewhere very vulnerable. She knew she was dressed head to toe in black and wore a hat, but was she really so androgynous? She was well aware of her lack of feminine wiles, having spent much of her life knee deep in muck and wellies. She hitched up her chin and glared at him now, too angry to remember to try and stay hidden. 'I'm twenty-four, hardly a girl.'

He looked sceptical. 'Crawling through undergrowth to trespass on private property is hardly the activity of a grown woman.'

The thought of the kind of women a man like this would know—a world away from Nessa—made her skin prickle with self-consciousness and her vulnerability turned into defensiveness. 'You're meant to be in France.'

Luc Barbier was shocked. And he was not a man who was easily shocked. But this slip of a girl—*woman?*— was talking back to him as if she hadn't just flagrantly invaded his private property with clearly criminal intentions.

'I was in France, and now I'm not.'

He allowed his gaze to inspect her more closely, and as he did he felt something infuse his blood...*interest*. Because he could see it now. Yes, she was a woman. Albeit slim and petite to the point of boyishness. But he could see her breasts, small and perfectly formed, pushing against the form-fitting fleece of her black top.

He could make out a jaw too delicate to be a man's, and wondered how he hadn't noticed it before. He also saw a very soft lower lip, which was currently caught between white teeth. He felt a very unwelcome stirring of desire and a need to see more.

'Take off your cap,' he heard himself demand before he'd even registered the impulse.

The small chin came up and that soft lip was freed

from white teeth. He saw the tension in her. There was a taut moment when he wasn't sure what she would do. Then, as if realising she had no choice, she raised a small hand and pulled the cap from her head.

For a moment Luc could only stare stupidly as a coil of long, dark red hair fell over her shoulder from where it had been stuffed under the cap.

And then he took in the rest of her face and felt even more foolish. He'd seen countless beautiful women, some of whom were considered to be the most beautiful in the world, but right now they were all an indistinct blur in his memory.

She was stunning. High cheekbones. Flawless creamy pale skin. A straight nose. Huge hazel eyes—flashing green and gold, with long dark lashes. And that mouth, lush and wide.

His body hardened, and the shock of such a reaction to this whippet of a girl made Luc reject the rogue reaction. He did not react to women unless it was on his terms. He was reacting because she was unexpected.

His voice was harsh. 'Now, tell me who you are, or I call the police.'

Nessa burned inwardly from the thorough once-over Barbier had just given her. She felt very exposed without her cap. Exposed to the full impact of him up close. And she couldn't look away. It was as if she were mesmerised by the sun. He was simply…beautiful, in a very raw, masculine way, all hard angles and sharp lines. But his mouth was provocatively sensual—the only softness in that face. It was distracting.

'I'm waiting.'

Nessa flushed, caught out. She diverted her gaze, focusing on a picture of a famous racehorse on the wall behind him. She knew she really didn't have a choice but to give him the information. The alternative was to give it to the Gardaí and, coming from such a small, close-knit community, she knew that word would go around within minutes as to what she had been doing. There was no such thing as privacy or anonymity here.

'My name is Nessa…' She hesitated and then said in a rush, 'O'Sullivan.' She snuck a glance back at Barbier and saw that he was frowning.

'O'Sullivan? You're related to Paddy?'

Nessa nodded miserably at what a disaster this evening's escapade had become. 'I'm his younger sister.'

Barbier took a moment to digest this and then he said, with a curl to his lip, 'He's sending his baby sister to do his dirty work?'

Nessa instantly rose to her brother's defence. 'Paddy is innocent!'

Luc Barbier looked unimpressed by her impassioned outburst. 'He's made a bad situation worse by disappearing, and the facts haven't changed: he facilitated the purchase of a horse from Gio Corretti's Sicilian stud. We received the horse a week ago and the one million euros duly left my account but never reached Corretti's. It's clear that your brother diverted the funds into his own pocket.'

Nessa blanched at the massive amount of money, but she forced herself to stay strong, for Paddy. 'He didn't divert funds. It wasn't his fault. He was hacked—they somehow impersonated the stud manager in Sicily and Paddy sent the money through fully believing it was going to the right place.'

The lines in Barbier's face were as hard as granite. 'If that is the case then why isn't he here to defend himself?'

Nessa refused to let herself crumble in the face of

this man's seriously intimidating stance. 'You told him he would be prosecuted and liable for the full amount. He felt as if he had no choice.'

Paddy's frantic voice came back into her head.

'Ness, you don't know what this guy is capable of. He fired one of the grooms on the spot the other day. There's no such thing as innocent till proven guilty in Barbier's world. He'll chew me up and spit me out! I'll never work in the industry again...'

Barbier's mouth thinned. 'The fact that he fled after that phone conversation only makes him look even guiltier.'

More words of defence sprang to Nessa's lips but she swallowed them back. Trying to explain to this man that her brother had been entangled with the law when he'd gone through a rebellious teenage phase was hardly likely to make him sound less guilty. Paddy had worked long and hard to turn over a new leaf, but he'd been told that if he was ever caught breaking the law again he'd serve time and have a criminal record. *That* was why he'd panicked and run.

Luc Barbier regarded the woman in front of him. The fact that he was still indulging in any kind of dialogue with her was outrageous. And yet her vehemence and clear desire to protect her brother at all costs—even at her own expense—intrigued him. In his experience loyalty was a myth. Everyone was out for their own gain.

Something occurred to him then and he cursed himself for not suspecting it sooner. He'd been too distracted by a fall of thick red hair and a slender frame. It was galling.

'Maybe you're in on it? And you were trying to retrieve the laptop to ensure that any evidence was taken care of?'

Nessa's limbs turned to jelly. 'Of course I'm not in on anything. I just came here because Paddy—' She stopped herself, not wanting to incriminate him further.

'Because Paddy...what?' Barbier asked. 'Was too much of a coward? Or because he's no longer in the country?'

Nessa bit her lip. Paddy had fled to America, to hide out with her twin brother, Eoin. She'd entreated him to come back, tried to assure him that his boss couldn't be such an ogre. Paddy's words floated back.

'No one messes with Barbier. I wouldn't be surprised if he's got criminal links...'

For a moment Nessa had a sickening sensation. What if Barbier really *was* linked to—? She quickly shut that thought down, telling herself she was being melodramatic. But then a sliver of doubt entered her mind— what if Paddy *was* guilty?

As soon as that registered she lambasted herself, aghast that she could have thought it for a second. This man was making her doubt herself, and her brother, who she knew would never do something so wrong, no matter what his trangressions had been in the past.

Nessa's jaw was tight. 'Look. Paddy is innocent. I agree with you that he shouldn't have run, but he has.' She hesitated for a second, and then mentally apologised to her brother before saying, 'He has a habit of running away when difficult things happen—he ran away for a week after our mother's funeral.'

Barbier looked utterly remote and then he said, 'I've heard the Irish have a gift for talking their way out of situations, but it won't work with me, Miss O'Sullivan.'

Anger spiked again. 'I'm not trying to get out of anything.' She forced herself to calm down. 'I was just trying to help by retrieving his laptop. He said that he could prove his innocence with it.'

Barbier picked up the slim silver laptop and held it up. 'We've looked at the laptop extensively and there is no evidence to support your brother's innocence. You've done your brother no favours. He now looks even guiltier and you've possibly implicated yourself.'

Luc watched as colour washed in and out of the woman's expressive face. That in itself was intriguing, when so many people he encountered kept their masks firmly in place. He couldn't recall the last time he'd felt free enough, if ever, to allow his real emotions to be seen.

Still, he wouldn't believe this award-worthy display of innocence. He'd be a fool if he did and her brother had already taken him for a fool.

Nessa sensed any sliver of hope dwindling. Barbier was about as immovable as a rock. He put the laptop down and folded his arms again, settling his hips back against the desk behind him, legs stretched out, for all the world as if they were having a civil chat. There was nothing civil about this man. Danger oozed from every pore: Nessa just wasn't sure what *kind* of danger. She felt no risk to her personal safety, in spite of Paddy's lurid claims or the security man outside the door. It was a much more personal danger, to the place that throbbed with awareness deep inside her. An awareness that had been dormant all her life, until now.

Barbier's tone was mocking. 'So you really expect me to believe that you're here purely out of love for your poor innocent brother?'

Fiercely she said, 'I would do anything for my family.'

'Why?'

Barbier's simple question took her by surprise and Nessa blinked. She hadn't even questioned Paddy when he'd called for help. She'd immediately felt every protective instinct kick into place even though she was younger than him.

Their family was a unit who had come through tough times and become stronger in the process.

Their older sister Iseult had kept them all in one piece—pretty much—after the tragic death of their mother, while their father had descended into the mire of alcoholism. She had shielded Nessa and her two brothers from their father's worst excesses, and had slowly helped him to recovery even as their stud farm and stables had fallen apart around them.

But Iseult wasn't here now. She had a much deserved happy life far away from here. It was up to Nessa to shoulder this burden for the sake of her brother, and her family.

She looked at Barbier. 'I would do anything because we love each other and we protect each other.'

Barbier was silent for a long moment. Then he said, 'So now you're admitting that you'd go so far as to collude in a crime.'

Nessa shivered under the thin covering of her fleece. She felt very alone at that moment. She knew she could contact Sheikh Nadim of Merkazad, Iseult's husband and one of the richest men in the world. He could sort this whole thing out within hours, if he knew. But she and Paddy had agreed they wouldn't involve Iseult or Nadim. They were expecting a baby in a few weeks and did not need to be drawn into this mess.

She squared her shoulders and stared at Luc Barbier, hating his cool nonchalance. 'Don't you understand the concept of family and doing anything for them? Wouldn't you do that for your own family?'

Barbier suddenly looked stony. 'I have no family, so, no, I'm not familiar with the concept.'

A pang of emotion made Nessa's chest tighten. No family. What on earth did that mean? She couldn't fathom the lack of a family. That sense of protection.

Then he said, 'If your family are so close then I will go to whoever *is* capable of returning either your brother or my money.'

Panic eclipsed Nessa's spurt of emotion. 'This just involves me and Paddy.'

Barbier raised a brow. 'I will involve whoever and whatever it takes to get my money back and ensure no adverse press results from this.'

Nessa's hands clenched to fists at her sides as she tried to contain her temper and appeal to any sense of decency he might have. 'Look, not that it's any business of yours, but my sister is going to have a baby very soon. My father is helping her and her husband and they don't have anything to do with this. I'm taking responsibility for my brother.'

I'm taking responsibility for my brother.

There had been a tight ball of emotion in Luc's chest ever since she'd asked if he understood the concept of family. Of course he didn't. How could he when his Algerian father had disappeared before he was born, and his feckless, unstable mother had died of a drugs overdose when he was just sixteen?

The closest he'd ever come to family was the old man next door—a man broken by life, and yet who had been the one to show Luc a way out.

Luc forced his mind away from the memories. He was beyond incredulous that this sprite of a girl— *woman*—was insisting on standing up to him. And that she wasn't using her beauty to try and distract him, especially when he couldn't be sure that he'd hidden his reaction to her. He hated to admit it, even to himself, but he felt a twinge of respect.

She was defiant, even in the face of possible prosecution. If she was calling his bluff she was doing it very, very well. He could still have the police here within minutes and she would be hauled off in handcuffs with the full weight of his legal team raining down on her narrow shoulders before she knew what was happening.

But it wasn't as if the police were ever first on Luc's list of people to turn to in this kind of situation. Not because he had more nefarious routes to keeping the law—he knew about the rumours surrounding him, and as much as they amused him, they also disgusted him—but because of his experiences growing up in the gritty outskirts of Paris. Surviving each day had been a test of endurance. The police had never been there when he'd needed them, so to say he didn't trust them was an understatement.

He liked to take care of things his own way. Hence the rumours. Added on top of more rumours. Until he was more myth than man.

He forced his mind back to the task at hand. And the woman. 'Where do we go from here, then, Miss O'Sullivan? If you're prepared to take responsibility for your brother, then perhaps you could be so kind as to write me a cheque for one million euros?'

Nessa blanched. One million euros was more money than she was ever likely to see in her lifetime, unless her career as a jockey took off and people started giving her a chance to ride in big races and build her reputation.

She said, as firmly as she could, 'We don't have that kind of money.'

'Well then,' Barbier said silkily, 'that gets us precisely no further along in this situation. And in fact it gets worse. Thanks to your brother's actions, I will now have to hand over another one million euros to Gio Corretti to ensure that he doesn't ask questions about why he hasn't received the money yet.'

Nessa felt sick. She hadn't considered that. 'Maybe you could talk to him? Explain what happened?'

Barbier laughed but it was curt and unamused. 'I don't need to fuel the gossip mill with stories that I'm now claiming fraud to renege on payments.'

Nessa wanted to sit down. Her legs were wobbly again and she felt light-headed.

'Are you all right?' Barbier's sharp question was like a slap to her face. She sucked in a deep breath. He'd taken a step towards her and suddenly the room felt even smaller. He was massive. And so dark. Possibly the most intimidating person she'd ever met.

She couldn't fight this man. He was too rich, too successful. Too gorgeous. She swallowed. 'I wish I could hand you over your money right now, Mr Barbier, believe me. But I can't. I know my brother is innocent no matter what his actions look like.'

Nessa wracked her brains as to what she could do to appease Barbier so he wouldn't go after Paddy. At least until Paddy had a chance to try and prove his innocence. But what could she offer this man? And then something struck her. 'Look, all I can do is offer my services in his absence. If you have *me*, then can't you accept that I'm willing to do all I can to prove his innocence?'

For a moment, Nessa's words hung in the air and she almost fancied that she might have got through to him. But then he straightened from the desk and the expression on his face darkened. He spat out, 'I should have known that veneer of innocence was too good to be true.'

That unnervingly black gaze raked her up and down, disdain etched all over his face. 'I must admit, I might have felt differently if you'd come via the front door dressed in something a little more enticing, Miss O'Sullivan, but even then I can't say that you'd be my type.'

Nessa struggled to understand—he couldn't possibly mean…but then she registered what she'd said and how it might have sounded. And, she registered that he was looking at her with disgust, not disdain. Her gut curdled as a wave of mortification rushed through her whole body, along with hurt, which made it even worse. She burned with humiliation and fury.

'You know I did not mean *that*.'

He raised an imperious brow. 'What did you mean, Miss O'Sullivan?'

Nessa had started to pace in her agitation and she stopped and faced him. 'Please stop calling me that—my name is Nessa.'

His voice was hard. *'Nessa.'*

The way he said her name impacted her physically, like a punch to her gut. She instantly regretted opening her mouth but *Miss O'Sullivan* was beginning to get under her skin. This man. This…*meeting*…was veering so far off course that she wasn't even sure what they were talking about any more, or what was at stake.

She tried to force herself to stay focused, and calm. 'What I meant, Mr Barbier, is that I will do everything in my power to convince you that my brother is innocent.'

CHAPTER TWO

LUC STARED AT Nessa O'Sullivan.

I will do everything in my power to convince you that my brother is innocent.

What kind of an empty suggestion was that? And why had it given him such an illicit thrill to see her act so shocked when he'd called her bluff? She'd blatantly offered herself to him—and then pretended that she hadn't!

He wanted to laugh out loud. As if she were an innocent. There was no innocence in this world. Perhaps only in babies, before they grew up to be twisted and manipulated by their environment.

His conscience smarted to think of how he'd told her she wasn't his type. He couldn't deny the pounding of his blood right now. He told himself it was anger. Adrenalin. Anything but helpless desire.

Luc knew he should have walked away long ago and left her at the mercy of the authorities, no matter what he thought of them. He had enough evidence now to damn her, and her brother. But he knew that wasn't necessarily the best option. Not for *him*.

She was staring at him, as if bracing herself for whatever he was going to say. She was throwing up more

questions than answers and it had been a long time since
anyone had piqued Luc's interest like this.

What did he have to lose if he contained this himself? It wasn't as if the local law enforcement could do
any better than the private security company he'd already hired to investigate the matter and track down
Paddy O'Sullivan.

One thing was clear. This woman wasn't going to be
walking away from here. He didn't trust her. Not one
inch of her petite form. Not after he'd seen how far she
was prepared to go. And she wasn't going anywhere
until he had his money returned and he knew there
was no damage to his reputation. If she was involved
in this crime, then keeping her close would surely lead
him back to the thief.

He folded his arms and saw the way her body tensed,
as if to steel herself. In that moment she looked both
defiant and vulnerable, and it caught at Luc somewhere
he wasn't usually affected. More acting. It had to be. He
would not allow her to make a fool of him.

'You say you want to convince me your brother is innocent?'

Nessa still felt sick to think that Barbier had taken
her words to mean that she was offering herself up, like
some kind of— She forced the thought out of her head.
Of course this man would never look at someone like
her in that way, but she didn't need to be humiliated.

She tipped up her chin. 'Yes.'

He was looking at her with unnerving intensity. She
really couldn't read him at all. Her mouth felt dry and
instinctively she licked her lips. His gaze dropped to
them for a second and her insides flipped. She ignored

it, telling herself her reaction to him was due to the heightened situation.

His eyes met hers again. 'Very well, then. You're not leaving my sight until your brother accounts for his actions and my money is returned.'

Nessa opened her mouth but nothing came out for a moment. Then she said, 'What do you mean, not leaving your sight?'

'Exactly that. You've offered your services in place of your brother, so until he or my money returns you're mine, Nessa O'Sullivan, and you will do exactly as I tell you.'

Nessa struggled to comprehend his words. 'So you're going to hold me as some kind of…collateral? As a prisoner?'

He smiled but it was mirthless. 'Oh, you're quite free to walk out this door, but you won't make it to your car before the police catch up with you. If you want me to believe that you have nothing to do with this, *and* that your brother is innocent, then you will stay here and do your utmost to make yourself useful.'

'How do you know about my car?' Nessa asked, distracted for a moment and not liking the way panic had her insides in a vice grip.

'You were tracked as soon as you parked that heap of junk outside my perimeter wall.'

Fresh humiliation washed over Nessa to think of her stealthy progress being watched in some security room. 'I didn't hear any alarms.'

He dismissed that with a curl of his lip. 'Security here is silent and state of the art. Flashing lights and sirens would unsettle the horses.'

Of course it would. Hadn't Nadim insisted on installing a similarly high-tech system on their own farm?

Nessa searched in vain for some way to avoid being forced to spend an unknown amount of time under this man's punitive command, even though she'd all but asked for it. 'I'm a jockey and I work at our family farm—I can't just walk away from that.'

Barbier's black gaze flicked dismissively over her body again before meeting her eyes. 'A jockey? Then how have I never heard of you?'

Nessa flushed. 'I haven't run many races. Yet.' In recent years she'd gone to university and got a degree, so that had taken her out of the circuit for some time. Not that she was about to explain herself to Barbier.

He made a scathing sound. 'I'm sure. Being a jockey is gritty, hard work. You look as if a puff of wind would knock you over. Somehow I can't really see you rousing at dawn and putting in a long day of the back-breaking training and work that most jockeys endure. Your pretty hands would get far too dirty.'

Nessa bristled and instinctively hid her hands behind her back, conscious of how *un*pretty they were, but not wanting to show Barbier, even in her own defence. She still felt raw after his stinging remark, *I can't say that you'd be my type.*

The unfairness of his attack left her a little speechless. Her family had all worked hard at their farm for as long as she could remember, getting up at the crack of dawn every day of the week and in all kinds of weather. Her family had certainly never lived a gilded life of leisure. Not even when Nadim had bought them out and pumped money into their ailing business.

'Who do you ride for, then?'

She forced down the surge in emotion and answered as cooly as she could, 'My family stables, O'Sullivans. I'm well used to doing my share of the work, believe it or not, and I've been training to be a jockey since I was a teenager. Just because I'm a woman—'

He held up a hand stopping her. 'I have no issue with female jockeys. What I do have an issue with are people who get a free pass on their family connections.'

If Nessa had bristled before, now she was positively apoplectic. She'd had to work twice as hard to prove herself to her own family, if not even more. But she was aware that to really prove herself she'd have to get work with another trainer. It was a sensitive point for her.

'I can assure you,' she said in a low voice full of emotion, 'that my being a jockey is not a vanity project. Far from it.'

She might have laughed if she were able to. Vanity—what was that? She couldn't remember the last time she'd worn make-up.

Barbier looked unimpressed. 'Well, I'm sure the family farm will cope without you.'

Nessa realised that she was damned if she walked out the door and and damned if she didn't. But there was only one way of containing the situation and making sure that the rest of her family weren't dragged into it, and that was doing as Barbier said. She wished she could rewind the clock and be safe at home in bed…but even as she imagined that scenario something inside her rejected it. Rejected the possibility of never having had the opportunity to see this man up close. The shock of that revelation made her stop breathing for a second, its significance terrifying to contemplate.

But the fact was that Nessa's blood was throbbing through her veins in a way she'd never experienced before. Not even after an exhilarating win on a horse.

Shame bloomed deep inside her. How could she betray her own brother, her family, like this? By finding this man so...compelling? Telling herself that stress was making her crazy, she asked, 'What will I be doing here?' She tried to quash lurid images of herself, locked in a tower being fed only bread and water.

Barbier's eyes flicked up and down over her body as if gauging what she might be capable of. Nessa bristled all over, again.

'Oh, don't worry, we'll find something to keep you occupied, and of course any work you do will be in lieu of payment. Until your brother resurfaces, his debt is now yours.'

Barbier straightened up to his full intimidating height and Nessa's pulse jumped.

'I will have Armand escort you back to your home to retrieve what you need. You can give me your car keys.'

This was really happening. And there was nothing she could do about it. Nessa reluctantly reached into her pocket for her keys and took the car key off the main ring, all fingers and thumbs. Eventually she got it free, skin prickling under the laser-eyed scrutiny of Barbier.

She handed it over, a little devil inside her prompting her to say, 'It's a vintage Mini. I doubt you'll fit.' Even the thought of this man coiling his six-foot-plus frame into her tiny battered car was failing to spark any humour in the surreal moment. She really hadn't expected the night to turn out like this...and yet she could see now that she'd been supremely naive to assume it would be so easy to infiltrate the Barbier stud.

He took the key. 'It won't be me retrieving your car.'

Of course. It would be a minion, despatched to take care of the belongings of the woman who was now effectively under house arrest for the foreseeable future.

Not usually given to dramatics, Nessa tried to quell her nerves. She was within five kilometres of her own home, for crying out loud. What was the worst this man could do to her? A small sly voice answered that the worst he could do had nothing to do with punishment for Paddy's sins, and everything to do with how he made her feel in his presence. As if she were on a roller coaster hurtling towards a great swooping dip.

Barbier turned away and opened the office door to reveal the huge burly man still standing outside. They spoke in French so rapid that it was beyond Nessa's basic grasp of the language to try and understand what they were saying.

Barbier turned back to her, switching to English. 'Armand will escort you home to collect your things and bring you back here.'

'Can't I just return in the morning?'

He shook his head, looking even more stern now, and indicated for her to precede him. Mutely, Nessa stepped over the threshold and followed the thick-set security man back out the way she'd come. In the courtyard there was a sleek four-by-four car waiting. Armand opened a car door for her.

For a second Nessa hesitated. She saw the entrance to the courtyard and a glimpse of freedom, if she moved fast. From behind her she heard a deep voice. 'Don't even think about it.'

She turned around. Barbier was right behind her and looked even more intimidating in the dark. Taller, more austere. His face was all hard bones and slashing angles. Not even the softness of that provocative mouth visible.

Nessa put her hand on the car door, needing something to hold onto. 'What happens when I come back?'

'You'll be informed when you do.'

Panic made her blurt out, 'What if I refuse?'

She saw the gallic shrug. 'It's up to you but you've

made it clear you don't want to involve your family. If you refuse to return I can guarantee that *that* will be the least of your worries. You would be an accessory to a crime.'

Nessa shivered again in the cool, night-time air. She had no choice, and he knew it. Defeated, she turned and stepped up into the vehicle, and the door closed behind her.

The windows were tinted and Nessa was enclosed in blackness as the bodyguard came around the front of the vehicle and got into the driver's seat. Barbier strode away from them towards the main building and she felt suddenly bereft, which was ridiculous when the man was holding her to ransom for her brother. *You put yourself up for that ransom*, a voice reminded her.

As they approached the main gates Nessa reluctantly gave Armand directions to her own home. They passed her lonely-looking car on the side of the road and she sucked in a deep breath, telling herself that if she could endeavour to persuade Paddy to return to prove his innocence, and prevent anyone else from getting involved, then this—hopefully!—brief punishment at the hands of Barbier would be worth it.

Nessa tried to call up her usually positive disposition. Surely if Barbier saw how far she was willing to go to prove her brother's innocence, he'd be forced to reconsider and give Paddy a chance to explain, wouldn't he?

But why was it that that seemed to hold less appeal than the thought of seeing Luc Barbier again? Nessa scowled at herself in the reflection of the tinted window of the car, glad she wasn't under that black-eyed gaze when her face got hot with humiliation.

When Nessa returned a short while later the stud was in darkness and quiet. Armand handed her over to a middle-aged man with a nice face who looked as if he'd just been woken up, and he was not all that welcoming. He introduced himself as Pascal Blanc, Barbier's stud and racing stables manager, his right-hand man, and Paddy's one-time immediate boss.

He said nothing at first, showing her to a small spartan room above the stables. Clearly this was where the most menial staff slept. But still, it was clean and comfortable, when Nessa had almost expected a corner of the stables.

After giving her the basics of the Barbier stud schedule and informing her that, naturally, she would be assigned to mucking out the yard and stables, and to expect a five a.m. wake-up call, he stopped at her door. 'For what it's worth, I would have given Paddy the benefit of the doubt based on what I thought I knew of him. We might have been able to get to the bottom of this whole nasty incident. But he ran, and now there's nothing I can do except hope for his sake and yours that he either returns himself or returns the money. Soon.'

Nessa couldn't say anything.

Pascal's mouth compressed. 'Luc... Mr Barbier... does not take kindly to those who betray him. He comes from a world where the rule of law didn't exist and he doesn't suffer fools, Miss O'Sullivan. If your brother *is* guilty, then Luc won't be gentle with him. Or you.'

Somehow these words coming from this infinitely less intimidating man made everything even bleaker. But all Nessa could find herself doing was asking, 'You've known Mr Barbier for long?'

Pascal nodded. 'Ever since he started to work with Leo Fouret, the first time he came into contact with a horse.'

Nessa was impressed. Leo Fouret was one of the most respected trainers in racing, with hundreds of impressive race wins to his name.

'Luc didn't grow up in a kind world, Miss O'Sullivan. But he is fair. Unfortunately your brother never gave him that chance.'

Luc didn't grow up in a kind world... The words reverberated in Nessa's head for a long time after she'd been left alone in the room. She eventually fell into a fitful sleep and had dreams of riding a horse, trying to go faster and faster—not to get to the finish line but to escape from some terrifying and unnamed danger behind her.

What on earth did she have to laugh about? Luc was distinctly irritated by the faint lyrical sound emanating from his stableyard, which was usually a place of hushed industry in deference to the valuable livestock. It could only be coming from one person, the newest addition to his staff: Nessa O'Sullivan.

Her brother had stolen from him and now she laughed. It sent the very insidious thought into Luc's head that he'd been a total fool. Of course she was in on it with her brother and now she was inside the camp. It made him think of the Trojan Horse and he didn't find it amusing.

He cursed and threw down his pen and stood up from his desk, stalking over to the window that looked down over the stables. He couldn't see her and that irritated him even more when he'd deliberately avoided meeting her since her arrival, not wanting to give her the idea that their extended dialogue the other night would ever be repeated. Now he was distracted. When he couldn't afford to be distracted.

He'd only just managed to convince Gio Corretti that the slight delay in money arriving to his account was due to a banking glitch.

Luc's reputation amongst the exclusive thorough-bred racing fraternity had been on trial since he'd exploded onto the scene with a rogue three-year-old who had raced to glory in four consecutive Group One races.

Success didn't mean respect though. He was an anomaly; he had no lineage to speak of and he'd had the temerity to invest wisely with his winnings and make himself a fortune in the process.

Everyone believed his horses were better bred than he was, and they weren't far wrong. The rumours about his background merely added colour to every other mis-conception and untruth heaped against his name.

But, as much as he loved ruffling the elite's feath-ers by making no apology for who he was, he *did* want their respect. He wanted them to respect him for what he had achieved with nothing but an innate talent, hard work and determination.

The last thing he needed was for more rumours to get around, especially one suggesting that Luc Barbier couldn't control his own staff. That he'd been stupid enough to let one million euros disappear from his ac-count.

Even now he still felt the burn of recrimination for finding Paddy O'Sullivan's open expression and in-fectious enthusiasm somehow quaint. He should have spotted a thief a mile away. After all, he'd grown up with them.

Luc tensed when he heard the faint sound of laughing again. Adrenalin mixed with something far more am-biguous and hotter flooded his veins. Nessa O'Sullivan was here under sufferance for her brother—and that was all. The sooner she remembered her place and what was at stake, the better.

'Who were you talking to?'

Nessa immediately tensed when she heard the deep voice behind her. She turned around reluctantly, steeling herself to see Barbier for the first time since that night. And she blinked.

The skies were blue and the air was mild but, in that uniquely Irish way, there seemed to be a mist falling from the sky and tiny droplets clung to Barbier's black hair and shoulders, making him look as if he were... sparkling.

His hands were placed on lean hips. Dark worn jeans clung to powerful thighs and long legs. He was wearing a dark polo shirt. The muscles of his biceps pushed against the short sleeves, and the musculature of his impressive chest was visible under the thin material.

He couldn't look more virile or vitally masculine if he tried. Nessa's body hummed in helpless reaction to that very earthy and basic fact.

'Well?'

Nessa was aghast at how she'd just lost it there for a second, hypnotised by his sheer presence.

She swallowed. 'I was just talking to one of the grooms.'

'You do realise you're not here to socialise, don't you, O'Sullivan?'

Tendrils of Nessa's hair escaped the hasty bun she'd piled on her head earlier, and whipped around her face in the breeze. Her skin prickled at her reaction to him and irritation made her voice sharp. 'It's hard to forget when I've been assigned little more than a cell to sleep in and a pre-dawn wake-up call every day.'

She was very conscious of the unsubtle stench of horse manure clinging to her. And of her worn T-shirt tucked into even more worn jeans. Ancient knee-high boots. She couldn't be any less his *type* right now.

A calculating glint turned his eyes to dark pewter. 'You assured me you were accustomed to hard work and you did offer your services in the place of your brother—if this is too much for you...' He put out a hand to encompass the yard around them.

Nessa stiffened at the obvious jibe. He was clearly expecting her to flounce out of here in a fit of pique. And yes, the work was menial but it was nothing she hadn't done since she'd started walking and could hold a broom. That, and riding horses. Not that he'd believe her.

She squared her shoulders and stared him down. 'If you don't mind, the yard has to be cleaned by lunchtime.'

Barbier looked at the heavy platinum watch encircling his wrist, and then back to her. 'You'd better keep going then, and next time don't distract my employees from their own work. Flirting and gossiping won't help your brother out of his predicament or make things any easier for you here.'

Flirting? For a second Nessa's mind was blank with indignation when she thought of the groom she'd been talking to—a man in his sixties. But before she could think of anything to say in her own defence, Barbier had turned his back and was walking away.

In spite of her indignation, Nessa couldn't stop her gaze following his broad back, seeing how it tapered down to those slim hips and a taut behind, lovingly outlined by the soft worn material of his jeans. He disappeared around a corner and Nessa deflated like a balloon. She turned around in disgust at herself for being so easily distracted, and riled.

Feeling thoroughly prickly and with her nerves still jangling, Nessa turned the power-hose machine back on and imagined Barbier's too-beautiful and smug face in every scrap of dirt she blasted into the drains.

'She's totally over-qualified, Luc. She's putting my own staff to shame, doing longer hours. I shouldn't even be saying this but the yard and stables have never been so clean.' Luc's head groom laughed but soon stopped when Luc fixed him with a dark look.

'No, you shouldn't. Maybe you need new staff.'

Simon Corrigan swallowed and changed the subject. 'Can I ask why we're not paying her? It seems—'

'No, you can't.' Luc cut him off, not liking the way his conscience was stinging. He was many things, but no one had ever faulted him on his sense of fairness and equality. But only he and Pascal Blanc knew what was behind Paddy O'Sullivan's sudden disappearance, and he wanted to keep it that way.

Nessa had been working at his stables for a week now. She hadn't turned tail and run or had a tantrum as he'd expected. He could still see her in his mind's eye—standing in the yard the other day, her back as straight as a dancer, face flushed, amber-green eyes bright and alive. That soft lush mouth compressed. Long tendrils of dark red hair clinging to her hot cheeks as she'd obviously struggled to keep her temper in check.

Her T-shirt had been so worn he could make out the shape of her breasts—small, lush swells, high and firm.

He could also remember the feeling that had swept

through him when he'd heard her carefree laugh. It hadn't been anger that she might be up to something. It had been something much hotter and ambiguous; a sense of possessiveness that had shocked him. It wasn't something he felt for anything much, except horses or business acquisitions.

'Where is she now?' Luc asked Corrigan abruptly.

'She's helping to bring the stallions in from the paddocks. Do you want me to give her a message?'

Luc shook his head. 'No, I'll do it.'

But when Luc got to the stallions' stables Nessa was nowhere to be seen and all the stallions had been settled for the evening. Feeling a mounting frustration, he went looking for her.

'You are a beautiful boy, aren't you? Yes, you are… and you know it too. Yes, there you go…' The three-year-old colt whinnied softly in appreciation as he took the raw carrot from Nessa's hand and she rubbed his nose.

She knew she shouldn't be here in the racing section of Barbier's stables, where the current thoroughbreds resided, but she hadn't been able to resist. She felt at peace for the first time in days, even as her body actually ached with the need to feel a horse underneath her with all that coiled power and strength and speed. But she wouldn't be riding again for a while.

'You were told to stay away from this area.'

And just like that Nessa's short-lived sense of peace vanished and was replaced by an all-too predictable jump in her heart-rate. She turned around to see Barbier standing a few feet away, arms folded. He was wearing a white shirt, and it made his skin look even darker. His hair touched the collar, curling slightly.

'I'm on a break,' she responded defensively, wondering if he was this autocratic with all his employees. But she had to admit that, so far, everyone seemed pretty content to be working here. She'd found out that the employee who'd been fired on the spot had been smoking weed and she'd had to concede that he would have suffered a similar fate on their own stud farm. Barbier had also enrolled the employee on an addiction course. It was disconcerting to realise that perhaps he wasn't as ruthless as she'd like to believe.

Barbier moved now and closed the distance between them before she could take another breath. He snatched the rest of the carrot out of her hand, frowning. 'What are you feeding Tempest?'

'It's just a carrot.' She pulled her hand back into her chest disconcerted by the shock his fleeting touch had given her.

He glared at her, and he was far too close, but Nessa's back was against the stall door and the horse. She was trapped.

'No one is allowed to feed my horses unless they're supervised.'

Her mouth dropped open and then she sputtered, 'It's just a carrot!'

He was grim. 'A carrot that could contain poison or traces of steroids for all I know.'

Nessa went cold. 'You think I would harm your horses?'

His jaw was as hard as granite. 'I'm under enough scrutiny as it is. I don't need the possible accomplice of a thief messing around with my valuable livestock. I don't know what you're capable of. How did you know that this is the horse?'

Nessa struggled to keep up. '*What* horse?'

Now Barbier was impatient. 'The horse I bought from Gio Corretti.'

Nessa swallowed. 'I had no idea, I just came in for a visit. He seemed agitated.'

Barbier's gaze went from her to the horse behind her and she took the opportunity to slide sideways, putting some distance between them. He put out a hand and stroked the side of Tempest's neck, murmuring soft words in French. Nessa's gaze locked onto his big hand stroking the horse, and she had to struggle not to imagine how that hand might feel on her. She'd never in her life imagined a man stroking her—she must be losing her mind.

The horse pushed his head into Barbier's hand and Nessa glanced at Barbier to see his features relax slightly. For a heady moment she imagined that there was no enmity between them and that he might not always look at her as if she'd just committed a crime. She wondered what he'd look like if he smiled and then she glanced away quickly, mortified at herself and afraid he would read her shameful thoughts on her face.

Barbier said, 'He's been agitated since he arrived, not settling in properly.'

Welcoming the diversion from her wayward imagination, Nessa replied, 'He's probably just pining for his mother.'

Barbier looked at her sharply, his hand dropping away. 'How would you know such a thing?'

Nessa flushed and kept avoiding his eye. How could she explain the weird affinity for horses that she shared with her sister and father? She shrugged. 'I just guessed.'

Barbier's voice was harsh. 'Gio Corretti told me and your brother that we might have issues settling the colt because he hadn't been separated from his mother until recently, which is unusual. That's how you know.'

Nessa looked at Barbier and saw the condemnation and distrust in his eyes. How could she defend a gut feeling? She shrugged and looked away. 'If you say so.'

Without realising it, Nessa's hand had instinctively lifted up to touch the horse again, until suddenly Barbier reached out and took it. Nessa jumped at the weird electricity that sparked whenever they got too close. She tried to pull her hand back but his grip was too firm. And warm.

He was holding her palm facing upwards, and asked grimly, 'What is this?'

She looked down and saw what he saw: her very *un*pretty hands, skin roughened from her training as a jockey and blistered from the last few days of hard work. Humiliated at the thought that he'd see this as proof she wasn't used to work, she yanked her hand back and cradled it to her chest again. 'It's nothing.'

She backed away towards the entrance. 'I should go—my break is over.' She turned and forced herself to walk and not run away, not even sure what she was running from. But something about the way he'd just taken her hand and looked so disapproving to see the marks of her labour made her feel incredibly self-conscious and also a little emotional, which was truly bizarre.

Nessa couldn't recall the last time anyone had focused attention on her like that. Her sister had done her best but she wasn't their mother. Their father hadn't been much use while he'd drowned his sorrows.

So they'd had to fend for themselves mostly. She hadn't even realised until that moment how much another's touch could pierce her right to the core. And for it to have been Luc Barbier was inconceivable and very disturbing. She didn't have an emotional connection with that man—the very notion was ridiculous.

Luc watched as Nessa walked quickly out of the stables and around the corner with an easy athletic grace that made him wonder what she'd be like on a horse. *Excellent*, his instincts told him, as much as he'd like to ignore them.

He was still astounded at the apparent ease with which she'd calmed Tempest, who was one of the most volatile horses Luc had ever bought. But also potentially one of the best, if his hunch about the colt's lineage was right. Certainly Gio Corretti had asked for top dollar, so he'd clearly suspected potential greatness too.

Luc turned back to the horse, who pushed his face into Luc's shoulder, nudging. Did Luc really believe Nessa would poison the horse? He held up the innocuous, gnarled carrot and eventually fed it to the horse with a sigh.

The answer came from his gut: no, she wouldn't poison his horse. She'd looked too shocked when he'd said it. But the fact was that, until her brother reappeared or the money did, the jury was out on Nessa O'Sullivan and he had to keep her under close scrutiny. He'd be a fool not to suspect that brother and sister were working in tandem.

Luc told himself it was for this reason, and *not* because her raw hands had twisted something inside his gut, that he was about to move her to where she could be kept under closer scrutiny.

CHAPTER THREE

'I'M MOVING YOU out of the stables and into the house.'

Nessa looked at Luc Barbier where he stood behind his desk. She'd been summoned here a few minutes ago by the head groom, Simon Corrigan, and she'd tried not to let the understated luxury of the grand old Irish country house intimidate her.

This was where Barbier's suite of private offices were based and now she stood on thick sumptuous carpet and was surrounded by dark oak panelling. Books filled floor-to-ceiling shelves. In contrast to the rather conservative decor, there was modern art on the walls that tickled at Nessa's curiosity. And behind Barbier, a massive window where Nessa could see the training gallops in the distance. An amazing view and one that made her yearn to be on a horse.

But she dragged her attention back to what he'd said. 'Excuse me?'

'I said, I'm moving you into the house.' He enunciated the words slowly, which only made his accent more noticeable. Nessa still couldn't get over the raw, untameable energy that emanated from the man, in spite of the luxe surroundings.

She felt a bit dense. 'Why?'

'My housekeeper has lost one of her household assistants and so I told her you would fill in.'

'Household assistant,' Nessa said slowly as it sank in. 'You mean a cleaner?'

Barbier grimaced faintly. 'I think they prefer the term household assistant.'

A faint burn of humiliation washed up through her body. 'This is because I went to see your racehorses.'

Barbier's jaw tightened. 'I'm not so petty.'

Nessa thought of being cooped up indoors cleaning floors and already felt claustrophobic. 'You accused me of potential sabotage.'

Barbier's jaw got even tighter. 'At this point in time I have no idea what you're capable of. You've put yourself in this position in a bid to convince me your brother is innocent. Mrs Owens, my housekeeper, needs someone to help her out—'

'And I'm just the handy house-arrest guest you can move about at will to wherever it suits you,' Nessa interrupted, feeling frustrated and angry.

'You're the one who is here by choice, Nessa. By all means you're free to walk out this door at any time, but if you do I won't hesitate to involve the local police.'

Nessa tipped up her chin, feeling reckless. 'So why don't you do it, then? Just call them!'

Barbier didn't look remotely fazed at her outburst. 'Because,' he said easily, 'I don't believe it serves either of our interests to involve the law at this point. Do you really want to drag your family name into the open and inform everyone of what your brother has done?'

Nessa went cold inside when she thought of the lines of pain already etched into her father's face. Indelible lines that would never fade even in spite of his much better mental state. She thought of Iseult's frantic worry and her husband, Nadim, who would un-

doubtedly storm in to take over—just weeks before
their baby was due.

Nessa looked at the man in front of her and hated
him at that moment. Hated the way he was able to hold
her to ransom so easily, and then that hatred turned inwards. She only had herself to blame. And Paddy.

She had taken responsibility and she couldn't crumble now.

She forced down an awful feeling of futility and said,
'No, I don't want anyone to know what has happened.
If I stay and do as you ask, can you promise that you
won't report what Paddy has done?'

Barbier inclined his head slightly. 'Like I said, it
serves us both to keep this to ourselves for the time
being.'

Nessa wondered why he was so reluctant to let this
get out, but then she realised that he would hardly like
it to be known that payment for a horse had gone astray.
It would put off potential sellers everywhere.

For a fleeting moment Nessa considered threatening
to leak this news in return for Barbier's assurance that
Paddy wouldn't be prosecuted. But she realised, without even testing him, that Barbier was not a man who
could be so easily manipulated.

Apart from which, she didn't have the stomach for
blackmail, and there would be no way that Paddy's reputation could remain unsullied. He might never get the
chance to prove his innocence, and with the stain of
possible theft and corruption on his record he'd never
get a job in the industry he loved again. It would ruin
him. Not to mention the disappointment of their father
and sister...

As if privy to her thoughts, Barbier said, 'You're
the only insurance Paddy has at the moment. His only

guarantee of any kind of protection. You walk out of here and that's gone, along with any sliver of doubt I may have about his guilt.'

Nessa's heart thumped hard at that. So there *was* a chance that Barbier might believe in Paddy, if she could just convince him to return and explain what had happened. She had to cling onto that.

Not even sure what she wanted to say but wanting to capitalise on any sliver of mercy she could, she started, 'Mr Barbier—'

'It's Luc,' he cut her off. 'I don't stand on ceremony with anyone, not even a suspected thief.'

He didn't trust her as far as he could throw her, yet he would still allow her to call him by his first name. Nessa didn't like how his bad opinion of her affected her. She'd never done a dishonest thing in her life— apart from creeping onto this property on that fateful night.

She told herself that she just didn't like anyone thinking badly of her—and that Barbier's opinion of her wasn't important. But that felt like a lie.

'Fine, I'll work in the house.'

The corner of his mouth tipped up ever so slightly in a mocking smile. 'I like how you give yourself the illusion of having a choice.'

Nessa controlled her facial expression, not wanting to let him know how much he got to her. 'Was that all?'

Now he looked slightly frustrated, as if he'd expected something else from her. After a moment he just said coolly, 'Yes, Mrs Owens will send for you and show you what she needs. You'll move into one of the staff bedrooms here.'

So she was to be completely removed from the realm of the stud farm and racing stables. Her heart contracted at the thought of being away from the horses, but at the same time an illicit fizz started in her body at the realisation that she'd be sleeping under the same roof as Barbier—*Luc*.

She'd never be able to say his name out loud; it felt far too intimate.

And not that she'd even see him, she assured herself. Not that she *wanted* to see him! She'd probably be confined to cleaning bathrooms and vacuuming hallways. Nessa left his office with as much dignity as she could muster.

En route back to her own quarters, she diverted and went to the paddocks where the stallions idly grazed the lush grass.

One of the huge beasts came over and whinnied, pushing his face into Nessa's shoulder. She dutifully pulled out the ubiquitous carrot she always carried and fed it to him, stroking his soft nose and feeling ridiculously at sea.

Being sequestered indoors and kept away from the bucolic expanse and the animals was more of a punishment than mucking out stableyards and stables ever could be. But Nessa couldn't convince herself that Barbier was doing it out of spite. He really didn't seem that petty.

Instead, she couldn't stop thinking about how he'd taken her hand in his and looked at her rough skin so fiercely the other day. She'd felt self-conscious ever since then. She curled her hands inwards now and shoved them back into her pockets, backing away from the horse.

As she walked back to the main buildings she told herself it was ridiculous to imagine for a second that Barbier had moved her away from the stables for any other reason than just because she was bound to serve out her time here however he willed it.

The man couldn't care less about her labour-worn hands, and, anyway, hot soapy water and housework were hardly going to be any less taxing or more gentle! She just had to get on with it and make the best of this situation until they could prove Paddy's innocence.

It took a long time for the heat in Luc's body to die down after Nessa had left his office. He'd had to battle the urge to push his desk aside and take that stubborn chin in his thumb and forefinger, tipping it up so that she presented her lush mouth to his. Silencing her in a way that would be unbelievably satisfying.

It was confounding. And irritating as hell. Especially as she was wearing nothing more provocative than a worn T-shirt, jeans and boots, hair pulled back in a messy ponytail and no make-up. Yet there was something very earthy and sensual about her that made her all woman.

That, and the defiant tilt of her jaw and the look in her eyes, effortlessly enflamed him. He had the same impulse when he was around her that he had with an unbroken horse. A desire to tame it, and make it bend to his will.

He'd never before become so interested in one woman. Women had never enthralled Luc beyond the initial attraction, and it usually waned quickly. He'd be the first to admit his experience of women hadn't been the most rounded. His mother had shown only the briefest moments of motherly love, before her addictions had swallowed her whole.

The girls in his milieu had been as gritty and tough as him, broken by their surroundings and circumstances. And if they weren't broken then they got out and went far away, exactly as he had done.

Sometimes, the women who frequented the social sphere he now inhabited reminded him of the girls and women of his youth. They were hard and gritty too, but hid it under a shiny, expensive sheen.

But Nessa was none of those things, which intrigued him in spite of his best instincts. And she was out of bounds, for many reasons, not least of which was her suspected collusion with her brother.

He knew without arrogance that she was attracted to him. He saw it in her over-bright eyes and pink cheeks, her taut body that quivered slightly in his presence. He felt fairly sure she must know that he was attracted to her—in spite of his words that first night. *I can't say that you'd be my type.* Apparently she was.

Yet she wasn't testing him by using their chemistry to try and leverage any advantage. He didn't think a woman existed who wouldn't. Unless she was playing some game. *That* was far more probable.

He stood at his window now, the view encompassing the gallops in the distance where his thoroughbreds were being exercised, and the stud farm just out of sight on the other side.

He had both sides of the industry here—racing and breeding. It gave him immense satisfaction to see it all laid out before him, except today, for the first time, there was a slight dilution of that satisfaction. As if something had taken the sheen off it. As if something was reminding him that he hadn't made it yet. Not really.

Luc scowled. He knew he hadn't made it yet, not completely. No matter how many winners he had or sired with his stallions.

He wouldn't have made it until he was respected by

his peers, and not looked at with varying degrees of suspicion.

It was the only fulfilment he wanted. He had no desire for the things most normal people wanted—family, security, love. What was love anyway? It was a foreign concept to Luc that came far too close to believing in trust, and such notions as fate and chance.

He couldn't understand Nessa's blind defence of her brother—unless she was getting something out of it too. It was inconceivable she was doing it out of pure affection or loyalty.

All that existed for him were the solid successes he'd manifested out of sweat and dogged ambition. The legacy he would leave behind would tell a different story from the one he'd been handed at birth. His name would endure as a gold standard in racing.

And yet now, for the first time, he had the disquieting suspicion that even if every one of his peers were to look him in the eye with the utmost respect, he'd still feel less than them.

A movement to the far right in the stud stableyard area caught Luc's eye and he welcomed the distraction. He turned his head just in time to catch a flash of dark red hair coiling down a slim back before Nessa disappeared around a corner. His reaction was instant and intense, making him scowl even harder at his body's lack of control.

His body pulsed with need. He should be pushing this woman further away, leaving it to his staff to keep her in check. But instead he was bringing her closer.

He was experiencing a kind of hunger he'd only felt once before, when he'd had his first taste of the wider world outside the gloomy Parisian suburbs and had made the vow to never end up back there again. He'd taken that hunger, and used it.

This hunger, however, would be crushed. Because it could do nothing to enhance his success, or his life. Resisting her would be a test of his will to not demean himself.

'Here—last job of the day, love, go up and do the boss's private suite. He's due back from Paris later this evening and I never had a chance to get around to it, what with the preparations for the party this weekend.'

Nessa took the basket containing cleaning products from Mrs Owens and hated that her skin got hot just at the mention of *the boss* and that he was returning soon. He'd been at his Paris stables for the past three days, which hadn't felt as much of a respite as Nessa had thought it would.

Angry with herself for still being so aware of him when he wasn't even here, she focused on feeling relieved that the day was nearly over. There was something particularly soul-sucking about doing housework all day, every day, and as Nessa had polished the silver earlier she'd revised her opinion that Luc Barbier wasn't petty.

They'd also been busy preparing for a huge party that was being thrown at the house that weekend, to launch the most prestigious racing event in the Irish season.

Just as the homely housekeeper was turning away she stopped and said, 'I've left fresh bedlinen in his room, so just strip the bed and remake it. Once you're done with that you're off for the evening.'

Nessa went upstairs to the second floor of the villa-style country house, still marvelling at the opulence.

It was about two hundred years old. All the bedroom suites were on the second floor. The first floor was taken up with Barbier's—*Luc's*—office and a gym. There was also a vast media room with a private cinema and informal meetings rooms.

The ground floor held the grand ballroom—prepared for the party now—with French doors opening out onto exquisite manicured gardens. It also had the main, and less formal, dining rooms and reception rooms.

The basement was where the vast kitchen and staff quarters were laid out. All in all a very grand affair. It certainly put Nessa's family farmhouse to shame, even though it too had been refurbished to a high standard since Iseult had married Nadim. It was a far more modestly sized house, though.

Nessa reached the second floor, and walked to the end of the corridor past all the guest rooms to where Luc's rooms were based. He had one entire wing, and she found she was holding her breath slightly as she opened the door.

His scent hit her instantly. Woody and musky. It curled through her nose and deep into the pit of her belly. Cursing herself for her reaction, she strode into the main reception room, dumping the basket of cleaning supplies and resolutely opening the sash windows to let some air in. She told herself the room was musty, not musky and provocative.

Still, she couldn't help but look around. The room was huge and open plan, with soft grey furnishings in muted tones. The same stunning modern art that she'd seen in his office was dotted around the walls, along with sculptures, huge coffee-table books on photography, art, and movies. More books than she'd ever seen in her life, ranging from thrillers to the classics.

The decor and objects reflected a far more cerebral man than Nessa would have guessed existed under Barbier's brooding, sexy exterior.

She had to force herself to remember why she was here and not give into the impulse to pluck out a book from the shelves and curl up on one of the sumptuous couches to read. She realised that she was more weary than she'd realised—the stress of the situation and hard work, mixed with nights of fitful sleep, wasn't a good combination. But she wasn't a wilting lily, and normally worked harder than most, so it annoyed her to find herself feeling tired now.

She scooped up the cleaning supplies and set to work dusting and cleaning. Eventually, as if she'd been putting it off, she went into the bedroom area. She opened the doors and the first thing that hit her eyeline was the bed. It was massive, dominating the room. Much like the man.

It was a modern bed with a dark grey headboard that reminded her ridiculously of his eyes and how they could turn dark silver. A detail she shouldn't even be aware of.

Apart from the bed there were some built-in wardrobes, a sleek chest of drawers and bedside tables. What was striking was the absence of anything of particularly personal value. No photos. No *stuff*. Just some clothes draped on one of the chairs and the rumpled bedsheets, which she avoided looking at.

Then she spied two more doors that revealed a walk-in closet and a luxurious bathroom complete with wet-room shower and a tub that looked big enough to take a football team.

Nessa set about cleaning the bathroom, trying not to breathe in his scent, which was everywhere. She picked

up a bottle of cologne and guiltily sniffed it before putting it down again hastily.

Disgusted with herself, she finished cleaning and
went back into the bedroom, pulling off the crumpled
sheets and trying not to imagine that they were still
warm from his body. *Would he sleep naked? He seems
like the kind of man who would...*

Nessa stopped dead for a moment, shocked at the
vivid turn of her imagination, and at the way she suddenly hungered to know what he would look like—
imagining the sexy naked sprawl of that big bronzed
body all too easily, and knowing her imagination probably fell far short of reality. Her pulse became slow
and hot.

She had to face the unpalatable fact that Luc Barbier
had succeeded where no other man had. He'd awoken
her hormones from their dormant state. *Their virginal
state.* And it was beyond humiliating that the first man
she should feel lust for was the last man who would ever
look at her like that.

She'd often wondered why she'd never felt particularly roused by other boys' kisses at university, and her
lack of response had earned her a reputation of being
standoffish. She'd closed inwards after that, choosing
to avoid exposing herself and risk being mocked.

Nessa made the bed as clinically as she could, ignoring the faint dent near the centre that indicated where
he slept. When she was done she made one more sweep
of the rooms to make sure she hadn't missed anything
and collected all the cleaning materials. She stepped inside the bedroom one last time to run her eye over the
now-pristine bed and was about to step back out and
shut the door when something caught her eye outside.

She went over to the window, putting the basket down for a moment. The view took her breath away; the sun was setting over the gallops, bathing everything in a lush golden light. There were no horses being exercised now, but Nessa could remember how it felt to harness a thoroughbred's power as it surged powerfully beneath her. There was a wide window seat and Nessa sat down, curling her legs underneath her, enjoying the view for an illicit moment.

Nessa suspected that she knew exactly why she had avoided physical intimacy until now. Their mother's death had profoundly affected everyone in her family: Iseult had grown up overnight to become their mother and much more, and the boys had gone off the rails in their own ways but had always turned to each other. Even though Nessa was a twin to Eoin, they'd never had that bond people spoke of.

Their father had gone to pieces.

But Nessa had been too young to do much but internalise all of her own pain and grief, too acutely aware of everyone else's struggles to let it out. She'd always been terrified of what might come out of her if she did. It had been easier to retreat emotionally, and concentrate on her dreams of being a great jockey.

But sometimes the pain in her chest—her unexpressed grief—took her breath away. And sometimes, when she looked at her sister Iseult with her husband and she saw their incredibly intimate bond, she felt envious of that relationship, even as it made her heart palpitate with fear. She couldn't imagine ever allowing herself to love someone that much, for fear of losing them. For fear of the devastation the loss would cause.

Up until now she'd avoided sex because getting close

to someone had seemed like too high a price. And yet, when she thought of Luc Barbier, the last thing on her mind was the emotional price.

Luc was tired and frustrated. He'd spent the last three days working intensively with one of his brightest hopes, a horse called Sur La Mer. He was due to race in a few weeks in France but none of his jockeys seemed capable of getting the horse to perform to his maximum ability. Luc would ride the horse himself if he weren't six feet four and two hundred pounds.

Luc was also frustrated in a far more difficult area—sexually. It was not a state he was used to. He didn't do sexual frustration. He desired a woman, he had her and he moved on.

But only one woman had dominated his thoughts in France. Nessa O'Sullivan. He'd gone to a glitzy charity auction in Paris that was abounding with beautiful women. Not one had piqued his interest. Instead he'd found himself wondering what Nessa would look like out of those jeans that seemed to be shrink-wrapped to her taut thighs. Or the series of worn T-shirts that did little to conceal her lithe body and firm breasts. Or what her hair would look like teased into luxurious waves, rippling down a bare back.

Dieu. He cursed himself as he strode down the corridor to his bedroom, relishing the prospect of a cold shower and bed.

But when Luc opened the door to his bedroom all of his instincts snapped onto high alert. An old habit from when his environment had spelled danger from sunrise to sunset.

He saw the basket of cleaning supplies first, on a table near the door. And then he saw *her* and his breath stopped in his chest. He wasn't entirely sure he wasn't hallucinating.

She was curled up on the wide window seat, fast asleep. Her knees were leaning to one side, and her head was leaning against the window as if she'd been looking at the view of the gallops.

He moved closer and his hungry gaze tracked down over her body—he was disappointed that she wasn't wearing the jeans and T-shirt combination that had enflamed his imagination. She was wearing the plain black trousers and black shirt that all his household staff wore. Flat, functional sneakers.

The shirt had untucked from her trousers, and he could see the tiniest bare patch of her waist and her paler than pale skin. Blood roared to his head and groin in a simultaneous rush.

He was incensed at her effect on him, and at his growing obsession with her.

As if finally becoming aware of his intense scrutiny, she shifted slightly and Luc looked at her face to see long dark lashes fluttering against her cheeks for a moment before her eyes opened sleepily. He watched as she slowly registered where she was, and who was in front of her.

Her cheeks flushed and those huge eyes widened until all he could see was dark, golden green. He wanted to slip right into those pools and lose himself...

A tumult raged inside him as she looked up and blinked innocently, as if butter wouldn't melt in her mouth. He might have almost believed for a second that she hadn't planned this little set-up.

'Well, well, well, what do we have here?' He looked her over slowly and thoroughly, fresh heat flooding his veins when he saw the thrust of her breasts against the shirt. It made his voice harsh. 'You would have been much more comfortable and made it easier for both of us if you'd stripped naked and waited in my bed.'

CHAPTER FOUR

NESSA LOOKED UP at Luc Barbier, who was towering over her with a dark scowl on his face and stubble on his jaw. For a blessed foggy moment, just before the adrenalin kicked in, his words hung harmlessly in the air between them.

His hair was tousled, as if he'd been running a hand through it, and he was wearing a white shirt, open at the neck, revealing a glimpse of dark skin. Awareness sizzled to life, infusing her with an urgency she felt only around him.

And then his words registered. It was like an electric shock or a slap across the face. Nessa was wide awake, and she scrambled off the window seat to stand on wobbly legs.

Her hair was coming loose from where it had been piled messily on her head to keep it out of the way. She was thoroughly rumpled, she smelled of cleaning products and he really thought…? Bile rose in her throat.

'How dare you insinuate such a thing?' Her voice was scratchy from sleep and she was burningly aware— even as she said that—of how bad this looked. She cursed herself for allowing her weariness to get the better of her.

Luc's head reared back, arms folded across his chest.

'I walk into my bedroom and find a woman, pretending to be asleep, waiting for me…like I said, they're usually in my bed and wearing a lot less but the message is essentially the same. They're here for one thing.'

Nessa was speechless at his sheer arrogance. Eventually she managed to get out, through waves of indignation and far more disturbing physical reactions, 'Well, I hate to burst your ego bubble but that was the last thing on my mind. I was cleaning your room, then I sat down for a minute and I fell asleep. I apologise for that. But I did not come here to…to…'

He raised a brow. 'To seduce me?'

Before she could respond to that, he continued as if she hadn't spoken. 'I might as well tell you now that kinky role-play doesn't really do it for me. I'm a traditionalist that way. When I make love it's intense, thorough and without the need for embellishment.'

A flash of heat went up Nessa's spine to imagine just how intense his lovemaking would be. Little beads of sweat broke out between her breasts and in the small of her back. Anger rose too. Anger that it was him who was firing up all her nerve-endings.

'I am not here to *make love* with anyone. My only crime was to fall asleep on the job and if you'll excuse me now I'll leave you in peace.'

She went to step away and out of his orbit but he caught her arm after muttering something that sounded very French and rude under his breath. His hand encircled her whole upper arm and his fingers were brushing the side of her breast. Nessa's pulse rocketed, and in the dim lights of the room—*night had fallen outside…just how long had she been asleep?*—all she could see were the forbiddingly gorgeous lines of Luc's face.

'Peace?' He almost spat the word out. 'I've had precious little peace since your brother absconded with one million euros and then his temptress of a sister turns up to play sidekick. Just what is your agenda, Nessa? What game are you playing here? Because I warn you now that you will get burned if you think you can play with me and get away with it.'

His dark intensity was totally intimidating, but somehow Nessa managed to pull her arm free and step away. Shakily she said, 'I'm not playing any games. I wouldn't know how. I really didn't come here with some nefarious intention to seduce you.'

She bit her lip to stop a semi-hysterical giggle from emerging. She wouldn't know how to seduce her way out of a paper bag, never mind a man like Luc Barbier. The very notion was ridiculous.

His mouth thinned. 'You really expect me to believe that you fell asleep like Sleeping Beauty in the fairy tale, waiting for her prince?'

Heat rushed into her cheeks—she *had* been mooning about his suite like some lovelorn teenager earlier. It wasn't like her at all. 'I don't believe in fairy tales,' she said stiffly. 'And don't worry, I know you're no prince.'

He put two hands on her arms now, swinging her around to face him properly. His eyes had turned to cold steel. 'What's that supposed to mean?'

'I…' Words got stuck in Nessa's throat. She couldn't seem to concentrate on anything but Luc's face above hers. The sensual lines were mesmerising. 'I didn't mean anything.'

Except she had, she realised. She'd just articulated it badly. This man was no prince, he was a marauding sultan, or a king. Uncultivated and suave all at once. Infinitely hard but also soft, as when he'd put a hand to his horse.

His mouth twisted. 'I might never be a prince, but you're in no position to look down on me, the sister of a common thief who thought she could seduce her way to paying back her brother's debt. Like I said, you could have saved a lot of conversation if you'd been waiting in my bed naked instead of playing out this elaborate charade of innocence.'

Nessa's hand had lifted and connected with Luc's cheek before she even realised what she'd done. Shock coursed through her system as the sting registered on her hand and Luc's face turned from the blow. All her anger drained away instantly.

He turned back slowly, face even darker now, a livid handprint showing on his cheek. Horrified, Nessa used his name for the first time. 'Luc, I'm so sorry. But I didn't mean it like that, and Paddy's not a common thief. He's really not—'

'Stop talking, you little hellcat, I don't want to hear another word.' His voice was rough.

Before Nessa could even think of uttering another word, Luc had pulled her right into him, so that her body was welded to his. All she could feel was whip-cord strength and heat.

All she could see were his eyes, fathomless and like molten steel. She realised he was livid and yet she felt no fear. She only felt an intense excitement. She opened her mouth but he said, 'Not another word.'

And then his mouth covered hers, and words were the last thing on Nessa's mind as heat fused with white light and poured into every vein in her body to create a scorching trail of fire.

Shock rendered her helpless to Luc's savage sensuality and her own immediately rampant response.

Luc's arm went around her back, arching her into

him even more, and his mouth began to move over hers. But this was no gentle exploration, and it left any other kisses she'd shared with boys in a far distant universe. This did not leave her cold, or unmoved. This was igniting her very soul.

It was mastery, pure and simple. And domination. And punishment. And yet despite all those things that should have had Nessa tensing and squirming to be free, she strained to be even closer, raising her arms to twine them about Luc's neck. If she could have climbed into his skin, she would have.

She opened her mouth under his, instinctively seeking a deeper kiss, wanting to taste him with every fibre of her being. His fingers threaded through her hair, catching her head, angling it so that he could give her exactly what she wanted, but on his terms.

He consumed her, demanding nothing less than total surrender, and Nessa knew only one thing: that she wanted to surrender, with no doubt or hesitation in her mind. It was as if every moment in her life had been building up to this conflagration.

She was drowning in liquid heat and could feel it, slippery, between her legs. Luc's mouth left hers and she heard a soft moan emanating from her mouth. He trailed kisses over her jaw and down her neck. Her head fell back, too heavy.

The only sounds in the room were harsh breathing and the *thump thump* of her heart. Luc's hand was on her shirt, deftly opening the buttons. Cool air hit her bare skin and her nipples drew into tight, hard points.

The world tipped on its axis and Nessa only realised moments later that Luc had sat down on the edge of the bed, bringing her with him so that now she sat on his lap. She was dizzy, and thought that this must be how it felt to be drunk: light-headed and euphoric.

He was pushing her shirt open, and she looked at him and saw an almost feral expression on his face. He cupped one of her lace-covered breasts. Breasts that had always felt very inadequate to Nessa. But now when she looked down she could see how she perfectly filled his palm. As if she'd been made for his hands alone.

He pulled down the lace cup, baring her flesh, and she bit her lip to stop from moaning, pleading. His thumb skated over one small hard nipple and it sent electric shocks through her whole body.

He looked at her and smiled and Nessa realised that he hadn't smiled at her once until now. And it was as devastating as she'd suspected it might be. Wicked, seductive, gorgeous and irresistible.

Lust and need cocooned them from reality, and for one wild second Nessa could almost convince herself that perhaps she was still asleep and this was all just a very vivid dream.

But she knew it wasn't a dream, and she knew that it was very important that she stand up and stop this.

Luc's head was dipping towards her breast and Nessa had never wanted anything more than to surrender completely to this moment, but something within her, some small sane voice, broke through. She put her hands on Luc's shoulders and levered herself off his lap, feeling like a foal trying to stand for the first time.

Luc just looked at her as if he couldn't quite believe she'd moved away, and Nessa realised she was half naked. She pulled at her shirt, scrambling to do up at least one or two buttons. The bare flesh of her breast chafed against the material, sensitised by his touch.

She forced out, through the clamour of her own de-sire, 'I didn't come here for this. I really didn't.'

Luc's body was hard and throbbed with a need to claim and possess, things he'd never felt for a woman before. Nessa was looking at him with wide eyes and flushed cheeks, and hair coming loose.

I didn't come here for this. Something slid into Luc's mind: the very rogue possibility that she *had* just fallen asleep while on the job. And then he dismissed it. She was playing with him and he would not be manipulated like this. He'd already exposed himself far too much. And the fact that she'd been the one to pull away, sig-nalling she was more in control than he was, was even more exposing.

Luc forced his blood to cool, and stood up in a fluid motion. Nessa took a step back. The thought that she was stepping back from him in case he touched her again sent something dark into his gut. And something far more unwelcome: a feeling of vulnerability, something that Luc had rejected long ago. He was invulnerable.

'Sleeping with me isn't going to improve your, or your brother's, situation. I told you already that I don't play games, Nessa, so unless you're willing to admit that we both want each other with no strings attached then get out of here.'

His voice was so cold and remote it skated over Nes-sa's skin like ice. She hated his obvious cynicism, and wanted to deny his claim that she would manipulate him to gain favour for her brother, but self-preservation kicked in at the last moment. She fled, taking the bas-ket of cleaning supplies with her.

When Nessa finally made it back to her room she closed the door behind her and rested against it. Her heart was still thumping out of time, and her whole body ached for a fulfilment she'd never needed before.

And she reeled with the knowledge that she'd almost lain back for Luc Barbier and handed him something she'd never handed anyone else. Her innocence. She'd almost tipped over the edge of allowing Luc to see her at her most vulnerable. A man who had shown her nothing but disdain and distrust.

Thank *God* she'd pulled back from the brink. She shivered now at the prospect of Luc looking at her when he'd discovered her virginity. She could already imagine the mocking look on his face, and how he would spurn her with disgust.

But then she thought of how he'd said, *Unless you're willing to admit we both want each other with no strings attached*, and she shivered again. But this time it wasn't with trepidation or humiliation. It was with an awful sense of illicit excitement.

Luc had turned the shower to cold, but that still hadn't cooled the lingering heat in his body. He couldn't believe how close he'd come to stripping Nessa O'Sullivan bare and taking her in a haze of lust.

She'd been the one to pull back. And even though Luc hadn't imagined the chemistry between them, it still got to him somewhere very vulnerable that she'd had more control than him.

He couldn't trust her, and yet he'd been about to sleep with her, complicating an already complicated situation even more. He shuddered to think of the hold she could have had over him after sleeping together. He hadn't yet known a woman who didn't try to capitalise on intimacies shared, even when they were only physical. And he had no doubt—in spite of her protestations otherwise—that she'd had an agenda.

He looked at himself in his bathroom mirror and scowled. If she thought that she could whet his appetite like this, and he would come running after her like a dog in heat, she was mistaken. Luc wouldn't be caught offguard again. She *was* resistable. Even if the pounding of his blood told him otherwise.

He pulled a towel around his waist and knotted it roughly, finding his mobile phone and picking it up. Within seconds he was issuing a terse instruction to the security firm he'd hired to seek out Paddy O'Sullivan, to step up their efforts.

Afterwards he threw the phone down and surmised grimly that the sooner they found Paddy and his money, the sooner he could get rid of the all too distracting Nessa O'Sullivan too.

Two nights later, Nessa was holding a tray full of champagne flutes filled to the brim, serving them at Luc's glitzy party. She was dressed in a white shirt and black skirt. The uniform of waiters everywhere. Hair up in a tight bun.

She could appreciate the breathtaking scene even as her arms felt as if they were about to drop out of the shoulder sockets. The unusually mild Irish spring day was melting into a lavender-hued dusk. Candles imbued the guests and room with a golden light.

She smiled in relief as some guests stopped and helped themselves to drinks on her tray, lightening her load marginally. And then her gaze tracked back inevitably to where one man stood out from the crowd—dark head and broad shoulders visible from every corner of the room.

Her main objective was to avoid coming face to face with Luc Barbier at all costs. The enormity of what had almost happened still sent shock waves through her body every time she thought of it. *So did the thought of a no-strings encounter,* added a wicked voice.

And even though she was trying to avoid him, she couldn't look away. Much like most of the women in the room, she'd noticed with a spurt of something suspiciously…possessive. He was dressed in a tuxedo and he was simply breathtaking. He was the epitome of virile beauty, but with that undeniable edge of something dark and dangerous.

As if reading her mind, two women stopped nearby and, in that way of seeing but not seeing Nessa, because she was staff, they were whispering loudly enough for Nessa to catch snippets.

'Apparently he's an animal in bed…'

'They say he was found on the streets…'

'Petty crime…'

'Only got to where he has because he slept with Leo Fouret's wife and the husband bought him off to keep him quiet…'

Nessa went still at that, something cold trickling down her spine. She hadn't heard that final, particular rumour before. Although, he *had* apparently left Leo Fouret's stables under less than amicable circumstances, before blazing a trail on his own.

The women moved away and then more guests approached Nessa, relieving her of her remaining drinks. She was only too happy to escape back to the kitchen to stock up. Just before she left, she cast one last glance in Luc's direction, but his head was bowed towards someone in conversation.

Lambasting herself for having listened to gossip, no

matter how inadvertently, Nessa forged a path through the crowd and away from Luc. She told herself that she wasn't remotely interested in what the women had been saying. And that she was truly pathetic to be feeling the tiniest bit sorry for him that he was surrounded by such fervent gossip in the first place.

There was no smoke without a fire, as her father loved to say on a regular basis. And from what she'd seen of Luc in action, she could almost forgive a married woman for falling under his spell.

'What on earth is Nessa O'Sullivan doing serving drinks at your party, Barbier? I'd hardly think she's short of a few bob!'

It took a second for Luc to register what the man beside him had said and when he did his wandering attention snapped into sharp focus. 'You know her?'

The man snorted. 'Of course I do—you forget Ireland is a small place. Her father is Paddy O'Sullivan, one of this country's best trainers—at one time. Before he hit the bottle and almost lost everything. Now of course they're back on top of the world, although I don't think Paddy will ever repair the damage to his reputation. Still, he doesn't need to now, not with the goldmine he's sitting on thanks to his son-in-law.'

Luc usually had an aversion to gossip but not this time. 'What are you talking about?'

Percy Mortimer, a well-known English racing pundit, turned to Luc. 'Nessa O'Sullivan is related to royalty—her older sister—who incidentally is also a very talented amateur trainer—is married to the supreme Sheikh Nadim Al-Saqr of Merkazad. He bought out their stud a few years back. Nessa's not a bad rider.

I've seen her in a couple of races over the years, but she doesn't seem to have made a proper impression yet.'

What the hell? Luc barely heard that last bit. Sheikh Nadim was a very serious contender in racing circles, and a billionaire. And Luc had had no idea that he owned a stables just down the road. *Nessa's family stud.* He reeled, although he didn't show it.

Percy was saying something else but Luc wasn't listening. His gaze was already scanning the crowd for a dark redhead. He'd seen her earlier—looking once again as if butter wouldn't melt, dressed in her white shirt and skirt. Even that small glimpse had been enough to cause a spike in his heart-rate.

Damn. Where was she, anyway?

Luc tried to move away but saw a group headed for him with Pascal leading the way. The look on Pascal's face told Luc that he had to stay exactly where he was.

Nessa would have to wait, for now. But he would track her down and this time there would be no games. Only answers to his questions. Like what the hell was she playing at, working for nothing to pay off her brother's debt when presumably she could ask for a handout from her billionaire brother-in-law?

Nessa's feet and arms were aching, and she knew she shouldn't be here, but after the party had finished and they'd been released, she found herself gravitating towards the stallions' stables. As if pulled by some magnetic force. As if that could help to ground her and fuse her scattered energies back together.

She'd been acutely conscious of Luc's every movement, all evening.

At one stage she'd caught his eye and it had seemed as if he was trying to communicate something telepathically. From the grim look on his face it hadn't been something particularly nice. And then, even though she'd skirted around the edges of the room, keeping far out of his orbit for the rest of the evening, she could have sworn she felt his dark gaze boring into her periodically.

She came to a stop in the middle of the stables when she realised that they were empty. She looked around and remembered belatedly that the stallions had been moved up to different paddocks and stables for a few days while these were being repainted and renovated.

There were white sheets piled high in a corner along with painting and cleaning paraphernalia. Nessa told herself it was just as well as she turned around to leave. The last thing she needed was to be caught again in the wrong place—

Her heart stopped when she saw the tall broad figure blocking the doorway, with only the moon behind him as a silhouette. Too late. *Luc.*

She could see that his bow-tie was undone and top button open, his jacket swinging loose and his hands in the pockets of his trousers.

He moved forward into the stables and she saw his stern expression revealed in the dim lighting. Immediately the space felt claustrophobic. Nessa's body tingled with awareness as he came close enough for her to see that there was also barely leashed anger in his expression.

She swallowed. 'I know I shouldn't be here—'

'That's not important. We need to have a little chat.'

Surprise robbed her voice for a moment and then she said, 'About what?'

Luc folded his arms. 'About why you've omitted to mention the not inconsequential fact that your sister is married to Sheikh Nadim Al-Saqr of Merkazad, *and* that he owns your stud farm.'

He continued, 'I'd imagine one million euro is short change to Sheikh Nadim Al-Saqr, so what the hell is Paddy doing jeopardising his career for a handout he could've begged off his brother-in-law, and why didn't *you* just pick up the phone to Nadim to sort this mess out?'

Nessa went hot and then cold as the significance of this sank in, and the realisation that someone must have recognised her at the party.

She said carefully, 'I didn't think it was relevant.'

Luc looked even more stern. 'Not good enough.'

Nessa swallowed. She knew she couldn't avoid an explanation. 'Nadim *did* buy our farm but he put it back into our name as a wedding gift for Iseult, my sister. It's ours again, he's just one of the shareholders. And I didn't want to involve him because this has nothing to do with Nadim or Iseult. My sister is due to have a baby in a couple of weeks and they don't need the stress.'

Luc stepped closer but Nessa was trapped, with a stable door at her back and nowhere to go. She was acutely aware of his tall, lean body and his scent.

'There's more to it than that,' he said. 'You and your brother avoiding asking for help just proves you're both involved in something that's gone beyond your control. I'm guessing Nadim wouldn't approve, and you don't want to bite the hand that feeds you.'

In a fierce low voice Nessa replied, '*No.* It's nothing like that. Why must you be so cynical and mistrustful?'

'Because,' he answered smoothly, 'I was born that way and nothing I've experienced has ever proved me wrong. Life favours the opportunistic. I should know.'

I was born that way. Nessa couldn't stop a rush of

curiosity and pity. The second time she'd pitied him this evening. But then she crushed it. Luc Barbier was the last man on the planet who needed anyone's pity.

He said, 'You could be free to walk away if you asked Nadim for help.'

Luc heard himself say the words even as something inside him rejected it immediately. Let her walk away? A hot surge of possessiveness rose up inside him. *He wanted her.*

She was looking at him, eyes huge, and for a second he could almost have imagined that she looked...*hurt.* A ridiculous notion.

Nessa shook her head and some long tendrils of red hair framed her face. 'No. I will not take the easy way out and cause my family distress. I promised Paddy that I wouldn't go to Nadim or Iseult.'

Luc was intrigued by this apparent loyalty. 'Give me one good reason why I shouldn't go to Nadim myself.'

An expression of panic crossed her face. 'I thought you didn't want this news to get out either!'

'I don't. But from what I know of the Sheikh, I think he would appreciate the need for discretion on his family's behalf. It would affect his name and reputation too.'

Nessa wrung her hands in front of her and it only drew Luc's attention to where the shirt strained slightly over her breasts. He dragged his gaze up.

'You have no right to involve them.'

Now he really wanted to know why she was being so stubborn on this. 'Give me one reason, Nessa, and make it a good one.'

She looked at him as if he was torturing her and then she answered with palpable reluctance. 'When our mother died Iseult was only twelve; I was eight. Our father couldn't cope with the grief. He went off the rails, and developed a drink problem. Iseult went to school, but she did the bare minimum so that she could take care of the farm, the horses and all of us.'

Nessa glanced away for a moment, her face pale. Luc felt at an uncharacteristic loss as to what to say but she looked back at him and continued. 'If it wasn't for Iseult shielding us from the worst of our father's excesses and the reality of the farm falling to pieces, we never would have made it through school. She shouldered far too much for someone her age…and then Nadim came along and bought the farm out and she felt as if she'd failed us all at the last hurdle.'

Nessa drew in a breath. 'But then they fell in love and got married, and for the first time in her life she's really secure and happy.'

'Married to a billionaire, conveniently enough.' The cynical comment was said before Luc had even properly thought about it, and it felt hollow on his lips.

Nessa's hands clenched to fists by her sides. 'Iseult is the least materialistic person I know. They love each other.'

Luc was a bit stunned by her vehemence. 'Go on.'

She bit her lip for a moment, and he had to stop himself from reaching out to tug it free of those small white teeth.

'My sister is truly happy for the first time in a long time. The only responsibility she now bears is to her own family. They had problems getting pregnant after Kamil so this pregnancy has been stressful. If she knew what was going on she'd be devastated and worried, and Nadim would do everything he could to help her. He might even insist on coming all the way over here, and she needs him with her now.'

She added impetuously, 'If you do talk to Nadim,

I'll leak it to the press about the money going astray. Maybe they'll be easier on Paddy than you've been.'

Luc just looked at Nessa for a long moment, and he had to admit with grudging reluctance that her apparent zeal to protect her family was very convincing. He'd never seen a mother bear with cubs, but he had an impression of it right now. And he didn't like how it had affected him when she'd mentioned her sister's happy family. For a second he'd actually felt something like envy.

It reminded him uncomfortably of when he'd been much younger and he and other kids from the flats would go into Paris to pick pockets or whatever petty crime they could get away with. Stupid kids with nothing to lose and no one at home to care what they got up to.

One day Luc had been mesmerised by a family playing in a park—a mother, father and two children. The kids had looked so happy and loved. An awful darkness had welled up inside him and he'd tasted jealousy for the first time. And something far more poignant—a desire to know what that would be like.

His friends had noticed and had teased Luc unmercifully, so he'd shoved that experience and those feelings deep down inside and had vowed never to envy anyone again. And he wasn't about to start now.

But eclipsing all of that now was the carnal hunger building inside him. He'd thought of little else but that incendiary kiss the other night. When he'd sought Nessa out after the party he'd told himself he could resist her. But the thick sexual tension in the air mocked him.

She called to him, even in those plain, unerotic clothes. She called to him, deep inside where a dark hunger raged and begged for satisfaction.

Suddenly it didn't matter who she was related to. Or if she was playing mind-games. She threw up too many questions, but there was only one question he was interested in knowing the answer to right now, and that was how she would feel when he sank deep inside her.

Luc closed the distance between them, and reached out to slide a hand around Nessa's neck, tugging her closer. Her eyes went wide and her cheeks bloomed with colour. She put a hand up to his and said, 'What are you doing?'

Luc's gaze was fixated on her mouth and he had to drag it away to look into those huge hazel eyes. 'Do you really expect me to believe that you're just an innocent who would do anything for her family? And that the other night was pure chance and chemistry?'

For a taut moment, Luc held his breath because he realised that some small kernel of the little boy he'd once been, yearning for something totally out of his orbit, was still alive inside him. He waited for Nessa to gaze up at him with those huge eyes and move closer, to tell him in a husky voice, *Yes, I'm really that innocent.* The worst of it was, he wasn't entirely sure that he wouldn't believe her.

But she didn't. She tensed and pulled back, jerking free of Luc's hand. Glaring up at him. 'I don't *expect* you to believe anything, Luc Barbier. You've got eyes in your head and if you choose to view the world through a fog of cynicism and mistrust then that's your prerogative.

'As for the other night—it was madness and a mistake. You won't have to worry why it happened because it won't happen again.'

Nessa had almost moved past Luc when his shocked brain kicked into gear and he caught her hand, stopping her. Every cell in his body rejected what she'd just said. She was walking away again. A savage part of himself rose up, needing to prove that she wasn't as in control as she appeared.

He pulled her back in front of him. 'You want me.'

She bit her lip and looked down. She shook her head. Luc tipped her chin up feeling even more savage. 'Say it, Nessa.'

She looked at him, eyes huge and swirling with emotion but Luc couldn't draw back now. Eventually she said with a touch of defiance, 'I might want you but I don't want to.'

Something immediately eased inside him. She glanced down again as if by not looking at him she could avoid the issue.

'Look at me, Nessa.'

For a long moment she refused but then she looked up, eyes spitting golden sparks, and it ignited the fire inside him to a burning inferno of need. He pulled her closer again. She put her hands up to his chest. 'No, Luc. I don't want—'

But he stopped her words with his mouth and used every ounce of his expertise to show her how futile her resistance was. Whatever else was happening around them, whatever she was saying, he could trust that this was true at least.

CHAPTER FIVE

NESSA WANTED TO resist Luc—she really did. She hated that he still patently believed she'd orchestrated the other night. And that he most likely didn't believe what she'd told him about her family.

But it was hard to think of all of that when his mouth was on hers and he was sliding his tongue between her lips and possessing her with such devastating ease. Big hands moved down her back to her buttocks, cupping them and bringing her in close to where she could feel the bold thrust of his arousal. For her. Not for one of the stunningly beautiful women at the party. *Her.* Nessa O'Sullivan.

He drew back then and Nessa realised she was welded to him. Arms and breasts crushed against his chest. One arm kept her clamped to him, not letting her escape for a moment. He undid her hair so that it fell around her shoulders. He looked at it for a moment as if mesmerised and something inside Nessa melted.

He wrapped some hair around his hand and gently tugged so that her head came back. And then he kissed her again, dragging her deeper and deeper into the pit of a fire that she knew she couldn't walk away from again. She'd barely been able to the last time.

He pulled her skirt up until she felt cool air skate over

her heated skin. He palmed the flesh of her buttocks and the place between her legs burned with damp heat.

She broke away from the kiss, breathing rapidly, and looked at him. Her heart was racing. She couldn't look away from his eyes. They held her to account and she couldn't lie.

'What do you want, Nessa?' His fingers moved tantalisingly close to the edge of her panties. Her breathing quickened. One finger slid under the material, stroking. Her legs were weak.

'Do you want me to stop?'

No! shouted every fibre of her being. Nessa couldn't explain it and wasn't sure if she even wanted to investigate it, but she realised at that moment that she trusted him. She wasn't sure *what* she trusted exactly. Maybe it was that he wouldn't lie to her or spout platitudes. And so she convinced herself that if she said yes to this… whatever it was…she'd be under no illusions that emotions were involved.

He drew back marginally. 'Nessa?' And there it was—a glimmer of concern, showing a side to this darkly complex man that she suspected not many people ever got to see. She knew he would let her go if she insisted, even if his pride demanded her capitulation. Even as they both knew she would capitulate all too easily. But, she wanted this man with every cell in her body. She'd never wanted anything as much.

'Don't stop,' she whispered, reaching up to wind her arms around his neck again, pressing her mouth to his. Luc didn't hesitate. He gathered her even closer and backed her into the stall behind them, where she'd seen all the white sheets piled up in readiness for the work.

Nessa felt a soft surface at the backs of her legs that swiftly gave way, and she fell into the pile of sheets.

Luc looked down at Nessa, sprawled before him. Her skirt was up around her smooth thighs, and her untucked shirt strained across her chest. Her red hair spilled across the white fabric. It was probably one of the least romantic settings for lovemaking, but it was one of the most erotic sights Luc had ever seen. He was no longer aware of anything but the pounding in his blood and the need he felt in every cell of his body.

A small voice tried to get through to him, to remind him that he was no longer this uncivilised man, but it fell on deaf ears as he started to take off his clothes with the singular intention of joining their naked bodies as soon as possible.

Nessa stared up at Luc. The intense expression on his face might have scared her if she didn't feel as though she might have a similar expression on her face. He pulled off his jacket, dropping it to the ground, and then his bow tie. He started to open his shirt and Nessa's eyes grew wide as his magnificent chest was revealed bit by glorious bit until he was naked from the waist up. She could hardly breathe.

He came down over her, arms bracketing around her body, and his head dipped to hers, mouths fusing again in a series of long, drugging kisses that made Nessa want more, much more.

By the time he was opening her shirt, she was arching her back towards him in silent supplication. He pushed apart the material and pulled down the lace cups of her bra, exposing her breasts to his dark gaze as he rested on one arm beside her.

'Si belle...' he murmured before dipping his head and surrounding one tight peak in wet heat. Nessa might have screamed, she wasn't sure. She just knew that Luc's mouth on her bare flesh was almost more than she could bear. And he was remorseless, ignoring her pleas for mercy.

His mouth moved down over her belly, and he pulled up her skirt so that it was ruched around her waist. He stopped for a moment and looked at her in the dim light, watching her expression as his hand explored under the waist of her panties before gently pushing them down her legs.

Nessa sucked in a breath. This was more exposed than she'd ever been in her life, and yet it didn't scare her. She felt exhilarated.

Luc's gaze moved down her body and his hand rested between her legs, cupping her. Slowly, he started to move his hand against her and Nessa gripped his arms like an anchor.

He watched her again as one finger explored in a circle, through her secret folds of flesh and then right into the heart of her. Nessa's back arched and she squeezed her eyes shut. It was sensory overload. Her legs were splayed and Luc's hand was a wicked instrument of torture, as one finger became two, stretching her.

She lifted her head. 'I can't…' Was that her voice? So needy and husky?

'Can't what, *chérie*?'

'Can't cope…what you're doing, it's too much…'

He smiled and it was the smile of the devil. 'It's not nearly enough. *Yet.* Come fly with me, *minou*. Come on…'

She didn't understand what he was asking, but then he flicked his finger against the very heart of her. She tumbled blindly over an edge she had no chance of saving herself from.

If Luc had ever wanted to assert his dominance, he just had. With pathetic ease.

It took a long moment for Nessa to come back to her senses. She felt undone but deliciously sated. And yet there was something deeper, throbbing with need inside her, an instinctive knowledge of something even greater to come.

'*Ca va?*'

Nessa opened her eyes to see Luc looking at her. If he'd looked smug or remotely triumphant she might have wakened from this craziness but he didn't. He looked slightly…fascinated.

She nodded. She didn't know what she was but it was better than *okay*.

Luc's hand moved up to cup her breast, fingers finding and pinching her nipple lightly. Immediately her body was humming again, as if she hadn't just orgasmed.

She realised that Luc's chest was within touching distance and reached out shyly to touch him. Tentative, but growing more adventurous when she felt how warm he was, and the latent steel of his body underneath.

'You really don't have to pretend, *minou.*'

He sounded slightly amused. Nessa's hand stopped and she looked at him. 'Pretend…what are you talking about?'

'Pretend to be some kind of innocent. I told you I don't get off on games. It's really not necessary. I want you, more than I've ever wanted anyone else.'

She wasn't pretending; she *was* innocent! His face suddenly looked stark, as if he hadn't meant to say those words, and treacherously it robbed her of any words of defence. Somehow she knew that if she said anything, this would all stop and she wasn't ready for it to be over.

So she did the most selfish thing she'd ever done

in her life and said nothing. She touched him again, placing her mouth over his blunt nipples and exploring with her tongue, feeling ridiculously powerful when she heard him hiss between his teeth and felt him catch her hair again, winding it around his hand as if he needed to restrain her.

It was an incredible aphrodisiac to know she had any kind of effect on Luc Barbier.

She explored further, down his body, tracing her fingers over abs so tight that her own quivered in response. And then she reached his belt. There was a moment, and then he said gruffly, 'Keep going.'

So she undid the belt, sliding it through the loops, then his button and the zip. She could feel the potent thrusting bulge under the material and her hand started to shake as she drew the zip down.

Luc muttered something in French and then he was standing up and pushing his trousers down and off, taking his underwear with them. And now he was naked and fully aroused and Nessa couldn't speak, taking in his virile majesty.

'Touch me.'

Nessa sat up and reached out, curling her hand tentatively around Luc's rigid erection. She found it fascinating—the silky skin pulled taut over all that potent strength. There was a bead of moisture at the top, and, acting completely on instinct, she leant over and touched it with her tongue, tasting the tart saltiness. Her mouth watered and she wanted to wrap her whole mouth around him but he was pulling her away saying, 'Stop…or I won't last.'

Luc's brain was so fused with lust and heat and need that it was all he could do not to thrust between the tempting lushness of Nessa's lips. All rational thought had gone. He couldn't wait. He needed to feel her whole body around him, not just her mouth.

He moved over her, between her spread legs, and for a second the way she was looking up at him, with some expression he'd never seen on a woman's face before, almost made him stop, and take a breath. This was too crazy. Too rushed. He needed to get his wits back...

But then he felt her hands on his hips as if guiding him into her and he was lost again, drowning in need.

Nessa was filled with a raw sense of earthy urgency so sharp and intense she found herself reaching for Luc, wanting to bring him closer. He knelt between her legs, spreading them wider with his hands.

Nessa was vaguely aware that her shirt was open, her breasts bared and her skirt ruched around her waist. But any selfconsciousness fled when the head of his erection nudged against where she was so hot and wet. She instinctively circled her hips up to meet him.

Nothing could have prepared her though for that first cataclysmic penetration. She felt impaled. Luc was too big. He looked at her for a moment with a line between his brows and her heart stopped. *Did he know?* But then he slid in a little further. The discomfort faded as he filled her more, all the way until she couldn't breathe.

As he started to move in and out he lifted her leg and wrapped it around his hip, making him move even deeper inside her. Nessa was clasping his shoulders, needing something to hold onto as tension wound into a tight ball deep inside her.

She'd never felt anything like the glorious glide of his body in and out of hers. She was utterly consumed with the moment and what this man was doing to her.

She wrapped both legs around him now, digging her heels into his buttocks, wanting, needing more. Sweat made their skin glisten and their breathing was harsh as they both raced to the pinnacle of the climb.

Luc's movements became faster and Nessa could only cling on for dear life as the oncoming storm hurtled towards her. He arched her up towards him and found a nipple with his hot mouth, sucking it deep, and at that moment Nessa was flung into the eye of the storm and she cried out a release that went on, and on, and on.

Luc went taut above her and she felt the warm rush of his release inside her but at that point her brain was too burnt out to think of anything else but the oblivion that extreme pleasure brought in its wake.

After a long moment, with Luc's body embedded in hers, Nessa felt as if she were claiming him. Immediately she rejected it as a ridiculous notion. Luc Barbier was not a man who would ever be claimed. That much was obvious.

She unlocked her arms from around his neck. His breath was warm against her neck. He moved then and she winced as tender muscles protested. He didn't look at her as he pulled away and stood up.

Nessa felt self-conscious and realised how wanton she must look, spreadeagled and with her clothes in total disarray. She started to pull her shirt back over her chest, and her skirt down, feeling cold. She had no idea how to behave in this unorthodox and totally new situation to her—post-sex etiquette. In a stables. On sheets.

Luc was just standing there, half turned away, like a statue. Nessa's hands stilled and she came up on one elbow. Something caught her attention, a long angry scar that zigzagged down Luc's back. She remembered feeling it under her hand in the throes of passion. But it hadn't registered fully.

She sat up. 'What is that on your back?'

Finally, he looked at her and his face was expressionless. Little alarm bells went off.

'My scar?'

She nodded, horrified to imagine him suffering such violence.

'It's a reminder from a long time ago to not forget who I am or where I came from.'

Nessa didn't like how it almost sounded like a warning. 'That sounds serious.'

Luc looked at her. 'My scar isn't serious. What is serious is that we didn't use protection.'

Nessa insides seized with icy panic when she remembered feeling the warm rush of his release. How could she have let that happen?

And then she ordered her sluggish brain to kick into gear and breathed a sigh of relief, tinged with something much more disturbing, like regret. Which was crazy. After her experience losing her mother, Nessa had never relished the prospect of becoming a mother that could die and potentially devastate her family. No matter how cute her little nephew was, or how envious she felt when she saw his special bond with her sister.

She'd taken birth control in college but had stopped soon after leaving, not deeming it necessary when it had never been necessary there. Now she felt supremely naive and foolish.

She forced herself to look at Luc. 'I'm at a safe place in my cycle.'

Luc made a mirthless, almost bitter sound. 'I'm supposed to take your word for it?'

Anger surged at herself for being so lax and at his accusatory tone. She stood up, pulling her shirt together and her skirt down, hair wild and loose. She mustered up every atom of dignity she could given the circumstances and said coolly, 'Well, you'll have to just take my word for it. There were two of us involved, so why weren't *you* thinking of protection?'

Because for the first time in a long time he'd been a slave to his base desires, and protection had been the last thing on his mind.

The realisation sent shards of jagged panic into Luc's guts. How could he have forgotten one of his most stringent rules? He, who had vowed never to have children because he had no desire for a family. Family was anathema to him. And to forget that with this woman, of all women? She was the one most likely to turn around now and use this for her own gain. He might as well have just handed her a loaded gun.

Except even now, Luc was still acutely aware of Nessa's state of déshabillé and how much he wanted to tip her back onto the sheets and take her again. He reached for his trousers, pulling them on angrily, disgusted with his lack of self-control.

He was in the grip of a tumult inside him that he didn't know how to decipher or necessarily want to. All he knew was that what had just happened between him and this woman left anything else he'd ever experienced in the dust. It hadn't just been mind-blowing sex. It had been something else. Something that had affected him on another level.

More disgust ran through him—he'd just done what he expressly forbade his own employees from doing. And now he'd made things exponentially worse by not using protection.

Nessa was looking at him and he realised she was pale. He knew he was being a bastard—it had been his responsibility to protect them. Not hers. He ran a hand through his hair. 'Look, I'm sorry. I just… I don't ever forget about something as fundamental as protection.'

She still looked pale and his chest felt tight. 'What's wrong?' *Had he hurt her?* He was so much bigger than her and the last thing on his mind had been taking care, or being gentle.

What's wrong? What's right? Nessa glanced away for a moment feeling ridiculously vulnerable, and even more so after his apology. She hadn't expected cuddles and a heart-to-heart after sex with this man—no matter how much lust had clouded her brain. But she also hadn't expected him to be so obviously angry with himself.

He hadn't even noticed that she was a virgin. He'd thought she was acting innocent.

She forced herself to look at him and for a second could have almost imagined she'd dreamed up the last hour. He was dressed again, albeit without his tie and jacket. She still felt thoroughly dishevelled and at a disadvantage, and suddenly she wanted to pierce that cool disdain and self-recrimination.

'I don't know what this is between us but I'm not proud of myself,' she said.

Luc looked at her with no discernible change in his expression, but then she saw the merest flash of something almost like hurt cross his face. He stepped closer, and she could see his eyes burning and a muscle jumping in his jaw.

'You might be related to royalty but if you were seated at a banquet table right now and dressed head to toe in couture, you would still want me. Lust makes great levellers of all of us. As does crime,' he answered.

It took a second for Nessa to absorb what he'd said. She couldn't believe he'd misunderstood her. He turned away at that moment and, in spite of the turmoil she was feeling, she reached out, wrapping a hand around his arm. 'Stop.'

He turned around.

She swallowed. 'I didn't mean that I wasn't proud because it was *you*. I meant that I'm not proud because I feel like I'm betraying my family.'

His lip curled. 'It's just sex, Nessa. Don't overthink it.'

She immediately felt silly for opening her mouth. She let his arm go and stepped back. 'Forget I said anything.'

She was about to step around him and make her exit to lick her wounds and castigate herself for being so weak but this time he took her arm, stopping her and asking harshly, 'What is that?'

Nessa looked around and for a second couldn't see what he was looking at behind them. But then she noticed the unmistakable stain of red on the white sheets. Her blood. Her virginal blood.

She went icy cold, and then hot with humiliation. Quickly she stood in front of it. 'It's nothing.'

He moved her aside and looked closer. If the ground could have opened up and swallowed Nessa whole she would have jumped right in.

He looked at it for so long Nessa wished she'd taken the chance to escape. But then he moved back, and there was such a mix of expressions on his face that she was stunned into silence.

Luc couldn't believe what his eyes had just told him, and yet he couldn't stop thinking about all the moments when he'd thought she was putting on some act with the shy tentative kisses, the self-consciousness, and the way she'd run the other night.

But what beat at his brain most of all had been that

moment, when he'd felt her body clamping tight around him. It had made him stop, and look at her, but the question had barely formed in his mind before her muscles had been relaxing to let him go deeper, and he'd conveniently blocked the half-formed question out, too desperate to sate himself.

She'd been a *virgin*.

That knowledge filled him with too many things to untangle now. One of which was a fierce feeling of satisfaction that he'd been her first. It was something he'd never imagined feeling in a scenario like this.

'Why didn't you tell me?'

She opened her mouth and closed it again, and that only brought Luc's attention to those lush lips and how they'd felt on his body.

'Well?' he snapped. She flinched minutely and Luc bit back a curse at himself. He felt unmoored, boorish. Out of control.

A hint of defiance came into her eyes and it comforted him. This woman was no wilting lily.

'I didn't think it was relevant. Or that you'd notice.'

Luc burned inside at that. He had noticed but had dismissed it. 'I don't sleep with virgins.'

Nessa folded her arms and said tartly, 'Well, you just did.'

He felt the burn of more self-recrimination. 'If I'd known I wouldn't have been so…rough.'

Amazingly, Nessa blushed and glanced away. 'You weren't too rough.' She hesitated. 'It was okay.'

'Okay?'

She looked back at him. 'I mean, I don't know, do I? It was my first time.'

Her words propelled Luc forward and he caught her arms in his hands. She felt unbearably slender and delicate all of a sudden. He was acutely aware of how petite she was. 'It was more than *okay*. I felt your body's response, and not everyone has that experience for their first time.'

She blushed even more now but she stared at him. 'I'll have to take your word for it.'

Luc was torn between laughing out loud at her sheer front and tipping her back onto the sheets to remind her exactly how unbelievably good it had been. But she'd be sore, and frankly he didn't like the strength of the emotions running through him. This was not a post-sex scenario he had ever experienced before. Usually there was a bare minimum of conversation before he left. Right now it was hard to let her go.

In fact, he was afraid that the longer they stood there, the more likely it was that he *would* take her again. Especially when she was looking at him with those huge pools of amber and green. Her face flushed and hair wild. Clothes in disarray.

Doing something he'd never done before—exhibiting any kind of post-sex tenderness—he put his hands to the buttons of her shirt and did them up, gritting his jaw when he felt the swells of her breasts underneath the material.

He stood back. 'You should go. Take a bath. You'll be tender.'

She swallowed and for a moment looked endearingly unsure. And unbelievably sexy.

'*Go*, Nessa,' Luc growled, aware of the tenuous grip on his control.

She looked around at the sheet and made a gesture. 'I should take—'

'I'll take care of it.' This was unprecedented territory for Luc.

Finally, she left and Luc watched her walk out, slightly unsteadily. Her skirt was still at an angle and all he could see were those slim legs and remember how they'd felt clamped around his hips. She was a lot stronger than she looked.

Luc tried to make sense of what had just happened but it was hard. One thing was sure, though: Nessa O'Sullivan had just managed to impact somewhere no one had touched him in a long, long time. And if he was to consciously allow her to gain any more advantage, then he'd be the biggest fool. What just happened...it couldn't happen again. No matter how much he wanted her.

Nessa stayed in the bath until the water cooled and her skin had started to pucker. There was tenderness between her legs but also a lingering buzz of pleasure.

She couldn't quite believe the sequence of events that had led to that frantic coupling on sheets in a stables with Luc Barbier.

Her whole body got hot just recalling how quickly they'd combusted. How easily she'd given in, and given away her innocence. And, how easily she'd justified it to herself. *And you'd do it again right now if you could*, whispered a wicked little voice. Nessa knew it was true. She wouldn't have the strength to resist Luc again, not after that. It was like experiencing paradise and then having to deny it existed.

And while he wasn't here right now, cosseting her and whispering sweet nothings in her ear, the way he'd told her to leave and take a bath, and how he'd done up her buttons for her, had made her feel pathetically cared for.

She cringed and wanted to submerge herself under

the water when she thought of how Luc had to be seriously regretting what had happened. Nessa cringed even more to think of him disposing of the evidence of her virginity.

He was a man used to sleeping with the most beautiful women in the world: experienced worldly women, not naive innocents like Nessa.

She took a deep breath as if testing for emotional pain and she let it out shakily. Her emotions were intact. Luc had impacted her on a physical level but that was all, she assured herself.

Liar, mocked a voice. Seeing those slivers of the more complex man under his stern exterior, and his gruffly tender treatment at the end had moved her more than she cared to admit.

If she saw any more evidence of *that* Luc, she wasn't so sure her emotions would remain untouched. And forming an attachment to Luc Barbier would be a lesson in futility and pain. Of that she was certain.

One thing was clear. The moment of madness just now couldn't happen again. Not that Nessa imagined for a second that Luc wanted it to. His self-recrimination had been palpable, and that suited Nessa fine. *It did*, she told herself. No matter what her newly awakened body might be aching for in secret places.

CHAPTER SIX

LUC LOOKED AT the figure riding the horse and couldn't believe what he was seeing. The boy—for it had to be a boy, he was too slight to be a man—was riding one of his prize thoroughbreds as if he'd been riding her all his life.

Jockey and horse were one entity, cutting through the air like a bullet. He'd never seen the filly perform so well. And he already itched to see what the jockey would be like on Sur La Mer, back in France. He just knew instinctively that he could be the missing link to get the best out of the horse.

Luc looked at his chief Irish trainer. 'Okay, who is he and where has he been before now, and can we retain him immediately?' Luc knew how rare it was to find raw talent like this.

Pete had come to him a few minutes ago and just said enigmatically, *You need to see this.*

Pete grinned. 'He's a *she*.'

'What the—?' Luc looked back and his skin prickled with a kind of awareness. The jockey and horse came around the nearest corner and as they thundered past him he caught a glimpse of dark red hair tucked under the cap and a delicate jawline. He recalled Percy Mortimer saying Nessa was a good rider.

Luc's nervous system fizzed immediately, even before Pete said, 'It's Nessa O'Sullivan.'

For the past couple of days Luc had been ruthlessly crushing any memories or reminders of what had happened in the stables. At night, though, when he was asleep, he couldn't control his mind: his dreams were filled with X-rated memories. He'd woken every morning with a throbbing erection and every muscle screaming for release.

He hadn't been at the mercy of his body like this since his hormones had run wild as a teenager.

It was galling; humiliating.

And here she was again, provoking him.

Pete was looking at him. 'Well?'

Luc controlled himself with effort. 'What the hell is she doing on my horse?'

Pete's grin faded. He put up his hands in a gesture of supplication. 'I've known Nessa for years, Luc. I know her whole family. They've been riding horses since before they could walk. Her sister and father are excellent trainers. I've seen Nessa race—she's not done many, granted, but she's got her licence and she's a natural. We were short a rider today and so I asked Mrs Owens if I could borrow her. I don't know what she's doing working for your housekeeper, Luc, but she's wasted there. She should be out here. All she's been waiting for is an opportunity to prove herself.'

If it had been anyone else but his trusted and very talented trainer, and if Luc hadn't seen her with his own two eyes, he would have fired Pete on the spot. And he wasn't about to tell Pete why Nessa was working at the house.

He looked back at the gallops to see the riders dismounting and walking the horses back to the stables. He spotted her immediately, the smallest of the bunch, immediately bringing to mind how tight she'd felt when he'd breached her body. *Virgin. No protection.* And he still wanted her with a hunger that unnnerved him.

Oblivious to what was going on in his head, Pete said, 'Luc, I think you should use her in the next race. Give her a chance.'

Luc looked at Pete, provocation and frustration boiling over. 'You've done enough for now. I don't care how talented a jockey she is, she knew better than to say yes to your request.'

Nessa was still buzzing with adrenalin after exercising the horse, and chatting with the other riders, some of whom she knew. They'd all been curious as to why she was here but she'd kept it vague.

She was in the changing room and had just pulled off her mud-spattered top when the door slammed open and she whirled around, holding the shirt to her chest. 'Do you mind?'

But it wasn't Pete or one of the other riders entering the ladies' changing room near the racing stables. It was Luc Barbier and he looked murderous. The door shut behind him with an ominously quiet click, and the room was suddenly tiny.

She'd deliberately avoided thinking about Luc's reaction if he found out. Apparently for good reason.

He stood before the door in worn jeans and a black polo shirt. He'd never looked more forbiddingly sexy. Nessa's insides melted even as she tried to ignore her body's response. Luc hadn't come near her for the past couple of days, making it perfectly clear that the other night couldn't have been a bigger mistake. And while

Nessa agreed on every rational level, she hated to admit that she'd been hurt by the dismissal.

Guilt lanced her now. Had she agreed to Pete's request to fill in for one of the jockeys, knowing Luc wouldn't approve, to provoke a reaction? Nessa was afraid she knew the answer to that.

'What the hell do you think you're doing?' Luc's voice was quiet, which made him sound even angrier.

Nessa lifted her chin, refusing to be intimidated, clutching her top to her chest. 'Pete was short a rider and so he asked me if I'd fill in. I was just doing him a favour.' *Liar*, mocked a voice. The thrumming of her pulse told her very eloquently why she'd done it.

'You knew very well that you weren't allowed to go near the horses. I don't let anyone that I don't personally vet myself near them.'

Nessa tried not to sound defensive. 'Pete knows me. He's seen me ride before. And it wasn't his fault,' she said hurriedly, having visions of Luc sacking him. 'I knew I should have said no…but I couldn't resist. It's my fault.'

Once again Luc was struck somewhere uncomfortable at how readily Nessa was able to take the blame from someone else. Her brother, and now Pete, who wasn't even related to her.

As if physically incapable of allowing space between them, Luc moved closer, seeing how Nessa's hands tightened on her top. He commented, 'It's not as if I haven't seen you before.'

She blushed. Amazingly. And it had a direct effect on Luc's body, sending blood surging south.

She scooted her head and arms back into her top but not before Luc had seen a generous amount of pale flesh and her breasts encased in a sports vest top. Her hair was caught at the back of her head in a bun, and he curled his hands to fists to stop from reaching out and undoing it.

She folded her arms over her chest and then said stiffly, 'I'm sorry. It won't happen again.'

Luc made a split-second decision. 'I'm afraid that's not really up to you.'

She looked at him. 'What do you mean?'

'There's a race this weekend; I want you to ride the same filly you were just riding.'

She went pale, and then colour washed back into her cheeks. It was fascinating to see someone so expressive. And then she looked suspicious. 'You don't want me near your horses. Why would you let me do this?'

'Because I'm not stupid enough to let someone as naturally gifted as you waste your talent, especially not when it might win me a race. I am, after all, running a business. And your brother owes me a million euros, which you have taken on as your debt. If you win, the money will go towards paying it off.'

Nessa was so stunned by what he'd just proposed she was speechless for a long moment. Eventually she managed to get out, 'I…well, thank you.'

Luc was brusque. 'You'll obviously work to Pete's instruction from now on.'

Then he turned to walk back out and Nessa blurted out, 'Wait.'

When he stopped at the door he turned around and she almost lost her nerve, but she forced herself to ask, 'What about what happened? The other night.' *As if he wouldn't know what she was talking about.*

She cringed inwardly. She hated that she'd felt compelled to ask. She hated that she couldn't be as nonchalant as him, and pretend the other night had never happened.

Luc looked remote. Almost like a stranger. 'What happened between us won't happen again. It was a mistake. You're here to pay off the debt through racing or until your brother returns my money, whichever happens first.'

And then he walked out and she felt as if he'd just punched her in the belly. She was breathless, and then she castigated herself. Hadn't he warned her, that first night in his room, that she'd get burned?

She had nothing to entice a man like Luc Barbier beyond that brief moment of craziness.

And here he was offering her the opportunity of a lifetime—a chance to ride for one of the great trainer/owners in the racing world. Luc might have a rogue's reputation but no one could discredit his amazing accomplishments, even if they weren't quite sure how he'd achieved them without a background steeped in the industry.

Nessa had to concede that, from what she'd seen so far, his incredible work ethic was responsible for much of his success. Without fail, he was up with his earliest employee, and probably one of the last to bed. She'd even seen him help with mucking out a stables one day, practically unheard of for someone at his level.

Nessa told herself she should be relieved that Luc had laid out in brutal terms where they now stood in terms of their short-lived intimacy. Conducting an affair with a man like him was total folly at best and emotional suicide at worst. Not to mention the guilt she'd feel.

But the most humiliating part of it was knowing that

if he'd kissed her just now, she'd have been flat on her back on the cold tile floor, showing not an ounce of restraint or control.

'I can't believe she's actually won.'

'Never fail to surprise us, eh, Barbier?'

'A female jockey? Who is she? Has anyone heard of her? Where did she come from?'

'Trust Barbier to come from left-field with a win like this...he just can't resist throwing the cat amongst the pigeons...'

Luc heard all the indiscreet whispers around him, but he was too stunned to care. Nessa had won the race. Unbelievably. On the horse with the longest odds.

She was coming into the winner's enclosure now, with Pete not far behind accepting his own congratulations. Luc caught the horse as she passed, stopping her momentarily. Nessa had a huge grin on her mud-spattered face and something turned over inside him.

He patted the horse and looked up at her, at an uncharacteristic loss for words. Her smile faded and he noticed how she tensed and something inside him rejected that. Normally he never had a problem congratulating his jockeys but this was different. It was *her*. Eventually he said, 'Well done.'

'Thank you. I can't believe it myself.'

That glimmer of uncertainty on her face reminded him of how she'd looked the other night when she'd stood before him all mussed and flushed after sex. His body tightened with need.

She was led on, and then slid off the horse to be weighed after the race. Luc watched her across the enclosure. She took off her hat and her hair tumbled down. A man behind him made an appreciative whistling sound and Luc spun around, glaring at him. The man blanched.

When Luc looked back Nessa was walking away from the podium and stewards with her saddle, presumably to go back to the changing rooms.

Pascal Blanc hurried over to him at that moment, shaking his head and smiling. 'Luc, this is incredible. Nessa is a sensation; it's all people are talking about, wondering who she is and where she came from. You've both been invited to a function this evening in Dublin, celebrating the racing industry in Ireland. I don't think I need to tell you how important this is.'

Luc knew exactly how important it was. So far the industry here had largely been closed to him socially, but one win with an outsider filly and a beautiful young female jockey and suddenly he was being granted access.

Yes, said a voice. *This is it.* And yet now that the moment had arrived, all Luc could seem to think about was not the potential for acceptance at last, but what Nessa would look like in a dress.

'Is it really necessary for me to attend?' Nessa's gut was churning.

'Yes, it is,' Luc said, looking frustrated. They'd returned to the racing stables after the race and Luc had just informed Nessa about the function in Dublin that night.

She couldn't even begin to describe the trepidation she felt at the thought of some glitzy social event. She'd never been a naturally girly girl and her few experiences of dressing up had invariably ended in failure when she'd seen how wide of the mark she was with current trends.

There'd been one memorable incident in university when she'd gone to a party and a girl had said snarkily, *I didn't know it was a fancy dress party.* After that, Nessa had given up trying to fit in. She wasn't cool, or fashionable, or blessed with any innate feminine wiles or sensuality. Luc had proved that in no uncertain terms.

'I don't have anything suitable to wear to an event.'

Luc glanced at his watch. 'I've asked a stylist to come from a local boutique with a selection of dresses. She's also bringing someone to look after hair and make-up.'

Nessa felt as if a noose were tightening around her neck. Luc was still dressed in a three-piece suit, in deference to the dress etiquette of the races. It was distracting to say the least, especially in the way that it seemed to be moulded to his muscles.

'Why is it so important that I go? I'm just the jockey. They won't know who I am.'

Luc took out his mobile phone and, after a few seconds of swiping, handed it to Nessa. She gasped. It was a headline on an online racing journal. *Two gorgeous fillies triumph at the Kilkenny Gold Stakes!* And there was a photo of a beaming Nessa astride the horse, being led around the winner's enclosure.

'Unfortunate headlines aside, you're a sensation. Everyone could see, just from that race, how talented you are.'

Nessa handed the phone back, feeling a little sick. She'd wanted to do well, but she'd never expected this level of attention. The euphoria of the win was draining away to be replaced with anxiety. She'd never liked being front and centre, and certainly not in an environment outside her comfort zone.

Her sister Iseult had struggled with this kind of thing

too, but she'd since blossomed into a poised and elegent Sheikha of Merkazad. Even so, she had confessed to Nessa that she still found it hard sometimes to pretend that she was comfortable with dressing up.

But Nadim loved her no matter how she looked or what she wore. A pang lanced Nessa to think of their bond. She felt very alone all of a sudden.

'What's wrong?'

Luc's question jolted Nessa out of her reverie. He was frowning down at her, and she hated the thought of him seeing an ounce of the vulnerability she felt. She was being ridiculous. It was just an event.

She tipped up her chin. 'Nothing is wrong. What time should I meet the stylist?'

'They'll be here within the hour. I've asked Mrs Owens to move you to a bigger bedroom suite to accommodate you getting ready. We may have more events like this to go to. I'll meet you at the front of the house at seven p.m.'

Nessa looked at herself in the mirror and blinked. *Was that her?* She felt the same inside, but on the outside she looked like a stranger. Her hair was pulled back on one side and trailed over her other shoulder in a rippling cascade of glossy waves. She wore a shimmering black dress that clung to her shoulders in a wide vee, and showed what felt like acres of pale flesh.

It was gathered under her breasts and fell in a swathe of material to the floor. Under the dress she wore spindly delicate high heels that made her walk with her chest out and with an unnatural arch in her back.

Her make-up was discreet, at least, but it made her eyes look huge. Her lips glistened with flesh-coloured lipstick.

The stylist stood back and looked at her critically. 'You look stunning, Miss O'Sullivan.'

'Call me Nessa, please,' Nessa said weakly, feeling like a fraud.

The stylist looked at her watch as the hair and make-up girl tidied up her things.

'It's almost seven p.m. You should go down to meet Mr Barbier.' The stylist winked. 'What I wouldn't give to swap places with you right now. He is *gorgeous*.'

The make-up girl giggled, clearly of the same opinion. Nessa forced a smile and desisted from saying that she'd be more than happy to swap places. But they wouldn't understand.

She made her way downstairs, careful in the high-heels. When she got to the hallway the door was ajar and she went out. Luc was standing with his back to her on the steps, his hands in his pockets, the jacket material pulled taut across his back. It reminded her of the scar she'd seen and how he'd dismissed it so enigmatically.

For the brief moment before he turned around Nessa could almost imagine she was one of those beautiful women who populated his world, and that this was a date. But then he turned around, and those dark eyes raked her from head to toe without an ounce of emotion or expression on his face and Nessa didn't feel beautiful any more. She was remembering how he'd told her that first night that even if she'd come via the front door and dressed to impress, she still wouldn't be his type...

For a second Luc almost didn't recognise Nessa. His chest tightened and his whole body went taut with the need to control his instantaneous response.

She looked beautiful. She surpassed anything he could have possibly imagined, and yet there was nothing showy about her. She oozed understated elegance in the long black dress. His body lit on fire when he registered the low-cut vee and saw how much of her skin was exposed, including the pale swells of her breasts.

He dragged his gaze back up, feeling a little dizzy. He saw her biting her lip, and looking anxious. 'Is it okay?' she asked.

Luc was a little incredulous. Did she really have no idea how gorgeous she was? His reaction to her, and his instincts urging him to believe this wasn't an act, made his voice curt. 'It's fine. We should go.'

Nessa tried not to feel disappointed by Luc's reaction as he turned away and went down the steps, towards where a sleek four-wheeled drive was parked. The other night was a mistake, not to be repeated, and this was *not* a date.

She made her way across the courtyard after him in the vertiginous heels, praying she wouldn't sprain her ankle. He was holding a door open and she got in gingerly, holding the dress up so it wouldn't get caught.

Luc walked around the bonnet. Nessa couldn't help observing how good he looked in the tuxedo. When he was behind the wheel he drove them a few short miles to where a helipad was located, away from the racing stables and stud.

'We're going in a helicopter?'

He looked at her. 'It's an hour's drive to Dublin. The event starts in half an hour.'

Nessa tried her best to look nonchalant and not shocked. When she stepped out of the car, though, she stopped. The grass was soft and damp after recent rain and she wasn't sure how to navigate the terrain in her shoes from here to where the helicopter was waiting.

Luc came around the front of the car and saw her, obviously assessing her predicament. Nessa was about to bend down and take the shoes off, but before she could do so Luc had lifted her into his arms effortlessly and was striding towards the helicopter where a pilot was waiting by the open door.

Nessa clung to his neck breathlessly, burningly aware of his hard chest and strong arms. Luc however showed no such similar awareness when he deposited her into the seat with a grim expression and did up her seat belt before she could object. His hands glanced off her bare skin as he adjusted it and Nessa's blood fizzed.

She was glad when he sat in the front beside the pilot because she didn't want him to decipher what she was thinking. He couldn't have made it more glaringly obvious that she was just someone he was tolerating, until such a time as she ceased to be a thorn in his side.

When they'd put on their headphones he turned around. 'Okay?'

She nodded rapidly and forced a bright smile wanting to leave him under no illusion that she was anything other than *okay* and completely unmoved by what had happened between them.

They took off and, as much as she hated Luc Barbier right now, she couldn't help feeling emotional when they swooped low over the River Liffey in Dublin's city centre and she saw the capital city glittering like a jewel in the dusky evening light. It was magical.

They landed, and Nessa was saved the ignominy of being carried again as she was able to walk to the car waiting for them. Luc sat in the back with her, and the plush interior, which looked huge, felt tiny with him so close to her.

The journey to Dublin Castle took ten minutes and soon they were pulling up in the majestic forecourt. Lights shone out onto the cobbles as a glittering array of people were disgorged from sleek cars. And Nessa—who had just won her first prestigious race on a thoroughbred horse—had never felt more terrified in her life.

Luc got out and came around to help Nessa out. She looked at his hand for a moment, hesitating, and then took it, letting him help her. As soon as she was standing, though, she let go as if burned.

Luc figured that he couldn't blame her after his less than gracious reaction to how she looked. He'd never been less charming. With other women he at least put on a show of being civilised. But with Nessa, he didn't know where to put himself.

When he'd picked her up to carry her over the grass to the helicopter it had been purely for expediency, but it had been torture to feel her slender frame curling into his, her arms around his neck. He'd been as hard as a rock for the entire journey.

It irritated the hell out of him that he'd made it more than clear that what had happened between them was a one-off mistake, and she didn't seem in the least inclined to try and change his mind.

Mind you, in a dress like the one she was wearing, she didn't have to do much. He was already aware of men around them looking at her twice. He was also aware of the way he felt inclined to bundle her back into the car, and take her straight to some private place where he could lay her out on a bed and make love to her as he *hadn't* done the first time.

Her first time. Surely, whispered a wicked little voice, *she deserves to know what it can really be like?*

Luc shut it down and put out his arm for Nessa to take. He had the feeling when she slipped her arm through his that she was only touching him to stay upright in those vertiginous heels. They added inches to her height and only made him more aware of how much closer her mouth would be to his.

Then he noticed how pale she was. He stopped just before they walked into the pool of golden light spilling out onto the beautiful enclosed courtyard of the castle. 'Is something wrong?'

She shook her head and glanced at him briefly, shooting him a fake smile. 'Everything is fine. Why wouldn't it be?'

'Because you look like you're about to walk the plank rather than walk amongst your peers at one of the highest profile society events of the year.'

She made an inelegant snorting sound. 'Peers? Don't make me laugh.'

Luc was shocked at the bitter tone to her voice. He'd never heard it before. But before he could ask her what she meant, a young officious woman in a long violet gown was coming forward to greet them. She was the PR lady. 'Mr Barbier, Miss O'Sullivan, we're so grateful you could both join us at short notice. Please, do come this way.'

They were led through the marbled foyer into a huge ceremonial room where the drinks reception was being held before the dinner. Luc noticed people turning to look, and how their eyes widened when they saw who it was. He usually would have wanted to snarl at them that he had as much of a right to be here as they did. But for the first time, he found himself not really caring how they were looking at him.

He was too distracted by the woman by his side.

They were served with champagne and Nessa took her arm out of Luc's. Perversely he wanted to take it back. She was looking up at him with a minute smile playing around her mouth. He said, 'What?'

'You said I looked as if I was about to walk the plank but you look as if you're about to take someone's head off.'

Luc relaxed his features, unnerved she'd read him so well.

'Haven't you been to this event before?' she asked.

Luc took a healthy swig of champagne and shook his head. 'No. They've never deigned to invite me. I was too much on the edges of acceptability for them.'

'So you don't want to be here?'

Luc looked out over the crowd and noted the furtive glances he drew. 'Whether or not I want to be here is beside the point. I've worked as hard as anyone here, harder, perhaps. I deserve to be respected and not stared at like an exhibit in a zoo. I deserve to be here.'

As soon as he'd spoken, he was shocked he'd let the words spill out. In a bid to divert Nessa away from asking more questions, he turned to her. 'What was that outside…? You made a comment.'

She flushed and took a sip of her own drink. Luc noted that her hands were tiny, with short, functional nails and clear varnish, unlike the elaborate claws many women sported. He also noticed that her hands looked softer already. His body thrummed with an arousal he was barely able to keep in check, especially when his taller vantage point gave him an all too enticing view of her cleavage.

'I didn't mean anything by it.'

Luc's gaze narrowed on her. 'Nessa…'

She rolled her eyes. 'I don't count these people as my peers, not really.'

'Why? You come from the same world. You have

a family lineage in racing to rival any one of these guests.'

'Perhaps. But that counts for nothing when you're losing it all. When my father got ill and the stud started to go downhill, most of these people turned their backs on us, as if we were cursed. See that man over there?'

Luc followed her eyeline to a portly man with a face flushed from drink. The man caught Nessa's eye and went even redder, sidling out of sight like a crab disappearing under a rock.

'Who is he?' Luc asked.

'He's P J Connolly. Used to be one of my father's oldest friends. They grew up together. He runs the state-owned stud. He was in a position to help us out but he never did. It was only when Nadim bought us out and the farm started to recover that we became personae gratae again.'

Luc was stunned. He hadn't expected to feel any sort of affinity with Nessa. He'd assumed she'd be air-kissing old friends and acquaintances within minutes, but she too knew how the cold sting of rejection felt.

She turned back to him then and looked up. 'How *do* you know so much about horses? I can't believe it was just through your work with Leo Fouret.'

Luc balked at her question. Most people were usually too intent on believing one of the many rumours about him to ask him such a question directly.

'Didn't you hear?' he said with a lightness he didn't feel. 'I'm descended from gypsies.'

Nessa just looked at him and cocked her head to one side as if considering it. 'I don't think so.'

A weight lodged in Luc's chest at her easy dismissal of such a lurid claim. At that moment the PR lady came back to them, smiling widely. 'Mr Barbier, Miss

O'Sullivan, there are a few people who would love to congratulate you on your win today. Please follow me.'

The weight in Luc's chest didn't abate as the woman led them further into the room. No one had ever looked at him as Nessa just had, without any guile or expectation for a salacious story.

CHAPTER SEVEN

NESSA WAS STILL irritated by the interruption earlier. Luc had looked as if she'd delivered an electric shock rather than asked an innocuous question. She was also still mulling over how he'd been deliberately ostracised from this milieu, and how it had obviously affected him.

They had just finished the sumptuous dinner when Nessa snuck a glance to where Luc was seated opposite her. He was talking to an older woman on his right-hand side, and as Nessa looked at him his eyes met hers and a shaft of sensation went straight into her gut.

She quickly looked away and put her napkin to her mouth, almost knocking over her glass in the process, in a bid to disguise that she'd been staring. When she could risk another glance, she saw the tiniest smile playing around the corners of his mouth, and it couldn't have been due to what the woman was saying because she looked all too serious.

Damn him. Nessa wanted to kick him. He must know exactly what his effect on her was—he'd been the one to awaken her, after all. She felt intensely vulnerable and averted her eyes from then on. Then the chairman got up to make a speech, so thankfully she could focus on that and not Luc. She tuned most of it out except the bit where he said, '…and we'd like to say welcome to our newest import, all the way from France. Luc Barbier stunned the crowds today with a spectacular win…'

Nessa looked at Luc and saw him incline his head in acknowledgement of the chairman's gushing praise. The expression on his face was cool, not for a second revealing anything. Nessa wondered what he was thinking. She was surprised at the affront she felt on his behalf that he hadn't ever been invited before now.

Then she got a mention too and her face flamed bright red as everyone in the room turned their attention to her.

When the speech was over the guests got up to go to a different room where soft jazz was playing. Nessa felt awkward standing alone, not sure if Luc was going to leave her to her own devices now that everyone was lining up to speak to him. She longed to take off the shoes, which were killing her, but to her surprise Luc came straight around the table and walked up to her.

'So, what was making you look so angry during the chairman's speech?'

Nessa blanched. She was far too expressive for her own good, useless at hiding anything. The thought of him noticing her reaction was beyond exposing. Luc wasn't budging, waiting for her reply.

She blurted out, 'Well, it's not as if you're *new* to the scene here, is it? You've been here for a couple of years, had plenty of horses in races and won more than your fair share, not to mention your accomplishments in France.'

Luc's tone was dry. 'This community is a tight-knit one. They don't allow entry purely by dint of your owning a stud and racing stables.'

'That's ridiculous. You have as much right to be here

as anyone. You have a brilliant reputation. Paddy—'
She stopped abruptly and bit her lip.

Luc arched a brow. 'Paddy *what*?'

She cursed her loose tongue. 'Well, you probably
won't believe me, but Paddy idolises you. You're all he
talked about for the first few months he was working for
you. To be honest I think part of the reason he's in hiding is because he's so mortified that he let you down...'

Luc looked at Nessa. He knew vaguely that he should
be working the room, capitalising on being welcomed
into the fold, but he was more intrigued by this conversation. Disturbingly he did seem to recall Paddy Jnr's
rather puppy-like manner and the way he'd followed
Luc around for the first few weeks. When Paddy had
first disappeared Luc had recalled his slavish devotion
and had seen it in a more suspicious light. But now...

Nessa went on. 'He thinks you're a maverick, and he
admired your unorthodox methods.'

Luc battled with the urge to trust what Nessa was
saying. 'You say one thing but his actions say something
else. They're nice words, Nessa, but I don't need staff
idolising me. I just need people I can trust.'

'Who *do* you trust?'

'Almost no one,' Luc answered and for the first time
in his life it didn't feel like something to be proud of.
Disgruntled at the turn in conversation, and not liking how Nessa's affront on his behalf made him feel,
he took her arm and led her into the other room where
couples were already dancing.

But as soon as they approached the dance floor she
became a dead weight under his hand. He glanced at
her and she was pale and had a terror-struck expression
on her face. Something sharp lanced him in his chest.
'What's wrong?'

She shook her head. 'I can't dance.'

'Everyone can dance. Even me.' He hadn't actually intended on dancing but now he was intrigued.

She started to pull away. 'No, really, I'll just watch. There have to be any number of women here who'd love to dance with you.'

Luc couldn't say he was unaware of the fact that a few women seemed to be circling, but apparently he was with the only woman in the room who *didn't* want to be with him. It was a novelty he didn't welcome.

He moved his hand down her arm to her hand and gripped it firmly and tugged her very reluctant body onto the dance floor.

Nessa felt sick. This was her worst nightmare. She hated dancing in public with a passion and could already hear the laughs and jeers of her brothers ringing in her ears. *Come on, Ness, you can't actually trip over your own feet—oops, she just did!*

'Really, I would rather just—' But her words dried up in her throat when Luc pulled her into his chest and put an arm around her back, then took her hand in his, holding it close to his chest.

Suddenly they were moving, and Nessa had no idea how her feet were even capable of such a thing, but suddenly she was being propelled backwards. No one was staring. Well, they were, but it was at Luc, not her.

Her tension eased slightly but then she became aware of how it felt to be so close to his body. Her eyeline was somewhere around his throat. She was still a full foot smaller than him, even in heels, and she felt very conscious of the taller and more swanlike women that glided past with their partners.

The more she thought about it, the more she had

to wonder if she'd hallucinated what had happened in the stables. Right now, aside from her own thundering heart-rate and physical awareness of him, Luc could have been a total, polite stranger.

And then he looked down at her and said, 'I never really congratulated you on your win today. If you perform like that again, you could be the face of a new generation of women jockeys.'

Had that been today? It felt like years ago. Nessa blushed, not expecting praise from this man. 'It could have been a fluke. If I do badly at the next race it won't help your reputation, or my career.'

Luc shook his head. 'You handled her beautifully. Where did you learn to ride like that?'

Nessa swallowed. The air suddenly felt thicker. She looked at Luc's bow tie. That seemed safer than looking up into the dark eyes that made her feel as if she were drowning.

'My father, before he got too ill. But mainly Iseult; she's got the real talent. I was never off a horse really, as soon as I got home from school and then every weekend when I came home from university—'

'You went to university?'

Nessa looked up. 'Iseult insisted we all go. She knew I wanted to be a jockey and she helped me, but she made sure I had something else to fall back on. The world of racing for female jockeys isn't exactly…easy.'

'What did you study?'

'Business and economics.'

Luc arched a brow. 'That's a little removed from racing.'

Nessa felt self-conscious. 'I know, and it kept me off the scene for a few years. But I didn't mind, really.

I wanted to learn how to take care of our business if anything happened again.'

'Even though your brother-in-law is a sheikh and rich as Croesus?'

Nessa gave him a withering look. 'None of us expect handouts from Nadim. Not even my sister, and she's married to him! And anyway, Iseult hadn't met Nadim by the time I began university, so things were still pretty grim. I knew I didn't have the luxury of doing what I wanted and following a precarious career path.'

Luc had to admit to a grudging respect for Nessa and what her family had obviously been through. Unless of course it was all lies designed to impress him. But as much as he hated to admit it, he didn't think it was.

Since he'd discovered she was a virgin and wasn't putting on some innocent act, it had shifted his perception whether he liked it or not. Also, he could verify her story pretty easily if he looked into it.

She looked up at him again and he saw something like determination in her eyes. 'You never did answer my question earlier…how you came to know so much about horses.'

Luc cursed the fact that they were so close and surrounded by couples. No escape. But then, what did he have to hide except a very banal answer?

'An old man lived in the apartment next to my mother's. He paid me sometimes to do odd-jobs for him, shopping, things like that. He used to be a champion jockey as a young man but an accident had ruined his career. I was always fascinated by his stories and the fact that every thoroughbred today is descended—'

'From just three Arab stallions,' Nessa finished. 'I know, that's always fasincated me too.'

'Pierre became a chronic online gambler but in spite

of knowing everything about every single horse's lineage and form he always lost more than he won. He taught me almost everything, including how to invest prudently, which was ironic because he never took his own advice.'

Nessa felt ridiculously emotional to think of a young Luc Barbier spending all that time with an old injured jockey. 'He sounds like an amazing person. Is he still alive?'

Luc suddenly looked more remote. He shook his head. 'He died when I was a teenager. Before he died, though, he gave me Leo Fouret's number and told me I should call him and impress him with my knowledge of racing, and that if I did he might take me on.'

Which he obviously had. Nessa was a little stunned. But before she could ask Luc any more questions she felt him pull her in much closer to avoid colliding with another couple. She'd almost forgotten they were on a dance floor, surrounded by people.

And then she felt it. The press of his body against her lower abdomen. His arousal.

She looked up, eyes wide, cheeks flaring with heat. Luc arched a brow in silent question as they kept moving, which only exacerbated the situation.

Nessa could hardly breathe. The previous conversation and revelations were forgotten. All she could think about now was the way he'd been so cold the other day in the changing rooms. *What happened between us won't happen again.*

She'd thought he'd meant he no longer desired her. 'I thought you said it wouldn't happen again.' Nessa had just assumed that her virginal state was a huge turn-off.

'I meant what I said,' Luc answered now.

Nessa was confused, and aroused. 'But...' She couldn't articulate it.

'But I still want you?'

She nodded dumbly, feeling completely out of her depth and clueless as to how to handle this situation.

Something stark crossed Luc's face. 'Just because I want you doesn't mean I have to act on it. I don't have relationships with staff.'

Nessa wanted to point out she was hardly staff, as she was working for free, but she was afraid it would sound pleading.

It was torture to be this close to him, knowing that he did want her but could act so cool about it. She was not cool. She was the opposite of cool. Her insides were going on fire and between her legs was hot and slippery.

Emotion was rising and bubbling over before she could stop it. She felt especially vulnerable after hearing his story about the old jockey. She pulled free of his embrace. 'You said you don't play games but maybe you lied, Luc. I think you're toying with me as a form of punishment. You know you're more experienced than me so maybe this is how you get your kicks.'

Nessa walked quickly off the dance floor—as quickly as she could in the heels. To her horror, she felt tears prick the backs of her eyes and she was almost running by the time she reached the foyer.

A man stepped forward. 'Miss O'Sullivan?'

It took her a second to recognise the driver. And then his eyes lifted to something, or someone, behind her. *Luc.* Nessa composed herself, aghast that she'd run like that. The last thing she wanted was for him to know he affected her emotionally.

The driver melted away again and Nessa turned around reluctantly. Luc caught her arm and tugged her over to a discreet corner. He was grim. 'I told you before that I don't play games. And I don't get off by denying myself, believe me—this is new territory for me.'

Nessa felt slightly mollified by that. Maybe she'd overreacted. And now she was embarrassed. If anything she should be rejoicing that he wasn't taking advantage of her lack of control around him.

She pulled her arm free, avoiding Luc's eye. 'It's late, and I promised Pete I'd be up early to train for the next race tomorrow.'

Eventually Luc just said, 'I'll have Brian drive you home. I have a meeting to attend tomorrow morning here in town so I'll stay the night.'

Nessa hated herself for the betraying lurch she felt, as if she'd been hoping that Luc might have said something else, like *stay*. She stepped back. 'Goodnight, Luc.'

He called Brian on his mobile phone and the driver reappeared. Within seconds of Luc delivering his instructions Nessa was in the back of the car, being driven swiftly away from Dublin Castle and back out to Luc's racing stables.

She cringed with humiliation the whole way because, whether he'd intended it or not, Luc had just proven that he might still want her, but she was the last woman on earth he'd take into his bed again. She might've felt like Cinderella going to the ball tonight, but wearing a pretty dress and dancing with a prince wasn't enough to make her a princess.

A short time later, Luc stood with a towel slung around his waist on the balcony of his opulent hotel suite. The moon reflected off the River Liffey where it snaked its way through Dublin city centre. He could hear late night revellers' shouts drifting up from the street. He took a sip of the finest Irish whiskey, but nothing could put a dent in the levels of his arousal. Not even the cold shower he'd just taken.

What the hell was he thinking denying himself the pleasures of female flesh? Even if it was Nessa O'Sullivan and she came with a million and one complications.

Because of the way she looks at you...and because of the questions she asks that reach right down to a place you don't care to analyse.

Luc cursed. He'd told her about Pierre. Pierre Fortin had been one of Luc's saving graces while growing up, teaching him about this fantastical world of horses and racing.

Luc had called his very first racehorse Fortin's Legacy, after his friend.

He never spoke about Pierre. It was too personal, too close to the bone. Sometimes grief for his old friend resurfaced, taking him by surprise with its intensity. But, for the first time, he felt as if he'd done a disservice to his friend by not talking about him more.

Luc cursed again. Tricky questions or no tricky questions, he still wanted Nessa. He realised now that denying himself the carnal satisfaction of taking her to bed again was doing nothing but messing with his head.

He wanted her on a physical level. That was all. And maybe if he reminded her of the physical, it would dissuade her from thinking about anything else. Like asking awkward questions that he wasn't interested in answering or thinking about.

Nessa came second in the next race. Not a win but very respectable all the same. Pete was ecstatic. As for Luc—his reaction, Nessa couldn't figure out, because his expression was always so unreadable and he'd given nothing away when she'd seen him on the sidelines after she'd finished the race.

A few days had passed since the function and she'd hardly seen him. Apparently he'd been in Dublin for meetings, and he'd also visited Paris in the meantime.

Nessa told herself that she didn't care, as she checked herself in the mirror of the VIP guests' bathroom. She pulled at the cream lace pencil skirt she was wearing, feeling overdressed. It had a matching top. Pascal had told her she'd need to dress up for the press, so she'd brought some of the clothes that the stylist had left for her from the night of the function.

She'd pulled her hair back so it looked as sleek as possible and had it in a low bun at the back of her head, and she wore one of those ridiculous-looking fascinator hats, set to the side of her head. She sighed, hoping she looked presentable, and made her way to the VIP room to meet Pascal.

When she got to the plush suite, however, it was empty. There were some refreshments lined up on a table but Nessa ignored her growling stomach and helped herself to some water, not wanting to be caught with a bun in her mouth and crumbs all over her clothes.

The room had an enviable view of the track where races were still being run, but it was blocked off from the other suites, making it very private.

She heard the door open behind her and turned around to greet Pascal and whatever press he'd brought with him but it wasn't Pascal. It was Luc, in his three-piece suit. Looking like the most uncivilised civilised man on the planet.

His dark gaze swept up and down and Nessa's skin

prickled with self-consciousness and awareness. 'Pascal told me to dress appropriately for the press.'

'You look very...*appropriate*,' Luc said. Nessa heard the unmistakable turning of the lock in the door, and her heart-rate increased as Luc prowled into the room like a predator approaching his prey.

Nessa took a step back and said nervously, 'Pascal and the press are going to be here any minute.'

Luc shook his head. 'He's keeping them busy elsewhere for a little while.'

Nessa felt confused. 'Why did you lock us in here?'

Now he was in front of her and looked very tall. And fierce, and sexy. Her body was reacting in spite of her best intentions to try and remain immune to his appeal.

'I locked us in here because I'm done denying myself where you're concerned.'

Luc put his hand around the back of her head, and before she knew what was happening she could feel her carefully constructed bun being undone and her hair was falling down her back. The silly, frivolous hat ended up on the floor.

'Luc, what are you doing?' Why did she sound so breathy?

In a silent answer, he pulled her into his body, tipped her face up and kissed her. Nessa had no defence for this sensual ambush. Her whole body ignited as if it had just been waiting for his kiss and touch.

Luc was like a marauding warrior, leaving no space to think about what was happening. All she could do was *feel*. Succumb. She'd wanted to experience this again so much, and now that it was happening she never wanted it to stop.

Before she could control herself her arms were lifting to wrap around his neck and she was arching her body into his, straining to get closer. His hands moved up and down her back, tracing her waist, going under her top to find the bare skin between that and her skirt.

But, like a cool wind skating over her skin, reality intruded, and she mustered up every ounce of strength she had to pull free.

Nessa was breathing as if she'd just run a marathon. Luc's eyes were burning and she belatedly noticed the stubble on his jaw. She could feel the burn on her skin like a mocking brand.

'What's wrong?'

'What's wrong?' Nessa wrapped her arms around herself defensively. 'You said this wouldn't happen again.'

His face was stark. 'I thought I could resist you, Nessa…but I can't. This will burn up, but then it'll fizzle out. It always does. Let me be the one to teach you how it can be, for as long as we want each other.'

She shivered inside. He'd already done a pretty good job of teaching her how it could be. There was something very illicitly enticing about the prospect of burning up with this man and then letting it *fizzle out*. But she had to be strong. She shook her head. 'I don't think this is a good idea.'

His jaw tightened. She spoke again before he could. 'I'm not just some convenient plaything you can discard and pick up again when it suits you.'

'Believe me,' he growled, 'there's nothing convenient about how I feel about this, or you.'

Nessa smarted. 'Well, I'm sure there are plenty of women who would be far more *convenient* than me.'

He shook his head and closed the distance between them, reaching out to cup her jaw, a thumb moving against her skin hypnotically.

'The problem is that I don't want any other woman. I only want *you*.'

Nessa's throat went dry. Luc Barbier telling her he wanted only her was more than she could handle. Treacherously, she could feel her resistance weaken.

Her heart thumped unevenly. As if trying to soothe a nervy foal, Luc gently cupped her face with his hands, tipping it up to him. He filled her vision.

'I want *you*, Nessa.'

Her mind raced. Could she really handle another intimate encounter with this man? He was already sliding under her skin in a way that mocked her for thinking she could separate her emotions from the physicality.

Dark grey eyes held her captive. 'This is just physical. Don't overthink it. It has nothing to do with your brother or the debt. This is just for us.'

He was saying all the right things to make her weaken even more. *Just physical*. She could keep her emotions out of it if he could.

Nessa was afraid she could no more refuse what Luc was offering than she could stop taking her next breath. She reached up and traced the hard sensual line of his mouth with her finger, overwhelmed that he wanted her so much.

A sense of fatality filled her. She knew she couldn't resist. She reached up and pressed her mouth against his in a silent gesture of capitulation, unable to articulate it any other way.

Luc didn't like to acknowledge the surge of triumph he felt when Nessa's mouth touched his. He didn't like to think of the swirl of emotions he'd just seen in her expressive green eyes. But it wasn't enough to stop him.

He wrapped his arms around her and backed her up against the wall so that he could fully explore that lush and sexy mouth that had been haunting his dreams for days now.

She was as sweet as he remembered. Sweeter. Her small tongue darted out to touch his, and went back again. He captured it, sucking it deep, making her squirm against him. His aching flesh ground into her soft contours and Luc knew that there was no stopping this now. He had to have her with a hunger that was unprecedented.

Somehow a sliver of cold realism entered his head and he took his mouth off Nessa's for a moment. 'I need you, here, right now...'

She looked up at him, eyes molten pools of desire. Slightly glazed. She bit her lip. 'Okay.'

Luc took his hands off her even though it was the hardest thing. 'Take off your clothes.'

Nessa shivered, feeling vulnerable for a moment, but then Luc started to disrobe and she couldn't take her eyes off him as he cast aside his jacket, waistcoat, tie, shirt, and unbuckled his belt.

In a bid to try and keep breathing, Nessa reached for the zip at her neck, but her fingers fumbled and were clumsy. Luc was bare-chested, his trousers open, showing the trail of dark hair that led down into his underwear. She couldn't function.

He stepped forward and said, 'Turn around.'

She did. His hand came to her zip, pulling it down, and then the top slid off from her front. He opened her bra and turned her to face him, pulling it off completely. The crowds outside the VIP box roared as another race was won, but Nessa barely noticed.

Luc discarded his trousers and she could see where the material of his underwear was tented over his erection. Her mouth watered.

'Your skirt. Take it off, now.'

The rough quality of his voice made the flames lick even higher. Nessa knew she should be feeling more self-conscious as she shimmied out of the skirt but she felt emboldened under Luc's appreciative gaze.

For the first time in her life she felt a very feminine thrill of power. It was heady to know she had this effect on a man like Luc Barbier, who was normally so in control.

As soon as the skirt pooled at her feet, she kicked off her shoes and dropped a few inches in height. Luc yanked down his underwear, freeing himself, and pulled her close, wrapping his arms around her and hauling her up and into him as his mouth landed on hers and he devoured her.

She loved the feel of his hard body next to hers. It made her feel delicate and soft. Her arms twined around his neck as she lost herself in his kiss and she wasn't even aware that he'd carried her over to a seat until the earth tilted and she realised he was sitting down and she was straddling his lap.

His hands felt huge on her back and his mouth was on a level with her breasts. He surrounded one hard peak in hot, wet, sucking heat and Nessa's head fell back. When his teeth teased her tender flesh she sucked in a breath, tensing all over.

His erection was thick and long between them. She reached down and touched him, feeling the bead of moisture at the tip. He hissed a breath and she heard the sound of foil being broken before Luc set her back slightly to roll protection onto his length.

He reached for her again, putting his hands on her hips. 'Sit up slightly...that's it...'

As he manoeuvred her into position over his body,

Nessa had never felt more animalistic, or earthy and raw. Luc ripped the side of her panties so they were no longer an impediment, and she felt the thick, blunt head of his erection against her slippery folds.

She had a moment of remembering the brief pain of his first penetration, but as if he were reading her mind his hand soothed her, up and down her back, and he said, 'Trust me, *minou*…it won't hurt again, okay?'

She nodded, bracing her hands on his shoulders as he slowly joined their bodies. Nessa couldn't look away from his eyes as, inch by inch, he filled her so completely that she couldn't breathe.

'You dictate the pace, *ma belle*…'

Luc's voice sounded strained and Nessa felt that rush of feminine power again as she experimented by moving up and down on his body, rolling her hips.

He huffed a laugh against her breast. 'You're going to kill me…'

But Nessa was too distracted by the building tension at her core and how, by moving faster, she could make it build and build. Luc was pressing kisses all over her bared skin, his teeth and mouth teasing her breasts unmercifully. Nessa's movements became wilder, more desperate, as she sensed the shimmering peak approaching. She was losing control. But just as she thought that, Luc took over, demonstrating his experience and mastery.

He clamped his hands onto her hips, holding her still as his body pumped up into hers, stronger and harder and deeper than before.

Sweat glistened on their skin, black eyes burning into hazel. Nessa couldn't hold on. She thought she might die, and then with one cataclsymic thrust she did, but it was an exquisite death that brought with it rolling wave upon wave of pleasure. It was so intense that she had to bite his shoulder to stop herself from screaming out loud and informing the entire racetrack what was happening in this room.

In the aftermath, Nessa couldn't have said how long she was slumped against Luc's body, wrapped in his arms. Her body pulsated rythmically around his, and it sent new shivers of awareness through her.

He gently tugged her head back. She was too sated and exhausted to care how she looked.

'Next time, we make it to a bed and do this properly.'

Next time. More shivers went through her body. *This is only just beginning.*

'Next time?' She injected her voice with a lightness she didn't feel.

Luc smiled and it was wicked and sinful and gorgeous. 'Oh, yes, there'll be a next time and one after that too…and possibly even one after that.'

He punctuated his words with hot, open-mouthed kisses along her bare shoulder. Weakly, Nessa blocked out all of the voices trying to burst the amazing afterglow bubble surrounding her and told herself that she could handle this. She could handle anything, as long as he didn't stop kissing her.

CHAPTER EIGHT

'THERE'S A HORSE at my stables in France that I'd like you to try riding. He's tricky and none of my jockeys there seem to be able to handle him.'

Nessa looked over at Luc from where she was brushing down Tempest, who she'd just been riding out on the gallops. Luc was dressed in his casual uniform of worn jeans and a long-sleeved top with boots. He leaned nonchalantly against the stable door, arms folded. He took her breath away all too easily and she had to focus to remember what he'd said. It had been two days since the X-rated interlude in the VIP suite at the track and her body still felt overly sensitised.

'Ok.'

Luc straightened up. 'When you've finished here go and pack—we'll leave in a couple of hours. We'll stay in my Paris apartment tonight for the function and go to the stables tomorrow.'

Nessa swallowed as she absorbed this information. 'The function?'

He nodded. 'We've been invited to the annual French sports awards. Apparently you're a sensation outside of Ireland too. Everyone wants to see you up close.'

Nessa quailed at that and distracted herself by asking, 'You said we'd stay at your apartment, is that appropriate?'

Luc came towards her and he said, 'It's very appropriate. What part of *next time* didn't you understand?'

He slid his hand around the back of her neck under where her hair was gathered in a messy ponytail and tugged her towards him, saying in a low voice, 'Maybe you need reminding…'

The stable and horse were blocked out as Luc's mouth covered hers. It was so explicit that all she could think about was heat and desperate need. She was barely aware of the brush falling to the ground or the horse moving slightly, jostling them.

Luc lifted his head after a few moments and it took a second for Nessa to open her eyes. *Damn.* She was toast, as well as being well reminded.

With a smug look on his far too gorgeous face, Luc backed out of the stable and walked away, leaving Nessa standing there feeling as if a bolt of lightning had just gone through her body.

She knew that it wasn't a good idea to allow Luc to affect her like this, for many many reasons, not least of which was self-preservation. But the thought of going to Paris with him was just too seductive to resist.

A few hours later, Nessa increasingly felt as if she were in a fairy tale. She'd been to Paris before, on a school trip, but it had been nothing like this. They'd flown in by private jet and then been whisked from the airport into the centre of Paris.

Nessa had noticed that, as they'd passed the graffiti'd high walls on the motorway on the outskirts of the city, Luc had seemed to tense and had looked resolutely out of the window at something she couldn't see.

But was there a more beautiful city than Paris, with its distinctive wide boulevards and soaring magnificent buildings? Especially at this time of year, on the cusp of summer and when spring's blossoms lined the ground like a multicoloured carpet. Not to mention the iconic structures of the Arc de Triomphe and the Eiffel Tower that Nessa could see through the open doors of her bathroom right now.

When they'd arrived at Luc's apartment, at the very top of one of those massive ornate buildings on a wide boulevard, he'd disappeared into a study to take some calls, and a friendly housekeeper had shown Nessa into a guest bedroom suite.

She'd shown her a dressing room that was full to the brim of a stunning array of clothes. Nessa hadn't really known how to react to the fact that Luc was evidently always prepared for his female guests, but it had certainly been sobering. It had been just as well, she'd told herself stoutly, as she hadn't even thought to pack a dress before leaving Ireland.

Now Nessa stood in her bathrobe on the small terrace outside the French doors, and pushed everything out of her head but *this* glorious magical view. Dusk was claiming the skies and the lights of the Eiffel Tower were just beginning to twinkle to life. As if someone had been waiting especially for her.

Nessa smiled and realised with a pang that it had been a long time since she'd felt such uncomplicated happiness. The minute she thought that, though, the smile slid off her face. *How* could she be feeling happy when her brother was still probably worried sick at the thought of ever showing his face again?

She'd tried calling him earlier but his phone had been

off, as it was every other time she'd tried. And her other brother, Eoin, was equally hard to track down.

Just then there was a light knock on the main bedroom door. Nessa's heart was pounding at the thought that it might be Luc, but when she opened the door, it was the housekeeper with two other women. Nessa breathed out.

'Mr Barbier has arranged for these ladies to help you get ready for this evening.'

Nessa forced a smile, the thought of the function making her feel slightly ill. Dublin was one thing. This was Paris. She would definitely need help. 'Thank you, Lucille.'

As the women set to work, Nessa tried to block out the insidious thought of all the other women Luc had had in this exact same spot, being preened especially for him.

'Luc, it's PR gold. They love her. The fact that she's so naturally talented makes her even more interesting. There hasn't been a buzz like this about a female jockey in years. The press have also discovered her family connection to Sheikh Nadim and his wife so now there's even more heat. Invitations are flooding in—you're officially accepted into the inner sanctum now. How does it feel?'

How did it feel? The conversation he'd just had with Pascal on the phone replayed in his head, as did that question. How did it feel to finally be experiencing a measure of the acceptance and respect he'd long since craved?

Curiously anticlimactic, if Luc was brutally honest. Even this view, which took in an exclusive slice of glittering Paris, left him feeling a little hollow.

Just then he heard a noise and turned around to see Nessa in the doorway of the room. And his heart stopped. She'd been beautiful before but now she was... *stunning*.

She wore a long, shimmering green gown. She was covered up from neck to toe and it had long sleeves, but it hugged every delicate curve of her body, highlighting her lithe sensuality. Her hair was up in a chignon and she wore simple diamonds in her ears.

She walked into the room looking nervous. 'I'm ready to go.'

There was a quality to her this evening that made her seem very vulnerable. Luc could tell how out of her depth she was, and he felt a very alien need to say something to reassure her.

Far too gruffly he said, 'You look very beautiful, Nessa.'

As she blushed and smoothed the dress at her hip, he noticed the slight tremor in her hand and it tugged on something very raw inside him. This woman could ride and master a thoroughbred horse, and yet *this* made her tremble?

'I'm not beautiful. You don't have to say that.'

He closed the distance between them in two long strides and tipped up her chin, searching her eyes. 'If you were anyone else I'd say you're fishing for compliments, but I think you really mean it. Who ever made you believe that?'

She pulled her chin free. 'Growing up with two brothers makes it hard to explore your feminine side, and our mother died when I was eight, so I never really had that influence.'

'What about your older sister, Iseult?'

Nessa shrugged. 'She was a tomboy too. And she was always so busy.'

Luc tried to contain his surprise. He'd never known a beautiful woman to not make the most of her assets, until now. Nessa was all the more refreshing for it. He felt in serious danger of taking her by the hand and leading her back to the bedroom to undo all that pristine hair and make-up. He felt unmoored.

He stepped back. 'We should go. The driver will be waiting for us.'

As they descended in the lift Nessa found it hard to douse the ball of warmth Luc's words had created in her chest. *He thought she was beautiful.* She knew he wasn't a man to make empty compliments, and for the first time in her life she actually felt something close to beautiful.

She took deep breaths to quell her nerves and tried not to be too aware of Luc in the small space. But he took up so much of it, effortlessly.

Their eyes met in the mirror of the door and any benefits of the calm breathing Nessa had been doing were gone in an instant. His eyes were like molten black pools, and there was a gleam so explicit that she couldn't breathe.

Everything tightened inside her and she wished she knew how to react in this situation. She could imagine that his other lovers—the ones who had also chosen dresses from the vast array he had—would turn to him now and twine their arms around his neck and say something sultry and confident.

They would take control. They might even press the Stop button and initiate an X-rated moment. Maybe he was waiting for her to do that? Overcome with insecurity, mixed with arousal, Nessa gabbled the first thing that came into her head. 'It was lucky that you're so prepared for your…er…women friends. There were a lot of dresses to choose from.'

His brows snapped into a frown at the same time as the doors opened. She stepped out and he took her arm, stopping her in her tracks. 'What's that supposed to mean?'

Nessa felt inevitable heat climb up from her chest to her face and cursed her colouring and lack of sophistication. 'The clothes in the dressing room. You obviously keep it stocked so your lovers aren't caught short.'

'Those clothes were for you. I had a stylist deliver them before we arrived. I don't entertain women at my apartment and I certainly don't keep a ready supply of clothes for them.'

Nessa was momentarily speechless. There was also a very dangerous fluttering feeling near her heart. He didn't entertain women at his apartment and yet she was here. She finally managed to get out one word. 'Oh.'

Luc looked grim, as if he'd just realised the significance of that too. He said nothing but just propelled her towards the entrance where the car and driver were waiting.

The journey to the hotel where the function was being held was taken in silence. Nessa was afraid of what else might come out of her mouth, so she kept it shut and drank in the view of Paris as they swept through the streets.

She had to remind herself that whatever overwhelming intensity she was feeling for Luc, it wasn't remotely the same for him. He was interested in her for a relatively brief moment, for some bizarre, unknown reason. If she hadn't burst into his life in such dramatic fashion out of a desire to protect her brother, there was no way she would have ever been sitting in the back of his car, dressed in a gown worth more than her annual income.

The sooner she kept reminding herself of that, the better. Because once Paddy sorted out this issue of the missing money, Nessa had no doubt she would be out of Luc Barbier's life so fast her head would be spinning.

A few hours later, Nessa was waiting for Luc in the foyer of the hotel. He was a couple of feet away, conducting a conversation with a man who had just stopped him. Nessa was glad of the brief respite. Luc had been right by her side all evening and she'd been embarrassingly aware of him, and even more acutely aware of every tiny moment he'd touched the base of her back or her arm.

Just then an accented voice said close to her ear, 'Isn't he the most beautiful thing you've ever seen?'

Nessa jumped and looked around to see an older but carefully preserved woman with blonde hair, her blue eyes fixated on Luc. There was something about the nakedly hungry gleam in her gaze that sent a shiver through Nessa.

'I'm sorry, do I know you?'

The women dragged her gaze off Luc and looked Nessa up and down disparagingly. 'You're this new jockey they're all talking about, I gather.' Her eyes narrowed. 'You're sleeping with him, aren't you?'

Nessa flushed. 'I don't think that's any of your—'

But the women grabbed her arm in an almost painful grip. She hissed at Nessa, 'He won't be tamed, you know. A magnificent beast like him will never be tamed.'

Nessa pulled her arm free and looked at the woman, feeling a hot surge of anger and something far more ambiguous. A fierce protectiveness. 'He's not an *animal*. He's a man.'

'Celeste. What a pleasure.'

Nessa's head whipped around to see Luc right behind her, looking sterner than she'd ever seen him, his glaze so black it was obsidian. Clearly it *wasn't* a pleasure.

The woman all but thrust Nessa out of the way and stepped close to Luc. 'Darling…it's been so long.' She laid a hand on his arm and a wave of revulsion went through Nessa to see the long red nails. It made her think of blood.

Luc picked off her hand and took Nessa by the arm, pulling her back beside him. 'Good evening, Celeste.'

He turned and they walked out. Nessa resisted the urge to look back at the woman. She had to be one of Luc's ex-lovers, but the thought of him with her made Nessa's stomach roil.

The car pulled away from the kerb and Luc reeled. He didn't like how it had made him feel to hear Nessa speak those words to that woman. *He's not an animal.* She'd looked ferocious, disgusted on his behalf. She'd had a similar expression on her face when she'd defended her brother so vociferously when they first met.

It impacted Luc in a very visceral way to think of Nessa standing up for him. He didn't need any of that.

He looked at her now and she was pale. His voice was harsh. 'You didn't need to say that. I can fight my own battles.'

She looked at him. 'She was talking about you as if you're not even human. How could you have ever been with her? She's awful.'

Luc felt disgust move through him. 'We were never lovers, even though she did everything in her power to seduce me. She's Leo Fouret's wife. I found her naked in my bed one night and she threatened to accuse me of rape if I refused to sleep with her. That's why I had to leave the stables. Leo Fouret knew what she was like and he offered to pay me off to leave and say nothing. I refused his money but I did take a horse.'

And why the hell had he just let all of that slip out? He didn't owe Nessa any explanations.

Nessa said slowly, 'That's why you reacted the way you did when you found me in your room.'

She continued, 'I'm sorry I opened my mouth but I couldn't help myself. You're *not* just some object.'

No one had ever jumped to Luc's defence before. A disturbing warmth curled through his gut. His anger was draining away. He said, 'In the end she actually did me a favour. If I hadn't had to leave Fouret's stables I might still be working there. That horse became my fortune.'

Nessa shook her head. 'I don't think so. I think you would have always made your fortune.'

Luc looked at her intently. 'You're like a fierce tigress.'

Nessa's cheeks got hot. She didn't know how to respond to that. She regretted letting that woman get to her, but the relief she felt to know that he hadn't been intimate with Celeste was almost overwhelming.

A thousand more questions were on Nessa's lips but then Luc said, 'You did well this evening.'

Nessa shrugged slightly, embarrassed. 'I felt like a bit of a fraud, to be honest. A couple of well-run races does not merit all that attention.'

Luc shook his head. 'You have a natural ability that anyone can see from a million miles away, and you're a beautiful young woman. It's quite a combination.'

She smiled wryly. 'I've been riding in races for a few years now and no one has ever commented before. I think the fact that I'm riding for you is the key. People are fascinated by whatever you do.'

Luc's jaw tightened. 'Fascinated in that way that drivers are when they pass a crash and have to look at the carnage.'

Nessa instinctively wanted to deny that but she knew he wasn't saying it for effect or sympathy. She'd seen how the guests had looked at him all evening. And no wonder, with that woman in their midst. It had to be exhausting, constantly having to prove himself.

Afraid he might see too much on her face, Nessa looked out of the window. They were driving along the Seine and Nessa noticed all the amorous couples. It tugged on a yearning inside her.

She couldn't imagine Luc stopping the car and taking her by the hand to walk along the Seine, and it shook her to realise she'd even thought of that. Whatever was between them wasn't about romance or emotions or love. But even as Nessa thought of that word, *love*, her heart pounded unevenly and she felt cold and clammy. Sick.

Oh, God. She was falling for him.

'Have you ever been to Paris before?'

Nessa jumped at his question and looked at him. *She wasn't in love with him. She couldn't be.* She forced down the panic she was feeling, assuring herself that the romance of Paris had infected her brain momentarily.

She said, 'Only once, a long time ago, on a school trip. I always wanted to come back some day—I've never seen anywhere more beautiful.'

Luc's gaze narrowed on Nessa's face. She'd been a million miles away just now, gazing wistfully out of the window.

His body was in an agony of sexual frustration after an evening standing by her side as countless people, mainly men, he'd noticed, had come and stared as if they'd never seen a woman before. He'd had to control the urge to snarl at everyone so he could pull Nessa into a quiet corner and muss up that far too tidy chignon and peel that dress from her luscious body.

And even though all he wanted right now was to drive straight to his apartment so he could do just that, he found himself leaning forward and instructing his driver to take a small detour.

Nessa looked at him when they came to a stop a few minutes later, after climbing the winding narrow streets as far as they could go in the car. 'Where are we?' she asked.

Luc was already regretting the impetuous decision even as he said, 'Montmartre. Come on, I want to show you something.'

He got out of the car and came around to help her out. Her hand slipped into his, and he had to grit his jaw at the surge of desire even that small, chaste touch provoked.

They walked the small distance up towards Sacre Coeur cathedral. It was late but there were still small knots of people milling around. Luc opened his bow tie and the top button of his shirt. He noticed Nessa shiver slightly in the cool evening air. He took off his jacket and draped it over her shoulders and she looked at him. 'Oh, thank you.'

They came around a corner and the full majesty of the iconic cathedral was revealed. Nessa stopped in her tracks. 'Wow. I'd forgotten this existed. It's so beautiful.'

'You came here on your trip?'

Nessa nodded, her eyes gleaming. 'Yes, but not like this. It's magical.'

He led her around to the front and then down the steps to the lookout points. Nessa sucked in an audible breath. Paris was laid out before them like a glittering carpet of jewels.

Luc realised how long it had been since he'd been here.

'This is stunning. Thank you.'

Luc was ridiculously pleased, which was ironic because over the years he'd presented women with far more tangible and expensive trinkets and had felt nothing when they'd expressed gratitude.

He gestured towards the view. 'I used to come here when I was younger, around age ten, eleven. We'd come in from the flats during the summer, peak tourist season. We used to take advantage of people's absorption with the view to pick their pockets, steal watches, that kind of thing.'

She turned to face him. His coat making her look even more petite, her hair a dramatic splash of red against the night sky.

'Were you ever caught?'

He shook his head. 'That's why they sent us in at that age. We were small and fast, able to disappear in seconds.'

'Who would send you in?'

'The gangs, older kids. We'd bring the haul back to them and if we'd creamed anything off for ourselves they'd know immediately.'

'So you grew up in the suburbs?'

Luc looked out over the city that had been witness to his single-minded ascent out of his grim circumstances. He nodded. 'Where I grew up is about as far removed as you can get from this view. It was a basic existence in not very pretty surroundings. School was a joke and gang life on the streets was our education.'

He looked at her, expecting to see that gleam women got in their eyes when they spied an opening to invite further intimacies but she just looked at him steadily. 'Is that when you got your scar?'

Luc's insides clenched when he remembered the stinging pain. He nodded. 'A rival gang surrounded me, and knives came out. I was lucky to escape with just a scar.' That had been the moment he'd realised that if he didn't get out, he might die.

'You said before that you had no family—did you really have no one?'

Luc's chest tightened. 'My mother died of an overdose when I was sixteen, and my father appeared for the first and last time to get a handout once he saw that I had money. I had no brothers, no sisters. No aunts, uncles, or cousins. So, no, there was no one.'

'Except for Pierre Fortin,' Nessa said quietly.

The tightness in Luc's chest increased. 'Yes. Pierre saved me. He died shortly after I'd received the beating that led to the scar and I took his advice to get out and contact Leo Fouret. If I hadn't done that, I think I might be dead by now.'

Nessa shivered at that. She could tell he wasn't being melodramatic. 'I'm sorry he's gone.' Her voice was husky.

He turned then to face her and for a second there was an expression of such rawness on his face that she was surprised he was letting her see it. And then he reached out and rubbed his knuckles along her jaw. Her breathing quickened in an instant.

'You're very sweet, Nessa O'Sullivan, or else you're a better actress than I've ever seen in my life.'

A sharp pain lanced her to think that even now he still distrusted her. She took her chin away, afraid of the emotion clogging her throat. 'I *am* sorry for your loss. You deserved to have someone in your corner and I'm glad he was there for you.'

Nessa felt exposed but refused to break eye contact. She was determined to show Luc her sincerity even if she had to brand it onto his brain through sheer will.

And then he reached for her, hands sliding under her arms and tugging her towards him until their bodies were flush and she could feel his arousal pressing against her.

Instantly words were forgotten. She got a sense of how much he'd been leashing his desire all evening and bizarrely felt comforted. Because he'd seemed completely in control and unaffected. But he hadn't been. He was just better at disguising it.

He said, 'I think we've talked enough. I've wanted to do this all evening.'

Before she could ask *what*, he'd started taking the pins out of her hair, until the heavy mass fell down around her shoulders and he dropped the pins to the ground.

He ran his hands through her hair and then cupped her face, tilting it up to his. In the split second before their mouths met, Nessa felt something incredibly poignant move through her as she realised she was one of those kissing couples she'd been so envious of earlier. And then Luc's mouth was on hers, his tongue was mating with hers and she could only clutch at his shirt to try and stay standing. She wasn't even aware of his jacket falling to the ground from her shoulders. She was burning up.

After long, drugging moments Luc pulled back and emitted a curse. 'I could take you right here, right now, but next time we make love it will be on a bed.'

He took her hand to lead her back the way they'd come, to the car. She grabbed his jacket up off the ground as they went, and her cheeks burned. If Luc had decided to make love to her there and then against that wall, she wouldn't have had the ability to stop him.

When they returned to the apartment Luc gave her no time to think. He led her straight to his bedroom. There was one small light burning in the corner, throwing everything into long shadows. His face was stark with need. Exactly how she felt.

He pushed his jacket off her shoulders to the ground and instructed, 'Turn around.'

She turned around, presenting him with her back. He pushed her hair to one side so that it fell over one shoulder, and then he pulled the zip down all the way to where it ended just above her buttocks. He undid her bra. She shivered with anticipation as he ran the knuckles of his fingers up and down her spine.

Then he pushed the two sides of the dress off her shoulders and down and it fell away from her chest. He turned her around again and peeled off her arms so that she was naked from the waist up.

Her nipples stiffened under his gaze, and when he brushed his fingers across the sensitised tips she had to bite her lip to stop from crying out.

He took his hand away. 'Undress me.'

Luc saw the almost drugged expression on Nessa's face. Sweat broke out on his brow at the effort it was taking not to rip the rest of Nessa's dress off her body, throw her onto the bed and sink himself so deep inside her he'd see stars. He had to exert some control before he lost it completely.

She lifted her hands to his shirt and undid each button with an air of concentration that he found curiously touching, tongue trapped between her teeth.

She pushed his shirt off and put her hands to his belt, then the button, and the zip. He was so hard he hurt. When she pushed his trousers down he stepped out of them.

'Your dress and panties. Take them off.' He sounded as rough as he felt, uncouth and desperate.

She pushed the dress down and it landed at her feet in a shimmering green pool. Then she pushed down her panties, revealing the enticing red-gold curls between her legs. She was blushing and not meeting his eye. He tipped up her chin until her eyes met his. 'You're beautiful, Nessa.'

'If you say so.'

'I do. Lie down on the bed.'

She crawled onto the bed and Luc bit back a groan at the sight. Then she lay down on her back. 'Open your legs.'

Shyly she did so and he could see where she glistened with arousal. It undid him. Luc tore off his own underwear and put his hands to her thighs, pushing them apart even more. He knelt between her legs and the scent of her almost drove him wild.

He kissed her inner thighs, and they quivered under his hands. Then he spread apart the lips of her sex and put his mouth to her, getting drunk on her essence. He'd never tasted anything sweeter.

She was moaning and trying to speak. 'Luc, what are you...? *Oh, God.*'

He smiled against her when he could feel the way her body was responding: melting, shivering, tensing. He was remorseless, ignoring her pleas to stop, but not stop. He thrust a finger inside her and she orgasmed around it, muscles clamping down so hard that he had to exert every ounce of self-control not to explode himself.

He sheathed himself and came over her. She looked up at him, dreamy and unfocused. 'That was…incredible.'

For a second, in spite of the raging hunger inside him, Luc stopped. There was something so open and unguarded in her eyes that he couldn't bear it. He felt as if she was looking all the way into the depths of his soul with that steady gaze—in a way no one had ever looked at him before. She was seeing too much.

'Turn over,' he commanded. When she blinked and a look of hesitancy came over her face he felt a sharp tug in his chest. He ignored it. Pushed it down.

He ran his hand down her body, cupping between her legs where she was so damp and hot and fragrant. 'Turn over, *minou*.'

She did and Luc pulled her back until she was on her knees. The delicate curve of her spine and buttocks was breaking him in two. She looked at him over her shoulder in an unconsciously erotic pose. 'Luc?'

He put his hands on her hips and pulled her right into his body. He saw her eyes widen and flare when he pressed against her. And then he was breaching her body as slowly as he could afford to go without going mad, feeling her snug muscles clamp around him and then relax to let him push deeper and deeper.

She let out a low groan, coming down on her elbows, bowing her head. Her hair was a bright fall of red against the white sheets. He saw her curl her hands to fists in the sheets, knuckles white as he drove into her again and again.

But as Luc could feel Nessa's body quickening towards her climax, he felt hollow inside. His own release was elusive. He realised he couldn't do it like this, no matter how exposed the other way made him feel. He pulled out, his whole body screaming in protest.

He turned Nessa around again so she was on her back. She was panting, skin gleaming with perspiration. 'Luc…'

'Look at me.'

She did, her eyes wide and trusting. Desperate for the release that he was withholding. He thrust into her again, just once, and that was all it took to send them both hurtling over the edge.

When Luc was capable of movement again he pulled free of Nessa's embrace, and went into his bathroom to dispense with the protection. He placed his hands on the sink and bowed his head. He felt momentarily weak, as if some of his strength had been drained away during sex.

He grimaced at the fanciful notion of Samson and Delilah. It was just the after-effects of extreme pleasure. *But*, a small voice reminded him, *you weren't able to climax until you were looking in her eyes. You needed that connection.* Luc had never sought that kind of connection before.

He went cold. The events of the evening flooded his mind and an icy finger danced down his spine.

He'd told Nessa more than he'd told anyone. He'd blithely let most of his sad history trip off his tongue without a moment's hesitation. He went even icier when the full significance of that hit him.

He'd lost sight of who she was. And what she could *still* be: an accessory to theft.

A hard knot formed in his gut. He'd become so blinded by lust for her that he'd lost sight of a lifetime of lessons, teaching him to trust no one. Luc's heart beat fast to think of how close he'd come to— He shut that thought down. He didn't trust her. They'd had sex. That was all.

He had to admit that since she'd been riding for him, the turnaround in public perception was phenomenal. That was the important thing here. Not his lust for her. That was a base instinct he couldn't afford to indulge again.

He also had to acknowledge the fact that, in spite of the reasons why she was there, she was a boon to his business. But she owed him this. Her brother had stolen from him and she had taken on the debt for herself.

A familiar feeling of ruthlessness settled over Luc like a well-worn coat. In spite of Nessa's innocence or apparent sweetness, he still couldn't trust that she wasn't taking advantage of his desire for her.

He would not be weak again.

CHAPTER NINE

NESSA COULD HEAR Luc in the bathroom. The shower was turned on. She opened her eyes in the dim light of the bedroom, unable to stop imagining water sluicing down over that powerful body. Between her legs ached pleasurably as she recalled the breathtaking feeling of Luc's body driving into hers over and over again.

She got hot when she thought of how he'd made her turn over, taking her from behind. There'd been something so raw and animalistic about it. It had also felt erotic, but she'd felt slightly unsure, out of her depth. She hadn't liked not being able to see his face, or his eyes. Until he'd turned her back and said *look at me*, and that was all it had taken to send her shattering into a million pieces.

The bathroom door opened and Nessa instinctively pulled the sheet up over her body, suddenly shy, which was ridiculous after what had just happened.

Luc stood in the doorway with nothing but a small towel hooked around his waist. Droplets of moisture clung to his sculpted muscles and Nessa's mouth watered.

'You should go back to your own bed now.'

Nessa sat up, holding the sheet to her chest. Humiliation rushed through her. Of course. What had she expected would happen? That Luc would come back to bed and take her in his arms again, whisper sweet nothings in her ears and want to cuddle?

'I don't sleep with lovers,' he said, as if he might not have been clear enough.

Nessa looked at him, unable to stem the blooming of hurt inside her. 'It's fine. You don't need to explain.'

She scooted to the side of the bed feeling awkward as well as humiliated as she searched for her dress, which lay on the ground a few feet away in a pool of shimmering green. She was just wondering how to get there without exposing herself even further when Luc appeared in her eyeline holding out a robe.

'Here.' He sounded gruff.

Nessa took it and pulled it on while trying to stay as covered up as possible. She hated herself for feeling so hurt by Luc's dismissal, by the confirmation that she was no different from his other lovers. *But you want to be different.* She stood up, belting the robe around her, squashing that thought. She didn't want to be different. *Yes, you do.*

Before Luc might see any evidence of the tumult of her emotions, Nessa plucked the dress up off the floor and walked to the door, avoiding his eye. She forced herself to stop, though, and turned around. 'Thank you for this evening. I had a nice time.'

Nessa had walked out of the door before Luc had a chance to respond. He waited for a sense of satisfaction that he'd made it clear that he had boundaries, but it wouldn't come. He thought of how awkward she'd looked just now at the door, avoiding his eye, clutching her dress. She wasn't like the women he knew. He felt like a heel now. Not satisfied at all.

If he was brutally honest with himself, he already regretted saying anything. He wanted to go after her, bring her back to bed and continue where they'd finished.

Luc bit off a savage curse and went back into the bathroom to take a cold shower. Damn Nessa O'Sullivan for sliding under his skin like this. The sooner his people tracked down her brother, the better.

Nessa couldn't sleep when she went back to her bedroom. She went out to the balcony and sat on the chair by the small table, looking at the view. She was such a naive fool. To have imagined for a second that Luc's opening up to her earlier that evening had meant anything.

It had meant nothing. He'd been on a trip down memory lane and she'd happened to be there.

It hit her then, with a cold, clammy sense of panic. She really was falling for him, and it was already too late. She had stood up for him in front of Celeste Fouret the way she would stand up for any of her loved ones. The thought that Luc might have interpreted her defence as devotion, and that had been why he'd sent her back to her own room, made her feel nauseous.

She knew now, with an awful sense of impending doom, that whatever emotional pain she thought she'd ever felt before would pale into insignificance once this man cast her aside. As surely he would.

Because Celeste Fouret had been right, after all. Luc Barbier would never belong to anyone. And certainly not Nessa. She was a brief interlude. A novelty for a cynical and jaded man, and she knew now that she had to protect herself before she got in any deeper.

The following morning Nessa got washed, dressed and packed before going in search of Luc. She heard movement coming from the main living area and walked into the room to see the dining table set and the housekeeper serving breakfast.

Sunlight streamed through the huge windows but it all paled into insignificance next to the image of Luc wearing a dark suit, sipping coffee and reading a newspaper, clean shaven. He looked every inch a titan of industry, and as remote as a rock in the middle of the ocean.

His dark glance barely skimmed over her, and Nessa was glad as it would give her the strength to do what she knew she had to for her own self-preservation.

Lucille told her to take a seat and that she'd bring her some breakfast. Nessa smiled her thanks, relieved that she wasn't entirely alone with Luc.

He put down the paper as she sat down. She felt self-conscious in her daily uniform of jeans and a T-shirt. She'd hung the glittering dress back up in the closet and had pushed down the dangerous spurt of emotion when she remembered Luc telling her she was beautiful.

'Did you sleep well?'

She looked at him and it almost hurt, he was so gorgeous. She nodded and told a white lie. 'Very well, thank you. Your apartment is beautiful. You're very lucky.'

Lucille came back and placed a plate down in front of Nessa with perfectly fluffy scrambled eggs with spring onions, salmon and buttered toast. Ordinarily her mouth would have watered but for some reason she felt nauseous. Not wanting to insult the Frenchwoman, she spooned a mouthful and ate, murmuring her appreciation to the beaming woman. When they were alone again Nessa put down her fork and took a sip of coffee, willing the faint nausea away.

Luc said, 'Luck had nothing to do with me having this apartment. It was success born out of hard work.'

Nessa shouldn't have been surprised that Luc didn't believe in things like luck, or chance. She hadn't either for a long time after their mother's death had rent their world apart. Until fate had stepped in, bringing Nadim into her sister's life, transforming their fortunes.

The hurt she still felt made her want to pierce a little of Luc's stark black and white attitude. 'Well, I do believe in luck. I believe there's always a moment when fate intervenes and you can choose to take advantage of it or not. Not everything is within our control.'

Luc's mouth tightened. 'Apparently not.'

Nessa wasn't sure what that meant. Incensed now, she said, 'Don't you consider Pierre Fortin to have been fateful for you?'

Luc looked at her. 'He gave me an opportunity and I made the most of it.'

Nessa resisted making a face at Luc's obduracy and made a stab at eating some more of the delicious breakfast, and tried to ignore the churning of her stomach.

Luc said, 'I have some meetings to attend in Paris today. My driver will take you to my stables just outside the city this morning, where you'll meet with François, my head trainer. He's expecting you. He'll see how you go on Sur La Mer and, depending on what he thinks, you'll ride him in the race next week. Or not.'

Nessa put down her fork. 'What if I don't perform well on Sur La Mer?'

Luc shrugged minutely. 'Then you'll go back to the stables in Ireland.'

She felt like a pawn being moved about at Luc's will. Into his bed, out of it…it was time to claim back her independence. She took a deep breath.

'Luc, I—'

'Look, Nessa—'

They both spoke at the same moment and stopped. Luc said, 'You go.'

Nessa's heart hammered. She swallowed. 'I just wanted to say that I don't think we should sleep together again. I'm here to do a job. I'd like to focus on that.'

Luc looked at her, eyes glittering like two black unreadable jewels. She'd never know what this man was thinking in a million years. He was too well protected. As she should be.

'I agree. I was going to say the same thing.'

'That's good,' Nessa said quickly, even as something curled up inside her. Some very pathetic part of her that had hoped that he might refuse to agree.

Then Luc stood up and walked over to the window. Nessa stood too, still feeling that nausea in her stomach. It got worse.

He turned around, hands in his pockets. 'As you said, you're here to focus on a job, a job that you've proven to have a great talent for. That's the most important thing now.'

Of course it was, because it was bringing the Barbier name respect and success. And as Nessa had learnt, Luc's business and reputation were everything to him. She couldn't begrudge him that. Not after everything he'd been through. But it was clear that he had no interest in anything outside that. Certainly not a personal life, with love, fulfilment, or family.

As if reading her mind, he said, 'My life isn't about relationships, Nessa. I don't have anything to offer you except what we've shared. There are other women who understand that and can accept it. You're different and, believe me, that's a good thing. But I don't do fairy-tale endings. For me…the novelty has worn off.'

The novelty has worn off. The sheen had gone from his naive virginal lover. Nessa should be thanking him for being so brutally honest, but she just felt incredibly sad, and sick.

She lifted her chin. 'I'm not as naive as you might think, Luc. And I don't believe in fairy tales either.' *Liar*… whispered that voice. Nessa ignored it.

'I'm ready to leave now, if you want to let your driver know.'

For a long moment there was silence and Nessa felt tension rise in the room. Eventually Luc said, 'Of course, I'll call him now and let him know you're coming down.'

So polite. So civil. So devastating. *So over.*

Nessa turned and left the room and when she reached her own bathroom she couldn't keep the nausea down any longer. She looked at herself in the mirror afterwards and saw how pale she was.

It was time to get a grip on herself again and forget anything had happened between her and Luc. Do the race, win the money, pay off Paddy's debt. That was her focus now. Nothing else.

Four days later Nessa was tired and aching all over from training so hard. François appeared at the door to Sur La Mer's stall where Nessa was rubbing him down and trying hard *not* to let her mind deviate with humiliating predictability to Luc Barbier.

She'd almost hoped that when she first sat on Sur La Mer, he'd throw her off. But he'd been a dream to ride and she'd connected with him immediately. François had been ecstatic.

Luc hadn't appeared once at the gallops to watch them train, but then one of the other jockeys had pointed to the CCTV cameras and told her that Luc often watched remotely from screens in his office.

Nessa knew he was at the stables because he'd returned from Paris the day after she'd arrived. The thought that he was watching her progress but avoiding any more personal dealings with her slid through her ribs like a knife, straight to her heart.

François was looking at her as if waiting for a response and Nessa blushed to have been caught out daydreaming. 'I'm sorry, did you want me for something?'

'It's Luc—he wants to see you in his office. It's in the main house on the first floor.'

The roiling in her gut intensified. The ever-present nausea that never seemed to quit. Nessa dusted her hands off and patted Sur La Mer before following François back out, careful to lock the stall door behind her.

He left her at the main door of the house and she went in, making her way up to Luc's office. The door was closed and she took a deep breath, hating that she felt so jittery and on edge at the thought of seeing him again.

She knocked lightly.

'Come in.'

She pushed the door open and Luc was standing behind his desk in jeans and a T-shirt. For a moment Nessa felt so dizzy and light-headed she thought she might faint. She clutched the doorknob like a lifeline.

'You wanted to see me?'

It was only then that she noticed he was on the phone. And he looked grim. He held the receiver towards her. 'It's Paddy.'

For a second she just looked at him. Her brain felt sluggish. 'Paddy…?'

Now he looked impatient. 'Your brother.'

Nessa moved forward feeling as if she were under water. Weighed down. It was shock. She took the phone and Paddy's familiar voice came down the line. 'Ness? Are you there?'

Luc moved away to the window.

Nessa turned away to hide the tears blurring her vision to hear her brother's familiar voice. 'Paddy, where are you? What's going on?'

Her brother sounded happy. 'Ness, it's all been cleared up. Well, not the money, I'll still owe Mr Barbier but he knows now it wasn't my fault. He's agreed to give me my job back and I'll start paying him back out of my wages every month. I'm going to do a course in cyber security too so we can prevent this happening again. He told me you're riding for him in a big race tomorrow—that's fantastic news, Ness! Look, I've got to run. I'm catching a flight home tonight. I'll call you when I get back and tell you everything. Love you, Ness.'

And the phone connection went dead. It was all over, just like that.

She looked at the phone for a long moment trying to gather herself and when she felt a bit more composed she turned around. Luc was standing in front of his window, arms folded. Nessa put the phone receiver back in the cradle.

She forced herself to meet his gaze. 'Can you tell me what's going on?'

He was still grim. 'It was Gio Corretti who realised what was happening, because it happened to him with another horse. Someone had hacked into his computer system so they could impersonate Gio's stud manager. They would then say something about a slight change in bank account details and the buyer would send the money to the hacker's account. That's what happened to Paddy. He'd suspected something, but by the time he'd figured out what had happened the money was gone and couldn't be traced. Then he panicked.'

Luc continued, 'Shortly after speaking to Gio Corretti, my security firm tracked Paddy down to the United States. He was staying with your twin brother.'

Nessa flushed with guilt.

Luc continued, 'I got in touch with Paddy to let him know he could come back. I told him never to do such a foolhardy thing like running away from a problem again.'

Nessa could feel Luc's barely leashed anger and almost felt sorry for her brother.

Luc unfolded his arms then and ran a hand through his hair. Nessa realised it was messier than usual and he looked tired. Stubble lined his jaw. She felt a spurt of pain when she wondered if he'd already taken a replacement into his bed. Someone whose novelty wouldn't wear off so quickly. Someone who knew the rules. Someone who didn't want the fairy tale.

He put his hands on his hips and looked at her. 'Obviously you're now free to go. I'd like you to run the race tomorrow on Sur La Mer but if you'd prefer not to, I will accept that. It's only fair. You have no obligation to me any more.'

Nessa blinked. She hadn't considered that. She felt a little panicky. 'But what about Paddy's debt? He said he still has to pay that back.'

'I told him the debt would be forgiven but he's insisting on paying it back for having been lax enough to be taken in by the hackers. Nothing I said would make him change his mind.'

Nessa's heart squeezed. Luc had been prepared to let the debt go. One million euros.

She made a decision, even though a part of her wanted nothing more than to turn around and walk away right now and go somewhere private where she could lick her wounds and try to get on with her life. She had to be professional about this and the race tomorrow was a huge opportunity for her.

'I'll run the race tomorrow. But if I win, or place, and there's any prize money I'd still like it to go towards the debt.'

'You wouldn't take it for yourself?'

Nessa shook her head. 'No. I don't want anything. I don't need anything from you. Are we done here?'

Every bone in Nessa's body ached with the need to be closer to this man. Have him touch her. It was agony.

Eventually Luc said, 'Yes, we're done.'

Nessa turned and walked to the door, but at the last second he called her name. For a heart-stopping moment she thought she'd heard some inflection in his voice and she couldn't control the surge of hope.

But when she turned around he was expressionless. He said, 'Wherever you go, or whatever you want to do in the future, you'll have my endorsement. I would retain you as a jockey at my stables here or in Ireland but I don't think you would welcome working for me.'

The thought of working alongside Luc Barbier every day for years to come, and seeing him lead his life as the lone wolf that he was, taking and discarding women as he went, was unthinkable. And it just drove home how unaffected by her he was.

She lifted her chin. 'Frankly, after tomorrow, Luc, I hope I never see you again.'

* * *

The following day before the race, Nessa was sick with nerves. Literally. Her breakfast had just ended up in the toilet bowl of the ladies' changing room at the racetrack. She cursed Luc Barbier as the source of all her ills and forced herself to just concentrate on getting through the race in one piece.

She'd booked herself on a flight back to Dublin later that night. Soon this would all be behind her.

She weighed out and made her way to the starting gate to line up with the rest of the horses and jockeys. She was oblivious to their curious looks. They were led into the stalls one by one. One horse started kicking and it took about three men to get him into position.

As Nessa waited on Sur La Mer, feeling his restlessness underneath her, she pushed all thoughts of anything else but the task at hand out of her head.

She took a deep breath. And then the gate snapped open and she unleashed the power of the horse beneath her.

As was becoming a familiar refrain, François said beside Luc, 'I don't believe it. She's going to win, Luc.'

An immense surge of pride and something much more tangled made Luc's chest swell and grow tight.

He watched as Nessa approached the last furlong, moving through the air like a comet. She looked tiny on the horse and something else moved through him, stark and unpleasant. Fear, for her safety.

When she'd stood before him in his office the day before, it had taken all of his control not to drag her into his bedroom like a Neanderthal and strap her to his bed so she could never leave.

He was going mad. She wasn't out of his system.

His system burned for her. But it was too late. This was it. She'd be gone within hours. *I hope I never see you again.*

He'd ruthlessly contemplated seducing her again, but he knew he couldn't do it. Much to his own surprise, it would appear he did have something of a conscience. Nessa wasn't like the other women. She was strong, yes, but soft. Her eyes held nothing back. She might say she didn't believe in fairy tales but he knew that, in spite of the obvious trauma of her mother's death and its effect on their family, there was still something hopeful about her.

She deserved someone who could nurture that hope. Never before had Luc been made so aware of his malfunctioning emotions.

But, as much as he could tell himself that he was doing this to protect her, he had the insidious suspicion that it was also himself he was protecting. He wasn't even sure from what, though.

'Luc, *look*! She's won!'

Luc saw Nessa shoot past the post and the usual sense of achievement and triumph when one of his horses won was tinged with something darker. '*Merde*, Luc, that horse is out of control…'

Luc went cold. He saw the other horses thundering over the line and spotted one that was riderless. It was going berserk. And it was heading straight for Nessa, who had slowed down and was turning around. Even from here Luc could see the huge smile on her face. A tendril of red hair falling from under her cap. Everyone was cheering.

But it was as if he were stuck under water and everything happened in slow motion. He saw the riderless horse rear up in front of Sur La Mer. Another jockey, still on his horse, tried to calm that horse down, but Nessa somehow got stuck in the middle. Sur La Mer bucked. There was a blur of movement, a huge collective gasp from the crowd and Nessa was off the horse and lying on the ground. Underneath the three horses.

Luc wasn't even aware he'd vaulted over the fence. All he could see was a horrifying tangle of horseflesh, hooves, and Nessa inert underneath it all.

The ambulance and paramedics were attending her by the time he got there and he only realised someone was holding him back when François' voice broke through the pounding of blood in his head.

'Luc! Leave them alone. They're doing all they can. Sur La Mer is fine. Someone has him.'

'I'm afraid I can only give out information to family or loved ones, Mr Barbier.'

Loved ones. That struck Luc forcibly, but he pushed down its significance. He was desperate to know if Nessa was all right and her family weren't here. *No*, said a voice, *because you took her away from them.*

Luc ignored the admonishing voice, and his growing sense of guilt. 'I'm not just her employer. We've been lovers.'

The doctor looked at him suspiciously for a moment but there must have been some expression on Luc's face because then he said, 'Very well. If you're intimately acquainted, then there's something you should know. Injury-wise, she was a very lucky young woman. She escaped from under those horses with just a badly bruised back. It could have been a lot worse.'

Luc felt sick when he thought of how much worse it could have been, how vulnerable she'd looked.

The doctor sighed heavily. 'However, there was

something else. I'm afraid we weren't able to save the baby. She wasn't even aware she was pregnant so I'm guessing it's news to you too. It was very early—just a few weeks. There's no way of saying for sure why the miscarriage happened; it could have been the shock and trauma, but equally it could have just been one of those things. Having said that, there's no reason why she can't get pregnant again and have a perfectly healthy baby.'

Luc stood outside the hospital a few minutes later, barely aware of the glances he was drawing. He was reeling. In shock. *Pregnant. A baby.*

He couldn't breathe with the knowledge that he'd almost had a family and in the same moment it was gone.

He'd spent so long telling himself a family wasn't for him that it was utterly shocking now to find himself feeling such an acute sense of…loss and grief.

He'd only ever felt like this a couple of times in his life. When he'd found his mother's dead body, and when Pierre Fortin had died. He'd vowed to himself he'd never let anyone close enough to hurt him again.

But this caught him unawares, blindsiding him.

The grief he felt for this tiny unborn child told him he'd been lying to himself for a long time. He'd blocked out the thought of children, not because of his own miserable upbringing, but because of the potential pain of losing someone again.

He might have believed he'd crushed the dream of a family. But it had remained, like a little kernel inside him. Immune to his cynicism. Immune to his attempts to control his life by creating so much wealth and success that he would never feel at the mercy of his environment again.

Family. Nessa had been pregnant with his child, and she'd almost died under those horses' hooves. He felt clammy at the thought of how close she'd come to serious injury. She'd been pregnant with his child because of *his* lack of care in protecting them both. She was his family now, in spite of the loss of the baby.

The doctor's words came back: *there's no reason why she can't get pregnant again.*

There, on the steps of the hospital, Luc was aware of his whole world view changing. The vision he'd always had for his life and legacy had been far too narrow. He could see that now.

Everything had just changed in an instant and he knew there was only one way forward.

Nessa was one big throbbing ache that radiated out from her back and all over her body, but most acutely in her womb. The place where her baby had been. A baby she hadn't even been aware of.

It was a particularly cruel and unusual thing to be told you're pregnant, and, in the same breath, that you're not.

How could she be feeling so much for something that had been so ephemeral? *Because it was Luc's. And because you do want the fairy tale. And because as soon as the doctor told you you'd been pregnant, you pictured a small child with dark hair. A child who would grow up secure and loved and who would take all of that dark cynicism out of his eyes. A child who would take away the terror you've always felt at the thought of your world collapsing around you again...*

Nessa squeezed her eyes shut at the surge of emotion that gripped her. She felt a tear leak out. But before she could wipe it away there was the sound of the door, and her heart clenched because she knew instantly who it was.

'Nessa.'

She quickly dashed the tear away, keeping her face turned towards the window. When she felt slightly more composed she opened her eyes and turned her head. And she knew straight away that he knew. The doctor had told him.

His suit was crumpled, tie undone, shirt open at the top. He came in and stood near the bed, eyes so dark that Nessa felt as if she might drown in them.

'I didn't know about the baby,' she said, hating the defensive tone in her voice.

'I know.'

The emotional turmoil of the past few hours and weeks and Luc's inscrutability made Nessa lash out. 'Do you? Are you sure I didn't do it on purpose to try and trap you?'

Something fleeting and pained crossed Luc's face but Nessa felt no triumph to have pierced that impenetrable wall. 'Once,' he admitted, 'I might have suspected such a thing but I know you now.'

He did. She'd let him right into the heart of her. And she resisted that now even though it was far too late. 'No, you don't. Not really. You have no idea what I want.'

Luc sat down on a chair near the head of the bed and sat forward. Suddenly he was too close.

'What do you want, Nessa?'

You, came the automatic response. She looked away from that hard-boned face. 'I want you to leave, Luc. My brother is coming from Dublin to help take me home first thing tomorrow.'

She heard a curse and movement and the bed dipped

as Luc sat down. Nessa couldn't move without extreme pain so she was trapped. She glared at him, seizing on as much anger and pain as she could to protect herself.

He looked fierce. 'We just lost a baby, Nessa. We need to talk about this.'

More pain gripped her. '*I* lost a baby, Luc. Don't try to pretend you would have ever welcomed the news.'

He stood up, eyes burning. 'What are you saying? That you would have never told me?'

Nessa was taken aback. 'I don't know. I didn't have to make that decision.'

'Would you have got rid of it?'

Nessa's hands automatically went to her belly and the answer was immediate and instinctive. *'No.'*

Luc seemed to relax slightly. He paced away from the bed for a moment, running his hand through his hair. Nessa's gaze couldn't help taking in his unconsciously athletic grace, even now.

He turned to face her again. 'I won't pretend I wasn't shocked by the news, and I can't blame you for thinking I wouldn't welcome it. I've never made any secret of the fact I don't want to have a family. I never wanted to be a father because my own was absent, so how would I know what to do?

'But now,' he said, 'things are different.'

Nessa's mouth was suddenly dry and her heart thumped. 'What do you mean?'

She had no warning for when Luc said in a very determined tone, 'I think we should get married.'

CHAPTER TEN

NESSA JUST LOOKED at Luc in shock. Finally she asked, 'Are you sure you didn't receive a head injury?'

He shook his head. He stood at the end of the bed, hands on the rail. 'I'm serious, Nessa. We would be having a very different conversation right now if you hadn't lost the baby.'

Sharp pain lanced her. 'Do you think it was my fault? I didn't know… I felt nauseous all last week but I thought it was just—' She stopped. She'd thought it was due to emotional turmoil. Not pregnancy.

Luc came and sat down near the bed again. 'No, Nessa. Of course it wasn't your fault. The doctor said these things happen. But the fact is that we almost had a baby and if you *were* pregnant there is no way we wouldn't be getting married. No child of mine will be born out of wedlock. I was born that way and I won't inflict the same unsure existence on my child.'

Nessa was desperately trying to read Luc, to absorb what he was saying. 'But I'm not pregnant, so why on earth would you want to marry me?'

As if he couldn't be contained, Luc got up and paced again. He stopped. 'Because this experience has made me face up to the fact that I'm not as averse to the thought of family as I thought I was. Having a child, an heir, it's something I'd always rejected. But I can see the benefits now.'

Nessa shrank back into the pillows. 'That all sounds very clinical.'

Luc came to the end of the bed again. 'I would love it to the best of my ability. I would give it a good life, every opportunity. Brothers, sisters. Like your family.'

It. Something in Nessa shrivelled up.

'What about me?' she forced herself to ask. 'Would you love me to the best of your ability?'

He waved a dismissive hand. 'This isn't about love—that's why it would be a success. We'd be going into this with eyes open and no illusions. I still want you, Nessa. And I can offer you a commitment now.'

He went on. 'We're a good team. These last few weeks have been a success for both of us professionally. We can expand on that, create an empire.'

'Just a few days ago you told me *the novelty had worn off.*'

'I didn't want to hurt you.'

'Well, you did,' Nessa said bluntly. She felt sick all over again at this evidence of just how far he was willing to go in a bid to achieve his ultimate ambition.

'As flattered as I am that you would consider me a good choice to be your wife and mother of your children, I'm afraid I can't accept.'

Luc's brows snapped together. 'Why not?'

'Because I don't love you.' *Liar.*

He didn't miss a beat. 'We don't need love. We have amazing chemistry.'

'Which you said would *fizzle out*,' Nessa pointed out.

A muscle pulsed in Luc's jaw. 'I underestimated our attraction. I don't see it fizzling out any time soon.'

'But it *will*,' Nessa all but wailed. 'And then what?

You take mistresses while our children see their parents grow more distant?'

She shook her head. 'I won't do it, Luc. Before my mother died my parents had a blissfully happy marriage. I won't settle for anything less. I'm very pleased for you that you've figured out what you want, but I'm not it. Go and choose one of the women who understand your rules. I'm sure one of them can give you everything you need.'

His words mocked her. *This isn't about love.* But it was. For her. And now that she'd broken her own rules and fallen in love, she knew she couldn't settle for anything less than what her parents had had and what she saw in her sister and brother-in-law's relationship. True selfless devotion. Trust.

Surely that was worth the fear of losing the one you loved? Even knowing that for a short time?

'Nessa—'

'I'm sorry, sir, you'll have to leave. She needs to rest now. Her blood pressure is going up.' A nurse had come in and neither of them had noticed.

Suddenly Nessa felt very weary. 'Luc, just go. And please don't come back. I can't give you what you've decided you need.'

For a long moment she thought he was going to refuse to leave. He looked as if he was about to pluck her from the bed. But then he lifted his hands up in a gesture of surrender. It was a very *un*-Luc gesture. 'I'll go, for now. But this conversation isn't over, Nessa.'

Yes, it is, she vowed silently as she watched him walk out.

The nurse came over and fussed around Nessa, checking her stats. She winked at Nessa and said, 'If you can't give him what he needs, just send him my way.'

Nessa forced a weak smile and laid her head back on the pillow. It was throbbing with everything Luc had just proposed. *Luc had just proposed.* But he hadn't. It wasn't a real proposal. He'd proposed a business merger. No doubt he saw the benefits of being related in marriage to Sheikh Nadim; it would place Luc in an untouchable place. Finally he would have all the respect and social acceptance he craved. And Nessa would be a side benefit of that. His wife, the jockey, who could be trotted out at social events as a star attraction. For as long as she won those races, of course.

And then bear his children, who he'd suddenly decided would be a convenient vehicle to carry on his name.

In a way she envied Luc—that he could be so coolly calculating and detached. She wanted to be detached. Not in love.

The nurse left the room. Just then Nessa's phone rang on the bedside table and she picked it up, expecting it to be Paddy. But it was Iseult, calling from Merkazad. She sounded frantic. 'Ness, what on earth happened? Are you okay?'

Nessa forced it all out of her head and told her sister everything. Everything, except how she'd fallen stupidly in love with Luc Barbier and lost his child.

It had been a week since Luc had seen Nessa in Paris and he'd since returned to the stables in Ireland.

He'd gone back to the hospital the day after their conversation to find her room empty and ready for the next patient. She'd already left for Ireland, with her brother. He'd since found out that her brother-in-law had arranged a private jet for them to go back to Kildare.

The image of Nessa being taken back into the bosom

of her protective family was all too vivid for Luc's liking. He hadn't liked the spiking of panic and the feeling of being very, very out of control.

He had to admit now that he'd had it all so very wrong. Paddy hadn't been a thief, and Nessa hadn't been an accessory. They were just a close-knit family.

Luc hadn't pursued her since then because she needed to recuperate, and he knew she also needed time to go over his proposal.

But there was no way that she was refusing his proposal the next time. Damn the woman anyway. From the very first moment he'd laid eyes on her she'd challenged him, thwarted him and generally behaved in exactly the opposite manner to which he expected. His blood thrummed even now as he looked out over the gallops and expected to see a head of dark red hair glinting in the sunshine.

It was inconceivable that he wouldn't see her here again, that she would turn him down. The chemistry between them was still as strong as ever. He would seduce her, and convince her to agree to his proposal. The alternative was not an option.

'What do you mean she's not at home?'

Luc glared at Paddy, who gulped. Luc had summoned the young man to his office to ask for directions to the O'Sullivan farm. It was time to bring Nessa back.

'She's gone to Merkazad. Iseult needed some help with the new baby. It's due any day now.'

Luc's blood pressure was reaching boiling point. 'But she's injured!'

Paddy looked sheepish. 'She said she felt much better already.'

He could imagine that all too well. Her sister said

she needed her, and Nessa jumped, without a thought for herself.

Luc made an inarticulate sound and dismissed Paddy. He paced his office, feeling like a caged animal. He needed Nessa *now*, and she was on the other side of the world.

A cold, clammy sweat broke out on Luc's brow and he stopped dead as the significance of that sank in. *He needed her.* When he'd never needed anyone in his life. Not even Pierre Fortin had impacted Luc as hard, and that man had given him a whole new life.

Luc assured himself now that he just needed her for all the myriad reasons he'd told her that day at the hospital. That was all. But the clammy feeling wouldn't recede.

He went to his drinks cabinet and poured himself a shot of whisky. He felt as if he were unravelling at the seams. He took another shot, but the panic wouldn't go away.

Eventually Luc went outside to the stables and staff scattered as he approached when they saw the look on his face. Pascal bumped into him and stepped back. 'Woah, Luc. What's wrong? Has something happened?'

Luc all but snarled at him and strode off. He went to the stables and saddled up his favourite horse, cantering out of the yard and up into the fields and tracks surrounding his land. He came to a stop only when the horse was lathered in sweat and heaving for breath. Like him.

He slid off the horse and stood by his head, holding the reins. This was the same hill he'd come to when he'd bought this place. He could remember the immense sense of satisfaction to be expanding his empire into one of the world's most respected racing communities.

Finally, he'd thought then, *I'll be seen as one of them. I'll no longer be tainted by my past.*

But as he stood in exactly the same place now, Luc realised his past was no further away than it ever had been. It was still as vivid as ever. He expected to feel frustration or a sense of futility because he knew now he'd never escape it. He waited, but all he did feel, surprisingly, was a measure of peace.

For the first time, Luc could appreciate that his past had made him who he was and there was a curious sense of pride in that.

Yet, this revelation left a hollow ache inside him because he had no one to share it with. He knew now that there was only one person he would want to share it with, and she was gone. A sense of bleakness gripped him.

Nessa had returned to the protection of *her* home, *her* family, and Luc had no place there. He had no right to claim her. For a brief moment they could have been together, but it had been taken away and he had no right to that dream with her.

She didn't love him, and if he had an ounce of humanity left he would not take advantage of their attraction to persuade her otherwise. She deserved someone far better than he would ever be.

The horse moved restlessly beside him, ready to return home, and Luc felt the bitter sting of irony. He wanted to go home too, but the home he wanted to go to didn't exist, because he'd spent his whole life denying that it could exist, or that he needed it. And now it was too late.

'Nessa, if you had told me about the baby I never would have let you come all the way here.'

Nessa's emotions bubbled up under the sympathetic

gaze of her older sister, who was sitting with her in one of Merkazad castle's beautiful courtyards. They'd just been served afternoon tea, which had remained untouched as Nessa had spilled out the last few weeks' events under the expert questioning of her concerned sister, who had noticed something was off.

Much as Nessa might have guessed, Iseult had already vowed to pay off Paddy's debt to Luc Barbier, and Nessa was glad she hadn't told Iseult before now. She would have been far too worried and insisted on getting involved. At least this way it was all over; whether or not Paddy would let Iseult and Nadim take on the debt was for him to deal with now.

'It's fine, Iseult. I'm glad I came. Really.' She adored her nephew, Kamil, a dark-haired imp of five going on twenty-five, who was as excited about the imminent birth as everyone else.

Iseult reached for her hand now, squeezing it gently. 'And what about Luc?'

Nessa sighed. 'What about Luc? He proposed marriage as a business merger, not out of romance or love.'

'But you do love him?'

Nessa desperately wanted to say no. But in the end she nodded, feeling her heart contract with pain.

Her sister sat back again, placing a hand over her rotund bump that looked ready to pop under her kaftan. Just then Kamil burst into the courtyard, holding his palm tablet and saying excitedly, 'Look, Auntie Ness, I found you on the Internet!'

He jumped up onto Nessa's lap and started playing the video of Nessa's last race. Iseult suddenly realised the significance and reached across, saying, 'I don't think Auntie Ness wants to see that one, Kami. Let's find another.'

But Nessa shot a smile at Iseult even as her heart was thumping. 'It's fine. I wouldn't mind seeing it anyway. I haven't looked back at it yet.'

The tablet was propped on the table and Kamil squealed with excitement on Nessa's lap as the race drew to a close and she won.

When Kamil wriggled off her lap to run off again Nessa barely noticed. And she didn't see the concern on her sister's face. Her eyes were glued to the screen and the aftermath of the race. She saw the riderless horse and then a flurry of movement, Sur La Mer bucking and then herself disappearing underneath the horses.

She had no memory of the actual incident, so it was like watching someone else.

A blur of movement entered the frame from the right. A man, pushing his way through, throwing people out of his way and shouting. The camera focused on him, zooming in. Nessa realised with a jolt that it was Luc, and that he was being held back by Francois while the medics cleared a space and worked on her.

Francois was saying something indistinct to him and then Luc turned around with a savage look on his face and shouted very clearly, *'I don't care about the damn horse, I care about her.'*

The video clip stopped then, frozen on Luc's fierce expression.

Nessa looked warily at Iseult, who arched a brow. 'That does not look like a man who is driven by ambition to marry a woman he sees only as a business opportunity, now, does it?'

'He's in the gym on the first floor, love. He's in there for hours in the morning and every evening. It's like he's trying to exorcise the devil himself.'

Nessa smiled her thanks at Mrs Owens. Her heart was palpitating—she'd come here straight from Dublin airport. Iseult had insisted she come home, all but bundling her onto the plane herself saying fiercely, *'You'll always regret it if you don't find out for sure, Ness.'*

Nessa had known herself that even if Luc did feel something for her, he wouldn't come after her. He'd been too hurt by his past. He'd never had anyone to depend on. Not really. And anyone he'd felt anything for had died.

It had only dawned on Nessa then that they actually had more in common than she'd ever appreciated. Fear of loss. Grief.

The difference was that she'd had a family around her and he'd had no one.

She stopped outside the door to the gym. It was too late to worry about how she looked in worn jeans and a long-sleeved top. No make-up. Hair up in a loose topknot. Impulsively at the last second, she undid it and her hair fell down around her shoulders.

All she could hear from behind the door was a low and muffled-sounding rhythmic *thump thump*.

She took a deep breath and opened the door into the vast room. All Nessa saw at first were a hundred complicated-looking machines. But Luc wasn't on any of those.

He was at the other end of the room punching a heavy bag, dressed in sweats and bare-chested. He was dripping with perspiration, a fierce frown on his face, hair damp. The scar on his back was a jagged line and Nessa's heart squeezed.

He gave the bag a thump so hard that Nessa felt the reverberations go through her own body. And then he stopped suddenly. She realised that he'd seen her in the mirror.

He turned around, chest heaving and gleaming. Nessa was breathless. She'd never seen him looking so raw. Unconstructed. Suddenly the thought of never being with this man again left her breathless with pain. She couldn't do it. Even if he didn't really love her.

He stood with an arrested expression on his face and she walked towards him slowly. As she came closer the expression was replaced with a smooth mask. He pulled off his gloves and picked up a towel, running it roughly over his face and the back of his neck. He pulled on a T-shirt.

'I thought you were in Merkazad.'

Nessa stopped a few feet away. 'I was. I came back.' *Brilliant, Nessa. As if that weren't patently obvious.*

He shook his head. 'Why did you go there? You'd just lost our baby, but you jumped to your sister's bidding with no thought of the pain it might cause you?'

Our baby. Not *it*. Nessa's heart clenched. 'It wasn't like that. Iseult didn't know about the baby, and I thought it would be a good idea to help out.'

'You were afraid I'd propose again.' Luc sounded grim.

Nessa nodded slowly. 'Part of me was afraid you'd insist…' And that she wouldn't be able to say no.

'Was my proposal so unwelcome?' There was a bleak tone to his voice now.

Nessa nodded, watching his expression carefully. Something flashed in his eyes and she recognised pain. As much as she hated to see it, it also sent hope to her heart.

She moved closer and saw a wary look cross his face now.

'But not because of why you think. I couldn't bear the fact that it was such a clinical proposal. To merge two names. To bolster your reputation and success. And just because you'd had a revelation about wanting a family.'

He shook his head and when he spoke his voice was rough. 'It wasn't just that.'

He looked at her, and the pain in the depths of his eyes was unmistakable now. 'I'm sorry for everything. You just tried to help your brother and I treated you as if you'd stolen from me yourself. Then I seduced you, when I had no right to take your innocence, an innocence that I didn't believe in until it was too late. I had no right to disrupt your life like that.'

He went pale. 'When I saw you lying under those horses, I thought I'd killed you…and then the baby. It's my fault you lost the baby, Nessa. If I hadn't asked you to ride in the race it wouldn't have happened. You were innocent of every charge I levelled at you.'

Suddenly Nessa felt cold. She put a hand to her mouth, horror coursing through her. 'You feel responsible? That's why you were so upset when you saw the accident. I thought…'

Nessa felt sick and turned away before he could see her. She'd never felt like such a fool. She tried to walk away as quickly as she could but a hand on her arm stopped her.

'You thought what…?'

Nessa blinked back tears and turned around, avoiding Luc's eye. 'I watched the race online. You ran over, and you shouted at Francois that you cared about me, and not the horse.' But now Nessa realised that of course Luc would care about any one of his jockeys more than a horse.

That was all it had been.

His hand tightened so much on her arm that she looked up at him. When she saw the look on his face she stopped breathing.

'You thought I just felt responsible for you?'

Nessa's humiliation turned to anger. 'Didn't you?'

His eyes were burning and she saw the same volatile emotion she was feeling reflected in their depths. But she didn't trust it.

'Believe me,' he said grimly, 'I wish that what I felt for you was just a sense of responsibility.'

'What's that supposed to mean?'

He dropped his hand from her arm as if suddenly aware he might be hurting her.

'I proposed to you in the hospital because I was too cowardly to admit that I nearly lost my whole life when I saw you lying under that horse. Of course I felt responsible, but I was also terrified.'

He took a deep breath. 'I was terrified I was about to lose the only other person I've ever truly loved in my life, but I couldn't admit that to myself even then.'

Nessa's heart stopped. She was afraid she might be projecting words from her heart onto Luc's lips. 'What are you saying?'

He took a step closer. He looked uncharacteristically vulnerable. 'I'm saying that I love you, Nessa. I think I've loved you from the moment we met, when I knew that I didn't want to let you out of my sight. But I know you don't love me and I told myself I wouldn't stoop low enough to seduce you again because you deserve more. I brought nothing but more loss into your life.'

Nessa shook her head, almost too afraid to move in case she shattered this delicate moment. 'First of all, it's no one's fault we lost the baby. It was just one of those things. Secondly, I lied to you. I *do* love you. So much that it scares me. And third of all, you brought nothing but richness into my life. You awakened me. You made me believe I was beautiful, you gave me the chance to be a jockey, you showed me Paris. That's where I knew I loved you.'

He reached for her and drew her to him as gently as if she were spun glass. 'Do you mean this?'

She nodded. 'I mean it with every bone in my body. When I told you I didn't love you at the hospital it was because I thought you were just consolidating your empire with a marriage of convenience.'

He shook his head, drawing her in even closer so their bodies were touching. A wave of need surged through Nessa. Luc's voice was full of self-recrimination. 'None of this means anything without you. I said it wasn't about love because I didn't know what love was. Until I went back the next day and you were gone. I was so sure I could persuade you...seduce you. And then I realised I wanted so much more.

'I want it all, Nessa. A real family. Even though it terrifies me. How do I know how to have a family when I've never been part of one?'

Nessa reached up and put her arms around Luc's neck. She felt stupidly shy all of a sudden. 'I can show you.'

He looked down at her, a suspiciously bright glint in his eye. 'It might take a lifetime.'

'I wouldn't settle for anything less.'

Luc suddenly looked serious. He framed her face with his hands. 'Nessa O'Sullivan, I'm never letting you out of my sight, ever again. Will you marry me?'

She nodded, a surge of joy spreading from her heart

to every part of her body. Tears made her vision blurry. 'Yes…yes, I will. I love you, Luc.'

'I love *you, mon amour.*'

Luc could feel Nessa's heart thumping in time with his, and as her mouth opened under his and he pulled her even closer he knew that this wasn't just a mirage, and that, finally, he'd found peace, love, and his true home.

EPILOGUE

'AND IT'S NESSA BARBIER, riding to glory again in the Kilkenny Stakes on Sacre Coeur, owned by her husband and brother-in-law...'

A short time later Luc watched as his wife rode into the winner's enclosure, mud-spattered face beaming. She wore the colours of the newly announced Barbier-Al-Saqr racing consortium—green and gold, a nod to Ireland and Merkazad.

His heart-rate finally returned to normal to see her in one piece. She saw him and her smile got even wider. She jumped off the horse gracefully and handed it to a groom before coming over to where he was standing with their two-year-old son, Cal, in his arms.

Flashes of light went berserk around them—the press still couldn't get enough of Luc and Nessa ever since their fairy-tale romance had become news. They'd been married almost two years ago in a modest ceremony in an old chapel on Luc's stud farm grounds in Kildare, and then they'd celebrated with a more lavish reception in Merkazad.

'You do know that every time I watch you race it takes about a year off my life?' Luc grumbled good-naturedly as he handed over his son, who was reaching for his mother with chubby arms.

Nessa cuddled him close and looked up at Luc. She had an enigmatic glint in her eye and then said *sotto voce*, 'Well, if it's any consolation it looks like this will be my last race for about a year, if not longer.'

Luc looked at her. The only other time she'd stopped racing was when they'd fallen pregnant with Cal, and even though the doctor had assured them that Nessa should be fine to race early in her pregnancy they'd both agreed that she wouldn't, in deference to what had happened when she'd first been pregnant.

A surge of emotion rushed through Luc as he reached for her. 'You're...?' He stopped, mindful of waggling ears.

She nodded, eyes shimmering with emotion. 'I'm late, so I don't know for sure yet, but I'm pretty certain.'

Luc pulled her and Cal into him, her free arm wrapped around his waist and his son snuggled up between them. His heart was so full he was afraid it might explode. He finally knew the true meaning of wealth and success and it had nothing to do with professional respect or money. It was *this*.

And then over Nessa's head he saw Nadim and Iseult with their two children walking towards them. Iseult was pregnant again with baby number three. *His family.* Luc finally felt like he belonged to something he'd never had the courage to hope for, and it still felled him sometimes. How lucky he was. How blessed he was. And now this, the seed of a new life in Nessa's belly.

Nessa looked up at him and for a brief moment before they were enveloped in their family, and congratulations, they shared a look of pure love and understanding. 'I love you,' he said, not caring about hiding his emotion.

'I love you too...'

The kiss they shared at that moment with their son between them was the picture used on the front pages of the newspapers the next day under the headline: *Love at the races...a true family affair.*

* * * * *

CLAIMING HIS
WEDDING NIGHT

LOUISE FULLER

To Jane Arnold. For Friday coffee and shopping; for making it up to Southwold so many times; and for being my friend.

Thank you.

CHAPTER ONE

SHE SHOULD BE PLEASED. Good publicity was what charities like hers survived on. Only it was doing more than surviving, Addie Farrell thought with a small smile of satisfaction as she glanced down at the newspaper. It was just five years since they had opened their doors to offer music to disadvantaged children in the city, but the way things were going, they might be able to open a second centre soon.

Addie frowned. The article was one hundred per cent approving—even the photograph was flattering. So why did she feel so deflated? Her smile faded. Probably because the glossy red curls tumbling over her shoulders and the nervous excitement in her blue eyes hinted at a different Addie—an Addie she had been a long time ago, for a few blissful months. The Addie she might still be now if Malachi King hadn't taken her heart and tossed it aside like some unwanted corporate gift.

Don't go there! she warned herself. The article was about her hard work and determination. It had absolutely nothing to do with her rat of an estranged husband. Or their foolhardy and doomed marriage.

That was all in the past now.

Her present—her future—was a world away from that dark place she'd slipped into after Malachi had broken her heart. And she had survived worse than his defection. Her muscles tensed as she remembered the car accident that had shattered her dream of playing the piano professionally. It had been devastating, but she had not given up and now she had the best job in the world: bringing music to children whose lives were a constant battle with poverty and neglect.

She sighed. Only that would keep happening if she got on and knuckled down to her admin.

Opening her laptop, she began clicking through her emails. Twenty minutes later she reached across the desk and picked up a pile of envelopes from her in tray. Glancing at the one on top, she felt her breath catch sharply in her throat, the beat of her heart suddenly swift and urgent. As though mesmerised, she stared blankly at the embossed logo on the front of the envelope.

King Industries. Owned by her very rich, very handsome and very estranged husband Malachi.

The blood was roaring in her ears, and for a moment she imagined tearing up the letter and hurling the pieces into the warm Miami air. And then, with hands that shook slightly, she tore it open and read the letter inside.

It took three attempts before her brain could connect the words to their meaning. Not that the letter was badly written. Quite the opposite, in fact. It was polite and succinct, informing her that, after five years of funding, King Industries would be withdrawing their financial support from the Miami Music Project.

Heart pounding, Addie scanned through the lines, her eyes inexorably drawn to the signature at the bottom of the page. Bracing her shoulders, she felt her chest squeeze tight as she stared at her husband's name.

Fury snapped through her bones like electric sparks. Was this some kind of cruel joke?

He hadn't been in touch for five years. *Five years!* Not a phone call, an email, a text.

Nothing.

This was the first time he'd contacted her since their wedding day and it was some stock letter telling her that he was cutting the funding for her charity! It was despicable! And so cowardly when he hadn't even had the guts to speak to her, let alone meet her face-to-face.

Somewhere beneath her ribs she felt something twist—a wrench, slight yet irrevocable. If she hadn't known better she might have thought it was her heart.

Her whole body was shaking and she felt a sudden spasm of helpless rage. Wasn't it enough that he'd crushed her romantic dreams? His support for her charity was the *one* good thing that had survived their marriage. Only now he wanted to wreck that too.

What kind of man would do something like that to his wife?

Her stomach cramped as she miserably remembered her wedding day, and how Malachi had promised to love her. Looking into her eyes with a shimmering heat that had made her heart quiver, he had made her believe he meant every word.

Gritting her teeth, she stared down at the face looking back up at her from the newspaper.

How could you have ever believed that he loved you?

Her face tightened. She'd known all about his reputation as a womaniser, a player of hearts as well as cards. But of course she'd believed him. Who wouldn't? That was what Malachi did best. He looked into your eyes and smiled, a gorgeous, curving smile, and he made you believe.

He made the gamblers in his casinos believe they would beat the tables.

And he'd made her believe that he loved her.

But he hadn't. Instead he had used her and exploited their relationship to improve his bad-boy image. Their marriage had been nothing more than a stunt conceived and executed by a man who had built a multibillion-dollar business by ruthlessly taking what he wanted. A man who liked playing games almost as much as he liked to win.

Her head snapped up and, lifting her shoulders, she eased her head from side to side, like a fighter about to step into the ring.

Maybe it was about time he found out what it was like to lose.

Breathing out slowly, Addie lifted up the letter and stared at it bleakly.

He might have had the 'house edge' during their relationship, but if he thought this letter would be the last word on their marriage he could think again. A lot had changed in the five years since they'd separated. She knew what lay behind his smile now, and she certainly wasn't the same lovestruck young woman he'd married.

Rapidly typing into her keyboard, she narrowed her eyes as she picked up her phone and quickly punched in the number at the top of the letter.

'Good morning! King Industries. How may I help you?'

Feeling her heart start to pound, Addie took a deep breath and said quickly, 'I'd like to speak to Mr King!'

'Could I take your name, please?'

Her shoulders stiffened. Gripping the phone tightly, she bit down hard on her lip. It was her last chance to change her mind. To leave the past sealed.

For a moment she almost hung up, and then, dry-mouthed, she closed her eyes and said hoarsely, 'Addie Farrell.'

There was a pause.

'I'm sorry, Ms Farrell, I don't seem to have you down for an appointment.'

'I don't have one,' she said, surprised and even a little

impressed by the firm, even tenor of her voice. 'But it's important—vital that I speak to him!'

'I understand that, Ms Farrell.' The girl sounded young, and a little nervous. But despite her youth she had clearly been well-trained. 'And I'll do my best to help, but Mr King doesn't speak to anyone without an appointment.'

Opening her eyes, Addie cursed softly. Of course he didn't. Malachi was the CEO. His calls would obviously be screened and only the most important would be put through to him. She gritted her teeth. But who could be more important than his wife?

Somewhere at the back of her head a voice was warning her to hang up, but it was muffled by the angry, insistent beat of her heart. 'He'll speak to me,' she said slowly. 'Just give him my name.'

There was another, longer pause. 'I can't do that, Ms Farrell. But I can certainly arrange an appointment. Or if you'd like to leave a message—'

Addie smiled grimly. 'Fine,' she snapped. 'Tell him it's his wife. I just wanted to remind him that it's our wedding anniversary tomorrow.'

There was a total, frozen silence and she felt an unexpected but welcome ripple of satisfaction wash over her.

'If you wouldn't mind passing that message on? I don't mind holding,' she said sweetly.

Outside the window of his private jet an ethereal pale blue sky stretched to the horizon. It was beautiful, humbling. But Malachi King was oblivious to the view. Instead his gaze was locked to the screen in front of him, his dark grey eyes moving swiftly over the columns of figures that filled the page.

'What happened on Table Twenty-five?' he asked

abruptly, looking up at the thickset, middle-aged man seated opposite him.

'There was an incident. A bunch of guys on a stag night got a bit messy. But I dealt with it. Nice and smooth, Mr King.'

'That's what I pay you for, Mike. To keep it all smooth!'

Glancing at the message on the screen of his phone, Malachi gave a small, tight smile. If only he could smooth out his parents' messy lives so easily. But unfortunately Henry and Serena King were showing no sign of giving up their decadent habits any time soon, and as their only son he had no option but to clean up after them.

There was a knock on the cabin door and both men watched in silent appreciation as a sleek brunette wearing the uniform of the King Industries private airline sashayed into the room.

'Your coffee, Mr King! Will there be anything else?'

Malachi's smile shifted. Breathing in sharply, he let his eyes linger on the almost ludicrous swell of the woman's bottom against the navy fabric of her skirt. He felt his body stir—

Will there be anything else?

Surely that was one of the advantages to owning your own plane? Sex with a beautiful woman at forty-one thousand feet? It certainly beat an in-flight movie and a packet of peanuts. He let his gaze drift over the woman's body. She was very beautiful. And desirable. But he would never sleep with her. Not only because she worked for him— that, of course, put her off limits—but because she was just too available. There was no excitement, no challenge in bedding a woman like her.

He didn't miss a beat.

'No, thank you, Victoria. Just the coffee.' His intonation was perfect, polite but neutral, making it clear that while he might remember her name that was the beginning and the end of their relationship.

He turned his attention back to his security chief. 'It all looks good, Mike. I'm going to chill for ten minutes, so enjoy the rest of the flight.' It was a dismissal, but again done with exactly the right blend of warmth and efficiency. Leaning back in his seat, he heard the door shut and, reaching forward, clicked the phone on the desk. 'No more calls, Chrissie.'

Closing his laptop, he breathed out slowly. Now he could enjoy the view!

He didn't really understand why but it was something of a guilty pleasure for him, watching the sky stretch out and away—a giant, vaulted ceiling of blue. Was it something to do with the colours? He frowned. Maybe. Or maybe it was because the serenity and calm was so unlike the chaotic debauchery of life with his parents.

He shifted in his seat, feeling it for the first time: that soft pressure, like a finger pushing against a bruise. A memory of eyes that exact colour, widening, changing from light to dark, cool to hot—eyes that set off a jangling alarm inside his head.

He gritted his teeth. He tried never to think about Addie. His wife. But this time of year, this month—tomorrow, in fact—always made him unusually tense. He had to dig deep to calm himself, to stop his nerves from ringing.

He jolted forward in his seat. The ringing wasn't inside his head. It was his phone. Mouth hardening, he stared at it in disbelief and then, frowning, snatched it up. 'This had better be good,' he said tersely. 'Or at least entertaining enough for you to have disturbed me—'

There was a short, tense silence, and then he heard his personal assistant breathe out nervously.

'I'm sorry, Mr King—I didn't want to do the wrong

thing. I wouldn't have bothered you, but she said it was important so I put her on hold. Is that okay?'

She! In other words, his mother. Gritting his teeth, Malachi felt a surge of irritation. But he couldn't really blame his assistant. Serena King could make a broken nail sound like a diplomatic incident if she chose.

Imagining his mother's likely mood, he grimaced. *Please let it not be something too sordid. Or illegal.* 'It's fine, Chrissie. I'll speak to her now,' he said slowly.

Better just to take the call, for Serena would not take kindly to being fobbed off after having been kept on hold. And her unkindness was not something he wanted to provoke.

'Yes, sir.' The girl hesitated. 'And Happy Anniversary for tomorrow, Mr King!'

Suddenly his jaw was clenched so tightly he could feel his teeth vibrating. His whole body was on high alert, his mind rewinding their conversation.

There was only one other person aside from himself who knew that tomorrow was his wedding anniversary. And it certainly wasn't his mother. He'd made damn sure that his parents had been kept well away from his marriage.

He breathed out slowly. 'I think we might be speaking at cross purposes.'

Glancing down, he saw that his hand was curled tightly over the armrest, the knuckles protruding whitely against his skin. With an effort, he splayed the fingers apart.

'Who exactly have you got on hold, Chrissie?'

She cleared her throat, and when she spoke again, her voice was high and nervous. 'I—I'm sorry, Mr King,' she stammered. 'I thought you understood. It's your wife. Ms Farrell!'

Malachi stared across the cabin. Outside the window the sky had clouded over. Everything was the same pure white as newly settled snow. The same pure white as the dress Addie had worn when she'd spoken her wedding vows. His throat tightened. His motives for marrying might have been a little self-serving—even a little manipulative. But either way, she'd promised to love and cherish and honour him. Only her promises had been as fragile and tenuous as the clouds breaking apart outside the window.

Why now? he wondered. Why, after all this time, had she chosen this moment to get in touch? For a moment random thoughts collided in his head—irritation, curiosity, disquiet—and then abruptly he sat up straighter.

'What a charming surprise,' he said smoothly. 'You'd better put her through.'

The phone line clicked and his stomach tensed as, for the first time since their wedding, he heard the light, clipped voice of his wife.

'Malachi? It's me. Addie!'

'Apparently so,' he drawled softly.

It had been five years, but nothing in his manner gave any hint of how unsettling it was to hear her again. Nor would it. Years spent playing high-stakes poker had taught him early and hard the value of never giving anything away. He grimaced. That and being Henry and Serena's son. It was just a pity he hadn't remembered that lesson when he'd first met Addie.

'It's been a long time, sweetheart,' he murmured. 'To what do I owe the honour?'

Addie felt the walls of her office shift and shrink around her.

In her haste to call him she hadn't considered how he might react. But now, hearing his voice, she felt confused and thwarted, for he sounded exactly as he always had: cool, smooth, in control. Almost as though the last five years had never happened.

She gritted her teeth. What had she expected? Anger? Outrage? That would mean being emotional, and Malachi King didn't *do* emotional.

Her hands felt suddenly hot and clammy and, closing her eyes, she gripped the phone more tightly. She might not like it, but the truth was that it would take more than hearing from his estranged wife to make Malachi lose his cool. After all, even when their marriage had been disintegrating he had been like the eye of the storm: calm, detached. Separate.

But that was all in the past now. This phone call wasn't about raking over their personal history. It was about her husband's despicable behaviour *now*. And its impact on children's futures. Breathing out, she opened her eyes.

'How can you even mention the word *honour* after how you've acted? And don't act so surprised to hear from me. I sent you an email ten minutes ago—'

She broke off suddenly, anger making her trip over her words, the misery and pain suddenly as fresh as it had been five years ago. How could that be? It didn't seem fair to feel like that. But then she had never really got over his deception. Nothing—not even her job—had ever really filled the void that Malachi had left.

A shiver ran through her body and she was grateful that he couldn't see her face, see just how strongly he affected her. Her eyes narrowed. There was no way she was about to give him the satisfaction of hearing it in her voice either and, trying to project poise and confidence, she said coolly, 'I know you're short on empathy, Malachi, and that you have the morals of a shark, but I didn't think even *you* would stoop this low.'

The plane was turning. They were making their descent. Frowning, Malachi flipped open his laptop, punching the keyboard, his face impassive as he searched through his emails.

'I feel your pain, sweetheart,' he said softly, 'and I wish I could help. But unfortunately I'm a little baffled as to what it is you think I've done.'

Despite the neutrality of his words, he felt her anger gritty on his skin. Five years of silence and she randomly decided to ring up and shout at him about his morals and his lack of empathy. He frowned again. For some inexplicable reason she had once managed to turn his world upside down and inside out. It was a little surprising, not to say unsettling, to discover that she could still do so.

But his surprise was forgotten as finally he found the source of her outrage. So *that* was why she was so upset!

Leaning back, he stared at the screen, his eyes fixed on his wife's name. In theory, their conversation was over. He could and probably should simply hand the matter over to his social responsibilities department but—his eyes gleamed—where would be the fun in *that*?

'As I'm sure you remember, I run a huge operation,' he said disingenuously. 'Perhaps you could explain exactly what it is you *think* I've done.'

Addie felt a flash of impatience.

First he pulled the financial rug from under her feet, and now he was pretending he didn't know anything about it. She might have been idealistic and eager enough to take his words at face value when they'd first met, five years ago, but thanks to Malachi she'd become an expert in double-dealing.

'Oh, please! Do you *really* think I'm that stupid? You can't bluff your way out of this one, Malachi. This is not some game of cards!'

'Indeed it is not. Card games have rules, and players don't tend to screech unfounded accusations at one another.'

The taunting note in his voice made her heart bang in her throat, and suddenly she was gripping the phone so tightly her hand hurt.

'They are not unfounded. And I'm not screeching,' she snapped.

Damn him. He was so infuriating! Always twisting the facts. And so impossible to pin down. Unless she concentrated hard she was going to lose track of why she'd rung him in the first place, and probably end up saying or doing something stupid. Although not as stupid as agreeing to marry him.

Her blue eyes hardened like water turning to ice. Reining in her temper, she said crisply, 'You signed the letter, Malachi. I have it in front of me.'

'I sign lots of letters,' he said smoothly. 'It could be anything. Dry cleaning. Overdue library book.'

Addie gritted her teeth. She had rung him in anger, *knowing* that right was on her side. Only now he was making her fury seem out of place—comical, even—as though she was trying to rob a bank with a water pistol. Worse, she could feel herself responding to the teasing note in his voice.

It was suddenly hard to breathe. Memories of the past were pressing in on her. Memories of the man she had loved—not just because of his staggering good looks but because he was cool and funny. *And flirty.*

She felt her insides tighten and a prickling heat began to spread slowly over her skin.

Even the most prosaic of words sounded warm and honeyed when spoken in that slow, sexy drawl of his. For a moment she allowed herself to picture his handsome face, that wicked gleam in those dark, hypnotic eyes, the slight upward curve to his gorgeous lush mouth—

Her heart was banging.

Don't forget the lies that spilled from that gorgeous lush mouth, she reminded herself coldly.

Particularly those he'd told her at the altar. Next time she felt like reminiscing over her husband's charms she needed to remember those lies and how they'd left her struggling even to get out of bed some mornings.

Gripping the phone more tightly, she lifted her chin. 'As you well know it's about the centre. So quit pretending that you had nothing to do with stopping my funding.'

Staring at the screen in front of him, Malachi shifted slowly in his seat, waiting, thinking, deliberating.

Until two minutes ago her letter had just been one of the many that were handed to him every week. And yes, he'd signed it. But did she really believe he would do such a thing to her charity out of malice? His face tightened. Probably, and he knew she had reason to think so, but he didn't like the fact that she thought so badly of him.

'You're right. I did sign the letter,' he said coolly. 'But, like I said before, I sign hundreds of letters every week. I don't read them all—or even write them, actually. Except those that are personal.'

'You mean like a letter to your *wife*?' Addie said acidly.

Malachi stared straight ahead. Her words stung, as she'd intended them to.

'I suppose I asked for that.'

Feeling a stab of pain, Addie breathed out slowly. 'Yes. You did.'

At least if he'd known nothing about the letter she might have been able to believe he would have acted differently. But how had he not noticed her name? Or remembered her charity? For a moment she contemplated asking him, but her pride forbade her from revealing the grinding ache of misery in her chest. Besides, what was the point? It was all too long ago to matter.

She heard him sigh.

'I can understand how it might have looked to you. But it's quite simple, really. We offer financial support to emerging charities for a fixed period—in your case five years. By that time we would expect the project to be up and running and the funding would be cancelled. My signing the letter was just a formality.'

A formality!

Her lips twisted.

What a perfect footnote to a marriage that had been nothing more than a business strategy—for Malachi, at least.

'So,' he said softly, 'is that it? Are we good? Or is there something else you want to discuss?'

Her stomach gave a lurch as his words ricocheted inside her head. What did he mean? *Something else you want to discuss.* Was he just being polite? But even if a prickling tension *hadn't* begun to spread over her skin she knew he wasn't. She could hear the dare in his voice, the challenge, fluttering between them like a ribbon in a breeze.

Damn him. If Malachi wanted to talk about their relationship he could bring it up himself. Speaking to him had been a necessary evil. But she absolutely, definitely wasn't going to make polite conversation with him. And she certainly didn't want to discuss their marriage.

Or did she?

Her cheeks grew warm. Ringing Malachi had been a spur of the moment act. Confronted by what she'd seen as a deliberate act of provocation, she'd been swept along in a rush of anger and outrage. Only now her anger was slipping away, and reluctantly she found herself acknowledging the *whole* truth.

That she could simply have ignored the letter.

Or let a solicitor contact King Industries.

Or asked to speak to someone other than Malachi.

But she hadn't because deep down, buried beneath the resentment and the pain and the hurt, she had *wanted* that chance to speak to him. She shivered. It had been reckless, stupid. But surely she could forgive herself that one moment of weakness. After all, didn't every disappointed lover have some tiny sliver of longing to hold on to their fantasy of love?

But that didn't mean she was ready to discuss her failed marriage with the man who had trampled on that selfsame heart. Any more than she'd been willing five years ago to share more than the barest details about herself —particularly those concerning her life-changing accident. It would have required a trust that simply wasn't there.

She breathed in sharply. Right now, however, there were other less personal but more pressing matters to resolve. Like getting her funding back.

'No. We're *not* good! I accept that you didn't personally choose to stop the funding but that doesn't change the fact that it has stopped.'

She paused. Despite her bravado her heart had started to thump inside her chest. It had been easier when anger had been driving her. But ranting and raging was clearly not going to persuade Malachi to rethink his decision. That would require a softer, more conciliatory touch. Appalled, she licked her lips nervously. *Stay neutral and stick to the facts*, she told herself quickly. The funding was vital, the centre's work lasting and beneficial, and of course his generosity would be much appreciated. But, first off she needed to test the water.

Lifting her chin, she said firmly, 'Which is why I'd like you to change your mind.'

Malachi leaned back in his seat, a predatory smile curling his lip. It was a reasonable request. But it was still a request. One that *he* had the power to approve.

Or not.

'As I explained,' he said smoothly, 'I receive many requests for financial support. You yourself know of many deserving charities in Miami.'

'I do,' she agreed hurriedly. 'But the work we do with the children is enormously valuable and unique to the city.'

Standing up, Malachi stretched slowly and stifled a yawn. Could he be bothered to drag this conversation out any longer? The amount under discussion would barely make a dent in his billions. He could have a new agreement written up in minutes, sign it and say goodbye to Addie for ever. Or he could simply refuse to renew the funding and hand it over to his lawyers. Either way, in a matter of minutes she would be off the phone and out of his life for good.

His chest ached. Except now that she'd finally made contact with him saying goodbye was the last thing on his mind.

'True enough,' he said finally. 'But, be that as it may, there would have to be exceptional circumstances for me to renew your funding.'

The phone twitched in her hand and holding it suddenly felt dangerous, as though it had morphed into a snake. There was a long, pulsing silence and Addie licked her lips again. His words were innocuous enough, but she could feel the danger shimmering behind them. Only, having come this far, what choice did she have?

She took a deep breath. 'What kind of exceptional circumstances?'

Her voice sounded taut and high—too high. To her strained nerves it sounded desperate, needy—hardly the image she was striving to convey. As far as Malachi was concerned she wanted him to think that she was doing just fine. Better than fine, in fact. She wanted him to imagine her as gorgeous and successful—and utterly out of his reach.

Breathing in sharply, she glanced down at the letter on her desk and scowled. 'What kind of circumstances?' she repeated more steadily.

Malachi stared in silence out of the window. The sun was turning the sky a pale gold. It was going to be another beautiful day. A small smile curled his lips.

'I don't know,' he said truthfully. 'But I imagine I would have to look into the case closely...' He paused, relishing the tension quivering down the phone line. '*Very* closely. In fact I would definitely have to meet with the applicant. In person.'

Addie held her breath. Her body seemed to have turned to liquid.

'N-No!' she stammered. 'I don't think that's a good idea.'

'But *I* do. I don't just hand out money to anyone, you know.'

'I'm not anyone!' she snapped. 'I'm your wife.'

Too late, she saw that she had fallen into his trap.

'Which is another good reason for us to meet,' he said slowly. 'We can talk about our marriage.'

Her office suddenly felt airless. Her nerves were shrieking like a car alarm. Suddenly he wanted to talk about their marriage? Was he mad? Or deluded?

'No, we can't! I won't. Dragging up the past isn't going to change anything,' she said shakily. 'We just have to accept it was a mistake—'

'Was it?'

Addie blinked. It had been a disaster. And Malachi knew that as well as she did.

'Yes. It was.' She spoke too quickly, the words keeping pace with her heartbeat. 'I can't imagine what I was thinking!'

'Can't you?'

She took a quick breath, almost like a gasp. His voice was slow and glowing with a heat that she could feel down the phone. A heat that crept under her skin and coiled around her heart so that suddenly she couldn't seem to breathe properly.

'That's probably because what we shared had very little to do with thought, sweetheart.'

He paused and she felt the heat spike inside her.

'Mostly it had to do with tearing each other's clothes off.'

Addie swallowed. Her hand felt damp against the phone. A drumroll of fear and longing was beating so loudly that for a second she thought it was coming from outside of her body.

'I don't remember,' she whispered.

'I don't believe you,' he murmured. 'I know you remember that time in the lift.'

She shivered. She did remember. Could remember it as if she were there now, watching herself and Malachi, his hand slipping beneath her dress, her body arching against his as she tugged feverishly at his belt.

With a pure effort of will she dragged her mind back to the present.

'Apart from being irrelevant to this discussion, it was all a long time ago. So, no, I *don't*,' she lied. 'Unlike you, Malachi, my life, like most people's lives, does not just revolve around sex!'

'You think? Then you're either excessively naive or an extremely bad liar.'

She heard the amusement in his voice.

'Sex drives *all* human life. What did you think our relationship was based on? A mutual love of seafood!'

Addie felt a dull pain start to throb in her chest. No. She hadn't thought it was based on seafood. Fool that she was, she'd actually hoped and believed that their relationship had been based on love. An ache spread through her chest, hot and dark like a summer storm. Only love required honesty and trust, not secrets and lies. And neither of them had ever told the other the truth.

'I don't like seafood any more,' she snapped. 'Nor do I want to listen to your one-dimensional views on relationships. And I especially don't want to discuss them, or anything else for that matter, with you in person.'

'Really?' he said in that slow, sexy drawl that made her blood hum and her skin turn to glue. 'That's a shame. You see, I was hoping you'd meet me for lunch so we could discuss your funding. You *do* want me to renew your funding, don't you, sweetheart?'

Addie stood up, pushing her seat back with such force that it fell backwards onto the floor. But she barely noticed, such was her panic to block out that seductive velvet-smooth voice. And the urgent response of her body to it.

'I'm not going to meet you for lunch, Malachi!'

'You think dinner might be better?' he said disingenuously, completely ignoring the fury in her voice. 'I'm happy to do either. What do you fancy? French? Or what about some ceviche? There's a great new Peruvian place just opened up.'

Dinner! A vein was pulsing painfully in her forehead and mechanically she pressed her fingers against it. 'I don't want to eat French or Peruvian,' she said shrilly. 'And I'm not meeting you for lunch or dinner or any other kind of meal.'

'Pity!' His voice was dark and loaded. 'Because that's the only way you're going to get your funding out of me.'

'Fine,' she snarled. 'Then I'll just have to get the money some other way.'

'I'm sure you will,' he murmured. 'You always were very *imaginative*, as I recall.'

Her temper finally snapped. 'You are disgusting and I never want to speak to you again.'

He laughed. 'I'm a little unclear. Did we agree on lunch or dinner?'

With a howl of fury, she hung up.

Still laughing, Malachi switched off his phone and dropped it onto the desk. He gazed thoughtfully across the plane's cabin, wondering what she would wear when he saw her again. For, whatever she'd said, their meeting was as inevitable as the sun rising and setting. His heart began to thump; his blood was pumping, slow and heavy. Nor was it hate that had made her hang up on him. It was fear. She was scared—scared of the connection between them and her response to it.

And so she should be.

His grey eyes flared and feeling his groin harden, he let out a long, slow breath as a trickle of anticipation ran down his spine.

She might not have been the perfect wife he'd imagined, but Addie had never been boring. On the contrary— she had been feisty and stubborn and impulsive. Which meant that lunch—or, better still, dinner—was a foregone conclusion. All that remained was for him to choose a restaurant and a tie.

And, letting out a sigh of satisfaction, he settled back into his chair to enjoy the view.

CHAPTER TWO

'NO. I QUITE UNDERSTAND.' Trying her hardest to keep the note of disappointment out of her voice, Addie picked up her pen and drew a line firmly through the last name on the list in her notepad. 'And thank you for giving me so much of your time.'

Flipping open her laptop, she scrolled slowly through the column of figures on the screen. Finally she let out a long, slow breath. It was hopeless. Despite all her efforts she had barely enough funds to cover next month's rent and a few utility bills. Even if she added in her meagre savings she certainly couldn't afford to pay her staff's salaries.

Leaning back in her chair, she bit her lip. If she told them what had happened she knew they would offer to forego their pay. But why should they? she thought angrily. Why should they suffer because she had let her arrogant, maddening ex get under her skin?

Her head was pounding. And it wasn't just because of her precarious finances. Speaking to Malachi again had stirred up feelings she had buried deep, deep down, and now she was battling emotions she still wasn't ready to acknowledge or resolve.

Her heart gave a lurch. It wasn't only her feelings she couldn't face. She'd spent the last five years more or less pretending that her marriage had never happened. Now, in the space of twenty-four hours, she'd been forced to confront not only her husband but the state of estrangement between them.

Sighing, she slumped back in her seat and reluctantly contemplated the mess she'd made of her private life. Since splitting with Malachi she'd focused her energies on work. Yes, she'd been on a few 'dates' but no man ever quite measured up to him. But then she hadn't just fallen for Malachi. She'd dived in headfirst, captivated not only by his looks and charm but by how he'd made her feel like her true self. The self she'd discovered through music and lost the night of her accident. Only through music had she felt able to be the real Addie—wild and free. And Malachi had made her feel like that too.

But not for long. Pretty soon she'd been out of her depth and drowning. Only by that time she'd become his wife.

Her pulse twitched and she shifted in her seat. It had all happened so long ago. So why were they still married?

As far as Malachi was concerned it was probably because he'd forgotten all about her until yesterday, when she'd called him, whereas she— Her face coloured painfully. She was still married because she was a coward. The thought of seeing him again had been just too painful. In the months following their separation she had vowed to confront him and demand a divorce, but she had always found a reason not to do so. And so the months had become years.

Five long years. In fact, tomorrow it would be five years exactly.

Remembering her wedding day—his tension, her confusion over his parents' absence—she felt a shiver of sadness. It was obvious even then that what they'd shared was nothing more than physical attraction.

She frowned. But her marriage wasn't the issue here. She needed money, fast, and if having lunch with Malachi meant that she got her funding then maybe she should just call him. No doubt he was sitting there in his office, smugly waiting for her to do just that. But she sure as hell wasn't going to help him choose a restaurant as if it was some kind of a date. Her eyes narrowed. She needed to do something to make it clear that she was meeting him on her own terms.

So why not surprise him at lunch? All she would have to do was follow him to wherever he was eating and confront him, and then finally she might wipe the self-satisfied smile from that gorgeous mouth of his. Easy!

Her breath jammed in her throat.

Easy?

One look from Malachi had once been enough to turn her into a rippling mass of desire. But not any more, she told herself firmly. For even if her body hadn't learned the consequences of falling for that shimmering, sensual gaze her mind had, she had more sense and pride than to let it happen again.

Was it only lunchtime?

His grey eyes widening with disbelief, Malachi glanced at the one-of-a-kind Swiss-made watch on his wrist. Unusually for him, the day had seemed to drag—and his mind was only half on work. The other half was picking over his conversation with Addie.

Leaning back, he smiled slowly, remembering the frustration in her voice.

She'd been good and riled. But it wasn't only exasperation that had made her so hot and bothered. He'd heard another kind of heat.

And just like that an image of Addie flared inside his brain. The soft pouting lips, glossy red curls and legs like a thoroughbred in the Kentucky Derby. All wrapped up in a take-it-or-leave-it manner that he'd had no choice but to take…

Breathing heavily, he shifted in his seat, remembering the feverish touch of her mouth against his, the heat between them blurring their edges so that it had been impossible to feel where she'd ended and he'd begun.

He smiled grimly. For most of his life he'd watched his mother and father use passion and emotion like poker dice, uncaring of the consequences. As an adult, away from their orbit, he'd sworn never to follow in their footsteps. *His* private life would be conducted in the realm of reason.

Only then he'd met Addie, and thrown away caution and control and broken every damn rule in the book.

A pulse began to beat in his neck and suddenly his chair felt cramped, confined. Standing up, he walked quickly across his office to the large floor-to-ceiling window that overlooked the gaming area of his flagship Miami casino. He breathed in sharply. There were nearly seven hundred gaming tables down there, not including the *club privé*, each one offering a change of fortune, a new beginning, a better life.

Watching people as they gave everything they had—sometimes literally—to the turn of a card or the roll of a dice seemed to him to represent the rawest, most pure expression of what it meant to be human. It was all there—hope and hunger, fear, and the desire to win. He found it fascinating, stimulating. But not as fascinating or stimulating as the thought of seeing his estranged wife again.

Staring down at the men and women, their faces tight with concentration, he felt a flicker of anticipation. She'd told him she never wanted to speak to him again. But she would. She'd have no choice. And not just because of the money.

His eyes gleamed.

So, where should he take her for lunch?

Snatching his jacket from the back of his chair, he tugged it on. Addie would no doubt refuse to meet him if there was even a hint that they would be alone together. A busy, open-plan restaurant would be better. His eyes gleamed again. He knew just the place.

Opening his door, he was met by the startled faces of his secretary, Chrissie, and her assistant.

'I'm going out for lunch.'

'But—'

The women glanced up at him in confusion.

'You're meeting Andy here at twelve-thirty,' said Chrissie. 'You always meet him.'

It was true. Most days he met his casino managers as they came on shift. But today was different.

'So it'll be a nice change for both of us,' he said smoothly. 'Call Eights. My usual table. And tell Andy I'm indisposed.'

'Would you like your car to be brought round to the front, sir?'

Malachi shook his head and smiled. 'No, thank you, Chrissie. I need a bit of fresh air.'

He ran a finger under his collar. After thinking about Addie, what he actually needed was a cold shower, but a tall chilled mojito might just be a tolerable alternative!

The restaurant was crowded with the usual mix of suave businessmen and glamorous, golden-limbed women. His table was set slightly apart from the other diners, with a view over the ocean. Like all the best views in the world, it was unchanging and yet never the same.

His choices made, he waved away the waiters and sat back, his eye drawn to the horizon between sea and sky, where dense black clouds hovered above the turquoise water. A storm was coming. According to the weather reports, it was due to hit land just after three. Not that he minded. A storm—bad weather in general—was good for business. But it meant that his lunch might have to be slightly curtailed.

His phone gave a small shudder and, turning, he glanced at it, his face expressionless. It was a message from Henry, asking him to call. But he didn't want his father's voice inside his head. Not when his mind was filled with thoughts of Addie.

He picked up his glass. The wine was an interesting choice, the crisp hint of apple surprising him. But it wasn't the wine that caused him to put down his glass. It was the woman walking through the restaurant towards him.

Like every other man in the room, he watched her intently as she wove sinuously between the tables. He felt a rush of excitement. *The weathermen had been wrong.* The storm had already hit town. And her name was Hurricane Addie!

Staring defiantly ahead, Addie made her way across the room. Walking into the restaurant, she'd felt a fluttering panic. It was one thing deciding in anger to gatecrash his lunch and cajole him into renewing her funding—quite another to confront him in cold blood. In theory, she could tell herself that she no longer cared about him and that he was just another businessman on her list. She could even remind herself that he was the man who had lied to her face and broken her heart. But all that reason and logic had been forgotten when she'd pulled open the door and stepped into the restaurant.

Despite the fact that the room was packed with diners, she spotted him in a heartbeat. No one but Malachi had that invisible but tangible push-me-pull-me energy. Radiating out from him like rays from the sun, it tugged her gaze across the room to where he sat, gazing out at the ocean like some buccaneer on the high seas. She breathed in sharply, her hand rising involuntarily, protectively in front of her, as though to ward off the full intensity of his masculinity.

He was even more beautiful than she remembered, with his dark hair falling across his forehead, that sculpted poet's profile and those eyes...the grey shifting and darkening like a constantly changing winter sky. He looked cool and relaxed in a tailored charcoal-grey suit that was a shade lighter than his eyes—and worth every cent of the billions of dollars he was rumoured to have made from his gaming empire.

Her head was spinning; the noise of the room sounded distant and distorted. But even though it was clear he still had the power to throw her off balance, she damn well wasn't going to reveal that fact to Malachi.

Her hands curling into fists, she walked purposefully towards him and stopped in front of his table. Her back felt as if it was burning beneath the combined female envy in the room, but her blue gaze was cool and scornful as they stared at one another in silence.

It was she who spoke first. 'You wanted to have lunch with me.' Her voice was husky, her cheeks flushed with colour. 'So here I am.'

'Yes, you are,' he said softly. He stared in undisguised appreciation at the clinging black dress. Or rather at the swelling curves beneath the fabric. 'You look incredible, sweetheart. Life must be treating you well. I feel like I should be the one asking *you* for money.'

Addie lifted her chin. 'Who knows? Maybe one day you will be.' She rested one slim hand on her hip. 'So, are you going to ask me to sit down? Or have you changed your mind?'

'In that dress? Not a chance. Come and join me.' Patting the seat beside him, he grinned as, ignoring his gesture, Addie sat down on the opposite side of the table.

As though her arrival had triggered some hidden switch, not one but two waiters immediately appeared beside them, and her shoulders lowered with relief as the daunting prospect of being on her own with him was temporarily postponed. But her reprieve couldn't last for ever and finally they were alone.

'I just want to make it clear that *I'm* paying,' she said quickly. Their eyes met—hers the same, rebellious blue as a teenage tattoo, his glinting, grey. 'It's only fair.'

His gaze fixed on her face and he stared at her thoughtfully, then shrugged. 'Fine. You can buy me lunch. But I warn you, I'm not a cheap date.'

Addie stilled. 'This is not a *date*, Malachi. And that kind of remark is why I'm buying lunch. So there aren't any mixed messages.'

He grinned. 'You know me, sweetheart. The only thing I like mixed are my cocktails. Speaking of which—at least let me buy you a drink. Do you still like Bellinis?'

She swallowed, feeling a stabbing within. And then a softness. 'You remembered…'

His eyes never left her face. 'Of course. I remember everything about you and our time together.'

The softness hardened and she shivered inside. Was that what their marriage had been to him? A portion of hours and days? Her heart began to beat faster.

'Good!' She swallowed. 'Then you'll remember how important my charity is to the children it helps. And, no, thank you. I don't want a Bellini.'

He waved a hand across the table at her negligently.

'Some wine, then? Or is my presence intoxicating enough for you?'

Tucking her legs beneath the table, Addie forced herself to meet his cool grey gaze. 'I don't drink at business meetings.' she said primly.

'Neither do I,' agreed Malachi, lifting the glass of wine to his lips. 'It's very unprofessional. But fortunately I don't class our meeting as anything other than a cause for celebration.'

She stared at him blankly. 'Celebration! I don't know what you're talking about.'

'Of course you do.' Beneath the restaurant's lights his eyes looked lighter, almost silver. 'It was you who reminded me.' He held out his glass and tapped it against her tumbler of water. 'Happy Anniversary, sweetheart!'

Addie felt her skin grow cold. His eyes were glittering with an emotion she didn't fully understand and, quickly turning her head, she fixed her gaze on the view of the ocean just as their meals arrived.

The food was both delicious and beautifully presented, but Addie found it impossible to enjoy her lobster salad.

'Even if it is our anniversary,' she said coldly, 'I hardly think that's relevant to today's discussion. Personally I'd be happier if we just stuck to the *real* reason why we're both here.'

'Of course,' he murmured. 'If it makes you more comfortable.'

Addie glowered at him. Comfortable! As if!

The only reason she was still sitting there was the children and her colleagues. Otherwise, had she not chosen to wear such ridiculously high heels, she would happily have turned round and run as fast as possible from that deceptively guileless face.

But breathing out slowly, she pressed her nails into the palms of her hands. At least she looked the part. Even if it had meant selling her bike. The important thing was that while she might need his help, *he didn't need to know that*. She looked cool and classy and in control. Not like a woman looking for a favour.

Now all she had to do was stay focused. But, glancing across the table, she felt a pulse leap in her throat as she looked up into his glittering grey gaze.

'You're very quiet, sweetheart. I thought you wanted to talk?' Lolling back against the leather upholstery, Malachi gazed at her intently.

She shrugged. 'I was just thinking.'

'Then I should probably be leaving!' His eyes, light and dancing, fixed on her face even as the corners of his mouth began to tilt upwards. 'A quiet woman is like a hand grenade. A quiet woman *thinking* is like a hand grenade with the pin pulled out.'

His curving smile waited for her reply and she licked her lips, her heart fluttering beneath his scrutiny.

And then, just in time, she remembered that there was an actual reason for her being there—other than just to gawp at Malachi's cheekbones. Feeling clumsy, hoping he didn't suspect the reason for her distracted behaviour, she pulled out a folded piece of paper from her bag and handed it to him.

'That's the original agreement.'

He took it and opened it. His face was impassive as he scanned the contents. Finally he looked up at her. 'It's strange, don't you think? The two of us? Together again?'

She'd been expecting him to refer to the letter. Instead, caught off guard, she had to force down the tangled mass of emotion that reared up inside her in response both to his words and the probing focus of his eyes.

'Th-there is no "two of us",' she said shakily. Her eyes darted away from him and round the room, seeking something solid and reassuring. Fixing on two burly businessmen at the bar, she felt her shoulders relax slightly. 'And we're not together.'

He smiled slowly. 'Then why are you scared?'

Her temper flared. 'I'm not scared.' She hesitated. 'Just a little apprehensive, I suppose.' She met his gaze defiantly.

'Would it help if I promised not to drop my napkin?' he said softly.

A warm tide swept over her skin, as hot and strong as a hurricane. But no hurricane could ever be as devastating or dangerous as Malachi King, she thought wildly. Her cheeks burning, she fixed her eye on the smooth white linen tablecloth. But she could feel his eyes, dark and implacable as granite, seeking her out.

'I'd rather you didn't bring *that* up now.' Her skin felt as if it was on fire; her heartbeat felt so loud she was surprised the other diners hadn't stopped eating to stare at her.

'When *would* you like me to bring it up?' he asked smoothly.

'N-never!' Her voice was trembling and she shook her head. 'It's just not appropriate!'

He shrugged, his face dispassionate. 'I don't remember you complaining at the time.'

His eyes were like the shimmering headlights of a car. She stared at him helplessly, hypnotised, horrified by her body's fierce, swift response to his words and the image they conjured up.

Had she *really* let him do that to her? In a *restaurant*? There was an ache low down in her pelvis. Her whole body was suddenly shaking and it felt as though her insides were being sucked into a whirlpool. A memory—perfect, impossible, spinning apart into a hundred shades of gold—slid into her head. It had been so wildly, shockingly exciting. Even now she could hardly believe it had happened. Or that she had let it. What had she been *thinking*?

She felt her chest tighten and her skin start to burn, for of course Malachi had been right. What they'd shared had had very little to do with thought. Their entire relationship had been founded on passion, in his arms she'd been fierce, wild, hungry for his touch; he had awoken the hot, sensual woman beneath the quiet, dutiful young pianist who'd practised her scales every day—

Her stomach dipped. But thanks to him that woman didn't exist any more.

Meeting his gaze, she gave him an icy stare. 'Do you want me to leave right now?'

His eyes flickered across her face and, reaching out, he picked up a piece of bread and bit into it with strong white teeth. 'Wouldn't that be a little premature? I thought you came here to discuss your funding? If you leave now, sweetheart, you'll go empty-handed. Besides...'

He gave her a slow, sexy grin that made something hot and scratchy scrape inside her.

'I'm sure you don't want to miss dessert.'

He was calling her bluff. He knew she had no choice but to stay. Meeting his gaze, her eyes narrowed into sharp shards of blue. He was so smug and annoying. How she hated him!

Except that she didn't.

Not unless that ball of hot liquid heat swelling inside her so that her ribs ached was how hatred felt.

She swallowed. Around her she could almost hear the air hissing when it came into contact with her overheated skin. Surely she wasn't supposed to feel like this—so breathless, so dazzled.

Watching him lounge back against the leather, his eyes gleaming with undisguised satisfaction, she felt a rush of pure white anger. 'I know what you're doing,' she said breathlessly. 'You're trying to make me lose my temper so that I'll leave.'

He raised his eyebrows. 'Is that right? You know, it never ceases to amaze me how women can misinterpret even the simplest statement and put some spin on it.'

'*Spin!*' It took every ounce of willpower she had not to throw the contents of her glass into his infuriatingly handsome face. 'You making vile innuendos is not *spin*,' she snapped.

'I didn't make any innuendos. I was merely recounting historical fact.'

His eyes were dancing with a malice that made her want to scream out loud. He was impossible. And this meeting was a farce.

'Well, I didn't come here to have a history lesson,' she hissed. 'Especially a highly selective and one-sided one.'

The waiter was back again. 'Was everything to your satisfaction, Mr King?'

'It was perfect, thank you. The scallops were sublime and my wife thoroughly enjoyed her lobster salad—didn't you, darling?'

My wife!

Startled, her eyes met his. 'Yes, I did.' Glancing up, she gave the waiter a perfunctory smile. 'It was delicious.' She waited, fuming, until the plates had been cleared away and they were alone again. 'Why did you call me that?'

His look of blank incomprehension made her want to throttle him with her napkin.

'Why *wouldn't* I call you that? That *is* what you are,' he said smoothly. 'Surely you didn't think you could just waltz back into my life and start demanding money but somehow avoid discussing our marriage?'

She shivered as his gaze fixed on her bare ring finger

but, refusing to be cowed, she drew back her shoulders and met his stare defiantly.

'I don't want to talk about our marriage.'

'Clearly,' he said softly. 'If you had, you would have got in touch over the last five years.'

She felt the blood drain from her face. 'There was nothing stopping *you* from getting in touch. And I didn't waltz back into your life and demand anything. I'm here because you *insisted* that I meet you and now you want to *dictate* what we talk about.'

Her voice echoed round the room and, looking up, she froze. The restaurant was no longer packed with diners. In fact she and Malachi appeared to be the only two people remaining, apart from the businessmen at the bar. She watched, her stomach clenching, as a waiter discreetly cleared a table and left the room.

'We need to leave,' she said hurriedly, glancing round again. 'Lunchtime service is clearly over.'

Glancing over his shoulder, Malachi shrugged. 'They can wait.'

Her eyes narrowed. 'You are *so* arrogant. These people have lives, Malachi. You can't just expect them to hang around for hours.'

'Why not? That's what they're paid to do,' he said casually.

She glowered at him. 'But not by you.'

There was a sudden, stinging pause. Glancing up, she saw that he was surveying her steadily, an odd light in his eyes. And suddenly the penny dropped.

'You own this place?' she croaked.

He nodded slowly, enjoying her shock. 'Yes, I do.' He paused, and there was a courteous edge to his voice that disguised the brutality of his words. 'That's why I chose to meet you here.'

She stared at him in confusion. For a moment her mind simply couldn't absorb his words. 'But you didn't choose to meet me,' she said slowly. 'I followed you here.'

He looked at her almost regretfully, and suddenly her heart was beating so fast she thought it would burst. Glancing over at the men at the bar, she felt her jawline tighten. Had she *really* thought they were businessmen?

She shook her head in disbelief at her own naivety. 'You had me followed. By them.'

Their eyes met—hers wide with outrage, his shimmering with satisfaction and her hands balled into fists. He was enjoying himself, the bastard!

He shrugged. 'It's their job. They spotted you outside the office.'

Heat was blistering her skin. He'd played her—acting as if he was surprised when all along he'd known she was coming. She felt a spasm of nausea. But was it that surprising, really? He'd always been good at pretending. Look at the way he'd convinced her that he loved her.

She stood up so suddenly that the men at the bar leaped off their stools.

'I should never have come here. As if you could *ever* behave like a mature, responsible adult—'

'Sit down.' Leaning forward, he spoke quietly, but the authority in his voice was enough to make her stop and look at him.

'Why? I don't want to talk to you.'

'Yes, you do. That's why you followed me.'

He leaned back in his seat, unfazed by her anger, and irritably she realised that despite her plans he was the one calling the shots. He always had been. It was just that she hadn't realised it until that moment.

'Come on, Addie. Sit down.' His voice had shifted, softened. 'Look, I'm going to give you your money. I always was.' Reaching into his jacket, he pulled out a piece of paper and slid it across the table. 'It's a copy of a bank transaction. It was wired to your account...' he glanced casually at his watch '...about twenty minutes ago.' His eyes flickered over her taut expression. 'Relax, sweetheart. You got what you came for. That *is* what you came for, isn't it?' He smiled. 'Now, why don't you just take a seat and we can both try and act like *mature, responsible adults.*'

Trying to keep what little remained of her dignity, she sat down and stared at him coldly.

His eyes gleamed. 'Go on. Take it.'

Reluctantly she reached out and picked up the slip of paper. Staring down at it, she felt her face drain of colour. 'This is the wrong amount.' She looked back down, then, blinking, lifted her head in confusion. 'This is double what I was expecting.'

His eyes didn't leave hers. 'Think of it as an anniversary present.'

Carefully she put the paper down on the table. 'That's incredibly generous of you,' she said hoarsely.

'I'm glad you approve.'

His tone was pleasant, but something in his eyes made a shiver of apprehension run down her spine and she glanced nervously at the slip of paper again, half feaing she might have imagined it. But it was definitely real.

'It really is very generous,' she said stiffly. 'I don't know what I'd have done if I hadn't got the money. It means so much to me. Thank you.' She breathed out. 'How long will it take to clear?' She knew she sounded gauche but she didn't care. If Malachi wanted to gloat—let him.

'Around two hours.' He paused and looked past her at the dark clouds and the grey swelling sea outside, and she felt that shiver of apprehension spike painfully through her skin. 'But before you start spending it I need to make a few things clear.'

She nodded. 'Of course. Do you want me to sign a contract? I can do that now.'

He turned and slowly, very slowly, smiled at her.

'That won't be necessary. You see, that money didn't come from King Industries. It came from me. From my *personal* bank account. And my terms are *personal* too.'

She swallowed—or tried to swallow at least—past the lump in her throat.

'What do you mean "personal"?' she croaked. Around her the air felt hot and leaden and the room was growing darker. 'What do you *mean*?' she repeated, and the lump felt sharp and jagged now.

His voice was soft, just as it had been when he'd promised to love and honour and cherish her for ever. But the lines of his face were knife sharp and harder than stone.

'I've been very patient, sweetheart, but you owe me a honeymoon.'

'I—I don't understand.'

His gaze swept over her slowly.

'Then let me explain. I want you to come away with me for a month. To be my mistress.'

His eyes locked on to hers, pinning her against the leather upholstery.

'Do that and you can keep the money. Who knows? There might even be a little bonus in it for you as well.'

CHAPTER THREE

THERE WAS A LONG, pulsing silence. Across the table, Addie stared at him in mute disbelief, unable to believe what she had just heard. Slowly she picked over his words inside her head, turning and twisting them like pieces in a jigsaw puzzle, trying to make a different meaning. But each time the picture was the same.

His *mistress*!

The word sounded even harsher inside her head than when he'd spoken it out loud and her breath snarled in her throat. Maybe she had misunderstood him. Or maybe he was joking. But as she stole a glance at his cool, implacable face she realised with a jolt of fear that he was making a serious suggestion.

'Are you out of your mind?' she said shakily.

She stared down at the slip of paper, still lying on the table between them, clenching and unclenching her hands in her lap.

He shrugged, his cool gaze boring into her. 'Everything in life has a price, sweetheart.'

'A *price*! What are you talking about, Malachi? You just offered me money for sex!'

His gaze drifted lazily over her pale, stunned face. 'How very unromantic of you. I thought I was offering you the honeymoon we never had.'

She was suddenly hot with rage. 'Oh, please! You know

exactly what you just said and it had nothing whatsoever to do with romance!'

Her words were tumbling from her lips so fast that she choked. As he gently pushed her glass of water towards her, she shoved his hand angrily away.

'I don't want any. I don't want anything from you.'

Stretching one muscular arm along the back of the banquette, he shook his head slowly. 'Now, we both know that's not true. Or are you saying that you want me to cancel that transfer into your account?'

Addie hesitated. She badly wanted to throw the money back in his face, but how could she? Without it the charity would struggle to pay the rent, let alone support the children. And she would lose a part of herself—the part she was most afraid to lose because it absorbed so much of the energy and emotion she had once given to performing. Once given to Malachi. Only she wasn't about to share that fact with him now.

Gritting her teeth, she lifted her eyes to his and he smiled slowly.

'See? Everything *does* have a price, sweetheart.'

He paused. His grey eyes watched her face with a satisfaction that made her want to scream.

'Besides, it's nothing you haven't done before.' His mouth curved, his grey eyes glittering provocatively.

She glared at him, her own blue eyes snapping fire. 'What? Sleep with a man for money?'

A muscle flickered in his cheek. 'I'm simply asking you to resume our relationship.'

'You are not! You're taking advantage of me.'

'No, I'm trying to negotiate a deal with you.'

'A *deal*? This isn't a deal. It's blackmail. And it's insulting—' Shaking her head, she pushed the slip of paper jerkily across the table towards him. 'I'm not some *escort* you pay by the day, Malachi! I'm your wife!'

'So *now* you want to talk about our marriage?'

His eyes held hers, so dark and dispassionate that suddenly she was frantic to leave. His crude proposal was bad enough. But she couldn't bear the thought of the two of them turning everything they'd once shared into something so twisted and ugly.

'No, I don't,' she said flatly. 'I don't want to talk to you about anything. In fact I've got a new deal for you. How about you keep your money? And I'll keep my pride.' Rising to her feet, she jerked her bag from the seat and glowered at him. 'Enjoy your honeymoon.'

'Addie—'

He was on his feet, reaching out for her. But, slipping away from his outstretched arm, she ran lightly across the restaurant and past the bodyguards. Yanking open the door, she stepped out into the street, her brain registering the black overcast sky just as a strong flurry of wind slammed against her.

Gasping, she tugged her thin jacket more tightly around her body and began to hurry down the rapidly emptying road. Her stormy encounter with Malachi had completely distracted her from the tempest raging outside, but now she realised that, like their relationship, the weather seemed to have taken a turn for the worse. Much worse!

She would have to get a cab, she thought despairingly as she glanced up at the swirling dark clouds. If she waited for a bus she'd be soaked.

Holding out her hand, she began to walk as quickly as her heels would allow, glancing back over her shoulder with increasing urgency until finally, hearing a car slow behind her, she turned with relief.

Only it wasn't a taxi. Her feet seemed to falter beneath

her as a sleek black limousine complete with uniformed chauffeur drew up alongside her.

Her heart lurched and she took a hurried step backwards as one of the bodyguards from the restaurant leaped out from the passenger side. For a moment she thought he might grab her, but instead, turning swiftly, he opened the rear door and she felt her bones turn to ice as Malachi stepped out onto the pavement.

Turning cold blue eyes on him, she breathed out sharply as another gust of wind slapped into her. 'Shouldn't you be packing?' she snapped.

'Addie, please. Do you really want to be doing this now? Here?' He flinched as a gust of wind sent a newspaper flapping past his head. 'It's been downgraded, but this is still a big storm. We need to get out of it.'

'I know that. That's why I'm getting a cab. And there is no *"we"*.'

She glanced away down the deserted street.

'There are no cabs.' Malachi stepped in front of her, his narrowed eyes at odds with the reasonable note in his voice. 'And it's getting pretty bad out here.'

As if to attest to the truth of his words, the first fat drops of water hit her face just as he reached out and touched her hand lightly.

'Let me give you a lift home, okay?'

Despite the chill of the rain, she felt heat explode inside her. The noise of the wind felt suddenly muffled, drowned out by the heavy thud of her heartbeat. But jerking her hand away, she gripped her jacket more tightly. It would have to be a Category 5 hurricane before she'd even *consider* getting into that car with him.

'I thought I made myself clear back at the restaurant.' She was having to shout now, against the buffeting breeze.

'I don't need anything from you, Malachi. So if you don't mind—'

'But I do. What if something happens to you? Imagine how that would look—'

Addie stared at him in disbelief, trying to banish the sharp stab of pain as his words dug into her brain. 'So this isn't about me and my safety. It's about you and your stupid image?'

For a moment she wanted to hurt him as he had hurt her. Was still hurting her. She clutched her bag against her chest, holding it in front of her like a shield as his eyes locked on to hers.

'I am worried about your safety.'

'So am I,' she snapped. 'Which is why I'm not getting in that car with you.'

All at once she was conscious of the calm surrounding him—as though his broad body was somehow absorbing the turbulence of the wind.

'Your choice, sweetheart. The back seat.' He smiled. 'Or the boot.'

Her hand tightened on the fabric of her jacket. 'Really! The *boot*? First you try and blackmail me—now you want to kidnap me!'

She watched the muscles in his arms swell against his beautifully tailored suit and instantly regretted her words. Knowing Malachi, he would have absolutely no qualms about tossing her into the boot of his car and, glancing down the street one last time, she made up her mind.

'Fine,' she said, through gritted teeth. 'You can give me a lift.'

His eyes glittered with what looked to her horribly like triumph and, willing herself to hold her temper in check, she edged past him. 'But just so you know—this doesn't change anything.'

Fuming, she slid along the leather as far as possible until she was pressed against the frame of the door. Already she was regretting her acquiescence, for despite the warmth and sanctuary of the car her nerves were singing, her body painfully alert at the realisation that she was about to be alone and up close with Malachi. It was asking for trouble.

But it was also too late to change her mind.

As he got in beside her she breathed out slowly, her eyes narrowing as he calmly gave her address to the chauffeur.

'Are you shivering or quivering?'

His voice broke into her thoughts and, turning, she scowled at him.

'Why do you care?'

'I was going to offer you my jacket.'

Her heart seemed to dissolve in her chest and a shivering heat crawled over her skin. 'Well, I'm not cold,' she said shortly. 'So you don't need to worry.'

'In that case you must be quivering.' He smiled. 'Dare I hope that it has anything to do with me?'

She knew he was teasing her but that didn't stop the sense of nervous unease she felt at his words. The sense that, despite her efforts to be poised and in control, she was making it transparently clear that her body still responded to him as it had always done.

Ignoring the burning in her cheeks, she lifted her chin. 'I'm sorry to disappoint you, Malachi, but it's been a long time since I was susceptible to your charms,' she said bitingly.

He tilted his head, his eyes skimming over her skin, sending ripples of heat in overlapping circles so that she was suddenly struggling to swallow.

'It's okay to admit it, sweetheart,' he said softly. 'I know you want me as desperately as I want you.'

Shoulders stiffening, she glared at him. Had he already

forgotten his despicable and offensive proposal that she be his mistress? Probably. But knowing Malachi, he thought it was a perfectly reasonable suggestion. She knew from painful personal experience that he was happy to exploit everything and everyone—even…especially…his own wife—for his own ends. Five years ago he'd used her image. Now he wanted to use her body.

The thought made her skin smart as though he'd slapped her.

'Don't flatter yourself. Right now I'm just desperate to get out of this car and away from you.'

Tipping his head back, Malachi laughed.

'Sorry, sweetheart, but you're stuck with me.'

'Only for as long as it takes your driver to get me home,' she snapped.

There was a short, pulsing silence, and through the rawness of her nerves she felt a drop of quicksilver shoot up her spine as he stared at her assessingly.

'We'll see.'

Her body was suddenly stiff and hollow and she felt a crack of fear open inside her.

'No, we will not! This is a one-off, Malachi.'

He shrugged, the muscles in his shoulders shifting against the fabric of his jacket.

'I see it more as a starting point.'

She shook her head slowly, her stomach lurching.

'For what? You paying me for sex.' Anger was flaring inside her once more.

'I just thought we could talk.'

'Look, Malachi, just because I accepted a lift from you, it doesn't mean I want to talk to you.' Fury rose up inside her. He was *so* insensitive. 'Why *would* I? After what you said in the restaurant?' She shook her head, the memory of his words making her hands ball in her lap. 'You insulted me!'

He stared at her in silence. It had been a spur-of-the-moment thing, asking her to be his mistress. Watching her walk towards him, the sight of her gorgeous body pressing against his eyeballs like a hot knife against butter, he'd made up his mind: he had to have her.

From nowhere, the idea had popped into his head, fully formed. But even now he wasn't completely sure why he'd actually gone ahead and suggested it to her.

Shifting in his seat, he gritted his teeth. Of course lust had obviously played a part. But there was more to his decision than just simple biology. When Addie had pitched into his life five years ago he'd seen her as an opportunity, a chance to have what he'd previously discounted as untenable, impossible. Before meeting her he'd never even wanted a wife—only she had been like an itch that wouldn't stop.

And then, realising how good she was for his image, it had been easy to persuade himself that she would make the perfect wife, her role in the local charity sector the yin to his yang as a ruthless, self-serving entrepreneur. Crucially, their partnership would help ensure a more positive reception for his new casino in downtown Miami.

His face stilled. But in the space of six months she'd turned his life inside out: she'd taken his heart and his name and discarded both. Worse, his failed marriage had unleashed a sense of disquiet and doubt that he'd never quite managed to shift, and her defection had left him smarting.

Now seeing her again, his body was aching with feverish sexual frustration. Persuading her to be his mistress had felt like the perfect solution, for it would solve his hunger *and* erase the feeling of powerlessness that was the legacy of their doomed relationship.

His mouth twisted. It was a feeling he loathed more

than any other. A grim, painful reminder of a childhood dominated by the dark chaos of his parents' lives. Addie had seemed like the perfect riposte to their world. Bright, smart, independent—and sexy, of course. Only despite that he'd given her his name, and access to a world of wealth and power, she'd turned out to be just as needy as his parents, only instead of disorder, she brought doubts and accusations.

Remembering how it had felt when she'd left him— the shock, the humiliation—his mouth tightened. It was a bitter reminder of what happened when he let lust not logic make his decisions. But it wasn't too late; he could still walk away. Only walking away would feel like cashing in his chips. His eyes narrowed. Besides, her impassioned refusal had simply sharpened his determination to change her mind.

Only it wasn't going quite as smoothly as he would like…

He breathed out slowly. 'I want you, Addie, and I'm willing to pay to have you.'

Their eyes met and heat crawled over the skin at the back of her neck. She should have been outraged, and part of her was, for his statement was shocking in its almost carnal brutality. Only she couldn't deny that another, greater part was trembling with raw, feverish longing.

It didn't seem to matter that she was no longer in love with him. He could still make her hands shake and her head spin.

She lifted her chin. *So could a waltzer at a funfair!* The difference was that when the ride ended, her heart and her pride would still be intact.

Gritting her teeth, she conjured up a memory of herself, face puffy with crying, slumped on her sofa beneath a duvet. *Remember that*, she told herself sternly. No amount of money or sexual gratification was worth those consequences.

Digging her fingernails into the palms of her hands, she raised her chin. 'But you can't have me, Malachi!'

She turned and glanced out of the window.

'This probably wasn't the best idea, so thank you for the lift but perhaps it might be better if you dropped me off here,' she said stiffly. 'I can look after myself.'

Malachi met her gaze. 'Is that why you're sitting all that way over there on your own?'

Watching her bite into her soft lower lip, he felt his groin harden. He could see the conflict in her eyes, could almost feel the nervous jolt of her pulse. She wanted what he wanted, but she couldn't admit it to herself—let alone him. Maybe it was time to switch tactics.

He let the silence between them lengthen again and then, shifting round, the better to watch her reaction, he said softly, 'So, are you demonstrating your independence? Or am I making you nervous?'

He had chosen his words intentionally, guessing that she would find it impossible not to rise to the implication that somehow he had got under her skin. His assumption was quickly and gratifyingly confirmed as she turned and glared at him, her narrowed gaze two slits of hostile blue.

'Nervous! Why would I be *nervous*?'

He shrugged, watching the slow rise of colour in her cheeks and the darkening of her eyes.

'Being here with me…' he murmured. 'Alone… There was a time when we couldn't keep our hands off of one another—'

He could hear her breathing, short and sharp and shallow, and felt a shivering rush of triumph dart over his skin. She was more than nervous. She was aroused.

'That was a long time ago,' she said stiffly. 'A lot's changed.'

'And a lot hasn't...' He paused, feeling his body respond to the provocation in her eyes and the pulse jerking erratically at the base of her throat. 'Like this...' And, reaching out, he stretched his arm along the back of the seat and lightly touched her hair. 'This hasn't changed one bit. It's still just as wild and beautiful.' Pulling loose a gleaming curl, he wound the hair round his finger.

Heart pounding, Addie shook his hand off. 'Actually, I've been thinking about going blonde. And short. *Really* short.'

With considerable difficulty, she tore her eyes away from his dark, shimmering gaze. Did he seriously think that one touch was all it would take? That just stroking her hair would be enough for her to melt into his arms and forget all about his appalling attempt to blackmail her? She caught her breath. Probably. He was so used to women throwing themselves at him. And, judging by the way her whole body was vibrating like a tuning fork, it appeared that she agreed with him. Or at least her stupid, treacherous body did.

'I could walk from here,' she said quickly, glancing out of the window at the rain-spattered pavement. 'It doesn't look that bad any more.'

She turned to face him and instantly wished she hadn't. Lounging negligently, his grey gaze seemed to hold her captive, so that even if she'd wanted to yank open the door and run as fast as possible from the dangerous, swirling undercurrents in the car, she would not have been able to do so.

'What?' she said hoarsely. 'Why are you looking at me like that?'

'Why do you think?' Slowly, with almost cat-like laziness, he leaned forward and picked up her hand, playing gently with her fingers.

She opened her mouth to tell him she didn't know or care, but somehow the words stayed stubbornly in her throat. Her mouth was dry and she could feel her pulse hammering in her wrists so hard that her hands seemed like living creatures. Drawing back, she pressed her spine into the upholstery of the seat.

'It doesn't matter what I think. None of this is real.' She shook her head. 'It's like you said. It's just us being alone together again.'

He was holding her softly, but his voice was softer still. 'Maybe. Only you seem pretty damn real to me—and so does how I'm feeling right now.'

Her blood felt as though it were thinning, growing lighter. If only she could fly, she thought desperately, fly far away. But neither fight nor flight was possible. Even thinking appeared to be a struggle.

Threads of heat were trickling slowly over her skin like warm syrup off a spoon and she stared at him helplessly, hypnotised by the languorous glow of his gaze. She wanted to lie back and close her eyes and breathe in his warm, masculine scent and believe what he was saying was true. How could it not be? When he said it in that voice…

For a moment she lingered over his words, repeating them inside her head: *How I'm feeling right now…*

And slowly she pulled her fingers away from his. It sounded true because it *was* true. Probably Malachi *did* feel like that 'right now'. But it would pass. No matter how beautiful and enticing it sounded, it was as transient as a winter sunset.

She shrank back inside her skin. 'But that doesn't make it right,' she said quietly.

She felt his gaze, fierce and fixed, on the side of her face.

'It makes it better than right. It makes it perfect. This

time, this way, it'll be good between us. There's no expectation. No promises or pressure.'

He made it sound so simple, so perfect. She could feel herself wavering.

Beside her, he inched closer, and looking up into the focus of his eyes, she saw a heat and intensity that seemed to melt her breath. She felt a rush of panic for those eyes told her what she already knew: that he still owned her sexually and now he was claiming her back.

'Stop it!' She lifted her hand and held it up. 'Stop saying these things. And don't come any nearer. I don't want you to.'

'Only because you don't trust yourself.'

Holding up his hand, he pressed his palm against hers, and the longing inside her seemed to split her apart.

'Why are you fighting this? You want me as much as I want you, Addie. Tell me you don't. Tell me I'm wrong.' In the depths of his eyes something flickered like the flare of a match—a small, bright flame of desire.

She knew she should speak, deny his claim. But she couldn't find her voice—and even if she could have done she wouldn't have been able to string her words together in any sensible order.

Heat was spilling over her skin like milk boiling over in a pan. And suddenly she wanted it to overwhelm her. To stop fighting and sink beneath the liquid warmth. His fingers were wrapping around hers, tugging her inexorably towards him, and she knew that they were going to kiss and she was glad…because sometimes kisses were less complicated than words.

Reaching up, she pressed her fingers against his lips, shivering as she saw his gaze darken with hunger. For a moment their eyes locked, and then she slid her hand up and over his jaw and into his dark silky hair, pulling his mouth feverishly onto hers.

At the touch of his lips she felt an ache—blissful, voluptuous—spreading out low from her pelvis, and then her hands splayed apart, her head spinning dizzily as he deepened the kiss.

Moaning, she arched her body towards him, her breath stuttering in her throat, a fissure opening up inside her as his tongue slid between her parted lips and his hands curved around her waist and thigh, pressing, probing.

'Addie...'

She heard him murmur her name, felt his hand slide inexorably up over the soft skin of her thigh and then higher, beneath the hem of her dress to the pulse beating insistently between her legs.

Her skin felt hot and tight; inside she could feel herself melting. Gasping, she leaned against the hard muscles of his chest, the hot, salt scent of him coiling round her skin so that she was shaking with longing, her whole body clamouring for more. Shuddering, she pulled at his shirt, tugging at it where it was caught beneath his waistband, lost in the quickening of her breath and the lambent heat pooling low in her pelvis.

He groaned softly. 'Stop, sweetheart...'

And then he said it more loudly, dragging his mouth from hers, lifting his hands away, and she stared up at him dazedly even as her disorientated brain began to absorb the full facts of the situation.

Her eyes opened and, face flaming, she stared in horror at her reflection in the window. How could she have let that happen? Was she out of her mind?

But blaming her mind for what had just happened was about as senseless as blaming the moon for turning the tide. However, any debate on the whys and wherefores of blame was going to have to wait.

Taking a quick breath, she looked up at him reluctantly. 'That shouldn't have happened,' she said slowly.

Leaning back against the seat, he watched her smooth down the hem of dress. 'And yet it did.'

Her cheeks grew hotter. 'It was a mistake.'

'And we learn from our mistakes?' he said idly, reaching out to take her hand.

'I have,' she retorted. 'I've learned that I shouldn't accept lifts from strangers.'

She tried to twist her hand away from his but he tightened his grip, pulling her towards him so that her body was pressed against his.

'But I'm not a stranger. I'm your husband.'

And, lowering his head, he kissed her again. She felt the same pull as before, the same ache, only stronger, more fervent, and she moaned softly.

'Come away with me, Addie.' His eyes were dark and fierce and compelling. 'There's things we need to talk about alone. Just the two of us. Please—say yes.'

She pressed her hand against her swimming head, staring at him helplessly, hazy with wanting him, with needing him, and then finally she nodded, for the sexual attraction between them was irrefutable, so why keep trying to suppress it?

'Say it!' His hands captured her face. 'I want to hear you say it.'

She hesitated. If she half closed her eyes and her mind to the tiny, nagging voices in her head, she could almost absolve herself from any responsibility for her actions.

Her breath tangled in her throat. But if she spoke, if she went into this now, agreed to this deal, then she would do so *knowing* that Malachi didn't love her.

She shifted in her seat. Maybe it would be easier that way. There would be no more broken hearts and shattered dreams. In fact dreams would come true for the children who learned to trust and hope and believe again through music. The charity she had founded, which had brought passion and pride back to her life, would grow and prosper. And maybe she needed to own this decision unlike last time when she'd been dazzled and docile and always one step behind.

Determinedly, she lifted her chin. 'Yes. I'll come away with you.' Her employee Carmen was always begging her to take a break. She would be happy to cover for her.

She felt the car slow as he kissed her again, his hands stroking her hair. Then, breaking the kiss, he looked down at her, his face catching the light so that her breath caught in her throat at the absurdity of his perfect cheekbones.

'It's not too late to change your mind.' Despite the teasing smile, his eyes were serious.

Her heart gave a lurch and she almost laughed out loud. Of course it was too late. It had been too late ever since that letter had turned up in her in tray.

Shaking her head, she lifted her chin. 'No. You're right—we do need to talk. Besides, I could do with a holiday.'

His eyes gleamed. 'You might need another one after we get back. This one could be quite...*strenuous*.'

Before she could reply he leaned forward and tapped on the window. And she felt the car stop.

Stepping onto the pavement, Addie looked up at the sky. The rain had stopped and a small, pale sun was edging out from behind the clouds.

She turned to face him, feeling suddenly awkward. 'So what happens now?'

Reaching out, he pulled her against him, sliding his

arms around her waist, and the touch of his strong hands
made her heart slam against her ribs.

'You go inside and pack,' he said mockingly. 'We leave
on Monday.'

'Monday!' She stared at him in shock, her ears buzzing.

He nodded. 'My driver will pick you up at nine. Try not
to keep him waiting too long.'

Addie was starting to feel somewhat overwhelmed, both
by the speed of these arrangements and this unsettling reminder of Malachi's wealth.

But, determined not to show her discomfort or lack of
sophistication, she merely nodded. 'Leave for where? New
York? France? The moon?'

Even to her own ears her voice sounded high and petulant, and she blushed as he laughed softly.

'The Caribbean. I own an island there—off Antigua.'
Glancing at her astonished expression, he grinned.

'Y-you *own* an island?' She had given up trying to play
it cool. 'What kind of island?'

'The usual kind.' He gave her a slow, teasing smile.
'White sand. Palm trees. Paradise on earth.'

Her head was spinning; questions were flying in every
direction. But he was already back in the car.

'Wait!' Stepping forward, she hammered on the window, her breath churning in her throat as it slid down.

He leaned forward, a teasing smile on his handsome
face. 'What's the matter? Are you missing me already?'

She frowned. Away from his touch, with the cooling
breeze on her skin, her head was clearing. 'I need to know
what to pack.'

He laughed, his eyes gleaming. 'It's a honeymoon,
sweetheart. You don't need to pack anything at all!'

CHAPTER FOUR

IN THE TINY bedroom of her apartment, Addie stood staring despairingly at the half-empty holdall on her bed. She had woken early and, after nearly an hour of lying in the darkness, had finally got out of bed with the intention of being calm and collected by the time Malachi's car arrived to pick her up. Yet somehow she wasn't anywhere near ready and, pushing down the swell of panic rising inside her, she sat down on her bed with a thump.

It was all happening so fast—too fast. Three days ago she hadn't seen or spoken to Malachi for five years. Now she was going away with him for a month. Alone. Today. This morning.

The thought was like a jolt of electricity passing through her body, and mechanically she began to fold her clothes and pack them in the bag.

After Malachi had driven off she'd felt exhausted—almost as though she'd just completed some arduous Herculean challenge. Lifting her hand, she pressed her fingers to her lips, remembering the bruising heat of his kisses.

Frankly, Hercules had it easy! She'd take defeating monsters any day over trying to resist the charms of her husband who, in his own devastating way, could cause the same mayhem and misery as any three-headed dog. Unlike the three-headed dog, however, he didn't serve some angry god. He was entirely self-serving and always, however reasonable he appeared, got exactly what he wanted.

Although, to be fair, she had wanted it too. Her cheeks grew warm. More than wanted it. It had been frantic, unstoppable, an almost primeval surge of need to feel his hands on her body again, his mouth on her mouth…

And he'd been the one to pull away, and it was only later that she'd realised how close she'd come to letting him make love to her in the back of his car.

It had been a shock to discover just how much she still wanted him. But a bigger shock was the realisation that instead of shame or regret she'd felt almost elated by what had happened. Elated and aroused. She bit her lip. Since splitting up with Malachi her job had more or less taken over her life. Sometimes she went to the gym, or met friends after work. But mostly she just ate her dinner on the sofa before falling into bed alone. There certainly hadn't been any romance.

Only now she was going to spend a month on a private Caribbean island. With Malachi. A man whose touch had tormented and tamed her.

She breathed out slowly.

She was almost certainly going to regret this trip. But those few snatched moments of release in the limousine had at least proved to her what she'd known but denied for so long. That she wasn't completely over Malachi; that in some intangible, incomprehensible way she still felt married to him.

She winced. Put like that, it sounded mad. But she wasn't living under any delusions. This 'honeymoon' wasn't some last-ditch attempt to save their relationship. Quite the reverse, in fact. It was a *coda*: a bittersweet and fitting finale to a marriage that had never been quite what it seemed—to her, at least. At least this time their relationship might actually be more straightforward, more honest, despite, or maybe because it involved a simple trade-off: sex for money.

This time her heart was definitely off limits. This deal would only involve her body—and only for a limited period. And, of course, a large amount of money.

She zipped the bag shut.

Did that make her shallow? Mercenary. Immoral.

No, it did not, she thought defiantly.

She'd never asked him for anything. Not a single cent. And she still hadn't. This was for her charity. But seeing him again had made her realise that she couldn't keep avoiding the past. Finally she was ready to bring an end to all the years spent wondering, hoping, aching. And that meant being with her husband one last time. She let out a long, slow breath. So why not make the most of it?

After all, there were a lot worse ways to spend a month than being on a private island with a sexy, handsome billionaire.

At the thought of Malachi's island she felt a flicker of fear. How was she going to survive the two of them being alone on a deserted island?

By sticking to the rules. Kissing was almost unavoidable and, knowing Malachi, if he thought she was trying to avoid kissing him he'd simply see it as a challenge. But there would be no touchy-feely stuff—the sort of things couple did without thinking—because this was a business arrangement and there was no point in blurring the boundaries.

She also expected to be treated with respect. Okay, he had the money, but this arrangement was only going to work if she made it clear that while her body might have a price she, Addie, was beyond even *his* wealth. The remnants of her pride required that she demand that at least.

And if it all got too unbearable she could always catch a plane back to Miami. She wasn't so destitute that she couldn't afford an airfare home!

Beside her on the bed her phone vibrated and, picking it up, she glanced at the screen and felt her heart jolt. The car would be arriving in twenty minutes. Just enough time to dry her hair and find her passport and double-check that Carmen knew she was in charge of the office for the next four weeks.

Thirty minutes later, wearing a short navy wraparound skirt and an embroidered cream silk blouse, she was sitting in the back of the limousine, trying her hardest to look as though it was something she did every day of her life. Tucking her legs to one side, she glanced down at her high-heeled navy court shoes and frowned. She hardly ever wore heels outside of work, and they were not the most practical footwear for a beach holiday, but she wanted a reminder of why she was there: a private nudge to herself that this was not personal but business. And, anyway, she needed the extra height if she was going to square up to Malachi's six-foot-two frame.

Feeling the car slow, she glanced out of the window and saw that they'd arrived at a large private airfield. And then her breath seemed to lodge in her throat as she saw the sleek white plane, emblazoned with the King Industries logo, gleaming on the runway. Beside it a line of stewards stood, waiting on the tarmac, all looking as though they'd just stepped out of the pages of Italian *Vogue*, and suddenly she felt like a rather unprepared understudy about to step on to a West End stage.

Who were they expecting? What had Malachi told them?

She would soon find out.

As the limousine swung smoothly to a stop and the door

beside her opened she took a deep breath, swung her legs out of the car and stepped onto the tarmac.

Immediately the nearest steward walked swiftly towards her, smiling. 'Good morning, Ms Farrell. My name is John. I'm the chief steward on this flight and I will be taking care of you today. Welcome to King Airlines.'

Inside the plane, Addie had to clench her jaw to stop it from falling open. She'd flown before. She'd even been upgraded to business class once. But this—

Trying not to gawp, she gazed slowly around.

It was not like the interior of any plane she'd ever travelled on. Rather than banks of seats with a central aisle, there was a large open-plan lounge area that spanned the width of the plane. Between huge leather sofas, vases filled with freesias stood on top of mirror-topped tables. There was also a bar!

Five minutes later she was sitting at one end of a sofa, sipping a perfect cappuccino from a fine bone china cup, when a door at the end of the cabin opened and Malachi sauntered towards her across the carpet.

'Sorry, sweetheart. This trip of ours has thrown quite a few balls up into the air. I needed to meet with some people just to make sure somebody catches them while I'm away.'

Before she had a chance to reply, he dropped down onto the sofa beside her and in one seamless movement took the cup from her unprotesting hands, jerked her onto his lap and kissed her so deeply that she came up gasping for breath. He tasted of sunlight and oranges, and despite the chill of the air conditioning his skin was warm.

'I missed you.'

His eyes were fixed on her lips and his face was so golden and perfect that for a moment she couldn't even remember how to speak, let alone what to say. She looked up at him warily as he grinned down at her, the brightness of the day lighting up the shards of silver in his eyes.

'This is where you're supposed to say, *I missed you too*!' he said softly.

She felt her insides tighten, every inch of her body responding to the pressure of his arm curling around her waist and the teasing note in his voice.

'It's only been two days.' She arched an eyebrow, hoping that she appeared more composed than she felt. 'You survived five years before that.'

'How do you know I survived?'

Something flickered across his face, too fast for her to catch.

'Maybe I was confined to bed. Weakened and distraught.'

'Then somebody very like you was out and about in Miami,' she retorted tartly. 'Attending civic functions and charity dinners. You might want to look into that when you get back. Identity theft is a serious business!'

His eyes glittered. 'I'm flattered you kept such a close eye on my whereabouts—'

'I did not—' she protested, but her voice frayed, the hot seam of words unravelling as his hand brushed against her blouse.

'I like this,' he murmured, fingering the silk. 'It's kind of demure yet sexy.'

As his gaze drifted slowly over her legs and down to her shoes, his eyes hardened in a way that made her stomach start to spasm.

'And I like those too.'

His hand slipped beneath her blouse, cool fingers sliding over her hot skin so that she stirred against him, feeling the shift in his breathing. And then, abruptly, he groaned and, gently tipping her off his lap and back onto the sofa, edged away from her.

'Damn it, Addie!' He was grimacing as though in pain.

'What is it?' She stared up at him dizzily, her head still reeling from the havoc his fingers had wrought upon her, feeling the absence of his warm body almost like an amputation.

Shaking his head, he gave her a wry smile. 'I've got a room full of people back there, waiting for me to sign off on a business plan, and you've got me so het up I'm not sure I can even spell my name—let alone write it.'

It took a couple of seconds for her to register what he was saying. That she would have to wait. Meeting his gaze, she saw the soft, taunting glimmer in his grey eyes and felt her temper start to flare. Was that how it was going to be? Him taking every opportunity to remind her that he was the one calling the shots.

Of course it was.

Right from the start Malachi had been the one dictating the terms of their arrangement. And, typical Malachi, he'd done it with a slow, teasing smile on that handsome face of his. And so of course, now she was here on his private jet, the ultimate symbol of his wealth and power, he would make her wait—presumably to demonstrate that no matter how equal the sexual attraction between them was, *he* was always in charge.

It was all she could do to stay sitting on the sofa. But she couldn't keep threatening to walk out on him like some Hollywood diva who didn't like her dressing room. The fact was she had agreed to this ludicrous charade, and she'd known right from the start that he was going to enjoy tormenting her. Her skin tightened as she remembered exactly how good he was at tormenting her. How he'd used to love to keep her hanging on so that she was frantic, wild, almost out of her mind with sexual need.

Dragging her mind back to the present, she gritted her teeth. The mature response—the *only* response—was not to dignify it with any response at all and so not give him the satisfaction of knowing that he'd got under her skin. But just because she'd agreed to come on this trip, it didn't mean she was some sort of concubine. She just needed to find a way to remind Malachi of that fact.

For a moment they stared at one another in silence, and then finally she shrugged. 'It's fine. I can entertain myself,' she said, reaching into her handbag. She pulled out a large paperback book. 'I thought this might come in useful on this trip,' she said sweetly.

His eyes locked on to hers.

'*Emotional Intelligence in the Adolescent Mind.* Sounds gripping. But I thought you were here to mess with my body. Not my mind.'

The thought of what form that *messing* might take made Addie's tongue stick to the roof of her mouth, but despite her hot cheeks she lifted her chin to stare at him. 'It's actually very interesting and informative,' she said loftily.

'I'm sure it is.' His eyes mocked her and, blowing her a kiss, he turned and sauntered out of the cabin.

He was back in less than half an hour. As he strode across the carpet every inch of him was humming with energy, like a racing car on the starting grid.

'All done!' His voice was hard with triumph. Collapsing onto the cushions beside her, he leaned over and picked up a handful of strawberries, tearing into them with white, even teeth. 'And now you have my full and undivided attention.' He plucked the book from her hand and dropped it casually onto the nearest table. 'Now, where were we?' His gaze slid down over her face, down lower to the pulse beating at the base of her throat. 'Oh, yes... Why don't you come over here and sit back on my lap?'

She stared at him in silence, too angry to reply in case she lost her temper. Did he think he could just swan back in and click his fingers and she'd come running? That she'd drop whatever she was doing or have it dropped by him.

She glanced across at the book. *Take control!* she told herself. *Show him that he can't walk all over you. He might have the plane and the limo and the money—especially the money. But he can't have you, not unless he works for it!*

'I've got a better idea,' she said slowly. Standing up, she smoothed her skirt over her thighs, watching his eyes drift down to the hem and then back up to meet her face.

'Why don't we get out of here? Go somewhere a little more private?' His gaze was suddenly so focused, so intense, it made her stomach curl into a knot. But, ignoring the pulse leaping in her throat, she smiled at him coolly. 'Shall I just pick a door? Or do you want to show me the way?'

Staring straight ahead, she kept her eyes glued to his broad back as Malachi led her up a floating spiral staircase to what must be the private quarters of the plane. She held her breath. He wasn't even touching her but already her skin was quivering, the blood slowing and thickening in her veins. She wanted him so badly—but more than that she wanted him to want her as much, even more than she craved him. To be in thrall to her. She wanted to have power over him, to get past that mask and beneath that beautiful, lazy smile and see that formidable self-control slip away.

Her muscles gave an involuntary twitch. They had reached the top of the staircase. There was a moment of tense, pulsing silence and then, pushing open a door, he stepped aside. After a fraction of a second she walked past him. It was another, slightly smaller lounge. There were a couple of gilt-framed mirrors on the walls and on top of several narrow, pale wood tables piles of paperback books vied with one another for space. Looking up, she found Malachi watching her, his eyes more black now than grey, and she felt her body respond to their darkening.

'So,' he said softly. 'Here we are. "Somewhere more private".'

His words snagged on her skin and, pulse jerking, she nodded, trying to stay calm. 'It feels different. Less—'

'Flashy?' For a moment he looked younger, more earnest.

'I was going to say formal,' she said carefully.

He laughed. 'How worryingly diplomatic of you.' He stared past her. 'Downstairs is just an extension of my office. It has to present a certain version of me. Up here is mine.'

Some of his tension had slipped away and she stared around, liking the comfort and the easy elegance. 'What's through there?' She gestured to a door at the other end of the room.

'It's a gym and a steam room.'

'What about up there?' She pointed to more curving steps that seemed to hang magically in the air. There was a moment of pulsing silence. He turned and his gaze slipped over her skin like warm silk. Suddenly she could feel her blood racing through her body like wild mustangs.

'Come and see.' He held out his hand.

She stared at it for a moment, letting his words hang in the air, needing a moment to clear her head of the pulsing beat of her heart.

Do it, she urged herself again. *Do it on your terms. Take control.*

Taking his hand, she slipped past him, turning at the

bottom of the staircase. 'I think I can find my way from here.'

She walked up the stairs slowly, his hand clasped in hers. At the top she stopped and stared—at a bed.

But only for a moment.

Then she turned and reached for him, her fingers curling into the fabric of his shirt, grabbing, tugging, pulling at buttons and hair and flesh. She'd caught him off guard, could feel he shook. But the next moment his mouth was on hers, fierce, bruising, heavy. Desperately she kissed him back, locking her arms around his neck, frantic with the freedom of being able to touch him, to kiss him, to run her fingers through his hair.

Catching the scent of his skin, she moaned softly, and her breath quickened as she felt his body move urgently against hers. She heard him groan and felt a rush of euphoria, and then suddenly his hands were on her waist, pushing her back and across the floor, his legs nudging and pressing between hers. She half slid, half fell onto the bed, pulling him with her, her mouth opening beneath the hard pressure of his lips.

His hands were at her waist, her thighs, her ribs— sliding all over her body, peeling away her shirt and her defences. Her breath felt hot in her throat, the tormenting touch of his mouth making her head swim and, moaning, she reached lower, pressing her hand against the smooth muscles of his stomach until she felt his body shudder.

'Malachi!' She whispered his name unsteadily and breathing in hard, she stilled as he raised himself up and stared down into her face, his grey eyes gleaming like polished steel.

'What's the matter?' he murmured. 'Have you lost your way?'

Addie shuddered. His fingertips, light and languid,

were sliding over the smooth mound of her belly, stroking, circling, caressing lower, and lower still, so that a
tingling, torturous thread of pleasure wove in and out of
her breathing.

Suddenly he lifted his hand and she couldn't stop herself
from whimpering. His gaze fixed on her face, his expression so hard and hungry and knowing that she squirmed
against the sheets. There was no way to hide how much
she wanted him to keep on touching her, how much she
needed to feel him on top and inside her.

'Malachi...' She swallowed, fighting to control the
need, the urgency in her voice, trying to hang on to the
liquid heat building inside her, her muscles clenching and
tightening.

'Addie—'

He let the word hang between them as she looked up at
him pleadingly and then, lowering his head, he licked her
shoulder, his tongue hot and measured as it snaked over
her collarbone, teasing the hollow at the base of her throat
until her body started to shake.

His fingers spread across the bare skin of her back,
expertly undoing her bra and freeing her swollen, aching
breasts. Almost choking on her own breath, she twisted
upwards, rubbing against his hips, goading him with her
body, wanting him to answer the ache clamouring inside
her. But, pushing aside the flimsy fabric, he dropped his
head and grazed her breast with his mouth, licking and
nipping, his tongue curling around first one nipple then
the other.

Finally she could bear it no more and she pushed his
head away, at the same time desperately reaching beneath
the waistband of his trousers to curl her hand round the
hard, straining length of his erection.

He jerked against her, his breath coming in ragged

gasps. Grasping her head, he began to kiss her again, each time deeper and deeper, until she thought she would melt with need. A slippery heat was trickling down inside her and helplessly she rolled beneath him, wanting to rid herself of that relentless, dragging ache, wanting, needing to feel him inside, *to finish what she'd started.*

She tugged at his belt urgently, her fingers tearing at the buckle, scraping his skin.

'Wait—wait, sweetheart. We mustn't—'

His hand caught her scrabbling fingers, holding them still, and she stared up at him dazedly.

'Wh-what?' Fighting to get her words out, she frowned. A haze of unfocused thoughts and fears were swirling inside her head. 'What do you mean?' Her voice was hoarse. She could hear her hunger for him, the scraped, raw longing. But she didn't care. She just wanted him—all of him. The heat and the power, the unthinkable, impossible bliss of his body stretching into hers.

He shook his head. 'Not here. Not now.'

She looked up at him, shifting restlessly, her whole body twitching with unfulfilled desire so that she had to bite her tongue in order not to beg him to make love to her.

His hand was curving under the back of her head so that his calm, assessing grey gaze held her captive. For a moment he studied her face and then, raising his hips, he let go of her hand and lifting himself off her body, he slid onto the bed beside her.

The cool air stung her skin.

But not as much as the cool, calculating expression on Malachi's face.

How could he look at her like that? She stared at him uneasily. And how had he found the willpower to stop? The thought that, unlike her, he had been cool-headed enough to break their frantic, febrile embrace was like a punch to the stomach. Cheeks burning, she breathed in sharply and pushed against his shoulder.

He made no objection as she shifted along the bed, tugging at her bra and blouse and pushing her skirt down over her naked thighs, shock at her own behaviour mingling with the humiliating realisation that, rather than taking charge, she had let her self-control go into a complete and very obvious meltdown. It had not been *him* begging *her* to ease the frantic demands of *his* body. Instead she had been the one whose whole being had been focused on satisfying her burning desire for him.

A discreet but insistent buzzing noise broke the silence between them and, rolling over, Malachi punched a button on a panel set into the wall above the bed.

'Yes.'

'Sorry, Mr King. Just to let you know we are approaching Antigua now, so if you wouldn't mind buckling up?'

'Yes, of course.' Hanging up, Malachi turned and met her gaze. 'We'd better go and take our seats.'

Smoothing his fingers through his hair, he tucked in his shirt and as though by magic was transformed back into a sleek, efficient business tycoon.

His eyes drifted over her dishevelled state. 'You might want to tidy up a little…'

Staring at her reflection in the bathroom mirror, Addie mechanically ran a comb through her hair. Her hand was shaking too much to put on any lipstick or eye make-up, so instead she tried to force her face into the same cool mask of detachment that Malachi could apparently achieve so effortlessly.

How did he do it? she thought helplessly. Even now, with her clothes straightened and buttoned up, and a door between them, her body was still a shuddering mass of sexual yearning, her brain barely functioning.

She moaned softly. She had so wanted to prove to him, to herself, that no matter how disparate their wealth and status they would come together as sexual equals on this trip. But the harsh reality was that she had simply managed to reveal how badly she still wanted him. She'd responded to him mindlessly, her hunger so intense, so desperate that she'd been ready and willing to surrender herself to his every whim—

She shivered. The trouble was that she couldn't do what he did. She couldn't blank off her mind from the passion, the hunger. How could she? Until her car accident her whole life had been about living emotions through music. Playing the piano demanded passion as much as discipline, poetry as much as practice.

Her mouth twisted. Sex with Malachi was evidently not going to be as straightforward as she'd thought. Not because she loved him. But because she appeared unable to switch off the mess of emotion that sex with Malachi provoked.

Her heart began to pound. But so what if she couldn't contain or control her feelings? Did she really want to become like Malachi? All warmth and charm on the outside, but utterly immune to real feelings.

No, she did not.

Her marriage to Malachi had already cost her five years of her life, her hopes, most of her pride and around six kilograms of weight. She wasn't about to sacrifice the essence of who she was to it too.

And she *would* survive this trip.

After all, she'd survived far worse.

Lifting her chin, she pulled out a lipstick and swiped it over her lips. She might come out of this affair emotionally battered and bruised, but she would come out of it as herself.

Turning, she pushed open the bathroom door and walked determinedly back into the cabin.

'Ready?' His voice was distracted, his eyes fixed on the screen of his phone.

She cleared her throat and waited for him to look up, watching his eyes narrow appreciatively as they switched from his phone to her glossy lips and long bare legs.

She met his gaze. 'I've never been readier,' she said slowly.

CHAPTER FIVE

STARING OUT ACROSS the turquoise-blue sea, Malachi felt a ripple of satisfaction break over his skin. Beside him in the speedboat Addie sat gazing out across the water, her long red hair blowing across her face, her slender legs curling against the smooth suede upholstery. He could imagine how they must appear to everyone around them: the perfect honeymooning couple on their way to paradise.

Beneath his expensive sunglasses his eyes glittered. Except that they weren't. Yes, his wife was *there*, her warm, seductive body just inches away from his. But, glancing at the pure line of her profile, he knew that her thoughts were far away. No doubt dealing with the unfamiliar sting of having her warm, seductive body turned down.

He shifted in his seat, his groin tightening uncomfortably. It might be rather more painful than he'd anticipated but he'd proved his point. She wanted him—and badly. Remembering those blue eyes dilating in helpless response, her body twitching beneath his, he felt a rush of triumph. Only it was tempered with a slight sense of relief, for he had come dangerously close to taking her there and then and he hated feeling that frantic. It was too raw a reminder of how his life had used to be, watching and waiting for his parents' parties finally to end.

But soon he would ease his body into hers. Only for now let *her* be the one feeling out of control.

As though sensing his thoughts, she glanced up and gave him an icy glare.

'Everything all right?' he said softly.

He watched her fingers curl into her hands.

'Everything's fine.'

'Really? Only you seem a little tense.' He gazed at her levelly. 'Is it the boat? I could rub your back if you think it would help...'

Oh, she was tense, all right. She'd tried and failed to cover it up, for he'd noticed the wary uncertainty in her eyes, the nervous flush of colour in her cheeks the moment she'd walked out of the bathroom. But there was no place on this trip for feelings—*her* feelings, for of course his weren't ever going to be a problem. He'd learned the hard way that life and particularly relationships were simpler, smoother, sweeter all round if emotions were removed from the equation.

His eyes fixed dispassionately on a distant speck of green and brown, rising out of the sea, and his mouth curled into a tight smile. It was the face he presented to any unfortunate gambler who got caught breaking the rules at his casinos.

And Addie had broken the rules. The first rule of the house.

She'd interfered with the run of play.

His mouth thinned. Or rather he'd *let* her interfere with it. Let her catch him off guard.

Beside her, Addie felt Malachi move, but she ignored him. She was still fuming over that last remark. Rub her back? She'd rather jump overboard. Or better still push him in. For a moment she allowed herself to picture Malachi walking a plank.

Imagining the splash he would make greatly restored

her spirits and, feeling able to face him again, she looked up and said sweetly, 'Everything all right with you?'

'Everything is fine.'

'Really? Only you seem a little restless,' she said.

He held her gaze. 'I was just thinking about poker.'

She glowered at him. Typical! So nothing had changed. She was still three steps behind him and he was thinking about cards. Carefully she turned her body away from his.

Gazing past Addie, remembering again how close he'd come to losing control, Malachi frowned. He'd been completely unprepared for the way she'd taken his hand and led him upstairs. More mind-blowing still had been how she'd kissed him. The touch of her lips on his had been like napalm—a flash of raw white heat, explosive, all-consuming. He'd been out of control, reduced to no more than a pulsing mass of heat and longing. And for that moment he'd wanted whatever she wanted and more.

His stomach clenched. Before he'd met Addie his mantra for living had been simple: work hard, play harder. By sheer effort and determination he'd transformed his family's casino business from a debt-ridden mess into a global brand. And to relax there had been women. All beautiful, sexy and disposable.

Until five years ago. Until Addie.

When, despite knowing exactly how damaging and abusive marriage could be, he'd gone ahead and married her. And he still couldn't quite understand why. It didn't make sense, not after his childhood with its ringside seat at his parents' marriage. Watching helplessly as they'd let sex and passion twist their lives—*and his*. He'd sworn never to do the same. A muscle tightened in his jaw.

But Addie had been so beautiful, so tempting, with that glorious red hair tangling about shoulders, her blue eyes pulling him in and under her spell, and just like that his promises had turned to air. Ignoring all his instincts, and every promise he'd ever made, he'd followed his libido up the aisle and married Addie, justifying it as a *commercial* decision: a merger of bodies rather than business.

It had sounded good inside his head—so good that he'd let himself believe it was the whole truth until, too late, he'd realised the scale of his mistake—and how badly sex had clouded his judgement.

But he wasn't going to let that happen again.

This time he held all the cards. He wasn't blind to the allure of her body, but this time it would be safely contained. Their arrangement would last a month, and there would be no meaningless romantic gloss. It would be like any other business arrangement. Only instead of paperwork and conference calls it would just be the two of them on a deserted island and a month of pure pleasure, designed to exorcise the sexual hold she still had over him.

Feeling suddenly immensely satisfied, he leaned towards Addie and pointed to where the dark clump of palm trees and other green foliage was rapidly growing larger.

'That's it. That's where we're going. Bar Jack Cay.'

She nodded and managed to give him a small, polite smile. But her head was spinning, her skin flushing hot then cold. It felt like seasickness but it wasn't. It was humiliation. Sitting in silence, gazing out across the water, she'd been able to pretend that she was on some other boat, maybe with friends. Those blush-making moments on the plane pushed to the back of her mind. But now that he'd spoken to her, his body leaning in, the faint smell of his cologne mingling with the sea spray, the whole embarrassing scene filled her head again.

What had she been *thinking*? She couldn't have made a bigger fool of herself if she'd planned it. Shrinking back against the seat, she felt her stomach twist with misery as she remembered her frantic behaviour, how desperate she must have looked. She might as well have worn a huge sign saying *'My sex-life is non-existent'* around her neck.

But far worse was the way she'd let him manipulate her all over again. Just as she'd done five years ago. She felt a rush of anger. Everything was such a mess, but one thing was clear. That despite what he'd said, or what they'd agreed, this arrangement clearly had more to do with power than desire. His power over her.

It was the first time she'd really understood what she had actually agreed to.

Her heart gave a jolt as the speedboat began to slow. Looking up, she found him watching her, and something in his cool, speculative gaze made her lift her eyes to meet his.

'Are we slowing down for a reason?' Her voice sounded curt, not at all like a bride on her honeymoon. But she didn't care. He was paying for her body—not for her to look as though she was madly in love with him. And it wasn't as though he would comment on her manner. He shied away from conversations that even hinted at the intimate or the personal.

With a chill, she remembered how he had refused even to acknowledge her doubts about their marriage. Like when she'd tried to find out why his parents weren't coming to the wedding. At first, he'd ignored her questions. Then finally, when she'd made it clear she wasn't going to drop the subject, he'd simply walked away. It had been the same at the reception, when having overheard a conversation about his motives for marrying, she had attempted to discuss it with him. He had withdrawn not just physically but emotionally and that was when she had known their marriage would never work.

But there was no point in thinking about any of that

now and, feeling his gaze on her face, she curled her arms around her waist, flattening out the emotion inside her.

'There are rocks up ahead.' He smiled, his eyes dancing maliciously. 'You can't see them, but they'd scuttle a boat this big. So we have to transfer to a dinghy.'

Ignoring his hand, she stepped past him into the smaller boat and, laughing softly, he sat down next to her, trapping her thigh against his, his arm draping around her shoulder as she stared mutinously down at the sea.

'I know the water's tempting, sweetheart, but don't you want to look at where you're going to be staying for the next few weeks?' he teased. 'Or are you trying to work out if you can swim home?'

Gritting her teeth, Addie lifted her head reluctantly and gazed at the island.

Up close, it wasn't quite what she'd been expecting. It was beautiful in a rugged kind of way, but truthfully, she had been expecting something a little more Robinson Crusoe.

But so what if the island was a little less pretty than her mental image of paradise? It was obviously completely untouched, which was surely closer to the true meaning of paradise. Surprised that Malachi would be sensitive enough to recognise that fact, she felt some of her anger fade.

'It's beautiful,' she said stiffly, managing a small, tight smile.

Smiling back at her, he reached out, and before she could protest he had taken her hand in his. 'I like to think of it as a little bit of Eden. Somewhere I can be completely uninhibited.'

Mesmerised by the shimmering molten heat of his voice, she wondered how such a short sentence could contain so much promise of pleasure and danger.

But of course paradise wasn't perfect, she thought dully. As well as cool streams and sunshine there were snakes. Or in this case one particular snake.

But as the dinghy slid through a narrow gap in the rocks she completely forgot her doubts, for in front of her was the most beautiful beach she had ever seen. At the end of a shell-shaped pool of clear blue water was a large curve of pale gold sand, fringed with picture-book palm trees. For a moment she stared in silence, struggling to find words to put into a coherent sentence as Malachi watched her stunned reaction.

'Is it a lagoon?' she said finally.

He nodded, his face impassive but his eyes suddenly intent. 'I'm guessing this is more what you were expecting to see.'

Before she could reply he lifted his hand and waved at a man and woman who were waiting at the end of a short wooden jetty.

'That's Terry Clarke and his wife, Leonda. They take care of everything on the island. Maintenance. Laundry. Cleaning. And Leonda enjoys cooking, so anything you fancy just tell her and she'll make it. But don't worry!' His eyes mocked her. 'We'll have plenty of time on our own, sweetheart. And plenty of space. Sixteen acres, in fact. Although not all of it is accessible.'

Sliding his arm around her waist, he pulled her against him.

'Imagine it. Just you and me in paradise. Alone. Doing whatever we want.'

His eyes seemed to reach inside her and suddenly her whole body was squirming with a flickering, treacherous heat. She didn't need to imagine what she wanted to do with Malachi. Since meeting him in the restaurant it had been playing inside her head like a slow motion erotic film.

But thankfully at that moment the dinghy bumped gently against the jetty, and with relief she climbed out of the boat and away from the gravitational pull of his gaze.

Terry and his wife, Leonda, were both charming. Having grown up on Antigua, they were well informed and enthusiastic about the Caribbean island experience. Still slightly stunned by the thought that this idyllic paradise was going to be her holiday home, Addie hardly managed to do anything other than make a few polite, meaningless remarks about the colour of the sand and her fondness for mangoes. Not that it mattered. Their attention was fixed on Malachi, and who could blame them when his handsome face looked so absurdly flawless in the pure, white sunlight?

Finally they were alone.

'The villa is this way!'

Pushing aside a tangle of foliage, Malachi stepped aside to let her pass.

Addie breathed in sharply. She had thought that nothing could surpass that first view of the beach, but the villa was quite simply stunning. A clean-lined, contemporary house, set on a bleached wood deck, it was surrounded by lush grape trees and looked across another, smaller lagoon.

'There used to be a colonial-style building here, but after Hurricane Helena came we had to rebuild everything. I actually prefer the look of this. It feels less intrusive. Come on, I'll show you around.'

Inside the villa, Addie had to pinch herself. It was luxury on a scale she'd never imagined, let alone seen. Five years ago Malachi had been wealthy, but his casino empire had only just started to expand, and although the money had been there it had been in the background. Gazing round at the state-of-the-art kitchen, at the understated glamour of the lounge area and the marbled luxury of the bathroom, she started to realise just how much he had changed over the last five years.

Watching her eyes widen at the sight of the huge open-plan living area, with its linen-covered sofas and vases of frangipani, Malachi felt his stomach twist. In the way of all wealthy and sophisticated people, most of the men and women of his acquaintance would have made a concerted effort not to notice, much less remark on their surroundings. But why? What was so wrong about being open and honest?

His eyes narrowed. He must have been out too long in the sun if he had to even ask himself that question. And while it might be amusing—charming, even—to listen to Addie go into raptures over the view from his bedroom window, it reminded him why their relationship had failed. Why it could never have worked. Her fervour for life was fine when carefully managed, as part of the overall package he had envisaged for their marriage. It had even played out well with the media, giving him a new, warmer, more caring image. But that was where it should have stayed. In public. He had no use for uncontrolled emotional outbursts in his private life.

No use for it.

No understanding of it.

And definitely no need for it.

'What's that over there?'

Addie's voice broke into his thoughts and, turning, he looked towards where she was pointing, over the lagoon to a wavering white line cut through the verdant foliage.

'I think it's a waterfall.' He squinted across the water. 'I seem to remember there being one.'

She frowned at him. 'How can you not know if there's a waterfall?'

He frowned. 'I *do* know. I just can't remember if that's

where it is. I haven't been round the island for years. When I stay I don't generally bother leaving the villa. I don't need to. There's enough to keep me entertained here.'

She gritted her teeth. By 'enough', he clearly meant some eager, sexually responsive female companion. It was a surprisingly unwelcome discovery, although she hadn't for one moment imagined that he had been single for the last five years. But did he have to rub in that fact here, now?

'If you're expecting some kind of sexual Olympics then I think you might be in for a disappointment,' she said tartly. 'Maybe you should have brought whichever woman you normally come here with instead.'

He stared at her in silence and then, smiling slowly, he leaned forward. 'You're the first and only woman I've ever brought here, sweetheart. The first and only I've ever *wanted* to bring here.'

It was true. He usually only visited the island on his way to or from a business trip, and he had certainly never brought a woman. Not even his mother. *Especially not my mother*, he thought grimly.

'I come here four or five times a year. As a reward for sitting through interminable discussions with people I'm only meeting so they remember my face.'

He smiled at her slowly, and suddenly her mouth was dry and her heart was pounding against her ribs. People didn't forget a man like Malachi King, his dark, restless gaze and pure, clean profile. And they always remembered his slow, devastating smile. She knew just how far someone would go to make Malachi King smile like that—and how much they would be prepared to sacrifice.

She had the scars to prove it.

The watch on his wrist made two small beeping noises and, grateful for the chance to break free of the tension swelling between them, she took hold of his arm and turned it gently.

'Is that the time?' she said quickly. 'No wonder I feel so hungry. Why don't we go down and I'll see if I can rustle up something to eat?'

Frowning, he pressed his hand against his forehead. 'I completely forgot. Leonda told me she'd left us some lunch. Nothing fancy, but I'm sure it'll be delicious.'

It was. A three-course cold buffet, all exquisitely presented. Leonda had also thoughtfully provided a handwritten menu, listing all the ingredients.

'I can't believe I offered to cook,' Addie groaned, gazing down at her plate.

'You didn't.' Biting into a barbecued rib with guava and tamarind, Malachi raised an eyebrow. 'You offered to *"rustle up something"*.'

He was impossible to resist. She tried to frown, but ended up smiling. 'You tricked me. You said she *enjoyed* cooking.'

His grey eyes gleamed. 'And she does. She also happens to be a Cordon Bleu trained cook who enjoys "creating dishes which combine colonial and Caribbean influences",' he drawled. 'Or so it said on her CV.' Grinning, he leaned across and speared a small, golden parcel. 'What is *this*?'

Addie glanced at the menu. 'It's coconut and shrimp tempura. It's delicious.' She sighed. 'I think I've eaten about forty already.'

He glanced across the table. 'Only another seventy to go, then.' He grimaced. 'I'm afraid Leonda seems to think I don't eat between visits, so she always cooks enough for a small army.'

Putting her knife and fork together tidily on her plate, Addie gave him a small, careful smile. As if her feelings were as easy to arrange as her cutlery. In her head being alone with Malachi had seemed quite straightforward: there was the sex and then there was everything else. She wasn't deluded enough to pretend that she wouldn't enjoy the sex part, but she hadn't expected the talking, the just being together to be anything other than extremely trying.

Only sitting opposite him now, it was hard to feel like that. Not just because he was stupidly good-looking, but because he was such effortless company. He was bright and well read and, mixing as he did with the rich and the famous, he had an endless supply of amusing and salacious stories.

But, while she might not hate him as much as she would or perhaps should, she needed to make sure their relationship had recognisable boundaries. Sex, by necessity, involved some amount of intimacy—maybe even a certain amount of tenderness. But this—the being together part—required her to be no more than civil. In fact, now might be a good time for her to introduce a more formal, less personal tone to their lunch.

Picking up her water glass, she took a breath and said quickly, 'Thank you.'

There was a flicker of surprise in his eyes as they met hers. 'For what?'

'For bringing me here. It's lovely. Truly.' She glanced out across the lagoon. 'So how did you find this place? I mean, it's so hidden away.'

He shrugged. 'It was an accident, really. I was actually looking to buy a yacht.'

She stared at him dazedly. He spoke about buying a yacht as though it was a carton of milk. And what kind of person chose whether to buy an island or a yacht? It was just another reminder of the differences between them.

She shook her head. 'So what happened?'

His eyes gleamed. 'I went for a swim.'

She stared at him, confused. Surely he couldn't have swam that far out to sea?

Glancing at her face, Malachi shook his head. 'Not here. In a hotel. In Vegas.'

Her eyes narrowed. 'How has that got anything to do with this island?'

He gave her a teasing smile. 'I was playing poker and Teddy Chalmers—do you remember Teddy?'

Addie nodded. She had met him socially with Malachi. He was a lanky middle-aged Texan real estate billionaire, with a penchant for land and property and a passion for poker.

'Teddy bet me this island that I couldn't jump into a pool at the hotel and touch the bottom.'

She frowned. 'That's crazy. Anyone could do that.' Her face stilled with suspicion. 'So why did he think you couldn't?'

Malachi grinned. 'Probably because of the sharks!'

'Sharks!' She stared at him in horror. 'Real sharks? With teeth?'

He laughed. 'The sharks were real, so I guess their teeth were too.'

Addie gazed at him, open-mouthed.

Smiling, Malachi reached for the wine bottle and re-filled his glass. 'Don't look so worried, sweetheart. I won.'

'What if you'd been bitten?'

He gave her an infuriating smile. 'I'm touched that you care.'

'I don't care,' she said quickly. 'I just can't believe you'd risk your life over some stupid bet.'

'I like to win.'

She glared at him. 'Winning isn't everything. And if you'd walked away what would you really have lost?'

He shrugged. 'My pride! Look, they were small nurse

sharks in a tank in a Vegas hotel. Honestly, I didn't think it was that risky. All I really had to do was focus on winning.'

Then Teddy Chalmers must be more stupid than he appeared, Addie thought slowly. Malachi might be the most charming person she had ever met, but he was also the most driven. Losing was simply not an option for him.

He held her gaze. 'I don't make a habit of it,' he said lightly. 'But I was twenty-four years old and I'd spent the best part of a year playing poker non-stop.' He breathed out slowly. 'And with those guys everything turned into a bet.'

Picking up his wine glass, he swirled the contents slowly around.

'When I finally came out here, though, it blew me away. Not the beach and the palm trees so much. But the peace—' His mouth twisted. 'There's something so pure about the sound of the waves, and the breeze and the birdsong.'

Something in his tone made her hold her breath. She stared at him, confused. Birdsong? Since when had that mattered to Malachi? Her heart gave a thump as she wondered what else he hadn't told her. But could she blame him? She'd hardly been open or honest with him, choosing to share only a carefully edited selection of details about her accident and home life.

Staring past him, she realised that they had never really known one another at all. That they had never trusted one another enough to do so. But why be so secretive now? It wasn't as if it mattered any more.

She glanced back at his face. 'I'm not usually a big fan of peace and quiet,' she said hesitantly. 'But this is the good kind.'

'The good kind? What's the *bad* kind?' he prompted his gaze fixed on her face, searching, curious.

She gave him a small, tight smile. It was so tempting

to believe that he was genuinely interested. Had she not known him as well as she did, she might even have hoped that he felt more than just a physical attraction. That he cared about her. But she knew that for Malachi a confidence shared was just a weakness to exploit. Only given their situation, what was there left for him to exploit?

She shrugged. 'I guess when I say "bad" I mean boring.' Pausing, she frowned, her sudden impulse to be open faltering in the face of his dark, dispassionate gaze. 'Which is what I'm being now, so—'

For a moment he stared at her in silence, and then slowly he reached out and pushed a strand of hair behind her ear. 'You might be a lot of things, sweetheart. Some of them are *exceedingly* challenging.' He smiled slowly. 'But I can safely say you have never once bored me.'

Her heart twitched, caught his smile like a fish on a hook. 'It's early yet,' she said lightly.

He grinned. 'Come on, I'm intrigued.'

She burst out laughing. 'Fine. But it's really not that exciting.' She hesitated. Except that it felt stupidly exciting to be talking to him about herself. To feel his eyes on her face, not as part of some kind of foreplay but because he was listening, actually listening to her. 'I suppose it's being here. It's made me think about the holidays I used to go on with my parents.'

'Where did you go?'

'To my aunt and uncle's farm in South Dakota. Every year for years. In the mornings my mum and my aunt would sew, and my dad and uncle would fix things, and in the afternoons they would all play bridge.'

Malachi nodded. 'It's a good game. Old-timers usually play a tight hand.'

Addie smiled. 'Not just old-timers. I play a pretty tight hand too.'

'But you didn't? Play, I mean? You said, "*they* would all play bridge".'

She stiffened. No wonder he was so good at poker. He missed nothing. Every glance, every word, every blink was noted and examined and weighed up.

She shook her head. 'No. I used to help my aunt feed the animals, and then I'd do my piano practice on this old keyboard my uncle rigged up in the barn. To be honest, it wasn't really that different to being at home—just quieter. Even quieter than in Wichita.'

'I've been to Wichita.' His face was calm, watchful. 'It's not Vegas, but it's not exactly a ghost town.'

Picking up her glass, she took a sip of water, her cheeks suddenly warm. She had never told him much about her family. She hadn't wanted him to know. Beside his glamour and raw animal energy, her home, her childhood, had felt so *ordinary* and she'd been embarrassed. But mostly she'd been scared. Scared that somehow he would see through her, past whatever it was that he thought he saw, and realise her ordinariness. For deep down she had never quite believed that he wanted her for who she *really* was.

She smiled. 'Wichita is fine. It was my home that was so quiet. You see, my parents were already old when I was born. My dad was nearly sixty when my mum got pregnant. I don't remember him ever being well. I always had to be quiet at home because he was sleeping, and I couldn't have friends over to play.' She smiled again, more weakly. 'I think that's why I got so good at the piano. My lessons at my teacher's house were the only time I was allowed to be rowdy!'

'Moving to Miami must have been a bit of a shock, then.' He was smiling still, but his eyes on her face were serious.

She nodded, wondering where he was heading with that remark.

'I suppose,' she agreed. 'But in a good way. I could be who I wanted to be. The real me. And Miami is such a warm, vibrant place. It's like there's a permanent party happening.'

The change in him was negligible. She might not even have noticed it but for the slight tightening of his mouth, the ripple of tension in his shoulders.

There was a small pause, and then he shrugged. 'You can get tired of partying!'

She looked up at his face, wishing that there were subtitles running across his forehead to give her a clue as to what was going on inside his head.

'I suppose you can,' she said carefully. 'I haven't actually been to that many.'

He shifted in his seat, abruptly switching his gaze across the veranda to the rippling blue water.

'I must have been to hundreds,' he said softly. 'My parents live to party. When I was a child, Henry, my father, kept a whole bunch of suites at the Colony Club. All weekend it would be open house. To get in, my parents just had to like you. My mother, Serena, once invited the boy who cleaned our pool because he could charm snakes.'

His face grew still and taut.

'He had other *charms* too!' He stared past her, then shrugged again. 'But not enough to keep my mother entertained. So somebody threw him out of a window. He landed in the swimming pool.' Glancing at Addie's horrified expression, he smiled tightly. 'I expect you're grateful they didn't come to our wedding now!'

She stared at him in silence. Yes and no. For a moment she considered asking him about their absence again, but the fierce dark glow in his eyes held her back.

'Wow! They don't sound like most people's parents,' she said finally.

His eyes narrowed. 'They're not. In fact I don't really think of them as parents. Serena was only sixteen when she had me, and Henry had just been kicked out of Dartmouth.' His mouth twisted. 'You could say we grew up together. And now there's a couple of calls I need to make, so why don't you take a shower or go for a swim?'

Disconcerted, she met his gaze. But there was no mistaking the discouraging tone of his voice. Nor the shuttered look in his eyes. The conversation was over.

In the end she took the shower. An hour later she lay on the bed, gazing out of the window. It had certainly been an interesting day. So much had happened—what with all the travelling and her failed attempt to seduce Malachi on the plane. Only even that felt so long ago now, and suddenly far less significant, pushed aside by his unexpected and uncharacteristic revelations about his life.

Thinking back to what he'd told her about his parents and their partying lifestyle, she bit her lip. *Would she be enough to keep him entertained?* Her pulse slowed and, stifling a yawn, she breathed out softly. She didn't have to be. This trip wasn't about partying and crowds. He wanted peace and birdsong. And *her.*

Or he would once he'd finished making his calls.

It was a comforting thought. Or it might have been had she not seen him sitting and staring out across the water, gaze unmoving, phone lying untouched next to where his fingers restlessly tapped the tabletop.

She tried to make sense of it. But after an hour her brain and body gave in to the heat of the day and finally swiftly, she fell asleep.

CHAPTER SIX

IT WAS THE light falling across her face and a feeling of not quite knowing where she was that woke Addie. Somebody had closed the cream-coloured blinds, but she knew without even pulling them open that it was morning.

Her stomach flipped over nervously and she kept her eyes closed, basking in the soft whiteness of the morning, delaying the moment when she would have to face the man lying on the other side of the bed. What exactly was the correct way to greet your estranged husband the morning after the night before?

Her cheeks grew warm. Except there hadn't *been* a night before, because she'd fallen asleep instead.

She held her breath, wondering how he felt about that fact.

But there was only one way to find out and, gritting her teeth, she opened her eyes and rolled over.

Beside her the bed was empty. And not just empty. The sheet and pillowcase were perfectly smooth. Unless Malachi had slept several inches above the mattress, he hadn't slept there at all.

Her heart gave a twitch as she noticed a paper rose on the pillow beside her. Unfolding it, she saw that it was a note from Malachi, written in his familiar bold, cursive script.

Sweetheart,
I'm sorry I didn't wake you last night, only I thought
you needed to sleep. I've got a couple of problems at
work to sort out, but breakfast is all laid out so help
yourself to what you want.
    Terry is dropping round this morning, so if you
need anything else ask him.
Malachi
PS—While I remember, the security pin is 2106.
You'll need it to open any doors or windows. You
shouldn't have a problem remembering it!

She read it again, and then twice more. Reading between every line, letter and punctuation mark. But the
words stayed stubbornly the same, and finally she dropped
the note onto the sheet beside her.

Of course she would remember the pin number. It
was their wedding anniversary. Her mouth thinned. No
doubt he'd chosen it to rub in the fact that this trip was a
travesty of the honeymoon they might have had, had she
not walked out on him. So much for the caring, sharing
Malachi of last night.

Frowning, and suddenly feeling as restless as her
thoughts, she pushed the sheet off. Rolling out of bed,
she padded across the floor into the wet room.

As she stood under the warm spray of water, snippets
of yesterday's lunchtime conversation with Malachi kept
popping into her head, each one seeming to contradict the
one before. It was so confusing. She couldn't seem to get
a clear picture of what he'd said. It was almost as though
she'd been talking to several different versions of the same
man. But who was the *real* Malachi King? And how could
she have been married to a man she knew so little about?

Then again, what did any of that matter now? He wasn't her concern any more.

Wrapped in a large fluffy towel, she walked back into the bedroom and gazed out of the window. It was another glorious day and it really was the perfect honeymoon location.

She lifted her chin. In another life, with another man, it might be, she told herself defiantly. But this was just a business trip. However, it was also probably going to be the only holiday she would ever spend on a private Caribbean island. So from now on she was going to make the most of every moment.

Selecting a new plum-coloured bikini, she covered it with a short crocheted dress—another recent purchase—and, pushing her feet into a pair of brightly coloured beaded sandals, did a twirl in front of the mirror. Glancing at her reflection, she gave a small, satisfied smile before turning and heading downstairs.

There was no sign of Malachi in the kitchen, but breakfast was indeed laid out on the wood-topped counter and, stomach rumbling, she picked out an almond croissant just as there was a knock at the front door.

Her first stupid thought was that it was Malachi. But why would he knock at his own door? And then, remembering his note, she realised it must be Terry. Feeling suddenly shy, she walked hesitantly into the hallway and pulled down on the handle.

Nothing happened.

'Sorry, Miss Farrell…' Terry's voice floated through the door. 'You need the code.'

'Oh, yes, of course. I forgot,' she said, hastily punching her wedding date into the keypad and mentally cursing Malachi for his malicious choice of number.

Her irritation was forgotten, though, as she saw Terry's broad smiling face beaming down at her.

'Good morning, Miss Farrell! And how are you today?'

Taking his hand, she smiled back at him. 'I'm fine, Terry. Thank you.'

'I saw Mr King this morning and he told me to drop in and make sure you have everything you need.'

'I do—but while I remember, would you please thank Leonda for the wonderful food?'

Terry grinned. 'I will, Miss Farrell. She's real happy, having you and Mr King stay for all this time. Normally he's only here long enough to read the morning paper—which reminds me: Mr King asked me to drop off today's newspapers.' Reaching down, he picked up a bag. 'There's some magazines in there too. Let me put them inside for you, Miss Farrell.'

Inside the kitchen, he glanced out of the window and up at the sky.

'Weather's looking fine. We might even get some turtles next week.'

'There are *turtles*?' Addie said excitedly. 'Do they come into the lagoon?'

He shook his head again and laughed. 'No. Turtles like to nest near open water, so their babies can reach the ocean real quick.' As though sensing her disappointment, he smiled. 'But they *do* nest on Finlay's Island. You won't have seen it from the boat, but it's only thirty minutes away. I keep an eye out at this time of year, so I'll let you know if I see any sign of them. Now, is there anything else I can do?'

Addie nodded. An idea had just occurred to her. 'Actually,' she began tentatively, 'there *is* one thing...'

Ten minutes later, Addie was relaxing on a sun lounger, a glass of iced tea in her hand, thoroughly enjoying a celebrity gossip magazine. Having arranged for Terry to take them on a tour of the island, she felt calmer—more in control.

More like herself.

She took a sip of her tea. It wasn't that she didn't have a sexy side, but she wasn't comfortable about it being her defining quality. And now it wouldn't be.

A shadow fell across her face and her thought jammed inside her head as, looking up sharply, her eyes collided with Malachi's cool, assessing grey gaze.

'Good morning,' he said slowly, his eyes roaming over her in a way that made her whole body twitch restlessly.

Dressed in a pair of linen trousers and a navy polo shirt that clung to the muscular outline of his chest and arms, he looked relaxed and cool despite the heat of the morning.

'Morning!' Putting her glass down on the table beside her, she gave him what she hoped was a casual smile. 'I hope you don't mind, but I did have some breakfast.'

'Not at all.' He glanced back into the villa. 'I might just grab some fruit. Can I tempt you with anything else?'

'Like what?' Her eyes flicked up and he smiled at her mockingly.

'I meant some more iced tea, or something else to eat.'

Licking her lips, wondering how he managed to make such a mundane suggestion sound so enticing and decadent, she shook her head. 'No, thank you. I had a…thing… you know…' Her mind was suddenly a total blank, his proximity playing havoc with her brain. 'A pastry—almond—almond croissant,' she managed finally.

'Then I'll be right back!' he said softly, his clear, teasing gaze leaving her in no doubt that he knew the effect he was having on her.

Gritting her teeth, heart pounding, she watched his broad retreating back with a mixture of longing and relief.

Moments later her breath seemed to punch out of her lungs as he dropped down lightly beside her on the lounger, the warm length of his thigh pressing against her naked leg.

'Why does everything taste so much better here than it does back on the mainland?' he murmured as he licked juice from his fingers. 'I know sugar's bad for you, but sometimes there's nothing better than that rush.' His eyes slid slowly over her face, fixing on her mouth. '*Almost* nothing anyway.'

Addie felt her stomach drop, and then a slow, prickling tension crept up her spine as he lowered his lips to hers and kissed her softly. Helplessly she arched against his body, feeling a quivering, featherlight pleasure steal over her skin, and then she breathed in sharply as Malachi lifted his head.

'Now, *that* is the correct way to say good morning!'

Staring down into Addie's dazed blue eyes, Malachi forced himself to blank off his mind to the clamouring of his body. His pulse was racing, and a fierce hot pressure was building in his groin. He had planned simply to kiss her, thereby reminding her of why she was sitting there, on *his* lounger, by *his* lagoon, looking so damn tempting. But now, with that red hair tumbling across her shoulders, her lips parted invitingly, it took every ounce of willpower he had not to scoop her up into his arms and take her right there and then.

Looking past her, he gritted his teeth, hating how stirred up she made him feel. He wanted her badly—so badly it felt like a toothache. But taking her now would only demonstrate that fact, and he'd arranged a little surprise for her that would be far more effective at enticing her into his arms.

He breathed out. Yesterday, after she had gone upstairs to lie down, he had fully intended to follow her. To give in finally to the hunger that had been growing inside him since the moment he'd heard her voice again.

Only he hadn't.

Oh, he'd wanted to. But he couldn't. His legs simply wouldn't move; it had been as if he was trapped inside his own body as once upon a time he'd been trapped as a unwilling onlooker at his parents' parties. How could he possibly have gone upstairs to Addie with that thought uppermost in his mind?

As for mentioning his parents to Addie—what had he been thinking? He shifted uncomfortably on the lounger. He'd worked so hard to suppress the hurt, to bury the memories. Now wasn't the time to let that darkness seep back into his life.

'Are you okay?' Looking up, he found Addie watching him warily.

He smiled, instantly back in control, and ran his fingers slowly down her arm, feeling her skin shiver beneath his touch. 'Of course. And you? Did you sleep okay?'

Her face stiffened. 'Yes. I did.' She hesitated. 'I'm sorry about falling asleep. I suppose I was more tired than I thought.' She frowned, not wanting to ask where he'd slept. Instead she said quickly. 'How did *you* sleep? Did you have a good night?'

It was not a night he would care to repeat, he thought grimly. And sleep had played a very small part in it. Having finally managed to clear his head enough to go and look for her, his erotic imaginings had turned increasingly feverish with every step, so that by the time he'd walked into the bedroom his body had been pulsing with desire.

Only of course she'd been fast asleep, her curled-up body seeming to emphasise her vulnerability and innocence. And, gazing down at her, he had cursed his timing. Waking a sleeping woman simply to gratify his sexual appetites was not something he could ever contemplate. But nor was lying next to *that* body when his mind was little more than a white-hot mass of sexually charged fantasies.

Which had left him tossing and twisting alone in a bed in one of the many spare rooms in the villa.

So, no. In answer to her question, he *hadn't* had a good night.

Or a particularly satisfying morning either. Having woken early and still painfully aroused, he had taken a long, cold shower, standing beneath the icy water until he simply couldn't feel his body any more. Stepping out of the shower, his libido once again checked and contained, he should have felt calmer.

His mouth thinned. Except that he hadn't. Instead he'd felt tense and on edge, his mind twitching with a whole set of new and unsettling feelings. Not least the realisation that Addie's presence appeared to be having an impact on more than just his libido. Staring down at where she lay in his bed, he'd felt more than thwarted lust. Maybe it had been the dark smudges beneath her eyes, or her slightly bitten fingernails, but something had twisted inside him and he'd felt a wholly uncharacteristic impulse to draw her into his arms.

He breathed out slowly. It didn't make any sense. But then what did in those strange early hours of the morning when the mind played tricks on itself? Once he'd finally bedded her he'd not only be free of this nagging physical ache but he'd also be able to think with his usual clear-headedness. After all, that was what sex did: it satisfied the body and soothed the mind.

He met her gaze. 'I always sleep well,' he lied, and watching her expression shift from curious to irritated, he felt a prickle of satisfaction.

That was more like it. Let her think she was a pleasurable diversion—not a compulsion that needed to be satisfied.

Feeling back in control, he stood up and, gazing out across the lagoon, he held out his hand. 'Come on! Let's go!'

Startled, Addie looked up at him. 'Go where?'

He grinned. 'To have a swim, of course.'

The lagoon was the perfect temperature and even though she was a fairly cautious swimmer, it would have been impossible for her not to enjoy herself. The warm water felt delicious on her skin, and everywhere there was something beautiful to look at. Tiny jewel-coloured fish. Shells of every shade of pink.

And Malachi.

Wearing nothing but a pair of navy trunks, his body was tugging at her gaze with the gravitational force of a black hole. She watched furtively as he pulled himself onto the deck, her eyes tracking the droplets of water trickling over his *café au lait* skin. He was shatteringly sexy.

Unfortunately at that moment he glanced over, and she felt her cheeks flame as she was caught in the act of watching him. Her breath faltered as he took a small run off the deck and dived back into the lagoon, cutting through the ripples towards her.

She stared at him dazedly, her brain melting. From a distance, his beauty was miraculous. Up close, it was as destabilising as an electromagnetic pulse and she could feel her resistance slipping away—

A shadow fell over her face at the same moment as a gust of air whipped up the water around them. Shocked, Addie gasped, her hand reaching out instinctively. Above them the unmistakable shadow of a helicopter hovered briefly, then swung away across the island.

'Don't worry!' Malachi's voice cut through the sudden

silence that followed the helicopter's departure. 'They're just dropping something off for me.'

She nodded. At some point she had ended up clutching his arm and, mortified, she withdrew her hand swiftly, ignoring the mocking glint in his eyes.

'I might just go and get some sunblock. I don't want to burn on my first day.' Averting her eyes from his wet, muscular chest, she slipped past him and swam hastily across the lagoon and levered herself out onto the deck.

He was beside her in a moment, smoothing back his wet hair. 'Would you like me to put it on your back?' he said solicitously.

'No. It's fine. I probably should cover up now anyway.' Backing away, she grabbed her dress and tugged it hurriedly over her head as, behind them, the helicopter rose up above the trees and then swiftly disappeared from view.

Gazing after it, she suddenly remembered her plans for the day. 'Actually, I thought we could go and have a look round the island this morning,' she said quickly, inching towards the villa. Anything to get away from his fabulous semi-naked body. 'You know… Explore a bit.'

There was a short, tense silence. Looking up, she saw that he was watching her, his face as unyielding to her scrutiny as ever. But something was glittering in his eyes that made her heart jerk in her chest.

'Why would we want to do that?' he said softly. 'It's just more of the same.'

He paused and took a step closer, his gaze darkening in time with the beat of her heart. Reaching out, he ran his thumb along her collarbone and, hooking the front of her dress, he tugged her towards him.

'There are far more interesting places I'd like to explore right here.'

His hand was grazing her breast, caressing, circling, making her stomach muscles curl into a ball.

'Which reminds me—I have a little present for you.'

She followed him inside, watching warily as he walked across the kitchen to the counter and picked up a beautiful cream box tied with pale gold ribbon.

He handed it to her casually. 'This is for you.'

She swallowed, her breath hot and scratchy in her throat. Where had that box come from? She didn't remember seeing it earlier.

As though reading her mind, he fixed his eyes on her face. 'I arranged for the chopper to drop it off this morning.'

Gazing into his narrowed grey eyes, Addie felt her stomach flip over. Of course, she thought weakly. It was just another example of the surreal, topsy-turvy world in which he lived. Where his every whim was magically and swiftly satisfied.

Trying not to think about how she fitted in with that particular revelation, she glanced down at the box she was holding. 'What is it?'

'Open it and see.'

Heart thudding, she tugged at the ribbon, struggling to undo it. Finally she pulled off the lid and, parting the feathery sheets of tissue paper, lifted out a short silk slip. It was pale gold, trimmed with delicate cream lace and utterly, utterly exquisite. She stared at it in silence, too stunned to speak.

'Do you like it?'

She nodded. 'It's beautiful, Malachi. I love the colour,' she said at last. Her cheeks grew warm. 'But I don't have anything for you.' And what would she give him anyway? she thought with a needle stab of pain. The man who not only had everything but valued nothing except winning?

'Oh, I wouldn't say that,' he said slowly.

He lifted his gaze, locking on to her flushed, startled face, and she felt a swirling liquid heat rise up inside as his eyes roamed over her body with open longing.

'Try it on.'

His voice was soft, and had he been touching her she might not have heard the authority beneath the seductive tone, for he wielded his body and her response to it like a weapon, ruthlessly using every kiss, every caress, to get what he wanted.

Only she must have wanted it too.

Or why else would she be hearing herself say, 'What? Here? Now?'?

His eyes met hers—dark, triumphant, like a runner who could see the finishing line.

He nodded slowly. 'Yes. Here. Now. Otherwise...' He paused, turning the word slowly over in his mouth, savouring it. 'How can I take it off?'

Something was wrong. *Yes. Here. Now.* His words were ringing inside her head like a series of off-key notes. But why? The slip was a present. A gift. A spontaneous gesture designed to give pleasure. Or was it? She had no reason to doubt him, but she couldn't shift the prickle of apprehension beneath her ribs. Why give her this today? Why not on the plane? Or yesterday?

Watching her in silence, his expression veiled, Malachi pictured her reaction, and inevitable surrender, feeling a rush of pre-emptive power. It was all part of the game. The game of seduction. And, like most games, it required nothing more than a cool head. And, of course, knowing when to make your move. It was a game he enjoyed playing. And winning.

Looking up, she found him studing her intently—and suddenly she knew why. His eyes had none of the heat or fire of a lover. Instead they were glittering down at her with a calculating coldness that made a shiver run down her spine.

She lifted her chin, her shoulders stiffening with suppressed anger. 'Why don't we wait until later?' she said coolly.

He frowned. 'Later?'

'Yes.' She met his gaze. 'You know I said I wanted to explore the island? Well I arranged with Terry for him to give us a tour this morning.'

His eyes were suddenly harder than stone. 'So unarrange it,' he said arrogantly.

This time it was unequivocal. It was an order—clear and direct.

She glowered at him, her anger as quick and cold as a flash freeze. 'I will not.'

There was a long, pulsing silence.

Malachi stared at her, his disbelief that she had actually rebuffed him rapidly switching to cold, hard rage. This wasn't how it worked. Did she seriously think for one moment that *she* could set the agenda for this trip? Or that he was remotely interested in looking around the damn island with her? She was here for one reason and one reason only. Clearly now was the time to remind her of that fact.

'Then I will,' he said coldly. 'I don't know what fanciful little idea you've got in that pretty little head about why we're here, but let me make it easy for you to understand. It has *nothing* to do with sightseeing.'

A muscle flickered in his jaw. He could feel his control slipping and it did nothing to improve his temper. He had wanted to demonstrate his composure in the face of her helpless desire for him. Only instead he was acting like a thwarted teenage boy.

'And even if it did, the only sight I want to see is *you*. In *that*.' He gestured to the slip hanging from her hand.

'You're a monster,' she said shakily.

'And *you* are a hypocrite. Making all this fuss—' His breath hissed through his teeth. 'We had an agreement. We still do.'

'I did *not* agree to this. To you snapping your fingers like some sexually depraved dictator.'

He shook his head. 'That's not what's happening here. You're just having a tantrum because I called you. In my house the rules are simple, sweetheart. Either fold or play.'

She stared at him in disbelief. Did he actually think this was like a game of cards?

'This is not a hand of poker.' She was practically shouting. 'This is you trampling all over my feelings.'

He shrugged. 'I don't care.'

It was his shrug as much as the cavalier tone in his voice that made something inside her snap. Her breath was suddenly choking her.

'Fine,' she snarled. 'Have it your way.'

Pulling her dress up over her head, she yanked off her bikini top, tugged the panties down from her hips and faced him—naked.

Malachi stared at her, his face hard with fury. 'What are you doing?'

'Me? Oh, I'm just getting ready for sex. That's why I'm here, isn't it?' Her voice was shaking, her breathing ragged. Dragging the slip over her head, careless of the delicate lace, she met his gaze. 'So where do you want to do it, then? On the table? On the beach?'

What was the matter with her? He shook his head, trying to control his anger, his confusion. 'You're being melodramatic!'

There was no reason for her to act like this. She'd agreed

to the deal. And the deal was about sex—not this raw emotion. So why was she making such a fuss?

She glared at him. 'No, I am not. I'm just being truthful. But honesty was never your strong point—was it, Malachi?'

'I never said you were just here for sex!' His voice was rough. He had finally lost his temper.

Swearing under his breath, he ran a trembling hand through his damp hair just as there was a knock on the door. He turned, frowning, and opened his mouth to say something. But Addie cut him off.

'Of course not. You never say what you mean to *anyone*! So why would today be any different?' Pressing her finger against her forehead, she pretended to think. 'Oh, I remember now. It's because I'm not just anyone. I'm your *wife*.'

'And I'm your husband. And you owe me a honeymoon and I always call in my debts.'

'You are *not* my husband. You're just a man who's blackmailing me for sex.'

He took a step towards her. The skin on his face was stretched tight; his arms were braced as though invisible hands were restraining him.

'If I'm blackmailing you, then how come *I'm* the one paying?'

She shook her head, her hands curling into fists. 'That's all you care about, isn't it? Money. And winning. I think you've lived and breathed that casino air for so long you think everything's like poker. That's why you're doing this. Why you've turned this, us, into some sort of sick fantasy game. You just can't help youself.'

Malachi stared at her in silence, his angry response stilled in his throat. He could *feel* her accusation, lodged beneath his skin like a poisoned dart. Hear it inside his head. Only it wasn't Addie's voice but his own, saying

words he'd never had the courage to say out loud. Words
he should have spoken long ago to people who should have
known better. His head was spinning. This wasn't meant
to be happening. He had just wanted to prove a point, but
somehow he'd become the nightmare he'd been trying to
escape from all his life.

He breathed in sharply, pushing aside that disturbing
thought. 'It's not a game—' he began.

'Yes, it is,' she spat at him. 'Only you don't even know
it. You actually think it's *normal* to manipulate your estranged wife into being your mistress. Or had it slipped
your mind that we are still married?'

His eyes were hard and gleaming, like polished steel.
'I hadn't forgotten. But having not heard from you since
your little outburst at our wedding reception, I'm surprised
you bothered to bring it up.'

'Why should I contact you?' Her eyes flared with pain
and anger. 'You lied to me.'

'I didn't lie,' he began. But she ignored him.

'And when I tried to talk to you about it you didn't want
to know—'

'It was our *wedding*.' His face was as set as stone. 'Fun-
nily enough I thought we might have other things on our
mind. Like celebrating!'

'Celebrating what? The fact that you'd made a fool out
of me. Or rather I'd made a fool out of myself. And now
I'm doing it again.'

She spat the words at him, wishing they weren't just
words but bricks—something that would hurt him as he
had hurt her. Was *still* hurting her.

'Calm down!' His eyes were glittering, their hostile
glare fixed on her face. 'Terry might hear you.'

'And you wouldn't want *that*, would you, Malachi?' Her
heart was thumping so hard she could hardly hear herself.

'You wouldn't want someone to actually hear what you're *really* like. How you use people. And exploit them. And hurt them.'

'Addie—' He started to speak but she shook her head.

'No. You've said enough.' She forced herself to meet his gaze. 'How can you think this is okay? Treating me like this? Like some whore?' The word stuck in her throat and suddenly she didn't care any more. Not about the deal she'd made with Malachi. Or the charity. Or Terry.

Blood roaring in her ears, she stared down at the slip sticking damply to her skin. She knew it was her body beneath the silk, but it didn't feel as if it belonged to her.

'You know, I thought nothing could ever feel as bad as when I found out I wouldn't be able to play the piano professionally.' It had been far worse five years ago, she thought dully. When she'd finally realised how ruthlessly Malachi had manipulated her love for him. The pain had felt like an actual wound.

How impossible it would have been then to imagine that she could sink any lower.

'It was like the end of everything.' Her voice trembled and she drew in a breath, pushing past the lump of misery in her throat. 'But I faced up to it. And I turned it into something good. Only you treating me like this—it's made me feel like I don't matter. That I'm nothing.'

It was true. She had never felt so utterly worthless. So tainted, so sordid.

'I don't even know who I am any more.' She swallowed, fighting to get her words out. 'I just know I don't like myself...this person I've become...' Her voice faltered and failed.

Malachi felt sick. He had known about her accident but he'd had no idea that it had robbed her of her dreams. She should have told him, he thought dully. Only why would she? Right from the start he'd made it clear that his past was off limits, and he'd never once encouraged her to talk about herself.

He stared at her in silence. She looked crushed, her face pale and trembling, her beautiful blue eyes clouded with pain. But it was her hands, clenched protectively in front of her, that made his body tense with shock.

He didn't like seeing her like that. He certainly didn't like knowing that he was responsible. The thought made him feel guilty, ashamed. He had turned their marriage into a game. He had trapped her and tried to manipulate her into doing what he wanted. He knew just how that felt, and yet he'd hurt her as he'd been hurt. His skin burned with shame.

'Addie—' Reaching out, he touched her hand gently, his heart twisting as she stiffened and shrank backwards.

'I can't do this,' she whispered.

With shock, he saw the sheen of tears in her eyes. He had never seen her cry and his throat felt tight. He didn't want to feel her pain. Didn't want to feel anything. But he had hurt her, and for the first time in a long, long time he wanted to face the pain. *Her* pain. Face it and erase it.

He took a step closer. 'Please listen to me, sweetheart.'

But, refusing to meet his gaze, she edged further away from his hand.

He stared at her uncertainly. What was he supposed to say? A cold, dull ache was seeping through his veins and he felt completely out of his depth. He'd spent most of his life avoiding scenes and confrontations, shunning anything remotely emotional, but as his eyes fixed on Addie's stricken face he felt his heart contract.

Suddenly his desires didn't seem all that important in comparison with comforting her. With helping her rebuild what he had so ruthlessly crushed.

He took a deep breath. 'I'm not a good person, Addie. I know that. But I swear it wasn't my intention to hurt you. And I can prove it to you if you let me. Please, Addie, let me make this right.'

'How can you?' she said flatly. 'Look what we're doing to each other. To our marriage. It's just so wrong—'

'It doesn't have to be like this.'

She heard him inhale and, looking up, saw that his eyes were fixed on her face, his expression strained.

'We can start over.'

For a moment she didn't reply and he held his breath, watching, waiting, until finally she lifted her head and sighed.

'I don't know what that means. But you'd better go and talk to Terry. I'm sure he's got better things to do than stand around on your doorstep.'

He nodded and walked swiftly into the hallway. She heard the door open and a muffled conversation. Moments later, the door closed and he returned.

'He's gone.' He met her gaze. 'Do you want me to go too?'

His face was set, and yet he seemed less self-assured than usual—as though he wasn't quite certain of her reply.

She gazed at him in silence. Was he playing with her? Or was he trying to make amends? Finally, she shook her head. 'No. I don't want you to go.''

He breathed out slowly. 'I meant what I said, sweetheart. About starting again.'

She watched in silence as, hesitantly, he reached out and touched her face.

'I want it to be good between us here.'

She bit her lip. 'Think about what's happening here, Malachi. I *sold* myself to you.'

Shaking his head, he stroked her cheek gently. 'Look at it this way: I can only afford you for a month.'

She gave him a tiny smile. 'Nice try! But I know a bluff when I hear one.'

'I'm not bluffing. You're a Royal Flush, sweetheart.'

He watched her face shift, the hurt showing through, and feeling a spasm of panic he reached out and grabbed her hands.

'I'm sorry. That was crass. I know you probably find this hard to believe, but not every thought I have is about poker.' He hesitated. 'Some are about you. Quite a lot, actually.' He felt her hands stiffen and, curling his fingers more tightly, he shook his head. 'I don't mean those kind of thoughts. I mean about *you*. The person you are.'

Addie stared at him in confusion. Was this really her uber-cool husband? He looked anything but cool. In fact he looked nervous, almost as though he didn't quite know what he was saying or doing.

She bit her lip. 'And who am I?'

His hands tightened around hers. 'You're a fighter. And a dreamer. Look at how you came back stronger after your accident.

'It stopped you from doing what you loved most but you didn't stop. You started a charity. Most people would have given up.'

Addie eyes him wearily. '*You* wouldn't.'

Her voice was quiet, but steadier, and he felt his heart lurch with hope. Maybe he hadn't ruined everything between them.

'No. It wouldn't have made me stronger. Or kinder.' But this wasn't about him. It was about Addie. 'I think you're one of the bravest people I know, sweetheart,' he said gently. 'And I'm really sorry for being such a jerk.' Tentatively, he slid his hand over her shoulder. 'Truly. I know it's not enough, but it's a start, isn't it?' He breathed out slowly. 'Please, can we try again? Please?'

His eyes met hers and finally she nodded mutely.

He made as though to pull her against him and then, breathing out slowly, he turned and, reaching round, picked up her clothes from the floor. 'Here. Put these on.'

Averting his gaze, he waited until she was dressed and then slowly wrapped his arms around her and pulled her close.

'Thank you.' Gently, he kissed the top of her head. 'And now, how about we go and take a look around this island?'

CHAPTER SEVEN

'So—do you have anything particular you'd like to do today?'

Leaning across the table to spear a piece of pineapple from a huge platter of fresh fruit, Malachi smiled at Addie. She held her breath. He was wearing a pair of dark blue swim shorts, and his long, muscular legs were sprawled out temptingly towards her. With his face tipped up to the sun and his dark hair falling loosely across his forehead, he looked impossibly glamorous, and intensely male, his lush beauty easily rivalling the tropical perfection surrounding them.

His eyes bumped into hers and he held her gaze so that she shifted restlessly in her chair. Her heart gave a twitch as he leaned forward, and for a moment she thought he was about to kiss her, but instead he picked up the coffee-pot and topped up their cups.

'Actually, I do have something in mind. I just need to make a couple of calls.'

Picking up her cup, Addie wished that it was her hands and not the sunlight caressing his smooth golden skin. That she could reach over and loop her arm around his neck, press her hot, hopelessly overexcited body against his—

But wishing was all she was likely to do.

Skin prickling, she sipped her coffee. Yesterday she had felt so unhappy, so diminished by the way he was treating her. Only then they'd argued, and he'd pushed aside his obvious desire to comfort her, and his tenderness had shifted something inside her, opened her up to him. But now Malachi seemed to be on some kind of mission to prove that sex was the last thing on his mind. Oh, he kissed her, and curled his arm around her waist, but whenever she leaned into him, hoping, longing, wanting more, he merely let his hands drift over her back or arms.

Breathing out, she sat up straighter and forced herself to smile, hoping that her face appeared more composed than her body felt. 'Great. That sounds great.'

He stared at her thoughtfully. 'I haven't told you what it is yet.'

Her fingers spasmed involuntarily against the cup.

'I know,' she said quickly. 'But I'm sure it'll be great—whatever it is.'

Leaning forward, he grinned at her—a long, slow, curling smile that made her heart flutter in her chest and her breasts ache.

'How very trusting of you. Then I think I'll keep it as a surprise!'

An hour later she was regretting that trust as they skimmed across the water in the speedboat towards—who knew where?

'Can you please give me a clue?' Turning round, Addie gazed up in frustration at Malachi.

Grinning, he shook his head, his arm curving around her waist. 'I don't want to spoil the surprise,' he murmured, squeezing her hand.

She glanced up at him, her blue eyes wide and wary.

He laughed. 'Trust me, sweetheart. I know what you like and you're going to love this.'

His fingers lightly caressed her belly through the thin fabric of her dress, and eyes half closed, she feverishly imagined what she liked doing with Malachi, her skin quivering at the thought of the two of them moving slowly together, bodies entwined—

Her pulse gave a jolt and realising she needed to get a grip, she glanced past him to where a mass of greeny-brown was slowly growing larger. 'Is that Finlay Island? Is that where we're going?'

Smiling, he shook his head. 'Two more minutes and all will become clear.'

At that moment, the boat curved around the island and Addie felt her mouth fall open. 'Wh-what is *that*?'

He was watching her, gauging her reaction.

'That is the *Pearl Diver*. She's a submarine and my most recent acquisition. I thought you might like to join me on her maiden voyage.'

Too jolted to speak, Addie gazed in disbelief at where the submarine lay in the water. Finally she recovered and, looking up at him, she shook her head slowly. 'Let me guess! You're planning to build the world's first under-water casino.'

His eyes gleamed. 'Now, why didn't *I* think of that?' Leaning forward, he ran a finger slowly under her chin, lifting her face to his. 'More importantly, why didn't my research and development team? Maybe I should give you a job there.'

She glanced at him sharply. Most likely he was joking. But then with Malachi it was impossible to know. Perhaps he thought he was offering her some kind of consolation prize.

Her stomach contracted at the thought of being down-graded from his wife to an employee but she managed to hold his gaze. 'Thanks, but I actually have a job I love.' She stared at the *Pearl Diver* and then back to Malachi, her curiosity piqued. 'So why did you buy a submarine?'

She couldn't resist teasing him. 'Did all those other nasty billionaires have one before you?'

The corners of his mouth tugged upwards. 'Well, now you come to mention it—'

She shook her head. 'You're impossible!'

His grey eyes searched her face and suddenly she was holding her breath. Finally, when she thought her lungs might burst, he shrugged.

'I just thought that as you liked exploring the island so much, you might want to take a look around under the water.'

'You did?'

Knots were forming in her stomach. Was that true? Had he really arranged this trip for *her*? Trying not to read anything into his words, she swallowed down the bubble of happiness rising in her throat and gave him a small, uncertain smile.

He smiled back at her. 'You seem a little surprised.'

'Yes—I mean, no!' She bit her lip. 'It's just that I didn't—you don't—I thought—' She took a breath. 'That's very considerate of you,' she finished, her voice trailing off as he stared at her assessingly, his gaze seeming to reach inside her in a way that made her nerves dance into life.

'Considerate...' Fingers tightening around hers, he turned the word over in his mouth as though tasting it. 'Is that what I am? And there I was, thinking I was being romantic.' He spoke teasingly but there was an intensity to his expression she didn't understand.

Addie felt her face still. Romantic! Once that had been her dream. And for a short time she had even believed it was possible. That Malachi was capable of loving her and of expressing that love. Now, with his hair falling across his forehead and those smoky eyes fixed on her face, it was tempting to believe there was some truth behind his teasing words. But of course there wasn't. Her face tight-ened. No matter how poetic his language the only hearts he was interested in were those on the front of playing cards.

She lifted her chin. 'I would swoon, only it's difficult when you're sitting down.'

His eyes narrowed, or maybe it was the sunlight play-ing tricks, for the next moment his face was smooth and untroubled and smiling. He said slowly, 'I'll just have to think of another way to sweep you off your feet.'

For a moment she could think of nothing to say. Could think only of how it felt to be the focus of his attention. To feel his smile and hear his laughter. It was like the sum-mer sun after a stormy spring.

She took a quick breath. *Now who was being poetic?*

Poetry was far from her mind twenty minutes later as she stood in the bedroom of the submarine's master suite. Instead, as a dizzying heat surged over her skin, she found herself thinking of the mind-blowing number of ways that she and Malachi could amuse themselves on a bed like that.

Feeling her insides tighten, she squeezed her thighs to-gether, the muffled thud of her heart suddenly competing with the rhythmic throb of the engine.

'You're shaking.' Malachi looked down at her, frown-ing. 'Are you okay?'

'I'm fine.' Looking up, she gave him a quick, tight smile. 'It's probably too much adrenaline. I can't believe this is happening. That I'm in an actual submarine. It doesn't feel real.'

Malachi stared down at her face. Her cheeks were flushed and her eyes dazed, and he felt his groin tighten. Almost half his life had been spent chasing the next thrill, the biggest risk, pushing boundaries— breaking rules. Yet nothing he'd done had felt as intoxicating as seeing her naked, unguarded excitement. Or knowing that he had made her feel like that.

His body stilled. A prickling heat was crawling over his skin. There was nothing between them but her dress and his shirt and shorts. He wanted her more than he had ever desired any woman *and she wanted him*. But he held himself back; it would happen…but when it did the time would be of her choosing.

'Oh, it's real, all right,' he said lightly. Loosening his grip, he held out his hand. 'Here. Let me prove it to you.'

Addie felt her stomach flip over as, handing her a small black remote control, he gave her one of his devastating smiles.

'See that button in the middle? The blue one? Press that.'

She pressed it. For a moment nothing happened, and then there was a whirring noise and the walls of the cabin started to move. Or rather they weren't walls, she saw now, but huge blinds. As they rolled slowly upwards she took a step backwards, her mouth dropping open.

On the other side of the window was the bluest blue she had ever seen. Only it wasn't just blue. It was white and gold and green and red. Stepping forward, she reached out and touched the glass with a hand that shook slightly. She had never seen colours like that. The coral was like a living rainbow. And everywhere there were fish of every shade and shape.

'What do you think?' Malachi was standing behind her.

She turned and shook her head. 'It's like another world,' she whispered.

'It's our world!'

His arm brushed against her body as he pointed past her and through the glass. 'See over there? That's the wreck of the *Creole Queen*. The Captain came across her last month. She's a three-master, sunk during a storm in 1785.'

He paused, his eyes roaming over her face. 'If you like, we could go and check her out. You never know—we might find some treasure.'

She looked up at him, her eyes wide. 'Is that possible?'

He grinned. 'I can't see why not. There are hundreds of wrecks out here. The odds are that some of them must have something of value on board.'

She nodded. 'That's true, I suppose.' She looked up at him and smiled, wanting to tease. 'But what happens if we do find some treasure? How do I know you won't steal my share?'

'How do I know you won't steal mine?' Slowly he ran a finger down her arm, making it impossible for her to concentrate.

She swallowed. 'You don't.'

For a moment she held her breath, mesmerised, as he stared at her thoughtfully, his face giving nothing away, his eyes revealing even less. Then slowly he smiled.

'In that case I don't think we have any alternative. We're just going to have to keep a very close eye on one another.'

The dive was incredible. Addie had only ever snorkelled before, but Malachi was an experienced scuba diver and a surprisingly patient teacher. Afterwards they ate a leisurely lunch on a secluded beach on another island chosen by the captain, and it was then that a wave of tiredness hit her head-on.

'I feel shattered,' she said, stifling a yawn as they headed back to the submarine. 'Is that normal?'

Malachi grinned. 'Completely. First dives always take it out of you.'

She sighed. 'I think I might just have a little lie-down. What are you going to do?'

His eyes gleamed. 'I'm going to have a little play at

being a submarine captain, but I promise I'll wake you in a bit.'

After he'd left, Addie took a shower and then lay down on the bed, closing her eyes with relief. Letting the soporific hum of the engine wash over her, she breathed out softly…

Waking some time later, she picked up her phone and stared groggily at the screen, frowning as she saw the time. She had slept for three hours! Sitting up, she pushed back the sheet—and then her eyes widened. Lying across the covers at the end of the bed was the most beautiful dress she had ever seen. It was full-length and blue, the same blue as the centre of a flame, and beside it was a pair of slightly darker high-heeled court shoes.

Heart pounding, she scrambled off the bed and picked up the dress. Slipping it over her head, she zipped herself up. It was cut into a deep V at the front, and the slit running up the side practically reached her pelvic bone. But it felt divine on, like a second silken skin. Grabbing hold of the wardrobe to steady herself, she pushed her feet into the shoes then turning, she took a step forward and stared at herself in the full-length mirror.

Was that really her? It took her several nervous glances to accept that it was. The dress fitted beautifully, but…

She glanced doubtfully down at her plunging cleavage.

'No, it's not.'

Her head snapped up, her body tightening automatically at the sound of Malachi's voice. Rooted to the floor, gripped by equal amounts of fear and longing, she stared helplessly at his reflection in the mirror. He was standing behind her in the doorway, wearing a beautifully cut dinner jacket, his white shirt unbuttoned at the neck, a bow tie hanging loose around the collar. In one hand he was holding a bottle of champagne, in the other a pair of long-stemmed glasses. He looked impossibly sexy and irresistibly glamorous.

'It's not too low. That's what you were thinking, wasn't it?'

She nodded, suddenly too shy to speak. He walked towards her slowly and her heart gave a jolt as he reached out and gently slid his palm around her waist, forcing her to face him.

His face was serious, his eyes dark and focused. 'You look beautiful, sweetheart. Far too beautiful for a two-bit hustler like me! And that dress fits you to perfection.'

She swallowed, trying to play it cool. 'Thank you. And thank you for getting it for me. But how did you know my size?'

He smiled—a sexy, curling smile that made her heart pound so hard she thought it would burst through her chest.

'It wasn't hard,' he said softly. 'I've been giving your body an awful lot of thought over the last few days.'

There was a tense, pulsing silence. Addie gazed up at him helplessly, the softness of his voice as much as the implication in his words playing havoc with her nerves.

Finally she managed to pull herself together. 'You did a good job. And you look amazing too,' she said hoarsely. 'I love that you haven't done up your tie.'

He grinned. 'I'd *love* to pretend it was a conscious fashion choice, but sadly it's just down to my incompetence. I did, however, manage to lay my hands on a bottle of champagne, so hopefully you won't spend the entire evening wondering how you got stuck with a loser like me!'

A loser! Addie gazed at him. She doubted Malachi had lost at anything—ever. She, on the other hand, would lose all self-control if they didn't leave the bedroom soon.

'Here!' He held out the glasses and, popping the cork, he poured the champagne. 'To the high seas! And sunken treasure.' He tapped his glass lightly against hers. 'Now, let's eat. I am *starving*.'

The meal was delicious: a starter of burrata salad followed by *taglierini* with shaved white truffles and a chocolate fondant for dessert.

'I'm so glad it's not fish,' Addie said, glancing out of the window at the darkened ocean. 'What if they'd looked in and seen us?'

Malachi grinned. He had taken off his jacket and his tanned muscular skin was perfectly offset by the pure white of his shirt.

'I think they'd be pleased you weren't eating *them*. It's a fish-eat-fish world out there.'

Laughing, she pushed away her empty bowl and took a sip from her wine glass.

'What are you thinking?'

'Nothing really!' Turning her head, she saw he was watching her, his face in the candlelight somehow softer, less guarded. 'Just how much the children would love this. You don't mind if I show them a photo or two, do you?' She gave him a small, tight smile. 'Otherwise they might not believe me.'

He shook his head, frowning slightly. 'No, of course not.'

'Thank you.' The easy atmosphere of moments earlier seemed to have disappeared. Confused, suddenly on edge herself, she lifted her chin. 'Sorry to bring up work. It just popped into my head.'

There was a short, strained silence.

'It's not just work, though, is it? For you, I mean.'

She looked up at him, startled. He was looking at her, his expression an odd blend of curiosity and appraisal.

'You really care about those children.'

'Yes. I do.' She was shocked at how fierce she sounded.

'They deserve it. Some of them—a lot of them—have such difficult lives, and they're so brave.'

'They're lucky to have you championing them.' He held her gaze. 'I can't think of many people I'd rather have by my side, watching my back.'

She held her breath. Then why had he pushed her away? She'd been by *his* side, watching *his* back. When all the time she should have been watching her own.

She shrugged. 'I'm not a saint. I get a lot back from them.'

Malachi stared at her. In that dress it would be difficult for any woman to look like a saint. He wondered if she had any idea how beautiful she was. How sexy. He wanted her so much. But for the first time in his life sex didn't seem that important. Not as important as hearing her story.

'Like what?' Leaning forward, he topped up her glass, then his.

Her face softened. 'Like having fun. And a purpose. After my accident I couldn't imagine doing anything with music. It hurt just thinking about what I'd lost. I was so miserable.

'So what changed?' His hand tightened around his glass. He hated the idea of her being that unhappy almost as much as he hated himself for not having known about it before.

'I did this workshop in a school and I realised that music isn't only about that one perfect solo performance. It's about sharing and creating.' She frowned. 'That's when I accepted that I wasn't going to have the life I'd planned. But I was going to have a life that *mattered*.' Meeting his gaze, she smiled weakly. 'Or at least one that wasn't as boring and lonely as lying in a hospital bed for weeks and weeks.'

He was staring at her intently and she fell silent. Malachi was unlikely to be familiar with the concepts of boredom and loneliness, let alone understand them. But after a short, stilted pause, he nodded slowly.

'That's why I started playing cards. Boredom.' He shifted, staring past her, his eyes suddenly cloudy. 'I must have been about seven. We were in Europe, visiting friends of my parents'.'

Abruptly he picked up his glass and drained his wine.

'I was always the only child, and my parents liked to party hard. Often they didn't surface until the afternoon, and I used to get so bored and then one day one of the valets at the hotel where we were staying taught me how to play patience. Then blackjack and then poker.'

His face tightened.

'I got real good, real quick.' He gave her a small, taut smile. That's the upside of living in hotels—there's always a bunch of people going on and off shift and a lot of them play cards.

Addie stared at him, trying to fit his words into the image of the Malachi she knew.

'I thought your dad must have taught you,' she said lowly.

He shook his head. 'No. He taught me other things, but I think those will keep for another day. Shall we have coffee?'

She said nothing, but her mind was buzzing with questions. Why had they never talked about his childhood before? And why were so many subjects off limits? Was it something to do with his father? Had they argued? Was that why his parents hadn't come to their wedding?

Pushing his chair back, Malachi stood and held out his hand.

Coffee was waiting for them in the lounge area.

Addie took a sip and frowned. 'What is that flavour?'

'Cardamom. If you don't like it I can get them to bring some different coffee.'

She shook her head. 'No, I like it. It's kind of spicy.' His eyes narrowed and she felt her stomach clench. 'M-maybe not spicy,' she stammered. 'More…hot without the heat.'

His gaze locked on to hers and she felt a shiver run down her spine as he reached out and ran his hand up and down her arm, grazing her breast with his knuckles.

'Hot without the heat? Sounds interesting.'

Heart pounding, she forced herself to meet his gaze. 'I'm talking rubbish. And I haven't even had that much wine. It must be all that oxygen earlier. I'll probably be seeing mermaids next.'

His hand stopped moving. It felt warm and steady on her arm, matching the warmth and steadiness of his gaze.

'I'm already seeing them. Or one, at least.'

Her breath felt suddenly thick and hot in her throat. 'It's just the dress…' she said hoarsely.

'No. It's this as well.' Gently he slid his hand up into her hair, threading it through his fingers. 'And these…'

Tilting his head, he brushed his lips across hers gently so that her head was swimming.

'You've bewitched me,' he murmured and, lowering his mouth, kissed her again more deeply.

It was the closest he would get to expressing any feelings of tenderness.

'So how come I'm at the bottom of the ocean in your submarine?' she whispered.

He smiled—a long, slow, curling smile that made her stomach disappear. 'Do you want me to take you back up to the surface?'

His eyes were huge and dark above her face, so that she felt as though she were drowning in them.

Slowly she shook her head. 'I want to stay down here for ever.'

'That could be arranged.' His voice was hoarse, his eyes burning into hers.

She stared up at him unsteadily. 'Wouldn't we run out of air?' she asked. She felt his fingertips graze her collarbone and slide slowly under the chin, lifting her face.

'Eventually. But we'd use it up slower if we shared.'

Her pulse was racing. 'How do you share air?'

'It's easy,' he murmured. 'You just do this.'

And, lowering his mouth again, he kissed her. She gasped, her lips parting, heat flooding her body. Clutching on to his arm, she felt her pulse jerk as his tongue probed her mouth. Heat, sharp and raw, flared up inside her, and suddenly her fingers were pulling at his shirt, tugging clumsily at the buttons.

Tangling her hands through his hair, she kissed him fiercely, pressing against the hard muscles of his naked chest. She felt him respond, deepening the kiss, his hand sliding around her waist, pulling her up against him. It felt so, so good. So right. No other man could make her feel this way. Only Malachi.

He broke the kiss. 'Are you sure?'

His face was tight with concentration, his arms shaking with tension and desire. The raw need in his voice reached inside her. Heart thudding, Addie breathed in shakily. Her eyes lifted and locked on to his and she saw that he was holding himself back, his muscles straining, his longing spilling over her skin like molten lava.

Dry-mouthed, Malachi held his breath. The last few days and nights his mind had been tormented by erotic images of Addie, but none had come close to how mind-blowingly sexy she looked right now. With her long red hair tangling around her shoulders, that incredible blue dress clinging to every curve like a second skin.

For a moment she stared at him, her eyes narrow blue slits, and then she nodded slowly and he felt his self-control slip away.

Pulling her to her feet, he scooped her into his arms. The blood was pulsing in his head. She was so soft in his arms, her body curving against his in obedient response to the heat of his lips and the touch of his hands. Striding across the floor, he pushed open the door to the bedroom and, kicking it shut, let her feet drop to the floor.

His fingers threaded through her hair, twisting and tugging it up from the nape of her neck. Whole body shaking, he pulled her against him, the sweet taste of her mouth tearing at his senses, and then he was walking her backwards, nudging her with his body, his knuckles scraping against the wall as they banged against it.

Lowering his lips, he licked her throat, tasting the salt on her skin as he grabbed her arms, stretching them high above her head, trapping her wrists with one hand, sliding the other down over her throat to her breast, his fingertips pushing beneath the satin, brushing lightly against a nipple.

Addie shuddered, her body straining helplessly against his, her belly hot and tight, and then she was arching upwards, whimpering, her fingers splaying apart as his mouth closed over her nipple, sucking the swollen tip.

Hearing her soft moan, Malachi nearly lost it. Groaning, lifting his mouth, he dropped her wrists and stepped back unsteadily.

For a moment he stared at her in silence, his breathing ragged, his gaze dark and fixed. Then slowly he reached out and touched her throat, running his hand lightly over her collarbone. With his other hand he reached for her zip and the heavy satin slid to the floor.

Malachi felt his whole body stiffen. She was naked except for a barely-there pair of panties. Looking at her, he could barely breathe. His blood was humming in his veins and then he was jerking her up against him, pushing her back against the wall. His whole body seemed to explode in a fireball of heat as he felt her hand tug at his belt, tearing the zip down, her fingers pulling the hard length of him free.

'Addie—'

Breathing in sharply, he felt her hand tighten around him, so that his body seemed to stretch out. His muscles started to spasm as he reached between her thighs, pushing aside the scrap of lace and opening her legs wider, dipping his fingers into the warm, slick heat.

Panting, eyes widening, Addie caught his hand, jerking it away. She guided him towards her, her body jolting up to meet his as he lifted her easily and thrust inside. Instantly she was lost, drowning in a shuddering, sensual heat. Eyes closed, she pressed against him, raising her hips as his fingers curled beneath her.

Tightening his grip, he pushed deeper still, opening her, stretching her. She bowed her back, meeting his thrusts, her nails digging into his shoulders, her breath quickening in time to the pulse clamouring between her thighs and then, shuddering, he groaned. And as she felt him spill inside her, her body convulsed around his.

Burying her head against the hollow of his shoulder, Addie breathed out unsteadily, letting her body go limp in his arms. She could feel his heart pounding, his skin damp against hers. Finally he shifted, gently withdrawing, and she felt his lips brush her hair. Somehow he got her onto the bed and she lay curled against his chest, his body damp and warm beneath her.

Staring down at her flushed face, Malachi grimaced. 'I didn't hurt you, did I?' He hesitated and then pulled her into his arms, pressing his face into her hair. 'I tried to stop but I just couldn't. I wanted you so badly.'

He had never felt that desperate. His breathing raw and uneven, he lifted his head, wanting, needing to see her face.

'I don't know what happens when I'm with you.'

She gazed up at him, stunned, mute, muscles aching. He looked as dazed as she felt. And was he really admitting that he'd just lost control?

She wanted to hear more—wanted to ask him what he meant—but she could hardly think straight, let alone speak. But it didn't matter, she thought, her eyes closing as she leaned into him. Just for the moment, nothing mattered except him and her and the beating of their hearts...

CHAPTER EIGHT

FINALLY! AN *ACE*. Feeling a twinge of satisfaction, Malachi placed the card on the table in front of him. Behind him, he heard Addie shift in her sleep and, glancing back at the bed, felt his breath catch in his throat. With her red hair gleaming in the silvery light flooding the bedroom she looked even more like a mermaid than ever.

For a moment he watched her sleep then, breathing out slowly, turned back to his cards. Addie might be sleeping soundly, but sadly he was not. And he couldn't quite work out why.

After she had got so upset, he had played it slow, choosing to wait, savouring the intensity and heat of his longing so that his desire had been raw and fierce. He had never wanted any woman as much as he had wanted her in that moment. Never waited so long for any woman. But it had definitely been worth the wait.

He should be feeling sated, satisfied. And yet here he was, wide awake, body twitching with lust, playing cards by himself in the moonlight.

It didn't make any sense. Sex was supposed to solve problems. Not create them. In his head, tapping into their passion had seemed like a foolproof solution to the niggling problem of the sexual hold she appeared to have over him. Only his plan didn't seem to be working out. Rather than killing his desire, having sex with her not only seemed to have heightened his libido but it seemed to be messing with his mind.

Take earlier. Usually, post-coital affection was something to be avoided, at best endured. But he had found it impossible to lie next to her and *not* hold her close. He'd actually had to get out of bed to stop himself from doing so.

Standing up, he walked softly across the room and stared down at Addie in silence. For the first time in his life sex didn't seem to be an end in itself. Instead it felt more like a means to an end.

He breathed out slowly. Something was happening. He was feeling things he hadn't expected or wanted to feel. Like the fact that this deal with Addie no longer seemed that important. Instead what mattered was spending time with her. Which was why he was going to take her with him to Venezuela, for the opening of his newest casino.

In the bed, Addie shifted onto her side, and then her eyelids fluttered open and she looked up at him drowsily. 'What's the matter?'

Gently he stroked her face. 'Nothing. I'm just not that sleepy.'

She smiled, her lips parting. 'Me neither.'

His eyes fixed on her face and there was a short beat of silence and then, sliding beneath the sheet, he pulled her soft, unresisting body against his and, capturing her mouth, kissed her fiercely.

'I'll have your twos, please!' Biting her lip nervously, Addie peered over the top of her sunglasses to where Malachi lay sprawled on the other side of the huge bean-filled lounger.

For a moment he stared impassively at his cards, and then finally he sighed and a wicked smile spread slowly over his face. 'Go fish! And I'll have *your* threes, please, sweetheart.'

'You are such a rat!' Shaking her head, she dropped her cards into his outstretched hand and picked up another from the deck.

Two minutes later it was all over.

Groaning, Addie rolled over onto her back. 'I can't believe I lost. *Again.* I thought you said you'd never played go fish before?' she said accusingly.

Shuffling the cards with the skill of a Vegas croupier, Malachi grinned. 'I haven't. Is that why you wanted me to play with you?' His eyes were watching her with amusement. 'So you could take advantage of me.'

Addie laughed. 'It did cross my mind.'

'It did, did it?' Reaching out, he grabbed hold of her hand and pulled her towards him, pinning her against the cushion with his thigh and his hand. 'Then maybe I should reciprocate.'

Her breath caught in her throat as he picked up a handful of glossy red hair, threading it through his fingers.

'Take advantage of *you* in some way.'

She stared up at him, tilting her head back to watch the play of sunlight on his face.

It had been a strange and strained few days. But Malachi seemed different now. Calmer...more relaxed. As though some tension had been eased. But then, she felt the same way too, so maybe it was just down to the two of them getting used to being around one another again.

Only it felt as if there was more to it than just the pair of them getting reacquainted. Her heart began to pound as she remembered how he had comforted her when she'd got upset. It was so out of character for him; he hated scenes, and yet he had shelved his obvious and pressing desire and let her talk—asking questions, listening to her answers.

Addie breathed out slowly. It was all so confusing. Almost as confusing as her feelings for Malachi.

She shouldn't really be enjoying herself. And yet if she just concentrated on living in the moment then the truth was that she had never been happier. *Not even when they were engaged and she'd thought Malachi actually loved her.*

She felt his gaze on her face and, pushing aside her thoughts, reached out and looped her arms around his neck. 'What do you have in mind?' she said softly.

'I'm not entirely sure,' he murmured and, shifting forward, he covered her mouth with his and abruptly all conscious thought was driven from her head.

Later, body aching, she lay curled against him, her fingers tracing the muscles of his stomach.

'So why are you opening a casino in Caracas, then?' Tipping her head back, Addie stared up at him curiously.

Frowning, Malachi shrugged. 'No reason other than I've been looking to expand into South America for a couple of years now.'

She nodded politely, barely listening. Her head was still reeling from the fact that he had asked her to go with him, and she wondered how this very public event fitted into their deal. Here, on this island, their relationship might be unorthodox but it was private. However, he could hardly parade her around as his mistress at some huge, social event.

Her heart skipped a beat.

But why did it matter? It wasn't as if she cared.

The answer to her question popped into her head, unwelcome and unwanted like a bill through a letter box. *Of course she cared. Not just about their relationship but about him.*

She breathed out slowly. It wasn't that much of a shock, but still—

It was strange, but even now, five years after they had separated, there was still this connection between them. Some sense of being more than married. It might not make any sense, and ultimately it didn't change anything, but that didn't stop it being the reason why she had never divorced him. Or why a tiny part of her wanted to stop being his mistress and go to Caracas as his *wife*.

His voice bumped into her thoughts and she stared up at him, trying to pick up the thread of their conversation.

'Sorry—I was…' She paused. 'It's just—are you sure you want me to be there?'

He stared at her thoughtfully. 'Of course.' His eyes were cool. 'I want to get my money's worth.'

There was a short, stilted silence, and then they both jumped as Malachi's phone rang.

Retrieving it from his pocket, he glanced momentarily at the screen and then answered it. 'Yes—no—I highly doubt that.'

Face blank, he shifted away from her, the muscles of his stomach suddenly taut and strained beneath her fingers, and after a moment of indecision she withdrew her hand. He stood and turned and, watching his shoulders tighten, she wondered who was on the other end of the phone. His voice was quiet, but she could hear a tension that hadn't been there before. With shock, she realised that he was struggling to maintain his composure.

Feeling as though she was intruding, she reached out and picked up a handful of sand, letting it run through her fingers.

Behind her, Malachi was winding up the call. 'Okay, that's fine. Just leave it to me. I'll sort it out.' He hung up.

Heart thudding, Addie stared at the back of his head, trying and failing to work out what had just happened.

'Is everything okay?' she said finally.

She was being polite. Clearly it wasn't okay—at least not if the prickly energy coming off him was anything to go by.

But when he turned he simply smiled at her. 'Everything's fine. It's nothing.'

She nodded mutely. It was the same smile he'd used when he was playing cards with her earlier. The one that was impossible to read. Probably it was the smile he used every day with anyone he wanted to keep at arm's length. She felt a stab of misery. The easy warmth between them had trickled away just like the sand between her fingers.

Slowly, she stood up. She could just leave it. He'd told her it was nothing, and even if it wasn't it was none of her concern. But there was something in that smile. Something in that voice that made her heart contract. And even though it was pointless to do so, she still cared about him. Still cared that he was hurting and upset.

She took a deep breath. 'Is it work?'

He stared at her. He was still smiling, but his eyes were the cool grey of a battleship.

'No. Work looks after itself. My parents, on the other hand, need a team of full-time minders.'

'Your parents?' Her pulse jerked. 'What's happened? Are they okay?'

He gave a casual shrug. 'I expect so. It's happened before. I'm sure it's fixable.'

He paused and she watched his expression shift and clear, like one of those drawing toys where with one shake the picture disappeared.

'But—' she began.

'Don't worry about it.' He interrupted her. 'It's nothing,

I promise. It certainly won't take more than a couple of hours to sort out. And thankfully they're only in Miami. The last time this happened they were in Cannes.'

Addie gazed at him in confusion. 'Are you saying we're going back to Miami?' she said hesitantly.

He looked at her in disbelief. 'No. There's absolutely no reason for you to be dragged into any of this. I'll go on my own. If I take the helicopter and leave now I'll be back this evening. Tomorrow morning at the latest.'

'But—' She frowned. 'Surely it would be better if I came with you.'

'Better?' he repeated. 'In what way would it be better?'

'I don't know. I just thought you might like to have a bit of support. Maybe I can help—'

'You want to help me with my parents?' Shaking his head, he laughed harshly. 'I see. I should warn you they're both tone deaf, so they might not be that responsive to music therapy.'

Addie stared at him, her breath hot in her throat, anger balling in her chest. It was like talking to a stranger, she thought wildly. A handsome, detached stranger. Instead of the man she had let inside her body.

'I don't understand,' she said slowly.

His face didn't alter but his eyes narrowed fractionally. 'You don't need to. This is *way* beyond your pay grade, sweetheart.'

She stared at him in silence, breathing unsteadily. Her whole body was suddenly trembling with anger. 'Is that right?' she said icily. 'Then maybe I should ask for a raise, because you're certainly not paying me enough to put up with *that* kind of remark.'

His face stiffened. 'You're overreacting,' he said softly. 'As I said before, there's no need for you to come to Miami with me.' His eyes met hers. 'If you really want to help,

stay here—and then we can go to Caracas together as
planned.'

'So you want me to come to Caracas but you don't
want me to meet your parents—' She broke off, suddenly
too angry and frustrated and upset to speak. 'If you're
so ashamed of me, then maybe I shouldn't be here in the
first place.'

He frowned, his face darkening. 'I'm not ashamed of
you.'

'Then what's the problem?'

'There *is* no problem. Except you. You're making it a
problem.'

'How? By wanting to meet your parents?'

'This—us—it has nothing to do with them.'

'Is that why they didn't come to our wedding?'

The words were out of her mouth before she could stop
them. The question he had refused to answer five years
ago. His parents' absence at their wedding had always
mattered to her. But now she knew that it had mattered
to Malachi too, for she felt the change in him even before
she saw it in his eyes.

'They didn't come because I didn't ask them.' His voice
echoed harshly between them. 'You wouldn't understand.
But then I'm not asking you to.'

'But you *are* asking me to go and watch you open your
new casino?'

He stared at her. 'Please try and be reasonable, sweetheart. The two aren't in any way connected—'

'If you say so,' she snapped. 'Just go, Malachi.' Picking
up her towel, she stalked past him. 'I'm going for a swim.
Have a nice trip.'

Wading into the lagoon, she stared fixedly ahead, too
furious even to register her beautiful surroundings. But
the water felt cool against her skin, and the soft breeze

and faint scent of frangipani was soothing, and slowly her anger started to fade.

Malachi was impossible. Rude and secretive and— *"'Please try and be reasonable, sweetheart!'"* she muttered.

It wasn't the most convincing impression of him, but it made her feel better, and suddenly determined not to let him spoil everything she began to swim with strong, firm strokes. Ten minutes later, smoothing the damp strands of hair away from her face, she glanced back at the beach, frowning. She was sure she had left her towel just under that palm tree…

And then her pulse gave a jolt as she saw Malachi standing at the edge of the sand, the towel in his hand.

Her footsteps faltered but then, lifting her chin, she marched towards him.

'Aren't you supposed to be on your way to Miami?' she snapped.

He didn't reply, just held out his hand. Pulse quickening, she stared at him warily.

'I know it looks like a towel,' he said quietly. 'But it's actually an olive branch.'

She didn't reply.

Malachi watched her face shift, saw her swallow and breathe in sharply. He could see the conflict in her eyes; the longing to believe his words, the hurt holding her back.

He was on the verge of trying again when abruptly she looked up at him and said, 'What do you want, Malachi?'

He cleared his throat. 'I want you to come with me. To Miami. If you still want to, that is.'

She held his gaze. Her blue eyes were no longer glazed and drowsy, as they had been earlier, after they'd made love on the beach, but dark and stormy. And hostile. Very, *very* hostile.

'I thought that was above my pay grade.'

Sighing, Malachi ran a hand over his face. His head was pounding, his stomach knotted with tension. Watching her walk away, he had felt a savage and unreasonable anger. Anger with his parents for messing up his time in paradise, anger with himself for letting his guard down. And anger with Addie for—

For what? For wanting to help him? For caring?

Picturing her face, he had felt his rage give way to shock as he'd realised what he'd seen but chosen to ignore. That she was worried about him. That she cared.

'I shouldn't have said that. It was rude and I'm sorry. It's just that I never— I haven't—' He stopped. Things were getting so complicated. How much should he say? There was so much she wouldn't understand.

She took the towel from his hand. 'I know,' she said quietly. 'I do know what it's like to have things inside your head you don't want to share. After my accident I got sick of people asking me what I was thinking. You don't have to tell me everything. Or anything. Not if you don't want to. I just didn't want you to have to deal with whatever it is on your own.'

He stared at her. 'Then come with me. That way I won't need to tell you. You'll be able to see it for yourself.'

'Okay. I'll come.' She gave him a small, tight smile as he reached out, his hand drawing her to him. 'But I'm warning you: if you start with that pay grade stuff again I might just push you out of the helicopter.'

Aside from the noise of the rotor blades, inside the helicopter cabin it was quiet—sombre, almost. Watching the lights of Miami grow closer, Addie was aware of nothing but Malachi's still, silent presence beside her.

It was clear that his parents were alive and well, and she

wondered what was serious enough to drag him over to the mainland. But, sticking to her word, she hadn't asked him any more about the phone call and he hadn't told her anything. However, he *had* held her hand during the entire three-hour flight.

After the peace of the island, downtown Miami felt crowded and noisy. But at least it was crowded with ordinary people, she thought nervously, staring out of the window as the limousine slid to a stop in front of the Marlin—one of Miami's swankiest and most exclusive Art Deco hotels. Malachi's parents were anything *but* ordinary. Having furtively searched for them on the internet, while he was talking to the pilot, she had been horrified to discover that Henry and Serena King were not only fabulously wealthy, glamorous and beautiful, they also hosted some of the most decadent parties around the globe.

Glancing at her reflection in the window, she felt a rush of panic. Her dress was short, black and cute, and it showed off her long legs, but it most certainly wasn't decadent. Maybe she should have worn the dress Malachi had given her instead. Her pulse shivered. Or maybe she should have just stayed on the island.

'Are you okay?' Malachi glanced down at her, his eyes roaming over her face.

'Yes. Why?'

He winced. 'Because you're cutting off the blood supply to my hand.'

'Oh, sorry.' Loosening her grip, Addie felt her heart start to thump loudly.

His eyes were dark and flickering with excitement, and there was a strange almost nervous energy about him that reminded her of how she had felt before playing in front of an audience: a mixture of fear and bravado and restlessness. But surely he didn't need to feel like that. After all, they were his *parents*.

Glancing away, she looked up at the smooth, curving hotel facade and frowned. 'I suppose I'm a little tense. It feels like I've been away for ever,' she said carefully.

He studied her face in silence, and then slowly pulled her up against him. 'Let me guess. You're worried about meeting Henry and Serena?'

She met his gaze. 'A little.'

'They're charming—and great company. I'm sure you'll fall under their spell. Everyone always does.'

He was smiling, but there was an undertone to his voice that she couldn't quite identify.

'I don't know if that's made me feel better or worse,' she said lightly. She squeezed his hand. 'Anyway, this isn't about me. It's about you—and I just want you to know that I meant what I said before. I'll be there for you.'

She glanced up at him, half expecting him to pull away or change the subject. But he didn't do either. Instead, after the briefest of hesitations, his fingers tightened around hers.

'I know.' His face softened and, lowering his mouth, he kissed her gently.

'Promise you'll stay close to me.'

She stared at him dazedly. 'I promise.'

It took nearly half an hour for them to make it up to the twelfth floor, where Malachi's parents were staying in the penthouse suite. Most of that was spent calming down the hotel manager, a tall, balding man who looked as though he was about to collapse but who eventually ended up offering them a magnum of champagne.

In the lift, watching the numbers counting up, Addie felt Malachi's gaze on her face.

'You look beautiful,' he said softly as with a slight shudder the lift came to a stop.

And then the doors opened and she caught her breath. Whatever she had been expecting, it wasn't this. The suite was huge, with high soaring ceilings. Six massive chandeliers swayed gently above a marble tiered fountain. But it wasn't the decor that had made her breath stop in her throat.

It was the people. Despite the room's size, it was packed. Women dressed in sequins and lace and men in dark suits were lounging on sofas or leaning against the walls; others were sprawled over chairs or one another. But all of them were wearing masks. *Masks!*

She glanced up nervously at Malachi but he was already leading her by the hand, weaving through the laughing, dancing crowd to the other side of the room to a table where two huge gold bowls sat side by side, each one filled with a selection of masks.

'I don't know which one to choose,' Addie said slowly. For some reason she couldn't bring herself to touch them.

'Then don't.'

His eyes were glittering and she could feel his body pulsing with that same nervous energy she had felt in the car, but his voice was surprisingly gentle.

'We don't have anything to hide.'

As they pushed their way through the mass of people, Malachi reached out and grabbed two glasses from a passing waiter. Holding the glasses up to the fountain, he let them fill with the bubbling liquid.

Tentatively, Addie took a sip from hers. 'It's champagne!'

Malachi nodded and stared away, across the room, his face twisting. To a casual observer the party might seem to be in full flow, but given the ratio of alcohol to people he knew it was just getting started. His skin was crawling. What was he *doing* here? And why had he brought Addie with him? Glancing over at her huge, shell-shocked blue eyes, he felt his stomach tighten painfully.

'Sometimes it's champagne and absinthe,' he said flatly. 'Then things get really out of hand.'

Nodding, Addie glanced round the room, sipping her drink nervously. 'Who *are* all these people?'

Malachi shrugged. 'Serena probably invited them. She hates small parties and she likes new people. And anything outrageous or forbidden.'

'And where are your parents?'

His face didn't alter but his eyes seemed suddenly to glitter more brightly.

'They'll be in one of the private rooms, having a party of their own.'

There was a crash behind her and a man wearing some kind of feathered headdress toppled over, hands flailing, his glass smashing to the floor.

Malachi reacted immediately. In one swift movement he had pulled her behind him and yanked the man to his feet. 'Get some air,' he said coldly, giving the man a little push, and then turning back to Addie, he said quietly, 'Come on. Let's go find Henry and Serena.'

They found them easily enough. At the end of a corridor four huge men wearing dark suits stood barring a door marked Private. And whatever was happening behind them, it was a lot quieter and more civilised than at the main party, Addie thought with relief. But as the door opened she felt her heart lurch. The room was dimly lit, and there were far fewer people. But most of them appeared to be in a state of undress and some of them appeared to be…intimately joined.

She barely had time to take in what she was seeing

when a beautiful blonde woman, wearing a shimmering dress that rippled over her body like molten silver, let out a scream and sashayed across the room towards them. Beside her, stumbling slightly, was a very handsome man with lipstick on his face and on his dress shirt. The woman gave a little wriggle, sending rainbows of light into the dark corners of the room, and kissed Malachi on both cheeks.

'Look, Henry! I'd said he'd come. I know you said we weren't to contact you, darling, but I don't deal with rude little men telling me what to do.'

'He's the hotel manager, Serena.' Malachi frowned. 'There's nearly two hundred people here. And the other guests are complaining.'

'How boring of them. And mean. Trying to spoil our fun.' Leaning forward, Serena ran her hand slowly over the lapel of Malachi's jacket. 'Not like *you*, darling. You can never resist a party, can you? And besides, you're so much better at managing those sort of people than Henry and I.'

Suddenly noticing Addie, she stopped.

'What exquisite hair! I had a red setter once, with fur that exact colour. It was my favourite dog. Mal, aren't you going to introduce us?'

Addie swallowed. *These were Malachi's parents.* Her heart began to pound. They were gorgeous. He had clearly inherited his high cheekbones from his mother and from his father his dark hair and those gleaming grey eyes.

'This is Addie.' She felt his hand on her back. 'Addie Farrell. Addie—this is Henry and Serena King.'

'What a sweet name,' Serena purred, and then, clapping her hands excitedly, she waved at one of the waiters. 'Four Brandy Alexanders. Make them doubles!'

Sipping her cocktail, Addie tried to look as though she was enjoying herself. Inside, though, she was in shock. All around her she was aware of the other guests, of bodies merging and soft moans, and of Malachi's taut profile and his hand gripping hers so tightly that she could feel her fingers going numb.

There was no love or tenderness in this room, just greed and narcissism and lust, and her heart contracted as she tried to imagine what it must have been like to grow up surrounded by these people. If this was his version of intimacy, it was no wonder he struggled so much to understand hers.

Watching Addie's hand tighten around her glass, Malachi tried to relax. He barely registered the other guests, or what they were doing; he'd seen it too many times before. Usually at his parents' parties he could find a place inside himself, somewhere to retreat. But with Addie beside him he had no choice but to stay focused, and it was as if he was seeing it all through her eyes—every sordid detail magnified and spotlit—and it sickened him.

As his gaze shifted from Addie's face to her tight fists, he felt her disgust too. Rage clawed at his stomach and reluctantly he let go of her hand. 'I've just got to talk to Serena and Henry for a minute,' he said slowly.

'Do you want me to come too?'

Meeting her gaze, he shook his head. 'I'll be right back. Just wait here.'

He turned to where his parents were draped over one another on a chaise longue, their eyes glittering like dark stars.

His mother smiled up at him mockingly. 'Malachi! Henry and I were just talking about you.'

Taking hold of his hand, Serena pulled him down onto the cushions beside her as his father stood up unsteadily.

'Darling,' she murmured. 'We *love* your little redhead.'

'Her name's Addie,' he said slowly.

'And it was so *clever* of you to find her. Henry is absolutely smitten.' Slowly, Serena ran her finger along his jawline. 'And you do look so like your father, don't you…?'

Malachi felt his skin grow taut; his pulse was pounding in his ears.

'She's with *me*, Serena.'

'Of course she is.' Her face hardened. 'It's just a bit of fun.'

He stared at her in shock. 'It's not fun. It's sick.'

His mother shook her head. 'Oh, dear. Somebody's having a tantrum.' She smiled at him coldly. 'And after all we've done for you.' She shrugged, her fingers curling under his chin. 'How very dull you are. Well, don't expect me to do your dirty work. You can tell Henry yourself.' Her eyes narrowed. 'If it's not too late.'

Glancing past her, Malachi felt his heart jolt. Across the room, his father was smiling at Addie, his face soft but his eyes dark and predatory. With the blood suddenly buzzing inside his head like a swarm of angry bees, Malachi pushed his mother's hand away from his face, stood up and crossed the room.

'Serena always likes the drinks too strong,' he heard his father say confidingly. 'Why don't you come with me? I can find you something soft to drink. Or maybe you'd like to lie down for a bit—'

He broke off abruptly, his mouth hanging open in fear as Malachi stepped in front of him, his face blazing with white-hot anger.

'The only one lying down will be you, Henry. In a hospital bed!' His voice was like ice. 'What the hell are you doing?'

Malachi drew a jagged breath. His body felt as if it was in free fall. Addie was staring at him, transfixed, but he couldn't bring himself to meet her gaze. Instead, grabbing her hand, he pulled her behind him protectively and turned towards his father.

'You couldn't help yourself, could you?' He shook his head, anger vying with pain, choking him, blistering his throat and mouth. 'Only you've gone too far. This isn't some stupid game. It's twisted.' Breathing out unsteadily, he took a step backwards. 'We're leaving. You have until three o'clock tomorrow to get out. But don't expect me to pick up the tab. This one's on you.'

Turning, he pulled Addie close, his heart jerking with relief as his arm curled around her soft body.

'And don't bother trying to contact me. There won't be any point. As of this moment, I never want to hear from you again.'

Later, Addie would wonder how they made it to the airport. She had no memory of leaving the hotel or getting in the limo or onto the plane. Nothing had seemed to register on her brain except Malachi's rage. She didn't think she had ever seen anyone so angry. His fury had been like the burning cold of an ice storm.

Gazing across the plane's lounge, to where he sat alone, she felt her stomach cramp. She didn't really understand all that had happened at the party. All she knew was that since getting in the limo she hadn't been able to reach him. That he hadn't needed her and certainly hadn't wanted her.

Slumped on a sofa, gripping a pack of cards in his hand, Malachi felt a wave of exhaustion wash over him. He had gone to the hotel to stop the police getting involved and he should have left after seeing the manager. Only he hadn't. He'd heard the music and the laughter and he'd been like a hunting dog following a scent. Only seeing Addie in the centre of that debauchery he'd immediately realised his mistake. Her shock, her horror, had been like a slap to the face. Yes, those guests had been happy to be there, and it had all been consensual, but it was so messed up. And then Henry had tried—

He gritted his teeth.

How could his father have done that? It had been obvious that Addie was with him. He shouldn't have even had to tell them that she was off limits. And then, of course, when he had, it had only spurred them on.

But he didn't care about them. Remembering Addie's face when his father had held out his hand, he felt sick. What if he hadn't been there? Anything could have happened. Imagining her fear, her confusion, he felt his chest tighten with a pure, savage rage.

Addie stood up. She felt tired—more than tired. She felt bruised by everything that had happened and too drained to fight for what Malachi clearly didn't even want to discuss. But she wasn't about to leave him alone. Slowly, she walked across the cabin.

'Where are you going?'

His words stopped her in her tracks. Hearing the strain in his voice, she stared at him uncertainly. 'I was going to get some water.' She hesitated. 'Would you like some? Or I could get you something stronger.'

'Something stronger.' His mouth twisted. 'So I can *drown my sorrows*?'

His voice was soft but she felt it slice through her like a knife.

'Maybe. Or we could talk—'

He shook his head. 'You think talking can change *this*.'

His face was pale, the skin stretched taut over his cheekbones as he laughed—only it didn't sound like a laugh. There was too much pain and anger there. And fear. But five weeks in a hospital bed had taught her to face fear;

to resist anger, to overcome pain. And, lifting her chin, she nodded.

'Yes. I do. But you don't want to. You'd rather sit there and wallow—'

'You know *nothing* about my life,' he snarled.

Her pulse was pounding in her throat. Clenching her teeth, she glared at him. 'Yes, I do. I know you jumped into a pool of sharks for a bet; I know you eat apples in the bath.' Her gaze shifted from his face to his hand. 'And I know you play cards when you feel tense or angry.'

He looked up at her silently and resentment surged through her. *He was impossible and this was hopeless.*

She turned to walk away.

'Addie.'

Looking down, she saw he was touching her wrist, his fingers trembling against her skin.

'Don't go. Please.'

She stood, staring past him. 'Why should I stay?'

He breathed out unsteadily. 'You said you'd be there for me.'

She didn't reply at first and then finally, after what felt like the longest moment, she sighed and sat down on the sofa.

He held out the deck of cards, his face strained, uncertain. 'What would you like to play?'

She shook her head. 'I'm not sure I can. My brain doesn't seem to be working.'

Nodding slowly, he half smiled. 'My parents have that effect on people.'

He let out a long, slow breath and his smile faded. She waited.

Finally, hesitantly, he reached out and took her hand, his face filled with angry bewilderment. 'I find it hard.'

The words sounded as if they were being dragged from him.

Her chest squeezed tight. 'What do you find hard?'

'Choosing not to be like them.' He ran a hand wearily over his face. 'For years I had no choice. Even when I was little they'd drag me to parties and nightclubs.' He paused and gave her another taut smile. 'They didn't see why having me around should stop them doing what they wanted. And if I was difficult, then they'd just leave me behind.'

'Where?' Addie felt her heart thump painfully hard.

He shrugged. 'With their friends. And by "friends" I mean the people who found it hardest to say no to them.' Glancing up, he caught sight of her face and his mouth twisted. 'I don't know what was worse. Worrying that they would never come back or knowing they would.'

She stared at him, feeling his pain, the fear of a little boy abandoned by his so-called parents, his dread of their return. 'Why didn't they get a nanny?'

'They did. But they never stayed for more than a couple of weeks. It got better as I got older.' His eyes met hers. 'I got better at managing them.'

She swallowed. 'Is that why you went back to Miami?'

He looked away. 'Yes. They can charm their way out of most situations. But sometimes, like last night, when they've gone too far and someone's threatening to call the police, I have to step in.' Smiling dully, he shrugged. 'It's irritating, but it's just easier and a lot less time-consuming if I sort it out.'

'And why did you leave? Tonight.'

She held her breath, sensing it was one question too many, but finally he turned to face her and the bleakness in his eyes almost broke her.

'I'd had enough,' he said quietly. 'Of their games. With

them, it's always a game. I just don't want to play any more.'

He fell silent.

Not trusting herself to speak, Addie sat mute beside him. How could anyone survive that kind of damage? It was almost worse than what had happened to her. That had been an accident. This had been deliberate, sustained. But the outcome was the same: a shattered life, a damaged soul. And she knew exactly what it took to repair that damage. It needed acceptance and hope and patience.

And love.

Her eyes suddenly filled with tears and she closed them quickly, trying to stop them from falling, trying to block out the truth. Except she couldn't. The truth was that she loved him—still, and so much.

And it was time for her to accept that fact.

She opened her eyes and concentrated on her breathing. But it was not the time to share it. Now she needed to keep her promise. To be there for Malachi. Without thinking, she reached forward and slid her arms around him. After a moment's hesitation his arms tightened around her. They held each other in silence, their hearts beating in time together, until finally Addie shifted free.

'Come on. Let's go to bed.'

Standing up, he glanced out of the plane's window and frowned. A pale yellow line was already edging the dark sky. 'I'm sorry, sweetheart, I don't think we're going to get much sleep. We'll be landing in less than an hour.'

She smiled. 'Who said anything about sleep?'

His eyes locked on to hers and for a moment, she stared at him, hypnotised by their fierce dark longing. And then he reached down and, scooping her into his arms, he began to carry her towards the staircase.

CHAPTER NINE

IT WAS LATE afternoon in Caracas. Staring out over the city from the balcony of Malachi's suite, Addie let the straps of her camisole slip down over her shoulders to catch some sun.

Two hands slid around her waist. 'Afternoon, sleepyhead.'

Her heart started to pound as Malachi kissed her shoulder, his lips drifting languidly down over her throat.

'You were sleeping so deeply I thought I was going to have to wake you with a kiss,' he murmured.

The hands round her waist were beginning to drift too, slipping under the silk camisole, circling and caressing the bare skin of her belly, then reaching up to stroke her breasts, caressing her nipples until she was shaking with desire.

Unable to stop herself, she moaned softly and she felt his body stiffen, his fingers stilling.

'You did that earlier,' she said hoarsely. 'That's why I was so tired.'

His hands were moving again, sliding slowly over skin.

'In that case I think you should lie down right now,' he said, and, gently he dragged her back into the suite and onto the huge bed.

Later, feeling warm and dazed, she lay beside him, watching him devour the brunch that had been delivered.

As he pushed the last forkful of eggs Benedict into his mouth, she gave him a mischievous smile and started clapping.

Draining his coffee cup, he grinned, eyes gleaming. 'I was hungry. And you want me to keep my strength up, don't you?'

Remembering their feverish lovemaking, she felt a melting heat ripple out from somewhere deep inside. *Yes, she did.* Only 'want' seemed too feeble a word to describe how fiercely she craved him.

'I'll try to be less demanding tonight,' she said lightly. 'Shouldn't you be getting ready?'

Rolling onto her side, she watched him get dressed. His pale grey shirt was still unbuttoned to the waist and she stared hungrily at the smooth, flat muscles of his stomach. Even half dressed, and with his hair still damp from the shower, there was a glamour to him that set him apart from other people, turned heads. It wasn't just his looks. It was something to do with that air of detachment, of being alone in a crowd.

Thinking back to his parents' party, she felt a rush of protectiveness. It was no wonder he had chosen to stay alone, or that he found it so difficult to let people get close to him. But he was changing. Look at how he had opened up to her last night. It might not have been his whole life story, but it had been a brief glimpse into what had made him the man he was. And it was the first time he had ever even hinted that he might need her. And surely with need came love?

She glanced up, her heart aching. She longed to tell him that she loved him but she knew it was too soon. She had barely come to terms with how she felt. If she sprung her feelings on Malachi it would be disastrous. Like trying to put a head collar on a wild mustang. She needed to follow her own advice and be patient. But there was nothing to stop her from showing she cared.

Trying to keep her face as casual as possible, she sat up, pulling the sheet over her breasts. 'How are you feeling?'

Stepping away from the wardrobe, he turned to face her, frowning. 'Fine. A little tired.' The corners of his mouth curled upwards.

She smiled back at him, then hesitated. 'I actually meant how are you feeling about last night?'

He was still smiling, but the smile was set and still. After a moment he shrugged. 'That's fine too.'

Turning away, he reached into the wardrobe and she stared at his back uncertainly. Was that it? Last night he had seemed so desperate, so tormented. But it was clear that as far as he was concerned the conversation was over.

'Which one?' He held out two ties for inspection. 'Or do you not like either of them?'

Pushing aside her thoughts, she looked up at him and frowned. 'What's it for again?'

He held her gaze. 'It's a meeting with the mayor and the council members.'

'The blue one, then.'

'I like the red one.'

'Then wear the red one.' Stretching out her legs on top of the sheet, she smiled up at him innocently, her eyes dancing. 'If you don't mind looking like a gigolo.'

He raised an eyebrow. 'A gigolo?'

She bit her lip. 'Maybe you could wear some of those nice stacked shoes we saw in that shop.

His eyes had narrowed and he was moving slowly towards the bed like a predatory animal. 'Anything else?'

'A manbag?' She gave a shriek of laughter as he grabbed hold of her leg and pulled her down the bed towards him, pinning her arms above her head.

'A manbag…' he repeated slowly, his eyes roving over her naked body. 'I'm not sure if I really see myself with one of those. But you might be right about the tie. In fact, I think you might look better wearing it.'

Too late, she read the intent in his eyes. 'No, Malachi—you can't!'

'Oh, but I can,' he said softly, and the heat in his gaze would have stripped the clothes from her skin if she hadn't already been naked.

With deliberate slowness he twisted the tie around her wrists and pulled it over the elaborate gilded bedstead, knotting it with one practised hand. Twisting, Addie tried to pull her hands free, but she simply managed to tighten her bonds.

'There,' he said softly, letting go of her wrists. 'I knew it would look better on you.'

He stared down at her, eyes dark with passion and unwavering, and she felt a hot ache spread out over her skin.

'You can't leave me tied up here, Malachi,' she said quickly, trying to push aside the thought that in all probability he could. 'What about when the maids come to clean the suite?'

He smiled, a long, slow smile. 'I'll tell them to leave it until tomorrow.'

'Malachi! Untie me.'

'What will you give me if I do?'

'You need to worry about what I'll give if you don't! Now, untie me!' She stared up at him, torn between wanting to laugh and wanting to give him a black eye.

He grinned. 'Is that right? I'm not sure you're in any position to be issuing threats here, sweetheart.' He sighed. 'However, fortunately for you, life has taught me that there is one absolute unbreakable rule when it comes to staying in hotels.'

He tugged at the knot and she slipped her wrists free.

'And that is, don't do anything to upset the housekeeping staff.'

She punched him gently. 'So letting me go has nothing to do with my persuasive charms, then?'

His eyes were still tinged with passion, but softer now. 'Believe me, you're *very* persuasive, sweetheart, but—' Grimacing, he sat up and twitched the sheet over her naked body. 'I have *got* to go to this meeting.' Seeing her expression, he shook his head. 'Don't look at me like that. I'd love to get out of this but I can't.'

His hand moved over the sheet, following the contours of her breasts and belly, and she felt her skin grow warm and tingling.

'You can find out what that feels like later.' Eyes glittering, he stood up. 'I'll even let you choose the tie.'

After he'd left, Addie spent a relaxing two hours in the hotel spa, having a facial and full-body massage. Malachi had left a message telling her that he had arranged for Lupita, a personal stylist, to come to their suite, and she arrived promptly, with several rails of beautiful clothes, an array of shoes and a box of jewellery that came with an armed bodyguard.

It was exhausting, but enormous fun. Lupita not only seemed to have met everyone who was anyone in Caracas, she was also talented at her job, knowing exactly which outfits would make Addie look and feel good.

Finally having made her choice, all that remained was to get ready.

Smoothing foundation over her skin, she stared at her reflection critically.

It was lucky that people could only see what was on the outside. And she was a lot less nervous about meeting

Malachi's guests than she had been about finally coming face-to-face with his parents.

She applied mascara, blinked and reapplied it.

But being nervous had some advantages. At least it meant she could hardly think straight. Certainly not about what everyone would be saying about her tonight. It had been different at the masked party. Everyone there had been hiding who they were. But tonight there would be reporters and photographers, and Malachi would be looking to generate as much publicity as possible for the opening of his first casino in South America.

Her heart gave a jolt of hope. But what did that mean for her? She knew what she wanted it to mean. She wanted to forget the past—forget this stupid deal and be his wife again.

But it was so much more complicated than that.

Thankfully her hairdresser chose that moment to arrive, and she was able to push aside her troubling thoughts.

An hour later Addie breathed out in relief as the young woman styling her hair stepped back and smiled.

'You look very beautiful, Ms Farrell.'

Turning her head from side to side, Addie stared into the mirror with pleasure. She had decided, on Lupita's advice, to put her hair up in a French pleat. It was not something she had ever done before, preferring the simplicity of a ponytail for work or a low chignon for more dressy occasions. But now she was glad she had followed the stylist's advice.

'Thank you!' She smiled up at the hairdresser.

The girl looked pleased. 'I think Mr King will be very happy,' she said shyly.

Addie took another quick glance at herself. Hopefully he would. She would soon find out.

* * *

Staring round the casino floor, Malachi felt a rush of satisfaction. The building had been derelict when he'd first seen it. Originally an opera house, it had been abandoned after a fire had damaged most of the stage, and then it had simply been left to decay. Only he had seen its potential. Not as an opera house. The capital city of Venezuela already had one of those. But as a casino.

It had taken six months just to clear the site and make it safe to work in. Another year to rebuild the interior and bring it up to modern health and safety standards. Then another five months painstakingly recreating the original gilded domed ceiling and setting up the casino floor.

His vision had been clear. No cool, contemporary chic. He had wanted old-style glamour. Gilt and glass and glitter. And it had been worth it, he thought triumphantly. It looked incredible: a gilded, show-stopping interior that mixed fin-de-siècle opulence with an unmistakable whiff of the forbidden and decadent.

And yet there was something that didn't feel quite right. Some detail he had overlooked. Something was missing, but he couldn't quite put his finger on it...

The next moment his uncertainty was forgotten as yet another swathe of local VIPs stepped forward to offer their congratulations. Twenty minutes later, though, he was staring round the room again, the famous King smile in place, while his brain clicked through the evening's schedule, looking for glitches.

Only there was nothing out of place. Frowning, he glanced up at one of the boxes he'd insisted be kept during the refurbishment, and caught a flash of red hair, a glimpse of long leg and felt his chest tighten.

Addie! She was here.

He was shocked by how happy that made him feel—
happy then stunned as he realised that *she* had been what
was missing. Abruptly his elation faded as the woman
turned and waved excitedly at a friend in the crowd. It was
not Addie. And her hair wasn't even red. He must have
been hallucinating! Seeing what he wanted to see.

His words echoed inside his head and he felt a mo-
mentary flicker of unease. Did he really want to see *her*
that badly?

Eyes narrowing, he gazed across the room. There were
so many beautiful women here tonight. Why was he ob-
sessing over Addie when he could just pluck one of them
out from the crowd?

Because he didn't want just any woman. He wanted
Addie.

His heart began to thump. But it was inevitable really,
he reassured himself. He'd been spending so much time
with her that he'd got used to having her around. And with
her glorious red hair and beautiful curving body she was
there for a very specific reason. To stand out—to be seen
by his side. Together they would be the most dazzling, the
most desired couple in the room.

He frowned. But where the hell *was* she?

And then he saw her.

And this time there could be no mistake.

She was standing at the top of the wide, curving staircase that led down to the main casino floor, the two bodyguards he had assigned to protect her on either side of her.

Caught beneath a pool of light, she looked beautiful.
More than beautiful, he thought dazedly. She looked like
a goddess. Her heels were black and high but her dress
was dark red and short, with long sleeves. It clung to her
curves as though she had been sewn into it.

But as she stared down into the crowded casino he felt

her hesitation, saw the uncertainty in her eyes. He was moving even before he realised he was doing so—striding across the room and up the stairs.

She saw him just as he reached her side, her ruby and diamond earrings catching the light as she turned to greet him.

He stared at her, his heart in his throat. Up close, she looked even more stunning. Her long hair was swept up, revealing her slim neck and flawless face, and suddenly he couldn't stand it any more. He had to touch her. More than touch—he wanted to lay claim to her.

Reaching out, he took her hand and drew her slowly towards him. 'You look beautiful, sweetheart. I think you should keep these.' Gently he touched her earrings. 'And that dress looks divine on you.'

She smiled then, her uncertainty fading, and it was as though they were alone; around them the swarming mass of people melted away.

'Thank you. I wasn't sure about the length. But I think covering my arms balances out my legs.'

He nodded. He had no idea what she was talking about. Just looking at her was throwing him off balance. 'I agree. Or I would if I knew what you meant.'

She pinched his hand. 'There are *rules*, you know. About clothing.'

His eyes gleamed. 'Has this got something to do with the tie—?'

'Malachi!' She glanced nervously over her shoulder, her body twisting, and suddenly he was too jolted to breathe, let alone speak.

Cut low and draped at the back, whatever rules she had been talking about, that dress was breaking all of them. His eyes bumped down the curve of her spine, his blood thickening and slowing, his thoughts a heaving mass of yearning, unfocused desire.

Trying to bring order back to the chaotic disarray of his body and mind, he dragged his eyes away from the smooth, golden temptation of her bare skin and gestured at a passing waiter.

'Here!' Back in control once more, he handed her a fluted glass of champagne. 'Let's go and mingle. There are some people I want you to meet.'

The rest of the evening was a blur of people and names. Addie felt as if she was floating. Beside her, one of the bodyguards held up a protective arm as guests spilled past them and she glanced up at him dazedly.

Bodyguard! When had she become the sort of person who needed a bodyguard?

The thought made her head spin. But then it was spinning anyway. She was so nervous she had barely even registered the gorgeous over-the-top decor—in fact, she'd been aware of very little except the sidelong glances that had followed her and Malachi as they made their way around the room, his hand resting casually on her back.

'They're all looking at us,' she'd whispered as he'd led her through the crowd.

'They're not,' he had whispered back. 'They're looking at you.'

But of course they hadn't been.

It was Malachi who was the object of their curious and admiring attention. He was the reason the hum of conversation tailed off. The reason men stood taller, waiters moved with even more swift efficiency and women—

She breathed in sharply. *All* the women were in his fan club, if the furtive, hungry expressions on their faces were anything to go by.

But of course they were. He was devastatingly handsome—and in a dinner jacket at his most desirable, with the stark contrast of black and white emphasising his flawless bone structure and restless grey eyes. Moreover, it was his night—his name on a thousand lips.

And she was the woman holding his arm. His wife.

Except that at no point had Malachi made that clear to anyone. Her heart began to pound. *Just who was she supposed to be tonight?* And was everyone else thinking the same thing?

Malachi stared across the casino floor, struggling to adjust his thoughts. Normally on an evening like this he would have been acting on autopilot: smiling, chatting, working the room. But tonight he just couldn't seem to concentrate. Not with Addie so close to him, the bare skin of her back so soft and tempting. If only he could peel off that dress and see the rest of her—

She was so beautiful, so desirable. Every woman in the room wanted to be her and every man wanted her. But she was his wife.

His wife.

So why not tell the world?

He glanced around the room. Everywhere he looked there were couples. Men and women holding hands, looking up at one another in excitement, sharing their happiness. His chest felt tight; his mouth was suddenly dry. He wanted to touch Addie and hold her close. But deep down he knew that they had no future. No sex, however perfect, was enough to make a marriage happy or healthy. He knew that better than anyone.

They were standing beside the roulette table. Beside him, the casino manager, Edgar, was talking to the young male croupier.

Malachi nodded at them. 'Are we busy?'

The croupier nodded. 'Yes, sir. Very busy. Roulette is very popular with the ladies.'

Malachi grinned. 'It always is.'

Beside him, Edgar cleared his throat. 'Would you like to play, Mr King? Or maybe…' Glancing past Malachi, the manager smiled politely at Addie, hesitated.

Malachi stared at her profile in silence, feeling her tension. He'd always known this moment would come: the moment when he would have to formally introduce Addie and he knew that she was waiting for his response. His chest felt tight. She was his wife, but he didn't believe in happy-ever-after.

He met her gaze deliberately. 'Addie, this is Edgar Baptista, my casino manager. Edgar, this is Miss Addie Farrell.'

Addie stared at him in silence as slowly the meaning behind his words filtered through her nerves. *Miss Farrell.* Not *Mrs King.* Not *My wife.*

'They want you to spin the wheel.'

She gazed up at him through the confused tangle of misery and disappointment. 'Spin the what?'

He gestured towards the roulette wheel. 'It's a tradition. It brings good luck to the house.'

'I'm surprised you of all people believe in luck,' she said lightly, pushing down the hurt in her chest. 'You'll be telling me next you believe in the tooth fairy.'

His eyes met hers: dark, mocking, compelling.

'We have a saying in the casino, sweetheart. Luck is for losers. But it seems a little churlish to point that out right now.'

He smiled at her then—one of those devastating smiles that made her heart beat too fast.

'Besides, everyone needs a bit of luck in their lives, don't you think? For when the odds are really against them.'

Only of course the odds never were against Malachi. How could they be? He was the man who set them.

Finally the evening was over. As they left the casino photographers crowded onto the steps, calling out to Malachi, cameras flashing on every side as he replied with his usual sangfroid.

'What do they want?' she whispered.

'They want to know who you are.' His eyes were cool.

'What did you tell them?' She swallowed, trying to hide her longing.

'I told them I wasn't going to do their job for them.'

It was a good answer. Plausible and playful. And evasive. A perfect bluff, in fact.

Her heart was hammering so loudly it took her a moment to realise that the press were still shouting at them.

'What are they saying now?' she said dully as he slid his arm around her waist.

'They want a photo.' He smiled down at her.

'Haven't they got enough?'

'They want a very particular kind of photo,' he said softly and, pulling her firmly against him, he lowered his head and kissed her.

Light exploded around them, and despite herself Addie felt her stomach curl as he deepened the kiss to the roar of the photographers. It was over in a moment.

Lifting his head, he smiled at her lazily. 'There. Now everyone's happy!'

Except she wasn't. Instead she felt restless, on edge—like a warrior getting ready for battle.

To Addie, the suite felt strangely still and quiet after the noise and drama of the casino.

Pulling loose his tie, Malachi walked slowly round her, studying her appraisingly, stopping behind her. Then, mov-

ing forward, he slowly began to stroke the back of her neck.
'So. Did you enjoy yourself tonight?'

Addie nodded. She couldn't run away from what had
happened at the casino, but already her skin was tingling,
her body leaning into his. 'It was fun. I'm just sad it's all
over—'

Her pulse jerked as she felt his lips brush against her
throat, and suddenly she was desperate for him to kiss
her properly.

'Don't worry,' he murmured, tipping her head back,
his mouth teasing hers. 'The fun's only just beginning...'

Staring up at the moonlight, Malachi walked slowly across
the rooftop terrace and sat down on a concrete bench. His
face was impassive but his head was in turmoil. It had been
a perfect evening. The casino had run like clockwork. All
the VIPs had gone home happy. Everything had gone according to plan.

And Addie—she had played her part to perfection. She
had been the most beautiful woman in the room. In that
dark red dress she had been more intoxicating than a bottle
of claret. All eyes had followed her around the room and
having her beside him, her arm curled through his, had
felt *right*. It had felt *good*.

His mouth twisted. Only that was the problem. He didn't
want it to feel good or right. Any more than he'd wanted
to feel so out of control when he'd seen her with his father.

The truth was he didn't want to feel anything at all.

A muscle tightenend in his jaw. He'd rather jump into
a pool of sharks. It would certainly be less dangerous.
Less painful. Although he knew he was probably alone
in thinking that way.

His stomach tightened. But that was the point. He *was*
alone. He always had been. And nothing and no one could

change that fact. Especially not a woman who had traded sex for money.

'Malachi—'

He turned.

Addie stepped forward, her face hesitant beneath the moonlight. 'Is everything okay?'

He nodded. 'Of course. I just needed some fresh air. Clear my head.' He frowned. 'You're dressed!'

She was wearing jeans and his dress shirt. Her face was flushed.

'I couldn't find you. I thought maybe you'd gone downstairs. Then I remembered about the roof garden, so I thought I'd check up here first.'

He smiled. 'I'm fine. I'm just a bit wired. It was a big night. Lots of things to get right.'

'You did a good job.' She smiled. 'It's a pity you can't give yourself some kind of reward.'

He took her waist in both hands and pulled her towards him. 'I did that earlier.'

She looked up at him, her eyes fixing on his face, her expression suddenly intent. 'Is that what I am? A reward?'

He stared past her, her words trapping him against the concrete, panic rising up inside. What the hell had he done? All those years he'd held it together, had never said a word about his parents or his childhood to anyone. Then Addie came back into his life, with her questions and her concern and her soft blue eyes, and all those barriers he'd built between the world and himself had come crashing down. And this was the consequence. This assumption that she had some right to cross-examine him, to expect answers.

But it was going to stop now.

'I like to think of you more as an asset.' He met her gaze levelly. 'Which reminds me—I'm flying down to Rio tomorrow. To look at a casino. I thought maybe you'd like to come with me. It's a beautiful city. Perhaps we could go to Buenos Aires and Santiago. Maybe even Acapulco.'

Addie gazed at him warily, trying to contain the chaos and confusion inside. Something was happening. Something she didn't quite understand. He was inviting her to go away with him and yet his manner was strangely detached, careless almost.

It had been such a tough couple of days. His parents' party had been horrible. But for the first time she had actually understood what had made Malachi the man he was. And afterwards he had needed her—not for sex, but for comfort and support. They had seemed so close.

Only now that closeness felt like an illusion, a trick of her senses, for all evening he had deliberately chosen not to acknowledge her as his wife. And now he was inviting her to go to Rio with him. Not even as his mistress but as an *asset*—

Her heart bumped against her ribs as though it was warning her to stay quiet. But she couldn't run away from this conversation. Not this time. Not after everything that had happened. 'I'd love to go to all those places. But how does that fit in with our deal?'

There. She had said it. She watched his eyes narrow fractionally.

Malachi stared at her in silence.

Their deal! A thread of anger and frustration uncoiled like a snake in the pit of his stomach. He could see the tension in her face, the doubt and unease, and he knew what she wanted him to say. But he would never say it. He couldn't.

His chest grew tight. He felt hard, cruel, knowing how much he was about to hurt her. But he couldn't give her what she needed.

Meeting her gaze, he smiled at her coolly. 'I'm not sure I understand the question, sweetheart. Nothing's changed except our location.'

He watched her eyes widen.

'I don't care about the location—' she began.

'So it's about the money?' he said smoothly.

It was as though he had slapped her.

'The money? No, it's not about the money!' she protested.

Her face was flushed and he could see a pulse beating at the base of her throat.

'It's about us.'

'"Us"?' he repeated softly.

'Yes. *Us*. You and me. Doing a tour of South America. How does that work, Malachi?'

She stared at him defiantly, but he heard the catch in her voice.

'I'm saying let's go to Rio. And then we'll take it from there. One day at a time.'

Her face shifted, softened. 'So you want to try again? Properly, I mean?'

He felt his chest clench painfully at the question. The hope in her eyes took his breath away. For a moment it made him hope and believe that it could work. That maybe he could need her and love her and care about her as she cared about him.

And then, slowly his hope faded, his eyes slid past her to the spiral staircase leading back down to their suite *and to escape*. It was no good. He might have let Addie get close, closer than anyone ever had, but he couldn't handle it. Couldn't handle caring or needing or loving. He'd tried for so many years with his parents and look where *that* had got him.

But she didn't need to share his fear and pain and guilt

and anger. Slowly, deliberately, he met her gaze. 'I don't remember saying that.'

Addie looked at him in confusion. 'You said we'd take things one day at a time. You just said it.'

'I meant carry on as we are one day at a time. Or a week at a time, if you prefer. Obviously there won't be the same financial terms, but I'm happy to give you an allowance.'

She felt dizzy; her breathing was all wrong—jerky and out of time. For a moment she felt flattened. Earlier, standing by his side in that beautiful gilded room, she had actually started to believe in them…in their future. But now she realised that whatever future they might have had it had ended before it had ever begun.

'A week at a time…?' she echoed. Her heart seemed to be shrinking, its beat slowing. Was he actually offering to keep her on as his mistress on a weekly basis?

'If you prefer.' He shrugged. 'We can see how it goes.'

She nodded mechanically, unable to speak. And then, glancing down, she realised he was still holding her by the waist. Breathing in, she reached down and pushed his hands away.

'You utter bastard,' she said slowly. 'What is *wrong* with you? How can you sit there and suggest this? That I be your mistress on some kind of zero-hours contract like I'm a chambermaid?' She shook her head; her stomach was churning.

His eyes were cold. 'You're being irrational. I'm simply offering the same deal with slightly modified terms. If it's the money that's a problem—'

'Go to hell!' she snarled. Her hands curling into fists, she took a step backwards. 'I can't believe this,' she whispered. 'I actually thought we could try again. That we could give our marriage a second chance. I must have been out of my mind.'

'If you thought I was going to renew my vows to a woman who slept with me for money, then I'd have to agree with you,' he said coldly.

Stepping forward, she slapped him across the face.

For a moment there was no sound except the distant downtown traffic and her frantic, uneven breathing.

Her eyes were wide and stunned, as though he had slapped *her*. 'I can't do this any more. I know loving you is hard. I did it before and it nearly broke me. I wanted to keep fighting for us. But I can't. I've got to think of myself now, and you will never give me what I need—how can you? You don't have it to give, Malachi.'

He took a step towards her, his eyes fixed on her face. 'You need to calm down.'

She stared at him, her whole body trembling. 'No. I need to leave.'

Turning, she began to walk, then run towards the staircase.

'We have a deal, Addie.' His voice was like ice.

Her foot was on the top step as she turned to face him. 'So sue me. And while you're at it you can divorce me too.'

And, grabbing hold of the rail, she ran lightly down the stairs.

CHAPTER TEN

STORMING BACK INTO the suite, Addie stared wildly around the elegant room, blind to its beauty. Tears of anger and disbelief were burning her throat and she barely knew what she was doing. All her efforts, every thought, every breath, were concentrated on one goal. Getting as far away as possible from the man who had broken her heart for the second time.

Even though it meant she would never see him again.

A wave of misery hit her head-on and she had to press her hand over her mouth to stop herself from crying out loud. For one mad moment she thought about running back upstairs to tell him she'd changed her mind.

But if she stayed, if she accepted his offer, what did she think was going to happen?

Surely she didn't actually believe that Malachi was going to wake up one morning and miraculously be in love with her? If love meant honesty and trust and sharing more than just bodies then he didn't know *how* to love. Seeing him with his parents, feeling his pain and confusion after their party, had felt like a defining moment in their relationship. As if from then on things would be different between them. Only it could never be any different. She saw that now—saw that he was way too damaged, too detached, ever to love her as she needed to be loved.

His insulting offer to renew their 'deal' had simply made that fact undeniable.

She let out a long, slow breath. Facing the facts, while not pleasant, at least made her options clear. She had made a mistake—a stupid, humiliating mistake—by agreeing to his stupid, humiliating deal. But at least she had only traded sex for money. To stay would be a far bigger mistake, for she would be trading her self-respect for a bunch of worthless dreams.

She wasn't going to give her heart to a man who thought a woman's role was to look beautiful and glamorous and provide sex. Nor was she going to shed any more tears.

Catching sight of her handbag, she snatched it up gratefully. It had everything she needed: money, and most important, her passport. She wanted nothing else—not even her own clothes; all of them were unwearable now anyway—sullied by that horrible, insulting offer he'd made to her.

Stepping into the waiting lift, she squared her shoulders. But as the lift slid slowly to a stop she felt some of her bravado fade. Now what? She couldn't just sit around in the reception area. But the hotel was nowhere near the airport. And although she might have braved public transport during daylight, she didn't feel confident about tackling the metro on her own in the early hours of the morning.

There was no avoiding it. She was going to have to speak to someone at the main desk about ordering a taxi. She certainly wasn't going to get to the airport otherwise. Her chest tightened. But there was no other way.

She walked quickly across the foyer. Behind the desk, the young receptionist looked up from her computer screen and smiled, and said in near perfect English, 'Good morning. My name is Carolina. How may I help you?'

Addie was about to reply when the girl's smile faded, a blush colouring her cheeks and brow. 'I'm so sorry. It's Ms Farrell, isn't it? You're staying in the Cruz-Rojas suite with Mr King.'

Nodding, Addie gripped the edge of the desk and forced herself to smile.

'Yes. That's right.' Horrified that the girl might be about to start asking questions about her stay, she said quickly, 'I wonder, would it be possible for you to order a taxi for me? To take me to the airport?'

Her lungs seemed to shrivel inside her chest as the girl shook her head apologetically. 'I'm sorry, Miss Farrell. We don't actually use taxis at this hotel. Most of our guests prefer their own transport.'

Addie felt her heart start to race. Of course they did. Like Malachi, they probably all had private cars with chauffeurs to take them wherever they wanted to go. She shivered. She would rather crawl over broken glass than go back upstairs to ask that monster for anything.

'But…' The receptionist looked at her earnestly. 'We *do* operate a complimentary limousine service to the airport. Would you like me to arrange one for you?'

'Oh, yes. Yes, please.' Addie felt a wave of gratitude wash over her. 'As soon as possible.'

She wasn't worried that Malachi would try and stop her. He hadn't even come after her when she'd stormed out of their wedding, and he hated scenes. But she felt so tired, and her self-control was slipping. She wasn't going to be able to hold it together for much longer—

'Miss Farrell?' It was the receptionist—Carolina. 'We have a limousine waiting for you outside. Your driver is Luis. Have a good trip.' She smiled shyly at Addie. 'Are you going somewhere nice?'

Addie nodded, emotion choking her.

Yes, she was. She was going home.

Everything was going to be all right. Soon Malachi King would be just a distant memory and she would marvel at the fact that he had ever had the power to hurt her.

Eyes narrowed, Malachi stared angrily across the empty roof garden. He couldn't believe what had just happened. What did she expect from him? In fact, why did she expect anything from him anyway?

His mouth curled in frustration. Throwing all those accusations at him and storming off like that. It was just like their wedding all over again.

And saying she wanted him to divorce her? The blood pounded in his ears. He had never even thought about a divorce. Probably he never would have if she hadn't thrown it in his face—

That thought was still uppermost in his mind when he felt his phone vibrate in his pocket. Skin tingling, half expecting it to be Addie, he pulled it out. Glancing at the screen, he felt his stomach tighten. It was a message from his father.

We're in New York, at the Aviation Club. Serena says to tell you we're having a party on Saturday. If you can behave, you're welcome to join us. Bring that sweet little redhead if you like. I attach a peace offering—

Malachi stopped reading. There was more—something to do with a money transfer—but he didn't care enough to finish the message. Opening up the attachment, he watched the bodies on the screen in silence. Abruptly, he switched it off.

He could almost hear Henry's cool, detached voice inside his head. *Bring that sweet little redhead if you like.* It knocked the breath out of his body that his father could actually suggest that. He had tried so hard to make it clear to Henry that Addie was out of bounds. So why—?

Lifting his head, he stared bleakly up at the moon, its pale, pure beauty making his heart contract. He knew why; he'd known why since he was a small child, only he had never wanted or been able to confront the truth before. But it was simple really.

For Henry and Serena drama and tension were more important than love and loyalty. For them life was a series of spectacles for which anything could be sacrificed—including their son's happiness. And when things—or people—got messy or boring, they simply got rid of them and moved on. The ground felt suddenly unsteady beneath his feet as he remembered what it had felt like: the unspoken threat, the fear that one day they would get rid of *him*.

Shakily he ran his hand over his face, panic swelling inside him. Only with shock he realised that he wasn't panicking about losing his parents.

But about losing Addie.

It hurt. Just thinking about her not being there.

Hurt because he loved her.

His heart gave a jerk as finally he faced the truth.

He loved her.

His face was impassive but his whole body was shaking. Why hadn't he realised?

He'd spent his entire life reading people. Spotting their weaknesses, their deceits and delusions. Yet he'd failed to notice that he was in love.

Worse, he had bullied and manipulated the woman he

loved into being his mistress, using her loyalty to her charity to get his own way.

For a moment he stood frozen and then he turned.

He needed to explain, to apologise, to tell her how he felt. Now. Before it was too late.

Heart pounding, he started to walk, then run towards the staircase.

But where was she?

Downstairs, Malachi stared uneasily around the empty suite. He had imagined Addie to be hurtling around the room, tossing clothes into her suitcase. Only the bedroom felt still and lifeless. Slowly he checked the other rooms, his pulse racing. But she wasn't there.

She couldn't have actually left—

Feeling sick on the inside, he checked the rooms again. And then his heart jerked as he pulled open the wardrobe door. Her suitcase was still there—and all her clothes and shoes. He felt almost numb with relief. She would hardly abandon all her stuff if she was leaving him. At the very least she would take her handbag.

Glancing round, his heart missed a beat. It was gone and so was Addie. His breath felt suddenly tight and panicky in his chest and, crossing the room in three quick strides, he picked up the phone and rang Reception.

'Mr King. How may I help?'

'Miss Farrell—' he began.

'Yes, sir. The limousine has already left.'

He went cold.

'Left? When? Where?' The stunned silence at the end of the phone echoed inside his head. 'Where has she gone?' he demanded hoarsely, not caring that he sounded nothing like his cool public persona.

'To the airport. She left ten minutes ago.'

He barely heard the receptionist's trembling reply. Inside his head one question was repeating itself over and over again.

What have I done? What have I done? What have I done?

More importantly, what was he going to do now?

Gazing up out of the window of the limousine, Addie watched the lights of an aeroplane move slowly through the night sky, growing smaller and smaller until finally they disappeared altogether. She sighed. Soon she would be on a plane just like that one and all this—this misery and mess—would be left far behind. In another country. In another life.

She glanced slowly around the luxurious cream leather interior of the limousine. All this luxury would be gone soon too.

But she didn't care. None of it mattered. She would have traded all of it to make Malachi love her. To make her marriage work. Her heart squeezed inside her chest. She loved him so much. But it hadn't been enough.

Sighing, she glanced at the clock on the limousine's dashboard and then closed her eyes. If she was lucky she might be able to catch a flight back home in the next few hours, but it was going to be a long night and an even longer day tomorrow. Only she wasn't going to spend it wallowing in the past and in self-pity. She lifted her chin. From now on, she was only going to go forward.

After what felt like no time at all, the limousine slowed, and opening her eyes, she glanced out of the window as it slid to a stop. She frowned. What the hell was the chauffeur playing at? They weren't at the airport: they were back at the hotel.

Leaning forward she banged angrily on the screen behind his head. 'Excuse me…er… Luis? What are you doing? I want to go to the airport!'

Frantically she tried to think of the words in Spanish, but before she could even muster up a basic sentence he had got out of the car and opened her door.

'What is going on? *Hablo—habla inglès?*' she said, staring up at him in frustration. 'No. You don't understand. I need to go the *airport*—'

Still holding the door open, the chauffeur stared impassively ahead. Realising she was getting nowhere, Addie slid past him and stalked angrily back into the hotel and up to the reception desk.

'Hello,' she said breathlessly. 'It's Carolina, isn't it? I'm sorry, but your driver—I don't think he quite understands what I want him to do. He was supposed to be taking me to the airport but he's brought me back here.'

The girl bit her lip. 'I'm sorry, Miss Farrell. But he was given new instructions.'

Addie gazed at her in frustration. 'What do you mean, new instructions? I thought he was *my* driver.' She pointed in exasperation to where Luis stood, still looking straight ahead.

'He—he is,' the girl stammered. 'But there was a change of plan.'

Addie shook her head. 'Not by me. So who changed it?'

'That would be me!'

There was a long, frozen pause and then Addie turned slowly round. Standing in the centre of the foyer, Malachi was watching her, his eyes fixed on her face.

'Then I suggest you change it back again,' she said through gritted teeth. Her heart was racing with anger.

Slowly he shook his head. 'That's not going to happen.'

'It's not up to you.' She stared at him furiously. 'You might be important to some people but you don't have any power in this hotel.'

He met her gaze. 'That's not strictly true. I *do* pay their wages.'

Her breath caught in her throat. 'Really?' she said coldly. 'By the day? Or by the week?'

A muscle flickered in his jaw. 'I think they're all quite happy with their contracts.'

'Lucky them,' she snapped. 'But, fascinating though this is, I'm sure you didn't drag me back here to discuss your staff's employment contracts. So what is it, Malachi? What do you want?'

'We didn't finish our conversation.'

'No, we did, Malachi. You just didn't have the last word.' She gave a tired laugh. 'Is that what this is about?' She shook her head, her mouth curving contemptuously. 'Fine, then—just say it. Go on.'

He glanced past her. 'Maybe we should take this somewhere a little more private.'

She felt the air punch out of her lungs. Shaking her head, she met his gaze. 'No. We should not. I'm not going anywhere with you, Malachi. So, short of abducting me, you're going to have say whatever it is you want to say right here.'

He stared at her in silence, his eyes never leaving her face. Finally he shrugged. 'As you wish.'

Glancing past her, he smiled.

'*Gracias, Carolina y Luis.* I can take it from here.'

Then before Addie had a chance to react, he had crossed the foyer and tipped her body up over his shoulders.

'Put me down!' Twisting, kicking, struggling, she beat her hands against his back. 'Malachi! You can't do this.'

She felt his arm tighten around her legs and then, hearing the lift doors open, she began to yell. 'Call the police! I don't care if he's your boss—'

The lift doors closed in front of her.

'You can't do this! Put me down!'

Abruptly he leaned forward and she slid ignominiously from his shoulder. Immediately she rushed at him, but he caught her easily, holding her flailing arms by the wrists.

'Calm down. I'm not going to hurt you. I told you—I just want to talk.'

Yanking her arms away, she ignored him. Opening her bag, she pulled out her phone. 'I am going to call the police and have you arrested, and you can see how you like talking to them—'

Taking her phone away from her ear, she stared at the screen irritably.

'Let me guess. No signal?' Malachi said helpfully. 'You won't get one inside the lift.'

'Fine!' she spat. 'I'll ring when we get to the suite.'

He nodded. 'That would work.'

Pausing, he turned and opened a small door in the side of the lift, slid a card into it and swiped it down.

'Only we're not going to the suite.'

The lift stopped moving.

Addie stared at him incredulously.

'Have you lost your mind?' she said finally. 'Why are you doing this?'

'I told you. We didn't finish our conversation.'

'There is nothing else to talk about,' she said furiously. 'Why do you think I left? I don't have anything to say to you.'

He nodded. 'I know. And you don't have to say anything. You just have to listen. I'll do all the talking.'

'It's too late, Malachi. If you wanted to talk to me you should have done it an hour ago.' Her eyes narrowed. 'In fact you should have done it five years ago.'

He leaned back against the doors, his face hardening. 'As I recall, you didn't give me a chance.'

She stepped towards him, her fingers curling into fists. 'That is *not* what happened. I tried to talk to you and you just walked away.'

'It was our *wedding*!' His face was taut. 'You were making—'

'What? A scene? Oh, I'm sorry—what was I supposed to do? I'd just heard two men talking about how lucky it was that your new wife had such strong ties with the local community. How it had made such a difference to getting your plans for a new casino approved.'

'That's not what happened,' he said savagely, and he stepped towards her, his eyes locking on to hers.

'So that *isn't* why you married me?' Her whole body was shaking with anger but her heart contracted painfully at the memory. 'Tell me I got it wrong. Go on. Tell me.'

Looking at his stricken face, she felt suddenly nauseous.

'You can't because it's true.'

'*No.*' His voice echoed loudly around the lift. 'I admit when I asked you to marry me I thought it would be good for business.' Tipping his head back, he breathed out sharply, his face twisting. 'But then things changed. I started to care about you—'

He took a step forward and with shock she saw that his hands were shaking.

'I missed you when you weren't there and I looked forward to seeing you.' He shook his head vehemently, his eyes dropping away. 'You have to understand, Addie.

I'd never felt like that before. I didn't know what I was feeling.'

She looked up at him uncertainly. 'What *were* you feeling?'

He shivered. 'Out of control. Scared.'

She bit her lip. 'Why were you scared?'

He clenched his teeth. 'Because I cared. About you. Only I didn't know how to deal with those feelings. When you got so upset it hurt to see you like that and I just wanted to get away. I didn't think you would leave—'

'I didn't think there was any point in staying,' she said flatly. 'I thought you didn't love me.'

His eyes met hers. 'I can see why you would think that.' Looking away, he ran a hand over his face. 'I grew up not knowing what love was. I didn't understand how to love someone or be loved. I didn't have relationships. I had sex. And sex was just a way of feeling things without actually having to care.'

His voice cracked.

'When I met you that changed. I started to see the world differently. But it was still all so new, and I found it hard.' He shook his head. 'I should have come after you.'

There was a lump in her throat. 'I was to blame too.' She bit her lip. 'I should have stayed and fought for our marriage.'

He breathed out slowly. 'Upstairs, you said you loved me and that you wanted to try again. Was that true?'

Hesitating, she stared at him in silence. But she knew the truth was written all over her face anyway. 'Yes. But I won't be your mistress, Malachi.'

He shook his head, his eyes damp, his face pale and strained. 'I don't want you to be my mistress.' Reaching out, he gently took hold of her hands in his. 'But I *do* want you to forgive me for blackmailing you. And treating you so badly.'

His hands tightened around hers.

'I'm so sorry, Addie. I know I don't deserve you, and I should have let you go tonight. Let you find someone kinder and better than me. But I can't. I know it's selfish, but I can't allow you to leave because I love you. And my life is nothing without you.'

Breathing out unsteadily, she looked down at his hands. 'Does that mean you're not going to sue me?' she said softly.

He shook his head. 'It wasn't a binding contract.'

She smiled weakly and then pulled away slightly.

'What about divorcing me?'

She felt her heart tumble over as he shook his head.

'Absolutely not.' Gently, he pulled her towards him. 'You're not getting rid of me that easily. You're my wife, and as soon as we get out of here I'm telling the entire world.'

She looked up at him, her mouth trembling. 'I don't know, Malachi. It all sounds perfect in here. But we can't stay in a lift for the rest of our lives.'

He grinned. 'It's tempting, but—trust me, sweetheart. I can make this work.' He frowned. 'Which is more than can be said for this lift...'

Her eyes narrowed. 'You broke the lift?'

He nodded. 'It would appear so. See that flashing light—that means it's locked.'

'Locked!'

He gave a helpless shrug. 'I was a little distracted.'

'So what happens next?' she asked slowly.

His eyes dropped to her mouth. 'We have to wait. Just for a couple of hours.'

She lifted an eyebrow. 'I see. I suppose we'll just have to think of a way to pass the time.'

His hands slid slowly round her waist. 'Do you have any ideas?

'Actually, I do.' She wrapped her arms around his neck and kissed him gently on the lips.

He drew away from her, his eyes softening. 'Me too.' Lowering his mouth, he brushed his lips across hers. 'Did I tell you that I love you, Mrs King?'

His hands moved over her waist, sliding under the shirt, warm palms touching her bare skin, and she felt her heart start to race.

'Yes, you did.' She closed her eyes. 'But tell me again.'

* * * * *

LET'S TALK
Romance

For exclusive extracts, competitions
and special offers, find us online:

 facebook.com/millsandboon

@MillsandBoon

@MillsandBoonUK

Get in touch on 01413 063232

For all the latest titles coming soon, visit
millsandboon.co.uk/nextmonth

JOIN US ON SOCIAL MEDIA!

Stay up to date with our latest releases, author news and gossip, special offers and discounts, and all the behind-the-scenes action from Mills & Boon...

 @millsandboon

 @millsandboonuk

 facebook.com/millsandboon

 @millsandboonuk

t might just be true love...

GET YOUR ROMANCE FIX!

Get the latest romance news,
exclusive author interviews, story
extracts and much more!

MILLS & BOON
MODERN
Power and Passion

Prepare to be swept off your feet by sophisticated, sexy and seductive heroes, in some of the world's most glamourous and romantic locations, where power and passion collide.

MILLS & BOON
Desire

Indulge in secrets and scandal, intense drama and plenty of sizzling hot action with powerful and passionate heroes who have it all: wealth, status, good looks…everything but the right woman.